Royal House of Corinthia
Royally wed…by Christmas!

This Christmas, Princess Arianna and Crown Prince Armando of Corinthia are facing the biggest challenges of their lives.

Pregnant Arianna flees to New York to find some privacy… only to find her very own Prince Charming!

Christmas Baby for the Princess
Available now

Crown Prince Armando needs a royal bride, so why can't he stop thinking about his assistant, Rosa Lamberti?

Winter Wedding for the Prince
Available now

You won't want to miss this delightfully emotional new duet from Barbara Wallace, brimming with Christmas magic!

WINTER WEDDING FOR THE PRINCE

BY
BARBARA WALLACE

First Published in Great Britain 2016
By Mills & Boon, an imprint of HarperCollins*Publishers*
1 London Bridge Street, London, SE1 9GF

© 2016 Barbara Wallace

ISBN: 978-0-263-92039-0

23-1216

Our policy is to use papers that are natural, renewable and recyclable products and made from wood grown in sustainable forests. The logging and manufacturing processes conform to the legal environmental regulations of the country of origin.

Printed and bound in Spain
by CPI, Barcelona

Barbara Wallace can't remember when she wasn't dreaming up love stories in her head, so writing romances for Mills & Boon Cherish is a dream come true. Happily married to her own Prince Charming, she lives in New England with a house full of empty-nest animals. Occasionally her son comes home, as well.

To stay up-to-date on Barbara's news and releases, sign up for her newsletter at www.barbarawallace.com.

For Second Lieutenant Andrew Wallace,
who commissioned five days after I typed
The End. Merry Christmas!

CHAPTER ONE

"THEN, AFTER THE children finish their sing-along, Babbo Natale will arrive to distribute presents. We were lucky enough this year to get each child something from their wish lists, even the girl who asked for a dragon and one thousand chocolate cookies. The internet is a wonderful thing." Rosa Lamberti looked up from her paperwork. "Are you even listening?" she asked the man in front of her.

Armando Santoro, crown prince of Corinthia, paused midstep to give her a narrow-eyed look. "Of course I did. Babbo Natale. Dragons. Cookies. Why do you ask?"

"I don't know, maybe because you have been wearing a path in the carpet for the past thirty minutes." Pacing like a caged panther was more like it. He had been crossing the hand-woven Oushak with long, heavy-footed strides that took advantage of his extra-tall frame. Between that and the scowl plastered on his face, she half expected him to start growling. "I have a feeling I could have announced a coup and you wouldn't have heard me."

"I'm sorry," he said, running a hand through his dark curls. "I'm a bit distracted this morning."

Clearly. Setting her paperwork aside, Rosa helped herself to a fresh cup of coffee. On good days, being the prince's personal assistant was a three-cup job. When he was distracted, the number increased to four or five.

"Don't tell me you're upset about your sister," she said. Only that morning, Princess Arianna had announced her engagement to an American businessman named Max Brown whom she had met in New York City. The details of the courtship were sketchy. According to Armando, the princess had taken off for America without a word why. A few days after her return, Max Brown forced his way into the castle demanding to see her. The pair had been inseparable ever since.

"No," he said. It was more a sigh than reply. "If Arianna is happy, then I am happy for her."

Happy was too mild a term. Rosa would go with delirious or ecstatic. The princess had lit up like Corinthia City on San Paolo Day when Max burst through the door.

Rosa suppressed a sigh of her own. Wild, passionate declarations of love and sudden engagements. It was all quite romantic. She couldn't remember the last time a man declared anything to her, unless you counted her ex-husband and his many declarations of disinterest.

Fredo had been very good at telling her she wasn't worth his time.

She returned to the question at hand. "If it is not your sister, then what is it?" she asked over the rim of her coffee cup. "And don't say nothing, because I know you." One didn't spend seven years of life attached to someone—four as a sister-in-law—without learning a person's tics.

An olive-skinned hand reached over her shoulder and took the cup before her lips had a chance to make contact. "Hey!"

Turning, she saw Armando already drinking. "You forgot the sugar," he said with a frown.

"I forgot nothing." What little was left of the warm liquid splashed against the rim as she snatched the cup free. "I'm on a diet."

"You're always on a diet. A teaspoon or two of sugar will not kill you."

Said the god of athleticism. He wasn't in danger of finishing out the year a dress size larger. Even sitting perfectly straight, she swore she could feel the button on her waistband threatening to pop.

Sucking in her belly, she said, "Stop trying to change the subject. I asked you a question."

"Did you just demand I answer you? I'm sorry, I was under the impression that you worked for me."

"Yes, but I'm family. That gives me special privileges."

"Like bossiness?"

"I'm not the one ruining a one-hundred-and-fifty-year-old rug." Reaching for the coffeepot, she poured him a fresh coffee of his own, making sure to add the two sugars before refilling her cup. "Seriously, Armando. What's wrong?"

This sigh was the loudest of the three. Taking the coffee, he came around to the front of the love seat and sat down beside her. Rosa did her best to squeeze into the corner to accommodate him. She didn't know if her brother-in-law kept forgetting she wasn't as petite as his late wife or what, but he always insisted on invading her personal space rather than taking a seat across the way. As a result, they sat wedged together, their thighs pressed tight. Rosa gave a silent thank-you for long jackets. It provided another layer between their bodies.

Oblivious, as usual, to the close quarters, Armando stared at the coffee she'd handed him. "Arianna's pregnant," he said in a dull voice.

No wonder they were rushing the engagement. "But that's a good thing, isn't it?" she asked. "Your father finally has another heir to the throne." It was no secret the king was eager to establish a third generation of Santoros to protect his family's legacy.

"It would be," Armando replied, "if Max Brown were the father."

"What?" Rosa's hand froze mid-sip. She would ask if he was joking, except this wasn't something to joke about. "Who…?" It didn't matter. "Does Max know?"

"Yes, and he doesn't care."

"He must love your sister very much." Took a special kind of love to marry a woman carrying another man's child. Certainly not the kind of love people like Rosa got to witness. People like her got a leftover kind of love. As Fredo had been so fond of telling her, she was flavorless and bland.

"Max's devotion is wonderful for Arianna, but…"

But it didn't erase the problems this pregnancy caused. "He or she can't be the heir."

Corinthian law stated that only the biological offspring of both parents could inherit the throne. Should anything happen to Armando and Arianna, then the title would skip to someone else, such as Arianna and Max's child or one of the distant cousins. Either way opened a host of complications.

"Not to mention that if the truth were to come out, that child would spend the rest of his or her life hounded by gossip and innuendo. Max and Arianna, too. The whole house of Santoro, for that matter."

"Unless Arianna and Max lie." Armando scowled at her suggestion. "What?" she asked. "You don't think that's happened before?" Not even the house of Santoro was that lily pure. In fact, someone trying to slip an illegitimate heir into the mix was probably the reason for the inane law to begin with.

"Whether it's been done before or not isn't the point," he replied. "Other generations didn't have tabloids or your wonderful internet."

Good point. Today, secrets couldn't last forever. Eventually the truth would come out, and when it did, there would be challenges. Corinthia would be plunged into a protracted legal battle that benefited no one.

"I take it you've already thought of trying to change the law," she said.

"Of course, but again, this isn't the old days, when

the king could change the laws on a whim. The ministers would want to know the reason for the change."

"All hail increased democracy," Rosa muttered. There wasn't much more that could be done, barring Armando remarrying and having children of his own, and a monk dated more than he did. The Melancholy Prince, the papers called him. The title fit. While Armando had always been serious, Christina's death had added an extra layer. It was as though he was suspended in permanent mourning. He never attended anything that wasn't an official event, and those he attended alone. Other than his sister, Rosa was the only woman in his life.

The prince had returned his attention to his coffee, studying the untouched contents from beneath thick lashes as if they contained the answer. Rosa couldn't help but indulge in a moment of appreciation. If he decided to date again, Armando's return to the dating world would be a welcome one. Even if he wasn't the future king of Corinthia, he was a man worthy of desire. Granted, he wasn't the most beautiful man in the country; his Roman features were a little too pronounced, although not so much that they looked out of proportion. Besides, she always thought a strong man should have strong features. Fredo, for all his self-importance, had had a weak chin.

The muscles in Armando's chin twitched with tension.

"You know King El Halwani," he started.

"That's a silly question." Of course she knew the

man. The sultan of Yelgiers was a frequent visitor. Corinthia and the tiny principality had a long history of economic and political relations. "What does he have to do with anything?"

"His daughter, Mona, is of marrying age."

"Is that so? I didn't know." Rosa's insides ran cold. Surely, he wasn't...

"A union between our two countries will be a tremendous alliance."

Did he say will? The chill spread down her spine, ending in a shiver.

Apology darkened his eyes to near black. "I called him this morning and suggested we discuss an arrangement."

"You—you did." Rosa set down her cup. The coffee she'd been drinking threatened to rise back up her throat.

Armando, remarrying.

She shouldn't have been surprised. Royalty lived a different kind of life than commoners like her. Marriages were arranged for all kinds of reasons: trade relations, military alliances. Why not to secure an heir?

The news still made her queasy. It was too quick. Armando wasn't the type to make rash decisions. For crying out loud, he'd waited a year before proposing to her sister, and they'd fallen in love at first sight. For him to wake up and decide he was going to marry a virtual stranger was completely out of character, looming scandal or no looming scandal. At the very least, he would have asked her what she thought.

But he hadn't. He hadn't sought her opinion at all. So much for being his right hand. Apparently the familiarity she thought they had developed over the past three years had been in her head.

She forced a smile. Pretended she was excited for his news. "I'm sure the people of Corinthia will be thrilled. As will your father."

"I'm not doing this for my father," he replied.

"I know. You're doing it to protect your sister."

"No, I'm doing it for Corinthia." His voice was sharp, the way it always was when his will was questioned. "I'm first in line. It is my responsibility to do whatever I can to ensure Corinthia has a long and peaceful future."

"Of course. I'm sorry." If there was anything Armando took seriously, it was his duty to his country.

Leaving Armando, she stood and walked toward the windows. The crown prince's suite overlooked the south lawn. The famed topiary menagerie remained green, but the grass had gone brown from the winter, and the flowerbeds were empty. Across the street, a pair of business owners were filling their outside window boxes with fresh evergreen—a Corinthian Christmas tradition. When they finished, a single white candle would be placed in the center, another tradition. Greens for life, light for the blessings of the future.

Apparently, Armando's future involved a bride.

What did that mean for her future then? For three years, it had been the two of them, prince and assistant, tied together as they both began lives without their spouses. Being there to help Armando had given her strength and purpose. She'd been able to rebuild the layers of self-esteem Fredo had destroyed.

What now? A new queen would mean new staff, new routines. Would she even have a place in Armando's life anymore? The grip on her chest squeezed tighter.

She watched as a *merli* poked at the barren grass looking for seeds. Poor little creature wasn't having much luck. She could identify. She felt a little like she'd been left wanting, too.

The thing was, she had always known there was the chance Armando would move on with his life. The news shouldn't be this disconcerting.

Then again, he should have told her. They were supposed to be friends. Family. They'd held hands at her sister's bedside and cried together. She let him drink her coffee, for God's sake. Why hadn't he told her?

"When are you making the announcement?" she asked. It would have to be soon if Armando wanted to draw attention from his sister. Depending upon how far along in her pregnancy Arianna had been when she met Max last month, there was a good chance the princess would start to show soon.

Behind her, she heard the soft clap of a cup against the coffee table, but she didn't turn around.

"We're making the formal announcement on New Year's Day."

What? When she thought soon, she didn't mean that soon. No wonder she couldn't breathe. In three and a half weeks, everything she'd come to know and rely on was going to change forever.

"Is everything all right?" she heard him ask.

"Of course," she lied. "Why wouldn't it be?"

"It truly is the best solution."

"I know." He had no reason to defend himself any more than she had the right to be upset.

Clearly, that didn't stop either of them from doing so anyway.

She was upset with him. Armando could tell because when she spoke, every third or fourth word had an upward inflection. Not that he was surprised. From the moment he made his decision, he'd worried she might see his remarrying as betraying her sister.

Staring at her back, he wished he knew what she was thinking. But then, she was good at hiding behind things. Her poker face was among the best.

"You know that if there was any other way…" he said.

"I know."

Did she? Did she know he'd been up half the night weighing options, or that, given his druthers, he would never remarry? He'd had his chance at love. Four wonderful years with the girl of his dreams. If the price for those years was spending the rest of his life in solitude, he'd been prepared. He didn't mind. After all, if he needed a companion, he had Rosa. She was better company than any consort might be.

Unfortunately, for men like him, what he wanted

didn't always matter. The mantle of responsibility out-weighed personal desire every time.

Leaving his coffee behind, he joined her at the window. "Corinthia's almost ready for the holiday," he said, noting the men arranging greenery outside. "They'll be lighting the candles tonight."

Rosa didn't answer. She stood with her hands clasped tightly behind her back, stiff and formal, like a proper royal servant, a pose she usually only struck in public. Armando didn't like it. He preferred the relaxed, irreverent Rosa who kept him on his toes and saved him from drowning in his grief.

After Christina died, he'd wanted to die, too. What good was living if his heart lay six feet underground? Rosa had been the only one who had been able to break through the darkness that filled his soul. She needed him, she'd claimed, to help her rebuild following her divorce. It was a lie, of course—Rosa was one of the strongest women he knew—but he let her think he believed the excuse. Helping her find a lawyer and place to live gave him a reason to drag himself out of bed that first day. Then, when she became his assistant, there were meetings and charitable initiatives and other projects she insisted needed his attention, and so he continued dragging himself out of bed. Until the day came when getting up was no longer a trial.

She'd kept him tied to the land of the living, Rosa did. Without her, he would still be lost in his grief. Or rather, lost even deeper.

Which was why he needed her support now.

"You never met my grandfather, did you?"

"King Damian? No." She wasn't so annoyed that she couldn't give him a side-eyed look. Of course she hadn't met the man. Illness forced him off the throne before Armando was born.

"He came upstairs to my room one night, a few weeks before he died, and got me out of bed so I could see what it looked like with candles lit in every window. I must have been seven or eight at the time. Corinthia City wasn't as developed as it is now. Anyway, he told me how all those candles represented Corinthians hoping for the future. 'One day you will be responsible for those candles,' he told me. 'It will be up to you to keep them burning bright.' I never forgot." The words were the weight pressing on his shoulders every time he saw a candle flickering.

He turned to look at his sister-in-law. "Father's aging, Rosa. I could see it this past month when Arianna disappeared. He's never truly gotten over Mama's death…" He paused to let the irony of his words settle between them. The curse of the Santoro men: to live a lifetime of grieving. "And I think he would like to step down, but he's afraid for the future. It's important he know that as his successor, I am willing to do whatever it takes to keep those lights burning."

"Including political marriage."

He shrugged. "Ours won't be the first royal marriage based on obligation rather than love." If anything, a man in his position was lucky to have spent four years with a wife he did love. "It would be nice, however, to know I have my best friend's support. Do I?"

The clock on the nearby mantel ticked off the seconds while he waited for her response. Unfortunately, her eyes were cast downward. They were the one feature that couldn't mask her feelings. In that way, she was like her sister. Christina had also had expressive brown eyes. Beyond their eyes, however, the two were dramatically different. Christina had been all passion and energy, with a beauty that commanded attention. Rosa was softer. Whereas Christina was bright like a star, her sister was more the glow of a candle.

Finally, her shoulders relaxed. "Of course you have my blessing," she said. "You know I can never say no to you."

Armando's shoulders relaxed in turn. "I know. It's my charm."

"No, it's because you're going to be king. I say no and you might have me thrown in the dungeon."

"As one does." He relaxed a little more. Rosa making jokes was always a good sign. "I'm serious, Rosa. Your support is important to me." Just thinking he might not have it had left a tight knot in the center of his chest.

A hand brushed his arm. Initiating contact with a member of the royal family was considered a violation of protocol, but he and Rosa had been together too long for either of them to care about rules. There were times, in fact, when he found her touch comforting. Like now, the way her fingertips seemed to brush the tension from his muscles. "You have it. Seriously. I just wish…"

"What?"

She shook her head. "Nothing. I'm being silly. You have my support, 'Mando."

"Good." Although he wondered what she had started to say. That she wished there didn't have to be a wedding? If so, Armando agreed.

But there was going to be a wedding, and he was glad to have his best friend's support.

Hopefully, she wouldn't change her mind when she heard his next request.

CHAPTER TWO

"I CANNOT BELIEVE you want me to attend a meeting with you and your future father-in-law. How is that possibly in good form?"

She had been complaining since yesterday. When he'd said he'd called King Omar, Armando left off that the sultan was in Corinthia and that they were going to meet for lunch the next day.

"And how is it no one was told of his visit?" she asked as they rode the elevator down to the first floor. "He's a visiting head of state. There are protocols to be followed."

"Since when do you follow protocol?"

"I always follow protocol when other royalty is involved. Exactly how long has he been in Corinthia?"

"Since Wednesday. You might as well get used to it," he added when she opened her mouth to speak. "Omar has decided to personally oversee the resort development." Such was the major difference between the two small countries. The Yelgierian royal family insisted on maintaining control of everything, while

Armando and his father preferred giving their subjects more freedom. "Between that and the upcoming…ar-rangement…" He couldn't bring himself to say the word *wedding*. Not yet. "I suspect Omar will be going back and forth quite a bit."

An odd looking shadow crossed her face. "With his daughter?"

"I—I don't know." Armando hadn't given his bride-to-be much thought. "I imagine she will, considering all the preparations that need to take place."

"Unless the wedding is in Yelgiers," Rosa replied. She was studying her shoes as she spoke, so he almost didn't hear her.

"True." He hadn't given much thought to logistics. Those kinds of details were usually up to the bride. "But it doesn't matter to me where the wedding takes place." Only that it did, and Corinthia's future was se-cure.

The elevator opened, and they stepped out into the guarded enclave near the driveway. Rosa's sedan had been brought around and sat running by the curb.

"I still don't understand why you need me for this meeting," she said as a guard stepped out to open the passenger door. "Surely, you can finalize your—" she glanced at the guard "—agreement without me."

"I told you, this meeting isn't about my 'agreement,'" Armando replied. "I'm meeting with him to discuss the development project." And perhaps finalize a few details regarding yesterday's telephone conversation. Sometimes she was a little too astute for his liking.

"You know I like to have you with me when I discuss business."

He waited until the guard shut her door and they once again had privacy. "Not to mention you are my favorite driver." The way Rosa handled a car made him feel comfortable. For a long time, just the thought of being on the road filled him with dread. He would hear the sound of an engine, and images of twisted steel filled his brain. But, just like she coaxed him back to the land of the living, Rosa had eased him onto the road.

Sometimes he wondered what his life would be like without her.

"So now I'm your driver," she replied. "If that's the case, maybe I should get a cap to wear."

"And have me listen to you complain about the hat ruining your hair? No, thank you. What you're wearing will suffice."

For a meeting she didn't want to attend, she was dressed rather nicely. As usual, her brown hair was pulled up in one of those twisty, formal styles she seemed to prefer, but unlike her usual skirt and blouse, she had on a brocade dress with matching jacket. A long one that seemed designed to hide a woman's shape. She wore those a lot—long, bulky jackets, that was. He wasn't a fan. It was as though she was trying to discourage attention.

"When's the last time you had a date?" he asked her. For the first time he could remember, she stripped the car gears. Turning her head, she squinted at him. "Excuse me?"

The question did sound like it came out of nowhere. It was just that looking at her, and thinking about how she continually hid her assets, had him curious. "I was wondering when was the last time you had been on a date."

"Why do you want to know?"

"No particular reason. Only that it dawned on me that I can't remember the last time you mentioned one."

This time she downshifted smoothly. "My being silent doesn't have to mean I'm not dating. How do you know I'm not simply being discreet?"

"Are you? Being discreet, that is." The thought that she might be seeing someone and had not said anything irritated him. At the same time, he found it hard to believe a woman as attractive as Rosa didn't have offers.

"Isn't that a bit personal?" she asked him. "It's called a private life for a reason."

"Yes, but you can tell me—we're friends."

His comment earned him a sharp laugh. "You mean like you told me about your plans to get married?"

"I did tell you."

"After the fact."

What was she talking about? "You were the first person I told."

The car slowed as she looked at him again. "I was?"

"Of course." He thought she knew that. "I told you how much your support meant to me."

"I know, but I didn't think…" Was that pink creeping into her cheeks? It was hard to tell, the driver's side being in shadow. "I'm sorry I snapped."

"I am sorry for prying. It was rude of me." He still would like to know, however. It was protectiveness as much as curiosity. To make sure she chose better this time around. While he didn't know much about her marriage, beyond the fact it had ended badly, he did know her ex enough to dislike him. Back when Christina was alive, Fredo and Rosa had attended a handful of state dinners. Armando found the man to be a narcissistic bore. He'd decided the man had to be a closet romantic or something, because how else could he have won a woman as soft and gentle as Rosa?

Then again, maybe Armando's first impression was right, since she'd divorced him. That Rosa, for her part, refused to talk about the man said as much.

"The answer is no," Rosa said, shaking him from his thoughts. "I'm not dating."

"At all?" He wasn't sure why he felt relieved at her answer. Perhaps because he feared a serious relationship might cause her to leave her job. "Surely you've had offers, though."

Again, she gave a strange laugh, although this one had less bite than the other. "Not as many as you would think. In case you didn't realize, my job eats up most of my time."

Was that truly the reason? The undercurrent in her laugh made him wonder. "Is that your way of hinting you need time off?" he asked. If so, it would be the first. Usually she had no trouble speaking up.

Another reason to question the excuse.

Rosa shook her head. "Not at all. At least not right now."

They'd reached the point in the highway where they had to choose whether to take the mountain pass or the longer, more circuitous route. Armando gave a slight smile as she turned onto the longer route. By mutual agreement, they hadn't driven the mountain road in three years. Feeling a warmth spreading across his chest, he reached over and gave her hand a grateful squeeze. Her eyes widened a little, but she smiled nonetheless.

"The truth is," she said, after he'd lifted his hand, "I haven't had a lot of interest in dating. I'm still working on getting to know myself again."

What an odd thing to say. Then again, maybe it wasn't so odd. Certainly he wasn't the same man following Christina's death, the hole caused by her absence impossible to repair. No doubt, Rosa's divorce left a similar wound.

She'd also lost a sibling. Sometimes, in his selfishness, he forgot that Rosa had suffered as much loss as he had. The idea that she might have been hurting as bad as he made his conscience sting that much more.

"Aren't we a pair," he mused out loud. "Three years removed, and we're still struggling to move forward without our spouses. What do you think that says about us?"

"Well, in your case, I'd say it's because you have a singular heart."

"I would think the same could be said for you."

"Hardly," she replied with a bark. "Do not insult my sister by even mentioning our marriages in the same breath. Fredo isn't fit to carry Christina's water."

On that they agreed, but to hear her say so with such forcefulness surprised him nevertheless. Usually when the topic of her former husband came up, she pretended the man didn't exist.

"What did he do to you? Fredo," he asked. Had he been unfaithful? Armando couldn't believe anyone married to Rosa would want to stray, but Fredo was a boor.

She shot him a look before changing lanes. "Who says Fredo did anything?"

The defensiveness in her tone. "Did he?"

"Water under the bridge," was her only reply. "My marriage is over, and I'm better off for it. Let's just leave things at that."

"Fine." Today wasn't the day to press for details and start an argument. That didn't mean he wasn't still curious, however, or that he wouldn't try again another time.

Rosa kept one eye on the rearview mirror as she moved from lane to lane. What had she been thinking bringing Fredo's name into the mix in the first place? Her marriage—or rather, her role in it—was her greatest shame; she would rather pretend it never happened than admit her own pathetic behavior. Especially to

Armando, whose pain and loss far outweighed hers. To hear him now, trying to equate the two...

At least he'd agreed to change the subject. Hopefully telling him she was working on herself satisfied enough of his curiosity. After all, it wasn't as though she was lying. She *was* rediscovering herself. Learning, little by little, that there was a capable woman inside her chubby shell. As her therapist one reminded, her value went beyond being her husband's verbal whipping post. And, while she was still a work in progress, she had begun to like herself again.

There were days, of course, when Fredo's insults haunted her, but his voice, once so prominent in her ear, was growing softer. If she learned anything from Christina's death, it was that life was too short to settle for anything, or anyone. She'd stupidly let herself believe she had no choice when Fredo proposed. Never again. She realized now that she deserved nothing less than unconditional love. Next time, if there was a next time, she wouldn't settle for anything less. There would be no settling the next time around. She wanted someone who loved her body and soul. Who made her heart flutter whenever she heard his voice, and whose heart fluttered in return.

She wanted what Armando had with Christina.

What he would eventually have with his bride-to-be. Sure, Armando's marriage might begin for political reasons, but time had a way of warming a person's heart, especially if the person deserved to be loved. Rosa had done some internet searching last night, and discovered Mona El Halwani was a caramel-skinned beauty whose statuesque body weighed at least forty pounds less than Rosa's. She was exquisite. A walking, talking advertisement for perfection.

How could Armando's heart not warm to perfection?

They left the city behind. The landscape around them began to change revealing more and more of Corinthia's old-world. Stone farmhouses lined the streets, their window boxes stuffed with fresh greens.

Seeing the candles in the windows, Rosa couldn't help but think of what Armando had said about being responsible for every light in every window. Such a heavy weight to grow up bearing—the future of your country on your shoulders. She suddenly wanted to pull over, wrap him in a hug and let him know he didn't have to bear the burden alone.

As if those words coming from her would mean anything. Providing solace was his future wife's job. Not hers. She might as well get used to the new hierarchy right now and just do her job.

An hour later, they arrived at the Cerulean Towers, the luxury high-rise that housed Yelgiers's development concern. It was as unheralded an arrival as King Omar's, with only the doorman to greet them.

The sultan was waiting for them in his penthouse suite. Tall and exceptionally handsome, he greeted Armando with the very type of embrace Rosa had considered earlier. "I have been awaiting this moment since yesterday's phone conversation," he said, clapping Armando on the back. "That our families will be forever joined warms my heart."

Rosa stifled a giggle as she watched Armando, clearly caught off guard by the effusiveness, awkwardly pat the man in return. His cheeks were crimson. "You honor me, Omar."

"On the contrary, it is you who honor my family by taking Mona as your bride. Your union marks the beginning of a long and fruitful alliance between our countries."

"Your enthusiasm humbles me," Armando replied as he disentangled himself. "My father sends his regards, by the way, and his welcome."

"Please send my regards in return. Tell him I look forward to the day he and I toast the birth of our grandson."

Rosa choked on the cough rising in her throat. All the effusiveness was making her insides cringe.

Armando arched his brow at the sound. "You remember my assistant, Rosa Lamberti," he said, motioning to her.

She started to bow only to have her hands swept up in the sultan's large bronze grasp. Apparently, his enthusiasm didn't only apply to Armando. "Of course. A man would never forget a beautiful woman. Especially one whose face makes the flowers weep." As the sultan pressed a kiss to her knuckles, Rosa heard Armando give a cough of his own. She waited until King Omar turned and flashed him a smirk.

He led them inside and to the penthouse dining

room. The table, Rosa noticed, had been set with a combination of Yelgierian and Corinthian colors, including a large centerpiece of greens, jasmine and dianthus, the official Yelgierian and Corinthian flowers. Meant to be a tribute to their merging families, the red and gold looked unexpectedly festive as well. There was wine chilling and a trio of uniformed waiters standing at the ready next to the sideboard.

"A working lunch," King Omar explained. "I thought it would be more efficient."

That depended upon your definition of efficient, Rosa thought, counting the silverware. Chances were she would be eating salads for the next week to make up for the excess.

"I am sorry Mona couldn't be here to join us," the king said as the waiters wheeled out the first course, a rich, spicy-smelling soup that had Rosa amending her plans to two weeks of salad. "I called and requested that she fly here this morning, but sadly, she told me she wasn't feeling up to traveling."

"She's not well?" Concern marked Armando's face. Rosa knew what he was thinking. If she was sickly, Mona might not have the stamina to meet the demands that came with being queen.

"The flu," King Omar replied. "Caught during one of her visits to our local children's hospital."

"One of?" Rosa asked.

"She spends a great deal of time there. Children's charities are among her passions. In fact, she recently completed her degree in children's psychology."

"Impressive," Armando replied.

"Public service is a duty our family takes quite seriously. We understand the responsibility that comes with power. Although of all my children, I have to say that Mona takes her responsibility the most seriously."

Smart, charitable and, guessing from King Omar's looks, beautiful. Rosa reached for her water to cool the heartburn stuck behind her breastbone. Call her a cynic, but Rosa thought the woman sounded too good to be true. If the glint in Armando's eyes was any indication, however, he was impressed.

"That is good to hear," he said, "as our family is extremely interested in social reform. Sadly, as beautiful as Corinthia is, the country is not without its blemishes. We are as susceptible to the problems of the world as every country. Disease. Drugs. Violence. We're currently working quite hard to stem the problems of domestic abuse."

"Interesting," King Omar replied. "How so?"

"Being an island country can be detrimental," Armando replied. "If women in trouble cannot afford airfare for themselves and their children, they often feel trapped. It's hard to start over when you're looking over your shoulder."

Omar replied, "Are there not laws in place to protect them?"

"Yes, but laws on the books aren't always enough," Rosa said. She could tell from the widening of the king's eyes he hadn't expected her to speak up over

Armando, but as always happened when the subject came up, she couldn't contain herself.

"Many of our villages are small and contain generations of connected families," Armando explained. "Women often fear going to the authorities because of their husbands' connections."

"I see," Omar replied. "You said you are working to change this? How?" Rosa wondered if he was thinking about his own small country with its tribal population.

"We've created a number of programs over the past couple years, but the one we're most proud of is called Christina's Home, which gives women who don't have the resources a place where they can escape."

King Omar frowned. "Are you saying you built a safe house?"

"Yes, although we prefer the term *transitional home*. We provide education, legal services and such to help them start over. Right now, we have one home, but our hope is to eventually have a network of two or three Christina's Homes that can address a variety of transitional needs."

During his explanation, the waiters replaced the soup with a plate of flaky fried pastries and salad of greens and roasted peppers that had Rosa extending her salad fast until after the new year. The sultan picked up one of the pastries and took a healthy bite. "Interesting name, Christina's Homes," he said when he finished chewing. "Named after your late wife?"

Some of the light faded from Armando's eyes. "Yes. One of the qualities that made her so special was the way she cared for the welfare of our people. By naming the shelter program after her, we're honoring her memory twofold. In name and in deed. It was Rosa's idea," he added. "She shares her sister's passion for helping people."

She had heard Armando make the same compliment dozens of times without reaction. Today, however, her stomach fluttered. She felt awkward and exposed.

"My sister always believed in taking action," Rosa said. Whereas she'd needed her sister's death before she found the courage to do anything. Reaching for her glass, Rosa hid her shame behind a long drink of water.

On the other side of the table, she could feel the sultan studying her. "This sounds exactly like the type of work my daughter would want to be involved with. How many families have you helped?" he asked.

"Too many to count," Armando replied. "Some only stay for a night or two while they make arrangements in another part of Europe, while others stay longer. This time of year is among our busiest, as we like to make sure circumstances don't prevent the children from enjoying the magic of the holidays. Every year we host a Christmas party for current and past residents, complete with traditional foods and presents."

"It's also when we host our largest fund-raiser," Rosa added. "The Concert for Christina's Home is broadcast nationwide and is fast becoming a tradition." Even though she felt ashamed about her own behavior, she was spectacularly proud of how her sister's legacy had taken hold. All those late nights she and Armando worked, neither of them willing to go home and face their sad empty lives. That the program thrived proved amazing things could come out of even the most profound sadness. It was almost as much of a legacy to their triumph over grief as it was a tribute to Christina.

"The program sounds exactly like the kind of work Mona would want to see continued." Rosa jerked from her thoughts just in time to hear King Omar mention his daughter's involvement. "I have no doubt she would be honored if you allowed her to help expand the work being done in your first wife's name."

Armando would never allow it, she thought as possessiveness took hold. Christina's Home was too sacred to let a stranger—even one he planned to marry—become involved. She looked across the table, expecting to find him giving her a reassuring look. Instead, she found him taking an unusually long drink of water.

"The people of Corinthia would appreciate that," he said finally. He looked to her, eyes filled with silent apology.

Rosa lost her appetite.

"He backed me into a corner," Armando said when they were on the elevator and heading back downstairs. "It would have been insulting to say anything other than yes."

Rosa didn't reply. Mainly because she didn't want to admit Armando was right. The king had practically forced his daughter's involvement on Armando. That didn't make it sting any less.

Christina's Home had been her idea as a way of honoring her sister. She'd been the one poring over the budget with Armando and massaging corporate donors. What made King Omar think his daughter could waltz in and become Armando's partner?

Because Mona was to be his wife, that's what. Next year at this time, it would be Mona helping Armando. Mona going over party plans in his dimly lit office while he shed his jacket and tie. Letting him drink her coffee when he grew punchy. For a man who could dominate a room of leaders, Armando managed to look like a sleepy cat when tired. So adorably rumpled. She'd bet Mona wouldn't be able to resist running a hand through his curls when she saw him.

Oh, for crying out loud, you'd think she was jealous, worrying what Mona did with Armando's hair. What mattered was maintaining control over a charity she'd helped create.

"Clearly, he thought playing up his daughter's generous nature would impress me," Armando replied. Busy adjusting his jacket, he thankfully missed Rosa's scowl. The man certainly had been eager to paint his daughter in a good light.

"Did it work?" she asked.

"Did what work? Singing his daughter's praises?" He gave his cuff a tug. "I suppose. It's good to know the future queen has a keen understanding of her responsibilities. Although right now King Omar is going out of his way to paint her in the most positive light possible. He's quite a salesman in that regard."

"You think he's exaggerating?" She was ashamed at the thrill she felt over the possibility of a problem.

The shake of Armando's head quickly squelched the notion. "Oh, no, the El Halwani dedication to social causes has been well documented. They are considered among the most progressive ruling families in the region."

Of course they were. No doubt the mythical Mona would be extremely dedicated to bettering Corinthian society, including helping Christina's Home. Next year, she would be the one working by Armando's side. While he left Rosa behind.

She pressed a fist to her midsection. Lunch truly wasn't agreeing with her. What started as a burning sensation had grown to a full-blown knot that stretched from her breast to her throat.

"Do you feel all right?" Armando asked. "You've been pale since lunch."

"Too much spicy food. My stomach wasn't expecting such an exotic lunch."

"Are you sure that's all?" he asked, turning in her direction.

Rosa hated when he studied her like that, like he could read her mind. She could almost feel his blue eyes reaching through her outer layers and into her thoughts. "I—"

The elevator doors opened, saving her from trying to tap-dance in close quarters. Quickly, she stepped out into the lobby. "Why would there be something else?"

she asked once she was safely a step or two ahead. "Can't a woman have a problem digesting spices?"

"Of course. She can also be hurt."

How was she supposed to respond to that? What could she say that didn't sound jealous and possessive? "I don't know what you're talking about," she said.

"I think you do." His fingers caught her wrist, stopping her from going farther.

In the center of the lobby stood an indoor fountain, ruled over by a small marble cherub. Maintaining his grasp, Armando tugged her toward the fountain edge, where he took a seat on the marble wall. "I think we should talk," he said, pulling her down next to him. "I know why you're upset, and I understand."

"You do?" Rosa doubted his did. How could he, when she wasn't 100 percent sure why she was reacting so strongly herself.

What she did notice was how the marble beneath them made her more aware of their close position than usual. She could feel Armando's body warmth radiating against her leg, even though the only parts of them touching were his wrist on her hand. And, she realized, looking down, that was no longer true.

Looking up again, she came eye to eye with Armando's gentle expression.

"Christina's Home," he said. "You're worried what will happen if Mona gets involved with the program."

Perhaps he understood after all. "It's just that you and I worked so hard to build something together…"

"Which is why I want you to know that I understand, and I promise—" Rosa gasped as he reached up to cradle her face between his hands "—I will never let anything, or anybody, take away your sister's legacy."

Christina, of course. What had she been thinking? She gave him a smile anyway, since his reassurance was well intentioned.

When he smiled back, an odd squiggling sensation passed through her.

"Good," he said. "I'm glad, because you know how much I would hate for you to be upset."

Smile softening even more, he fanned his thumbs across her cheekbones. "I would be lost without you, you know."

He held her cheeks a beat longer before getting to his feet. "Now that we've settled that, do you feel up to driving?" he asked.

"Absolutely," she replied.

As soon as Armando started toward the front door, however, she pressed her hand to her stomach to quell the odd quivering sensation that had sprung up.

CHAPTER THREE

WHEN ROSA AND ARMANDO first conceived of Christina's Home, they wanted to build a place that the late princess would have built herself. Therefore, the home was a sprawling stone villa set at the end of a gated access road. State-of-the-art security assured residents the privacy and safety they needed to rebuild their lives, while acres of grass and gardens gave their children the chance to be children.

For this year's Christmas party, thanks to local businesses and designers eager to earn a royal blessing, the central dining room had been transformed into a winter wonderland. In addition to the traditional Corinthian red and green window boxes, there were "snow"-covered evergreens lining the walls and animated snowmen with motion detectors that brought them to life. There was even an indoor jungle gym modeled after the ice castle from a famous children's movie. All afternoon long, kids had been laughing as they hurled themselves down the indoor "ice" slide into a pile of fake snow.

Rosa stood at the back of the room, near the parti-
tion that blocked the corridor and kept the chaos contained to the single room. Near to her, a giant window
looked out on snow-covered mountains, including
Mount Cornier, whose winding roads had been Christina's final destination. During his dedication speech,
Armando said that the view guaranteed the princess
would be forever looking down on her legacy.

Rosa wondered what Christina would think if she
knew her older sister had spent the last several days
fighting a disturbing awareness when it came to Armando. All of a sudden, it seemed, someone had flipped
a switch and she was noticing things about him she'd
never noticed before, such as how elegant his fingers
looked when gripping a pen or the how the bow in his
upper lip made a perfect V. What's worse, each detail
came with an intense collection of flutters deep inside
her, the source of which was a place long dormant.
Why, after all this time, she would suddenly and inex-
plicably be attracted to the man, she didn't know, but
there it was. Nature's way of ensuring her self-esteem
didn't get too strong, probably. No worries there. Not
with Fredo's voice renting space.

"Next year, we are hiring an actor." The object of
her thoughts poked his head around the barricade. Rosa
tried not to notice he was clad only in a white T-shirt.
"I am making it a royal decree."

"You realize you said the same thing last year," she
replied.

"Yes, but this year I mean it."

"You said that last year as well." Along with the year before that, when the official shelter was still being built and they housed families at the Corinthian Arms hotel. "You love playing Babbo Natale and you know it." Interacting with the children under the Christmas tree was one of the few times she saw him truly relax. Not to mention it kept them both from feeling maudlin on a day that was supposed to be joyful.

Armando mumbled something unintelligible. "What?" she whispered.

"I said, then at least get me a better beard next year. This one makes my skin itch."

"Yes, Your Highness."

"Be careful. Mock me and Babbo will put you on the naughty list."

"Oh, goody. Naughty girls get all the good gifts."

"How would you know? Is there something you're not telling me, Signora Rosa?"

"I'll never tell." Rosa immediately clamped her jaw shut. She didn't know what horrified her more, the flutters that took flight at his question or her flirty response. To cover, she made a point of studying her watch dial. "Are you almost ready? I think the natives are getting restless."

"I thought Arianna and Max had them under control." The party was serving as the couple's first official appearance. Currently, the princess was playing carols on the shelter piano while her fiancé led the crowd in a sing-along. He was already proving a people's favorite with his movie-idol looks and exuberant off-key singing.

"They are," she told Armando, "but you know children's attention spans. Especially children who have been gorging on cake and gelato."

"The Christmas cake was delicious, was it not?"

"Mouthwatering," she replied, hoping he didn't notice the catch in her voice. Truth was, she had been more transfixed by the way Armando licked the frosting from his fork.

Their conversation was interrupted by the arrival of the future Prince Max. "I have been asked when Santa might be arriving," he said. "We're running out of Christmas songs. If he doesn't arrive soon, I may have to break out the 1940s standards."

"Please no, not that," Rosa replied. She leaned back to look behind the screen only to find herself inches away from Armando's bearded face.

"Never fear, Babbo Natale is here." He grinned. "Ready to see who has been naughty or nice. Should I start with you, Signora Rosa, since you seem to think the naughty list is the place to be?"

Too bad she wasn't wearing a beard, if only to hide her warm cheeks. She had to settle for looking down and adjusting the hem of her white sweater. "I'm sure there's much more interesting people on that list than me," she said. "Besides, you don't want to keep the children waiting for their presents much longer or we could have a riot on our hands."

Proving her point, one of the youngsters spotted

his red hat poking out from behind the screen. "It's Babbo!" he yelled out. "He's here!" Half a second later, the rest of the children started cheering his arrival as well. The mothers had to corral their children to keep them from rushing the cloth screen.

"Looks like I'm on," Armando whispered. He stepped out, and in the blink of an eye, every trace of reluctance disappeared as the prince threw himself into his performance. "Ho, ho, ho!" he called out. "*Buon Natale!* One of my helpers told me I might find some good boys and girls here. Is that true?"

"Yes," the kids screeched at the top of their lungs.

"Wonderful. Because I happen to have a sack full of toys that I brought especially for them."

Someone dragged over a folding chair from one of the tables, and he perched on it as regally as if it were an actual throne, despite the fact his athletic frame dwarfed the chair. "Let me see," he said, reaching into the velvet sack he had brought with him, "who is going to be first?"

At the chorus of "Me!" that rang through the room, Armando let out a deep rumbling laugh worthy of the Babbo himself.

Rosa's heart warmed at the sight. She had known from the very beginning that playing Santa would be a balm for Armando's grief, but it never ceased to amaze her how good he was at the job. He made sure every child got special one-on-one time with Babbo, he treated them as miniature adults, going along with the pretense for the children's sake. He was going to make a wonderful father.

When he had children with Mona. Beautiful, royal children. A wave of envy, fierce and cold, sent her spirits plummeting.

Max, who she didn't realize had disappeared, returned carrying a pair of paper coffee cups. "All this time I've been thinking Babbo Natale was some old-world European tradition and it turns out he's a more athletic version of Santa Claus," he said, tilting his head to where Armando was teasing a young girl with a stuffed rabbit. "I feel cheated."

"If it makes you feel better, there are Corinthians who embrace Befana."

"What's that?"

"An Italian witch who arrives on Epiphany."

The American's lips turned downward. "A witch on Christmas?"

"More like a crone. She brings treats."

"In that case, yes, I do feel better." He handed her one of the paper cups. "Turns out marrying the princess comes with some benefits. I mentioned wanting an espresso and the caterer made me two. You look like you could use a cup."

"Thank you." Caffeine sounded like just what she needed to perk her sagging mood. "Speaking of Arianna, where is she?"

"Putting up her feet in the back room," he replied. "Sitting on the piano stool for so long was hard on her back."

"She should have said something."

"Are you kidding? You know what Arianna's like when it comes to pianos. She was having way too much fun." From the center of the room, a child let out a high-pitched squeal. "Sounds like they're having fun, too," he noted.

"Who? The children or Prince Armando?"

"Both. I think this is the first time I've actually seen Arianna's brother smile. Granted, I've only known him about a week, so I might be misjudging…"

"No, you're not," Rosa replied, thinking of the media's nickname. "Prince Armando isn't known for his jovial side in public. This is definitely one of the few events where he truly lets himself relax and enjoy the moment."

"Hard not to enjoy yourself when you're around children," she added, as out on the floor Armando scooped up another toddler. "Although some people can't shake their mean streaks no matter what. If they could, we wouldn't need a place like Christina's Home." Wives wouldn't be made to feel like second-class citizens simply because they weren't perfect or, heaven forbid, carried a few extra pounds.

"Tell me about it," Max said. The bitterness in his voice surprised her. "Only thing that made my old man happy was a bottle. Or smacking my mom."

Rosa winced. "Some people need to mistreat their loved ones to feel better about themselves."

"That sounds like personal knowledge."

"A little."

He paused to look at her over his cup. "Your father was an A-hole, too? Pardon the language."

"No, my ex-husband." Normally, she avoided talking about Fredo, especially here at the shelter where there were women who had suffered far worse than she, but it was hard to brush off a kindred spirit. "And the word you used is a very apt description."

"I'm sorry."

Rosa stared at her untouched espresso, grateful he didn't press for more. But then, one of things about a kindred spirit was they didn't want to share either, so not asking worked to their benefit. "Me, too," she replied. "But at least when I finally worked up the courage to leave, I had people to turn to. I'm not sure what I would have done otherwise." Most likely, she would be with Fredo still, fifty pounds heavier and with her self-esteem completely eroded.

"So Christina's Home is more than a memorial to your sister then," Max said.

"My sister would have been the first person to say we need places like Christina's Home," she replied. She also would have been horrified to learn about the truth of Rosa's marriage. "But yes. If someone like me, with connections to the king, of all people, had trouble working up the courage to leave, I can't imagine what it is like for a woman who has no one."

Max's tight smile said he knew but wasn't going to talk about it. "At least you left eventually. More power to you."

Much to Rosa's relief, he tossed his crumpled paper cup into a nearby trash bin, indicating the conversation was over. "I better go check on Arianna and make sure she's truly resting. She's only just over the morning sickness stuff, and I don't want her pushing herself more than she needs to."

"If she's anything like her brother, she will," Rosa replied. "When the Santoros make a commitment, they do so one hundred and ten percent. It's ingrained in their DNA."

"No kidding. I almost lost Arianna because of it," Max replied. "Wish me luck getting her to put her feet up."

"Good luck," She waited until he'd moved away before letting her smile fade. Talking about Fredo had taken the edge off her holiday cheer.

"Is it true?" a familiar voice asked.

Armando stood behind her, still in costume. His eyes were like bright blue glass amid all his fake white hair. "What you told Max about Fredo, is it true?"

Dammit. How much had he heard? Rosa wanted to look anywhere but at him and those eyes filled with questions and…and pity. Exactly what she didn't want to see. God, looking her reflection in the eye was hard enough. How was she supposed to look at him every day if he saw her as some kind of…of…victim?

"I'm going to get some more cake," she announced. She didn't want to talk about Fredo right now, and cake never asked questions.

"Rosa, wait." He chased after her, catching her hand just as she got to the serving table.

"Armando," she whispered harshly, "the children."

Armando looked around, saw several of the youngest ones watching their interaction, and released her hand. "Why didn't you tell me?" he asked.

"Because…" She didn't finish. The anguish in her eyes answered for her, and it nearly kicked the legs out from under him. "It's in the past. What does it matter now?"

It mattered to him. If he had known, he might have done something. Stopped it somehow.

All those nights discussing the shelter… He'd thought Rosa's passion lay in memorializing her sister, but he'd been wrong. While he had been waxing sympathetic about the women they were helping, Rosa never said a word. How long had she suffered? Why hadn't he or Christina noticed? Were they so caught up in their own worlds they missed the signs? Or had Rosa been skilled at hiding them? His stomach ached for wondering. The strength it must have taken for her to walk away, the courage.

He took a good long look at the woman he'd been calling his right hand these last three years. She looked the same as always, and yet it was as though he was seeing her for the first time. What else didn't he know about her?

Suddenly he wanted to be free of the party so the two of them could talk. He had so many questions.

Before he realized, he was taking her hand again. The anguish flashed in her eyes again. "Armando…" she pleaded.

Fine. He wouldn't push her right now. That didn't mean the conversation was over. He had too many questions—was too angry and ashamed of himself—to let the subject drop. "Just tell me one thing," he asked. "Did Christina know?"

She shook her head. "No."

In a weird way, he found himself relieved. He wasn't sure how he would feel if he'd discovered Christina had known, but apparently Rosa had suffered in silence. If only he'd known…

Someone tugged on his hem of his jacket. "Babbo, Babbo, Babbo!"

Damn this costume. Biting back a sigh, he instead turned to see what his visitor found so urgent.

A pair of blond pigtails and giant brown eyes looked up at him. Armando recognized the girl from earlier, a five-year-old named Daniela who had gotten a circus play set. In fact, she held one of the set's plastic elephants in her hand. Quickly he cleared his voice. Wasn't the child's fault she'd interrupted an important moment. "Ho, ho, ho, Daniela. You're not trying to get another early present out of me, are you?" he asked, hoping his voice sounded lighthearted.

The little girl shook her head. "You're standing under the mistletoe."

What? He looked up and saw the familiar sprig of

white berries dangling from a ceiling panel. "And you want a kiss from Babbo, is that it?"

Again, Daniela shook her head. "You have to kiss her," she said pointing behind him. Slowly, he turned to Rosa, whose hand he still held. Which was the only reason she was still standing there, if the look on her face was any indication.

His eyes dropped to her lips, causing his pulse to skip. He hadn't kissed a woman since Christina's death.

Meanwhile, some of the older children who had been standing near the refreshment table figured out what was happening and began chanting in a singsong chorus, "Babbo's under the mistletoe. Babbo's under the mistletoe." The little devils. The lot of them were old enough to know his true identity, too. Probably thought it would be funny to make the prince kiss someone. He looked back at Daniela.

"Aren't I supposed to kiss the person who caught me under the mistletoe?" he asked. A quick peck on the little girl's cheek to quiet everyone.

"No. It has to be her. She was the one standing with you."

"Kiss her. Kiss her," the other children started chanting. Didn't they have parents to teach them how to behave?

"Babbo has to leave to go back to his workshop," Rosa said. In the short time since he'd turned toward her, her expression had transformed from wanting to flee to sheer terror. Armando's ego winced. Surely the idea of kissing him couldn't be that terrible?

"Daniela is right, signora," he said. "Tradition is tradition. You wouldn't want to break tradition, would you?"

"I—I suppose not." Her gaze dropped to her feet. She had very long lashes, he realized. Reminded him of tiny black fans.

"Good." It was only one small kiss. The two of them could argue about its awkwardness tomorrow morning.

Still holding her hand, he slipped his other arm around her waist and pulled her close. It was, he realized, the first time he'd ever put his arms around her, and he discovered her body was as pleasantly soft and curvy as it looked. The swell of her behind rested just beneath his splayed fingers, and it seemed to dare him to slip his hand lower. Instead, he focused on her lips, which were apparently as dry as his mouth had suddenly become, because she was running her tongue across the lower one. Her lips looked pleasantly soft and full, too.

"Kiss her. Kiss her," the children chanted.

He dipped his head.

The kiss lasted five seconds. When he stepped away, Rosa's cheeks were bright pink, and he…

His lips were tingling.

He didn't know what to say. "I—"

"Gelato," Rosa cut in. "I—I mean, we need to check the gelato." She turned and hurried toward the kitchen.

"Rosa, wait," he called after her, but she disappeared behind closed doors without turning around. Apparently the moment hadn't erased her desire to flee their discussion.

"Are you all right, Babbo?" Daniela asked. The little girl's eyes were wide with concern.

"That's a good question, Daniela." Looking back to the kitchen door, Armando ran his tongue across his lip, which tasted faintly of espresso. Was he?

CHAPTER FOUR

BY TIMING HER comings and goings around Armando's schedule, Rosa was able to avoid the man for much of the next week. She was being a coward, yes, but she needed the space considering the way she'd reacted to Armando's kiss.

Hardly a kiss. A peck under the mistletoe. Yet here she was, reliving every detail from the way his lips tasted—like breath mints—to the sensation of his artificial beard against her skin. He was right—it scratched.

She was running her finger across her lips again. *Stop it, stop it, stop it.* Balling her fingers, she tried hammering her fist against the chair arm in time with her silent chant, only the rhythm was too similar to *Kiss her, kiss her, kiss her.* Before she could help herself, the chants had switched.

Apparently her increased awareness wasn't going away any time soon.

It was all so awkward and weird, this sudden realization that Armando was a man. She could only assume his getting married caused her subconscious to wake up as far as dating was concerned. Why else would her chest be filled with a hollow, jealous ache whenever she thought about it? She wanted what Armando would have. Or so she was telling herself. She didn't want to contemplate the other reason for her reactions.

As for Armando...the kiss obviously hadn't fazed him. He'd left a note the other morning saying that Mona would be attending the Christina's Home concert on Friday night. Escorting the woman to his late wife's memorial concert would certainly let Corinthia know he was ready to move on.

Hammering her fist on the chair arm again, she sat back and took another look at the morning's paper. In the upper left-hand corner ran Mona's photo with a headline that read Our New Princess? A small story on the inside page reported on Armando's growing closeness with the Yelgierian royal family as of late, and implied there would be a marriage announcement soon.

"We missed you last evening." Princess Arianna strolled into the office without notice, knocking not being a royal requirement. She was dressed casually—for her, anyway—in a simple black skirt and flowing pink silk blouse. In deference to her pregnancy, the hem hung untucked. "At the tree lighting," she added. "You didn't attend."

The tree lighting, when King Carlos lit the tree in the palace's grand archway, marked the official start of Corinthia's holiday season. Until last night, Rosa had attended almost every one. Next to the shelter festival, it was one of her favorite Christmas traditions.

"I'm sorry," she said. "I simply had too much work to do to get away."

"Funny, Armando didn't mention you were working. In fact, he didn't seem to know where you were."

But he hadn't been looking for her, either. "I worked at home," she replied. "Armando...that is, he didn't know I was behind."

"Is that so?" Rosa tried not to react when the princess looked down at her pristinely organized desk. People with neat desks could be busy, too.

"Maybe he should get you some help. It's not fair that you have so much work that you have to miss a Corinthian tradition."

"That's not necessary, Your Highness. I'm caught up now." That was all she needed, to look like she couldn't handle her workload.

"Glad to hear it," Arianna replied, "because I would kill Armando if you were too busy to celebrate with us next week. Which reminds me, you are coming to the dinner, are you not?"

"I— Are you sure you want me there?" The dinner was a private affair for family and dignitaries the night before the ceremony.

"Of course I do," Arianna replied. "You're family, aren't you?"

"Technically, no."

"Close enough. You're an important part of Armando's life, and therefore you're important to all of us."

"How can I say no after that?" Rosa replied, surprised to feel a lump in her throat. It had been a long time since someone had said she was anything other than a stupid waste of time. And while the idea of spending an evening watching Armando and Mona get acquainted left a sour taste in her mouth, the princess was smiling such a sweet, sincere smile, Rosa didn't have the heart to decline.

Besides, she would have to face Armando—and Mona—eventually. Maybe seeing them together would kill the weird feelings she was having.

Meanwhile, Arianna's smile grew broader upon Rosa's acceptance. "I'm so glad. Max's best friend from New York is coming, too, and I can't wait for the two of you to meet. Not for romantic reasons," she added when Rosa started to say something. "I just think he needs a dinner partner who will keep him on his toes."

"Oh. Thank you, I guess." She couldn't imagine keeping anyone other than Armando on his toes, but if Arianna thought so, she would try.

"It's a compliment, I assure you." Perching on the edge of Rosa's desk, Arianna turned the newspaper around. "Future princess, huh? Wonder where they came up with that idea?"

"I read the article. It's mostly speculation."

Arianna arched her brow. "I'm going to blame your naïveté on not having enough coffee. Armando hasn't dated since Christina passed away, and out of the blue the press start speculating on the exact woman he plans to marry? Impossible. Someone whispered in a reporter's ear. The only question is who is doing the whispering—Armando or King Omar. My guess is on Armando."

Rosa didn't understand. Princess Arianna's explanation about a leak made perfect sense, but she would think King Omar the more likely source, not her brother. "Why would His Highness leak information about his private life?"

"Because I know how my big brother's mind works. I'm starting to show. It's obvious to anyone who can add that I've been pregnant longer than I've known Max." A soft smile curled her lips as her hand patted her abdomen. She glanced back at the photograph. "This is Armando's way of diverting attention away from my growing bump."

Made sense. After all, he'd arranged a marriage to prevent scandal. Why not arrange for a little well-timed tabloid gossip, too? "He's trying to be a good king," she said.

"That's Armando. Corinthia and family first."

Responsible for every light in every window. "He takes fulfilling his duty very seriously," she replied.

"Always has," Arianna said. "Although he's gotten worse the last couple years. Sometimes I think he's decided that if he can't be happy anymore, he'll make sure everyone else in Corinthia is."

Rosa's heart twisted at the thought. She didn't know what bothered her more, Armando falling for his wife or him going through the motions for the rest of his life.

"Speaking of my brother, what do you think?"

It took a moment for Rosa to realize the princess was talking about Mona herself. Took a lot of discipline, but she managed to swallow the sour taste in her mouth before replying. "I wouldn't know, Your Highness."

"Please," the princess replied. She added an eye roll for good measure. "Don't go into acting, Rosa. You're terrible."

"But I really wouldn't know," Rosa replied honestly. "I haven't met her. She's very beautiful, though. And her father certainly speaks highly of her."

"Fathers usually do," Arianna replied. "According to mine, I am the purest creature to ever walk the earth." Her grin was nothing short of cheeky as she pointed to her midsection. "I think I'll wait until I've met the woman to see if she lives up to her advance praise. Armando says she's attending the concert tonight?"

"Yes. She is supposed to arrive late this afternoon." Rosa had been trying to figure out an excuse to avoid her arrival all week.

"You don't look happy about the idea."

"Excuse me?" So much for keeping her thoughts private. She really was a terrible actress.

"No worries," Arianna replied. "I understand. This is a concert for your sister, and here's Armando infringing upon her memory by introducing his future wife."

"No, that's not the reason." Everyone was so quick to blame her loyalty to Christina. Armando thought the same thing regarding the shelter party. The simple, shameful truth, however, had nothing to do with Christina.

"What is the reason then?"

Rosa opened, then shut her mouth. What did she say? She couldn't very well tell Armando's sister the truth—that she was dreading a night of simultaneous jealousy and embarrassment.

Fortunately the telephone saved her. When she heard the voice on the other end, her eyes widened.

"That was King Omar's secretary," she said when she hung up. "Apparently his daughter hasn't completely recovered from the flu and is feeling too ill to fly."

"Meaning she's not coming tonight?"

"I'm afraid not." Rosa's stomach took a happy little bounce at the news, even though she knew it shouldn't.

From Arianna's expression, she didn't do a good job of hiding her reaction, either. "Armando will be disappointed," she noted.

Immediately Rosa was ashamed of herself. "Yes," she said, "I imagine he will be." He no doubt meant for this appearance to be Mona's introduction to the Corinthian people.

"Where is my dear brother, anyway?" Arianna asked. "I came by because I wanted to talk to him about a rumored cut to the arts endowment budget."

"According to the note he left on my desk, he is at the swimming pool doing laps."

"Really? Max is swimming laps right now as well." With surprising spryness for a pregnant woman, the princess hopped off the desk. "I was planning to go visit him after I spoke to Armando. Why don't the two of us go together and you can tell Armando about Mona's cancellation?"

See Armando. At the pool. That happy little bounce turned into a shiver as she pictured a muscular and wet Armando emerging from the water like a men's fragrance advertisement come to life. "I thought I would send him a text…" she started.

"Don't be silly. I don't feel like waiting for him to check his messages before talking to him about it. Come down with me, and we will tell him in person."

This was the downside of working for royalty. It was impossible to refuse when they decided a plan of action. Suppressing a sigh, Rosa pushed to her feet. "After you, Your Highness."

Maybe she'd get lucky, and Armando would stay in the water while they talked.

The pool was an Olympic-size addition built in what had been an unused greenhouse on the edge of the palace gardens in the mid–twentieth century. When his children were younger, King Carlos had the aging facility refurbished, transforming what had been a bland indoor pool into a paradise filled with flowers and soothing flowing water. The bamboo and hibiscus served as more than decoration—they created a foliage privacy wall so that the royal family could relax in peace. For as long as Rosa had known Armando, the room had been one of his favorite places. Since moving into the palace, Max, had taken to visiting the pool as well.

A block of hot humid air hit Rosa when she opened the door to the building. It'd been a while since she'd visited Armando in his sanctuary, and so she had forgotten how much of a contrast there was between here and the garden path that connected the two buildings, especially during the winter. She could feel her shirt starting to stick against her skin in the dampness, destroying every bit of flowing camouflage. Wasn't worth pulling the garment free, either, since it would only cling right back.

A shout called her attention toward the pool where Armando and Max were splashing their way from one end to the other.

"Looks like they are racing," Rosa remarked.

"Of course they are. They're men," Princess Arianna replied. She did peel her shirt away from her skin. "This is the first time I've ever watched Max swim. I didn't know he was such a good swimmer."

He was definitely the faster of the two—his pale body was a good length ahead—but Armando had better style. His bronze shoulders rose up and down in the water, like a well-tuned piston. Rosa envied how he could be graceful both on land and in the water.

Unsurprisingly, Max reached the wall first. When he realized Arianna and Rosa were standing there, he pulled himself out of the water.

"Well, isn't this a pleasant surprise?" he said, leaning forward to give Arianna a kiss. From the way he twisted his body, he was doing everything he could not to let his wet body come in contact with hers.

Rosa couldn't help but look him up and down. The man was definitely as well built as his movie-star looks implied. Princess Arianna was a lucky woman.

Armando's voice sounded behind her. "Next time, we do more. We'll see if you're so fast when you have to make a turn, eh? Can someone hand me a towel?"

Someone being her, of course. Rosa should have known he wouldn't stay in the water. There was a large white one draped over the back of a nearby chair. Steeling herself for what she was about to see, Rosa grabbed it and turned around.

Oh, my.

Forget fragrance ad come to life. Try sea god.

Anyone who met the man could tell Armando was well built simply from the way his clothes draped his body. What the clothes didn't show was how virile he was. He made Max Brown look like a young boy. Awareness spread from her core as she took in the muscular, wet body, its contours glistening under the lights. Droplets clung to his chest hair, like tiny crystal ornaments. Wordlessly, she watched as he wiped them away with the towel, her breath catching a little on each stroke across his skin.

If she couldn't stop thinking about a peck on the lips...

"Rosa?"

She jerked her attention back to his face to find him

looking at her with unusual intensity. "Is everything all right?" he asked. "You looked flushed."

Because you're beautiful. "It's the heat," she replied. "It's like a sauna in here."

"Well, the room was designed for people in bathing suits." He wrapped the towel around his waist, and Rosa let out a breath. Never did she think wearing a towel would be modest. "I said I was surprised to see you. You've been avoiding me."

He'd noticed? Of course he had. She hadn't exactly been subtle about staying away. "No, I haven't," she lied anyway. "There is a lot going on, is all. I have been very busy coordinating the various year-end events."

"Right. Coordinating. I understand," he said in a voice that said he didn't believe her in the slightest. "Why are you here now, then? Did something happen?"

His eyes had not just dropped to her lips and back. He was a man about to marry an amazing beauty. The last thing he would waste time on was their mistletoe kiss, unless he was remembering her foolish bolt through the kitchen door.

"I—" Rosa began. This would have been so much easier if Arianna had let her send a text. Thanks to his half-dressed state, the moment felt far more intimate than it was. What was more, the princess wasn't even talking to Armando. She and Max had taken themselves to one of the many lounge chairs, leaving her and Armando alone.

"King Omar's office called. Mona is still feeling ill and won't be able to attend the concert tonight."

"Oh."

That was an…odd reaction. Detached and almost relieved sounding. Surely that couldn't be the case. "I thought I should let you know as soon as possible in case this affects your plans for the evening."

"You could have texted."

"Arianna wanted me to tell you in person."

"Oh." That answer did come with a reaction. A conspiratorial smile that said he understood exactly what had happened. They usually shared dozens of such smiles during the course of a normal week. Seeing this one made her feel all melty inside. She'd missed his company, dammit.

"Anyway…" She cleared her throat. "If you would like to cancel…"

"Cancel? Why on earth would I cancel?"

"I only thought that with Mona not attending…" Seeing his frown, she left her answer hanging. "Never mind."

"Never mind is right. I can't believe you even suggested I wouldn't attend." He headed toward a bench by one of the bamboo trees where a robe and additional towels lay. As he brushed past her, his bare shoulder made contact with hers, and Rosa's insides turned to jitters at the feeling of dampness through her blouse. It was as close to skin against skin as she'd felt in a long time.

"You're right," she replied, rubbing the goose bumps from her arms. "I don't know what I was thinking. This morning's newspaper article speculating on your marriage must have skewed my reasoning."

He was flipping a towel around his neck when she asked. Gripping both ends, he cocked his head. "What does that mean?"

"It means, I know it was to be an important public appearance for the two of you." The first step in establishing the seriousness of their relationship."

An odd look crossed his features. "Right. I forgot about the gossip column. It would have been nice to have Mona make an appearance, but seeing as how the marriage is all but a fait accompli, it's not completely necessary.

"Besides," he added as he reached for his robe, "it's not as if the people aren't used to seeing me attend events alone.

"You're still attending, right?" he asked, shrugging into the robe.

"Of course. It's my sister's memorial concert. I wouldn't miss it for the world." Not even Mona's presence would have stopped her. "I can't believe you asked."

"What are you talking about? You asked me the same question two minutes ago. And, considering I haven't seen you all week, I didn't want to assume."

There was a bite to his comment that took her aback. She thought they had addressed this. "I told you, I have had a lot to take care of this week."

"Coordinating. So you said." He tugged on his terry-cloth belt before looking her in the eye. Rosa tried not to squirm, but the intensity of his stare was too unnerving. He was trying to see inside her again. "Look, I know why you have been avoiding me," he said.

"You do?" Heaven help her, could they go back to talking about Mona? Please? Not only was her embarrassing reaction to their mistletoe kiss the last thing she wanted to talk about, this was the last place where she wanted to not talk about it—in a steamy pool house with him wearing nothing but a bathrobe.

"I owe you an apology."

"You do?" she repeated. For what?

"It was…rude…of me to confront you the way I did. Regarding Fredo. I put you on the spot, and I shouldn't have."

"I see." She had forgotten their argument about Fredo, her mind focused on their kiss. Apparently, circumstances were the other way around for Armando. He wasn't thinking about the kiss at all. Which was a good thing, right? Meant she didn't have to avoid him anymore.

There was no reason for her insides to feel deflated. "Th-thank you," she replied. "I appreciate that."

On the other side of the pool, Arianna and Max lay side by side in one of the lounge chairs. Max had slipped on his bathrobe, and the two of them looked to be in deep conversation. Whatever problem Arianna had with the budget seemed to have taken a backseat to her fiancé. They looked so happy and engrossed with each other. Maybe it was talking about Fredo, but looking at them left Rosa aching with envy. What she wouldn't give for a man who listened to what she had to say with interest instead of patronizing her or putting her down. Someone who respected her and didn't continually remind her of her many, many flaws. *You're fat. You sound like an idiot.*

A girl could dream, couldn't she? Even if the odds of a woman like her finding someone like Max Brown were slim to none. Heck, the only person she knew who fit her bill was… Max.

She turned back in time to discover Armando was studying her again. Only this time, instead of feeling like he was looking inside her, she broke out in a tingling, achy sensation that cut through her stomach to deep below her waist.

"Get dressed," she said abruptly. "I mean, you need to get dressed and I… I should get back to the office. I'll see you when you return."

Spinning on her toe of her shoe, she turned and headed toward the pool house door. Arianna was right about her acting skills. At least this time, her excuse sounded better than having to double-check gelato quantities.

"Rosa, wait."

Armando chuckled when Rosa turned around. She looked like an animal trapped in the headlights of an automobile. Wide-eyed and hesitant. And damn if he didn't find it appealing.

"Are you bringing a guest to the concert?" he asked.

He could tell she didn't know what to make of his question. "You mean, do I have a date?"

"Exactly. I was curious if, after our conversation the other day, you weren't inspired to…improve…your social life."

Was that a blush creeping into her cheeks or simply a flush from the warm air? "You're curious about a lot of things lately."

About her, he was. It disturbed him to realize he didn't know her as well as he thought. Like the proverbial onion, there were layers he'd yet to peel back, and dammit if he didn't want to see what lay beneath. "Are you?" he asked.

"No," she replied after a pause. "I haven't had the opportunity to…improve…anything. I've been busy."

"Why don't we sit together, then?"

Rosa nearly choked. "Together? As in sit with you in the front row of the royal box?"

"Why not? Now that Mona isn't attending, the seat next to me will be empty."

"Yes, but I always sit behind you at royal events."

A rule of her own making. Armando couldn't care less about seating arrangements. In fact, it sometimes aggravated him the way Rosa would stick herself in the background, as though she were afraid to take up space. "Well, tonight I'd like you to sit in the front row with me."

"I—"

"As you said, this concert is as important to you as it is me. Tonight will be the last concert I will host before I get married. This is our opportunity to pay homage to Christina together one last time."

A shadow darkened her features. Using Christina was a low blow, but her sister's memory was the one thing Rosa couldn't resist. "I suppose," she said in a soft voice.

"Good, it's settled. We'll attend together. I will pick you up at your apartment at seven."

"Fine. Seven o'clock," she replied. "Is there anything else?"

Yes, she could try to sound a little excited. "Feel free to take the afternoon off. I know how you women like to primp for these things."

"Thank you," she replied. Armando wondered if she was grateful for the extra preparation time or the chance to avoid him a little longer. Just because she seemed to accept his apology didn't mean she wasn't still upset with him, as her reluctance to attend the concert together showed.

He watched as she turned and continued to the door. Damn, but he hated those long blazers of hers. This one was charcoal gray and went to the hem of her skirt. If there was one thing he'd noticed over the years it was that Rosa had an unparalleled walk, as good as any of the runway models in Milan. Whenever she moved, she led with her pelvis, causing her hips to swivel from side to side. And, because unlike a runway model, she carried some actual meat on her bones, her bottom half undulated with a fluidity that was amazingly sensual. Reminded him of wine swirling in a glass.

Except when she wore those blasted blazers. If she tried to wear one tonight, he would burn it.

"Was that Rosa leaving?" Arianna asked when the door clicked shut.

"I gave her the afternoon off," he replied. "She's attending the concert with me—that is, we're going to cohost the event." The other way made it sound like a date, which this wasn't. No matter how his body had reacted when she said yes.

"What a nice idea," his sister said.

"I thought we should since Mona is unable to come." And it would be their last opportunity.

Did his relief upon hearing Mona had canceled make him a horrible person? One would think he would want to spend time with his prospective bride. Wasn't that why he'd invited her to the concert in the first place? So they could get to know each other?

And then he could start fantasizing about her rather than about the kiss he'd shared with Rosa.

He shoved that last thought to the back of his mind where it belonged. He was not fantasizing about Rosa. Not really. She was his sister-in-law, for crying out loud. His sex drive had reawakened, that was all. A man could only live as a monk for so long, and Rosa happened to be the woman who was there when his inner male returned.

As for tonight, it was only fitting they cohost the event. To honor Christina.

And if he wanted to make sure she had a proper time? Well, that was simply because she deserved an enjoyable evening and had nothing to do with wanting to make her feel special.

Nothing at all.

CHAPTER FIVE

WHAT HAD SHE been thinking? Rosa smoothed her hands along her hips. When she tried it on, the saleswoman flattered her to Rome and back with a pitch about how this dress's straight cut accentuated her figure rather than making her look large and hippy. Flush from the ego boost, Rosa had let herself be talked into going against her normal style. It wasn't just the silhouette that was out of character; it was the bright red color and slightly bare shoulders, too. *Live a little*, she'd thought at the time. *No one's going to care what you wear.*

That was before she knew she would be sitting in the front row.

Next to Armando.

As his date.

Not a date. Calling tonight a date made the evening sound like it was something special rather than two friends attending an event together. Which the two of them had done dozens of times before. The only thing different about tonight was the seating arrangement.

And the fact he was picking her up.

And that the concert would be broadcast across all of Corinthia. With her seated by Armando's side, which would make her look like his date.

Had he known that when he asked her?

Her palms started to sweat. Moving to rub them on her skirt, she caught herself in time.

Squaring her shoulders, she turned left, then right, looking for any unshapely bumps or bulges. The saleswoman had been right about one thing—the dress certainly emphasized her shape. Daily walking had made her legs firm and toned, while good old control-top undergarments had firmed up the rest. She looked, dare she say it, not that bad. If only the dress weren't bright. So attention seeking.

What makes you think anyone is going to be looking at you?

Three years and Fredo's voice was as loud as ever in her head, taking her confidence and crushing it into bits.

You're a cow. You're an embarrassment.

The last thing she wanted was to embarrass Armando.

Maybe she had time to change. The black dress from last Christmas, he had liked that one, hadn't he? Or the navy blue one she wore two years ago with the sequined bodice. Could she still fit into it?

She never stressed like this over dresses before.

Then again, she'd never been Armando's date before. Not a date, she quickly amended.

Just then her living room clock chimed seven. Barely

had the last clang sounded when the doorbell rang. Rosa jumped. What the— Three years of having to hustle him out the door, and the one night he had to get ready without her, he was on time?

She opened the door to find him with one shoulder propped against the door frame. Naturally, he looked amazing, the stiff white collar gleaming against his darker skin. In a flash, Rosa's mind peeled off the clothing to picture the man she saw swimming this morning. All six feet three inches of carved muscle.

"Hi." The greeting came out a breathy whisper, far too intimate sounding for the circumstances. She cringed inwardly.

Armando eyes widened. "You look…"

She knew it. The dress was too bright.

"Gorgeous," he finished. "I mean it, that dress is…"

"Thank you. The woman at the boutique talked me into trying something different."

"Good for her. You should wear red more often. The color suits you."

Rosa hoped so, because now her cheeks were the same color as her dress, a combination of modesty and embarrassment over her reaction. This wasn't the first time Armando had ever paid her a compliment, yet awareness ghosted across her skin like it was. Made her feel more feminine and beautiful than she had in years. "You look nice, too," she told him, looking up through her lashes. "Very…regal."

"Damn. I was going for dashing."

Mission definitely accomplished. Almost. "One little

thing," she said. His tie was crooked. "You never can get your tie proper," she said, reaching up.

"That's because you weren't there to help me," he replied, lifting his chin. "Arianna had to tie it for me."

"Well, that explains why it's better than usual."

Rosa felt his warm breath on the top of her head as she adjusted the tie. Despite having done this dozens of times, she'd never noticed the distinctness of his aftershave until now. Reminded her of a wood after summer rain, earthy and cool. The kind of scent that made a person want to run barefoot through the moss.

Or comb their fingers through their hair.

"There." Smoothing his collar, she stepped back before her thoughts could embarrass her again. "Much better."

He gave her a smile. "Whatever would I do without you?"

"Spend eternity with a crooked tie, for one thing." Once again, her body reacted as though he weren't making a comment he'd made before. This was ridiculous. Tonight was really no different from any other night. Why, then, was she acting as though it was? Surely she wasn't so desperate for male validation that her subconscious needed to assign deeper meaning to everything Armando said and did. "I just need to get my wrap and I'll be ready to go."

"You're not…"

"What?" She'd not gotten more than a few feet before he spoke. Turning around, she caught the hint of a blush crawling down his cheekbones.

"You're not going to put on some jacket and wear it all night, are you?"

"No. Just a velvet wrap for when we're outside. Why?"

"No reason," he replied quickly. "It's...well, I'm not as big a fan of jackets as you are."

"I wouldn't be either, if I had your rock-hard abdomen." Rosa squeezed her eyes shut. Please say she didn't speak those words aloud.

Armando chuckled as he sauntered toward her. "You were looking at my abdomen, were you?"

"Not on purpose. It's difficult to ignore a man's torso when he's standing in a bathing suit."

"I see. Well, I'm glad you found my torso to your satisfaction."

"That's not what I meant."

"Oh?" He reached around her to lift her wrap from where it lay draped on the back of her chair. "What did you mean, then?"

"Simply that your midsection doesn't need camouflaging."

"Neither does yours," he replied, laying the velvet across her shoulders. "You worry too much about your weight. Curves are to be celebrated. There's a reason Botticelli didn't paint stick figures, you know," he added, low in her ear.

Rosa's knees nearly buckled at the way his breath tickled her skin. "I'll try to remember that."

"Please do. There's nothing worse than listening to a beautiful woman denigrate herself."

"Nothing?" Rosa asked, trying to react to the word *beautiful*. He'd handed her more compliments in the past five minutes than she'd had in the last decade.

His returning smile was devastating. "Well, maybe not as bad as reviewing the revised energy regulations or listening to Arianna complain about the arts endowment, but definitely bad." He held out an arm. "Shall we?"

No matter how many times Rosa told herself that technically this evening was no different than any other, Armando and the evening kept proving her wrong. To begin with, there was a lot of difference between sitting in the rear of the royal box and sitting with the crown prince. In the past she would take her seat several minutes before the performance and patiently wait along with everyone else for Armando to take his seat. Tonight, she was the one hanging back while the audience assembled, the one receiving the applause as she entered the box at the Royal Opera House. Really it was Armando receiving the applause, but standing by his side, she couldn't help but feel special, too.

Armando himself was contributing to the feeling as well. She couldn't put her finger on how, but there was something about his behavior tonight. He was solicitous, charming. Flirtatious, even, peppering his conversation with subtle touches and low, lilting commentary. The skin behind her ear still tingled from their conversation in her apartment. *Curves are to be celebrated.*

She squeezed her knees together.

"Everything all right?" Armando asked, mistaking her shifting as discomfort.

"Just sitting up straight," she replied. "I don't want to get caught on camera slouching."

"Fortunately, most of the time they stay focused on the orchestra, or so I've been told. I was afraid you might not be having a good time."

"Why would you think that?" she asked, doing her best not to frown as she turned toward him.

"I don't know, perhaps because you've been avoiding me all week. I wasn't sure if you were still angry with me."

"I was never angry with you. I had a lot to do, is all."

"Then you weren't annoyed that I asked about Fredo?"

He was kidding, right? What was it that drove him to introduce awkward conversations at the most inopportune times?

"I know," he added when she opened her mouth, "you don't want to talk about him right now."

No, she did not, but now that the door was open, she figured she should at least give him a quick explanation. "Nothing personal. In my experience, anything to do with Fredo will only spoil a good time." As far as she was concerned, her ex was an ugly cloud she'd rather forget.

She started as a hand settled atop her forearm. Looking up, she noticed Armando wore a pleased expression. "Does that mean you're having a good time?"

"Very."

"Good." His hand squeezed her arm and then remained. "I'm glad. You deserve the best evening possible," he added in a low voice. His whispered breath caressed her jaw, reminding her of gentle fingertips. Thankfully, the house lights had started to dim, hiding how her skin flushed from the inside out.

Onstage, the conductor emerged from behind a curtain, drawing another round of applause. After bowing to Armando, the man stepped on his dais and tapped his baton. Like a well-trained army, the musicians raised their instruments. A moment later, the room filled with the delicate hum of violins.

"Don't tell my family," Armando whispered in her ear. Between the dark and the hand on her arm, the innocent comment sent a trail of goose bumps down her spine. "But I do not like classical music."

"Since when?" Considering the way his sister and late mother had revered music, the confession wasn't just shocking, it was almost treasonous.

"Since ever," he replied. "Why do you think Arianna is the only one who still plays the piano? As soon as I could, I stopped lessons and haven't touched a keyboard since."

"I didn't realize." Both that he disliked classical music and that he played piano. Keeping her eyes forward, she leaned her shoulder closer to his. There was something naughty about whispering together in the dark. "How long did you have to take lessons?"

"Twelve very long years."

That long? "Why didn't you stop sooner?"

"Because it was expected I would become a master."

Expected. Sadly his answer didn't surprise her. So much of what he did stemmed from expectations or tradition. Even this concert, in a way. Made her wonder how long it had been since he did anything purely for fun.

She settled back against her seat as the music crescendoed over them. "Does this mean I'll need to poke you in the ribs to keep you from nodding off?" she whispered.

"Don't be silly. I never fall asleep."

"Never?"

"Okay, not since I was twelve. I have a secret trick."

"What's that?" she asked.

Behind them, Vittorio Mastella, the head of security, gave a sharp cough, and Rosa bit her lip. Because it was the crown prince doing the whispering, no one was going to say anything directly, but apparently the security chief had no problem delivering a subtle hint. Armando smiled and winked. "I'll tell you after the concert," he whispered.

They spent the rest of the concert in silence. Unlike Armando, Rosa did enjoy classical music, although purely as an amateur. She hadn't had many opportunities to enjoy it when she was married, since Fredo would only attend a concert if there was business involved. The few times they did attend, however, were some of the best memories of her marriage. She would sit in the dark and let the music send her to a world far away, to a place where she was beautiful and happy. Like the Rosa she used to be.

As the music washed over her tonight, she realized she already felt beautiful and happy. Whether it was the dress or Armando's appreciative words or the two combined, she was content with herself for the first time in a long time. More than content—it was as though she'd woken up from a long sleep and remembered she was a woman. Her body was suddenly aware of even the lightest of touches. Armando shifted in his seat, and the brush of his pant leg against her ankle left her insides aching. It did not help that he shifted in his seat a lot. Nor the fact that his hand lingered on her forearm till midway through the concert, his long fingers absently tapping a melody against the lace. The more he tapped, the more she couldn't stop remembering how he looked climbing out of the pool. Did he know what he was doing to her? The thoughts he was putting into her head? She had no business thinking of Armando this way, like a strong, desirable man. He was… Armando. Her boss. Her brother-in-law. Her future king.

And yet, his fingers kept toying with her lace sleeve, and she kept feeling beautiful, and the fantasies played in her head until the concert ended.

Until the lights in the hall brightened and she looked down at the orchestra seats only to find herself looking into the eyes of the one man capable of washing all her confidence away.

Fredo.

* * *

Armando noticed the moment the smile disappeared from Rosa's face. It was inevitable, seeing how he couldn't stop stealing glances at her all night long. He'd always considered her attractive, but tonight was different. With her hair clipped loosely at her neck, and that dress... She had to stop wearing those damn blazers and sweater sets. A body like hers, all soft curves made for a man to run his hands down, should never be hidden. Of course, he'd always known she had a good figure. What surprised him was that he was thinking about hands and curves. Apparently he wasn't as sexually dead as he thought.

Now he followed her line of sight, zooming in on Fredo Marriota immediately. Rosa's former husband was looking up at her with an expression of surprise and disbelief. Armando watched as, despite having a date of his own, the man openly assessed Rosa's appearance. It was clear seeing Rosa in the royal box irritated him. His stare was callous and sharp and made Armando's jaw clench.

At first, Rosa appeared to shrink under her ex's scrutiny, reminding Armando of the conversation he'd overheard at the shelter. Her display of weakness lasted only for a moment, because the next thing he knew, she'd reached inside herself and found a backbone. Her shoulders straightened, and she met Fredo stare for haughty stare.

Shooting Fredo a side glance of his own, Armando made a point of slipping his hand around Rosa's waist and pulling her tight to his side. "Well played," he whispered. From Fredo's vantage point, it must have looked like he was nuzzling her neck, since the man immediately blanched. "I had no idea he would be here."

"Me neither. But then again, this is a large networking event, so I shouldn't be surprised."

"He doesn't look very happy to see the two of us together."

"It has more to do with seeing me in a capable position," Rosa replied. "What are you doing?"

He'd leaned close again, so he could talk in her ear. "Playing with him." The man could use a reminder of what he'd lost. "Every time I lean close, his eyes bulge like a frog's, or haven't you noticed?"

"I noticed. So has everyone else in the theater, for that matter. How will you explain to Mona if your picture ends up in tomorrow's paper?"

Mona, whom he hadn't thought about once since Rosa opened her front door. "She will understand," he replied.

"Are you sure? I don't want to cause trouble between you."

And Armando wanted to put Fredo in his place. She moved to break free; he held her tight.

"I am positive," he said. "I hardly think Mona's the jealous type." One of the reasons he'd selected her was her decidedly implacable nature. "Your ex-husband, however, looks as though someone stole his favorite toy." Reaching up, he pretended to brush a stray hair from her cheek. To make Fredo seethe, he said to himself. Still, he felt an unfamiliar tightening at how her skin turned pink where his fingers touched.

"Insulted, more likely. I'm sure in his mind, I attended with you on purpose just so I could make him look foolish."

"But that's…"

"Ridiculous? Not to him. Do you mind if we leave now? The car is probably waiting out front." She turned in his grip so that her back faced the orchestra, essentially dismissing the man they'd been talking about. Trying to dismiss the topic altogether, Armando suspected.

"Of course." Casting one final look over her shoulder, he guided her from the box to the door where Vittorio and other members of the royal contingent waited patiently.

"Will His Majesty be heading anywhere else this evening?" Vittorio asked as they passed.

"Just home," Rosa answered for them, forgetting she wasn't his assistant tonight. "I mean, my apartment building first, and then His Highness will be heading home."

"Actually…" Armando took another look behind him before looking back at Rosa. Despite her proud stance, the standoff with Fredo had taken a toll. The glow she'd maintained all evening had faded. He hated seeing her evening end on such a sour note. "We will both be returning the palace."

"We will? Why?"

He smiled. Was it a trick of the light or were Rosa's

eyes always this soft and brown? What would they look like lit by hundreds of Christmas lights? Would they sparkle like chocolate diamonds?

He would find out soon enough.

"Royal decree," he teased in answer to her question.

Her eyes narrowed. "What does that mean?"

"It means it is a surprise."

Normally, Armando wasn't one for surprises. It had been years since he did anything remotely spontaneous, and while in the scope of things, this surprise wasn't anything dramatic, he still found himself energized by the idea. He couldn't remember the last time he'd been excited. Bouncing on the balls of his feet, rapid pulse excited. Yet here he was, wrapped in a haze of exhilaration.

All over what was really something very silly. Didn't matter. He still looked forward to his plan.

Because he wanted to be sure Rosa's evening ended on a positive note.

It had nothing to do with wanting to see her eyes under Christmas lights.

"Have I told you that I do not like surprises?" Rosa remarked when the car pulled into the underground entrance behind the palace.

"Since when?" he replied. "I seem to recall you and your sister planning all sorts of surprises together before she and I got married."

"Correction, Christina planned surprises. I was there solely for support and labor. My life was unpredictable

enough. The last thing I needed was more unpredict-
ability."

He didn't answer until the driver had opened the
door and they stepped onto the pavement. "Unpredictable. You mean Fredo." Her comments from earlier
had stayed with him. They, along with the comments
she'd made to Max at the shelter, were forming a very
ugly picture.

Her steps stuttered. "I don't want to talk about Fredo
right now," she said, looking to her shoes.

She never did, Armando wanted to say. That she
continued to shut down the conversation when he asked
hurt. Childish, he knew, but he needed her to open up
to him. Why wouldn't she? They were family, were
they not?

Except the appreciation running through him as he
watched her walk ahead of him didn't feel very famil-
ial. All women should move so fluidly.

Good Lord, but his thoughts were all over the map
this evening.

At least he wasn't the only one having appreciative
thoughts, he said to himself as he caught the overnight
guard stealing a glance in Rosa's direction. Yet again,
his mind went back to Fredo, and he wondered what
was wrong with the man that he could find fault with
a woman as likable and attractive as Rosa.

Looking at her now, standing by the elevator with a
bag clutched to her chest, her gaze contemplative and
distant, something inside him lurched. She really was
beautiful.

"I'm sorry if I upset you," he said. Thus far, the excursion wasn't going as planned.

"No, I'm the one who should apologize. Here you are trying to do something nice, and I'm being difficult."

Unlike at the concert hall when he'd pretended in front of Fredo, this time there was real hair clinging to her cheek. Armando brushed it free with the back of his hand. "You couldn't be difficult if you tried."

"I hope you don't expect me to say neither are you," she replied, ducking her head.

"Why not? It wouldn't kill you to lie, would it?"

"Possibly."

Normally, the banter diffused any tension that was between them, but this time, the air remained thick as they stepped on the elevator. Armando wasn't completely surprised. A strange atmosphere had been swirling around them all evening.

At nearly four hundred years old, the grand palace of Corinthia could be broken into two major sections—the original front section, which was open to the public, and the royal residence and offices, which resided in the more modern rear section. When the elevator doors opened, Rosa instinctively headed toward the offices. Chuckling, he grabbed her hand and tugged her toward the original castle.

"Okay, I admit I'm curious now," she said. "Isn't this section of the building closed this time of night?"

"To the public. It is never closed to me. Come along."

In the center, a quartet of stairways came together in a large open area known as the grand archway. Armando literally felt a thrill as he led her toward one of the staircases. Below them, the floor below the archway was pitched in blackness.

"Now," he said, pausing, "I need you to wait here and close your eyes."

"And then what? You will push me down the stairs?"

"I might, if you don't do what I say."

He waited until she obliged, then hurried down the darkened stairwell. Thankfully, years of childhood explorations left him with indelible memories of every nook and cranny. He located everything in a matter of minutes. When he finished, he positioned himself at the bottom of the stairs.

"All right," he called up. "Open your eyes."

Rosa's gasp might have been the most beautiful noise he had heard in a very long time.

CHAPTER SIX

HE'D LIT THE Corinthian Christmas tree.

Rosa had seen the official tree many times in her life, but this was the first time she'd ever seen the archway illuminated solely by Christmas lights. She gazed in marvel at the towering Italian spruce. The theme this year was red and gold, and somehow the decorator had managed to find golden Christmas lights. As a result, the entire archway was bathed in the softest yellow.

From his spot at the bottom of the stairs, Armando smiled at her. "What do you think? Do you still not like surprises?" he asked.

Rosa's answer caught in her throat. Standing there in the golden glow of the trees, he looked a tuxedoed Christmas god, beautiful and breathtaking.

"Amazing," she whispered. She didn't mean the lights.

"You missed the ceremony the other night, so I thought I would treat you to a private one. I realize as surprises go, it's a little underwhelming…"

"No." She hurried down to join him. "It's perfect."

He'd lit more than the tree. The phalanx of smaller trees that stood guard around the main one sparkled with lights, too, as did the garlands hanging from the balustrade.

"I had to skip the window candles," he told her. "They're too hard to light without a step stool."

"I'll forgive you."

Unbelievable. She sank down on the bottom step to better study the room. This was the first time she'd seen this space so quiet. Because it was the palace hub, the archway was a continual stream of noise and people. Sitting here now, in the solitude, felt more like she was in an enchanted forest filled with thousands of golden stars. There was a feeling of timelessness in the air. Watching the shadows on the stone walls, it was easy to imagine the spirits of Armando's ancestors floating back and forth among the trees. Generations of Santoros connected by tradition for eternity.

And he'd created the moment for *her*. As if she were someone important. The notion left her breathless.

"Why..." she started.

"I didn't want your encounter with Fredo to be how you ended your evening. So now, it can end with Christmas trees instead."

Rosa's insides were suddenly too full for her body. She was being overly romantic, getting emotional over a simple kindness.

But then, there'd been so many simple kindnesses tonight, hadn't there.

Armando wedged himself between her and the banister and stretched his legs out in front of him. "When my sister and I were children, we would sneak in here after everyone went to bed and light the trees," he said. "When it came to Christmas, Arianna was out of control. She couldn't get enough of the Christmas lights."

"Neither could you, it sounds like."

He shook his head. "You know Arianna. She acts first and thinks later. I had to go along if only to keep her from getting into trouble. Did you know she used to insist on sneaking into our parents' salon to try and catch Babbo Natale every year? I spent every Christmas worried she was going to knock over the tree on herself or something."

Rosa smiled. "Taking responsibility even then."

His sigh was tinged with resignation. "Someone had to."

The Melancholy Prince, thought Rosa. Told as a child he carried the responsibility for a nation. When, she wondered, was the last time he had done something purely because doing so made him happy? She already knew the answer: he'd married her sister. While Christina was alive, he had at least shown glimpses of a brighter, lighter self. Now that side of him only appeared when Rosa arm-twisted him into situations that required it. Like playing Babbo.

Until tonight. Even though at his age lighting the palace couldn't be called mischievous, his face had a brightness she hadn't seen in years. You could barely see the shadows in his blue eyes. The look especially suited him. If she could, Rosa would encourage him to play every night.

Again, he had done this *for her*.

"Thank you." She put her hand on his knee and hoped he could feel the depth of her appreciation in her touch.

"You're welcome." Maybe he did know, because he covered her hand with his.

"Christina and I used to wait up for Babbo, too," she said, looking up at the twinkling treetop. "Her idea, of course. I was always afraid he would be mad and switch us to the naughty list. I don't know why, since Christina would have talked our way out of it." No one could resist her sister, not even Santa Claus.

"True." He nudged her shoulder. "Your arm-twisting skills aren't half-bad, either. I bet you could have done some sweet talking, too."

"No, I would have stuttered and fumbled my words. I would have been the one who fell down the stairs, too. I might still, if I'm not careful. Grace is not my middle name."

Armando drew back with a frown. "Are you kidding? You're one of the most graceful women I've ever met."

"I—I am?"

"You should watch yourself walk out of a room sometime."

"You do know, now that you've said something, I'll never walk unconsciously again?"

"Sorry."

"No, I am. Putting myself down is a bad habit. I'm getting better, but conditioning takes time to overcome. Hear something enough times, and it becomes a part of you."

"Yes, it does," he replied. Like Armando and responsibility.

Together, they sat in silence. Rosa could feel the firmness of Armando's thigh against hers. Taking its cue from the hand resting atop hers, the contact marked her insides with warmth that was simultaneously thrilling and soothing. She selfishly wished Fredo would appear again so that she might feel Armando pull her tight in his arms, the way he had at the concert hall, and indulge in even more contact.

Instead, he did her one better.

"Fredo is an ass," he muttered, and she stiffened, afraid he'd read her thoughts. "I know," he said. "You don't want to talk about him, but I have to say it. The guy is a class-A jerk."

She could end the discussion right there by not saying a word, but the indignation in his voice on her behalf deserved some type of comment. "Yes, he is, although he can be charming when he needs to be."

"They always are. Isn't that what they told us at the shelter? It's why a lot of very intelligent women who should know better find themselves trapped."

A woman who should know better. That certainly described her. Rosa could feel Armando holding back his curiosity. Trying so hard to honor her request in spite of the questions running through his head.

From the very start of their friendship, he'd treated her with kindness and respect. More than any man she'd known. Most people—her parents, even—thought she was crazy to leave a wealthy, successful man like Fredo; they couldn't understand why she wouldn't be happy. But Armando had never judged her. Never asked what she thought she was doing. He trusted that she had a reason.

Perhaps it was time she offered him a little trust in return.

"I never told anyone. About Fredo," she said softly.

"Not even Christina?"

She shook her head. "Although I think she knew I was unhappy. Thing is, for a long time I thought the problem was with me. That if I wasn't such a fat, stupid fool, my marriage would be better."

"What are you talking about? You're none of those things."

"Not according to Fredo. He never missed an opportunity to tell me I was second-rate." Looking to her lap, she studied the patterns playing out in the lace. Tiny red squares that formed larger red squares, which then formed ever larger squares. She traced one of the holes with her index finger. "Didn't help that Christina was everything that I wasn't. I loved my sister, but she was so beautiful…"

"So are you."

Armando's answer made her breath catch. "You are," he repeated when she looked at him. "Your face, your eyes, your figure. The way you walk…"

"Regardless," she said, looking back to her lap. She wasn't trying to fish for compliments, even if his comments did leave her insides warm and full enough to squeeze tears.

"The point is for a long time I believed him. Same way I believed him when he reminded me how fortunate I was that he was willing to take me off my father's hands."

"I'm going to shoot the bastard," Armando muttered.

It was an extreme but flattering response. Rosa found herself fighting back a smile. "There's no need. Your performance tonight wounded him more than enough."

Armando shook his head. "He deserves worse. If I'd known—"

"Don't," she said, grasping his hands in hers. This time he wasn't talking about her not sharing, but about his not stepping in to defend her. She wouldn't have him feeling guilty because her shame kept her from speaking up. "I told you, I didn't want anyone to know."

"But why not? I could have helped you."

"You and Christina were in the middle of this great romance—I didn't want to ruin the mood with my problems. And then, after Christina died, you were grieving. It wasn't the time. Besides..." Here was the true answer. "I was ashamed."

"You had nothing to be ashamed about."

Didn't she? "Do you know how hard it is to admit you spent nearly a decade allowing someone to strip you of your self-respect because you thought you deserved it?" Even now, the regret choked her like bile when she thought of the power Fredo had held over her. Power she'd given him. A tear slipped from the corner of her eye. She moved to swipe the moisture away only to have Armando's thumb pass across her skin first. When he was finished, his hand remained, his palm cupping her cheek. "No one ever deserves to be abused," he said.

"I told you, Fredo never struck me."

"You know as well as I do abuse doesn't always come from a fist."

So her counselor always told her. Words could cut deep, too.

Armando's touch was warm and comforting, calling to her to lean in and absorb its promised strength. "Took me a long time to learn that," she said. "I figured as long as I wasn't sporting a black eye, I didn't have a right to complain. Besides, when it was happening…" Her voice caught. How she hated talking about those years out loud. Admitting she thought she deserved everything Fredo did and said.

Armando's fingers slid from her cheek to her jaw, lifting her face so their eyes would stay connected. The smile he gave her was gentle and understanding. It told her that he wouldn't ask for details.

Knowing she had a choice gave her the strength to say more.

"It catches you by surprise, you know? At first, it's subtle. Constructive criticism. An outburst over something you did that doesn't seem worth fighting about, because, well, maybe you didn't communicate well enough. Meanwhile, your parents are telling you how lucky you are that such a successful, handsome man wanted to be with you, and you start to think, *he's so charming and agreeable with everyone else—it has to be my fault.* That you are the one letting him down by being inferior."

Armando squeezed her knee. "You are not—"

"I am also not Christina," she said, anticipating his protest.

The feel of his touch against her skin was too enticing, so she turned her face away. As his hand dropped, a chill rushed in to fill its absence. She stared at the Christmas lights. "Life is not always easy when your baby sister is a great beauty," she told him. "Soon as she walked in the room, I ceased to exist."

"That is not true."

"Isn't it?" She had to smile, weak as it was, at Armando's protest. He, the man who fell in love with Christina the moment he laid eyes on her. "The day you met her, at the reception, did you know I was standing with her?"

He stiffened. "That was different."

No, it wasn't. "You were not the first person to lose their heart at first sight, 'Mando. Just the first one whose feelings she reciprocated."

They fell silent again. Out of the corner of her eye, she saw Armando studying his hands, a scowl marring his profile. "Do not feel bad. It was just the way things were. Christina was extraordinary." Whereas Rosa was merely average, a fact she was only now starting to realize was a perfectly fine thing to be. Not everyone could be Christina. To hold a grudge against her sister for being special would have been a waste of energy.

For some reason, talk of her sister's superiority made her think of Mona, another winner in the beauty and character lotto. Someone else with whom Rosa couldn't compete. Not that there was a competition.

Next to her, Armando shifted his weight on the stone step. "You really believed Fredo was the best you could do?"

"Silly, I know." Shameful was more like it. That a bully like Fredo was able to chip away at her self-esteem the way he did. "But Fredo had me convinced I would be a lonely nothing without him. Not only was he doing me a favor by being my husband, but I had no other options. Everything I had—money, a home— were because of him. If I left, I would have nothing."

"What made you change your mind?"

"Strange as it sounds, it was Christina's accident," she told him. "I was sitting at her bedside, holding her hand, thinking how unfair it was that someone like her, whose life was wonderful, should die when there were so many like me who could go in her place, and suddenly, I heard her voice in my head. You know that voice she used when she got exasperated."

Armando gave a soft chuckle. "I certainly do."

"Well, that voice told me life was too short and unpredictable to waste time being miserable, so take back control. So I divorced Fredo as soon as I could."

His hand found hers again. "I'm glad," he whispered.

"Me, too." Who knew where she would be if she had not? Certainly not sitting on the steps in a lace ball gown surrounded by an enchanted palace wonderland. Armando would be but a distant part of her life. Her insides started to ache. The idea of a life without Armando was…was…

Right around the corner. The thought struck her, hard. Mona would be taking him away forever.

Before she realized, there was moisture rimming her eyes. "I'm sorry," she said, sniffing the tears back. "Here you are trying to end the evening on a happy note, and I go and spoil it by acting maudlin."

"You didn't spoil anything. I'm honored you trusted me enough to finally tell me."

"Trust was never the issue, Armando. I told you, I was ashamed. And afraid," she added in a small voice.

"Afraid? Of me?"

She closed to her eyes. "Of seeing pity in your eyes." That last thing she wanted was Armando looking at her like a victim. She couldn't bear it.

"Never in a million years," she heard him say. A wonderful promise, but… She squeezed her eyes tighter.

"Rosa, look at me." Rosa couldn't. She didn't want to know what she might see.

But Armando was persistent. Capturing her face in his hands, he forced her out of hiding. "Rosa, look at me," he urged. "Look me in the eye. Do you see pity?"

Slowly, she lifted her lids. Armando was gazing at

her with eyes blue and nonjudgmental. "I would sooner cut them out than look at you with anything less than admiration."

"Little dramatic, don't you think?"

"Not in this case. What you did took courage, Rosa. Courage and strength. If anyone needs to fear judging, it's me for not being worthy of your friendship."

"You'll always be worthy," she whispered. This time, it was she who reached across the space to touch his face. His cheeks were rough with the start of an early beard. For some reason, the sensation aroused her, as if the whiskers were scratching inside her and not her skin. She wondered if her touch had shifted something inside him as well, because the blue began to take on different shades. What had been light was slowly growing dark and hooded.

"You're wrong."

Focused on the shifting of his eyes, Rosa nearly missed his words. "Wrong?"

"Thinking you're not special. You couldn't be more wrong. You're smart, strong. Beautiful." It'd been too long since someone had said such lovely words to her, and the way Armando said them was so sincere that Rosa melted with pleasure.

"I wasn't looking for compliments," she said.

"Not compliments. Truth."

Rosa nearly sighed aloud at his answer. The moment must going to her head, she decided. Why else would she think Armando's gaze had dropped to her mouth? Or long for him to move closer?

"We—" She started to say that they should say good-night, but her mind was distracted by the way Armando's lips curled into a smile. He whispered something. It sounded like Fredo was an idiot, but she couldn't be sure. Next thing she knew, those beautiful curved lips were pressed against hers.

Rosa's breath caught.

Her heart stopped.

Her eyes fluttered shut, and her hand slid to the curls at the back of his head. Sweet and lingering, it was a kiss worthy of a fairy tale. Only it was Armando whose lips were gently coaxing a response. Armando whose fingers trailed down her neck to caress the base of her throat.

A moment later, he pulled away, leaving her dazed and confused. *What...?*

"Mistletoe," he said, pointing upward. "Be a shame to ignore tradition."

Dazed and mute, Rosa simply nodded. Looking up, she saw nothing. If the mistletoe was there, it was hidden in shadows.

Armando lifted her hair off her shoulder, tucking it neatly to the base of her neck. His smile was enigmatic. There was emotion playing in the depths of his gaze, but what it was, Rosa couldn't tell. She wasn't used to seeing anything but sadness in his eyes, so perhaps it too was the shadows playing tricks.

In a way, she felt like the whole evening had been one giant illusion from the moment Armando knocked on her door. Everything had been too romantic, too close to perfect to be anything else. For five wonderful hours, he'd made her feel desirable and special. Like a princess. There was no way those feelings could last. As soon as she said good-night, reality would return.

The question was, would their relationship return to normal as well? Or would this newfound awareness continue to simmer inside her?

"It's getting late," Armando said. "We should get you home."

And there it was—reality. Armando was already standing, a hand out to help her to her feet. Although she tried to fight it, desire pooled in the pit of Rosa's stomach the moment his fingers closed around hers, answering her question.

"Are you all right?"

Naturally, he would notice and show concern. Her fantasy evening wouldn't be complete otherwise.

"Everything's perfect," she replied. Except for one tiny problem, that was.

She'd just realized she was falling for him.

Armando called for the car to be brought around, then accompanied Rosa downstairs. Back in the bright light, he saw that the front of her hair had worked loose from its clip, the result of their kiss. The strands begged to be brushed away from her skin, and he had to clench his fists rather than give in to the temptation.

The driver was waiting when they stepped outside. Upon seeing them, he opened the door and snapped to attention. "Your Highness." He sounded surprised.

"Just walking Rosa out," Armando replied. For a second, he had the crazy idea of joining her on the ride, but steeled himself against that temptation as well. There was no telling what he might do pressed against her in the darkened backseat.

As it was, he had to go upstairs and make sure there really was mistletoe.

"I'll see you Monday?" he asked instead.

"Of course."

"And no more avoiding each other?"

You couldn't blame him for asking. The last time, just mentioning her marriage had her dodging him for days. Who was to say what this last conversation might cause. Especially considering her expression—part dazed and part shadowed.

Mirrored how he felt inside.

They exchanged good-nights, then the driver closed the door. As Armando watched the rear lights disappear into the darkness, he kicked himself for not stealing another kiss.

What excuse would he give, though? There was definitely no mistletoe hanging above them this time, and "I want to be close to you" sounded too much like a line, even if it was true.

The kiss upstairs had been born from admiration. When they were establishing the shelter, he'd heard story after story of women who found the strength to walk away despite being told by their abusive husbands that they would never survive on their own. To leave and start over took real courage. But then, he'd always known Rosa was strong. Hell, he'd been drawing on her strength for three years.

She was wrong, too. Years of verbal debasement were abuse; she might not have had bruises, but she'd been hurt nonetheless. Fredo's rising financial career had just ground to a halt. No way would Armando reward the man after what he did. Telling Rosa she was an embarrassment? Killing her self-esteem? If only he could throw people in the dungeon.

"Pardon me, Your Highness. Is something wrong? It's just that you've been standing in the middle of the driveway for a while now," his security guard added when Armando turned to look at him, "and I was—"

"Lost in thought," Armando replied. First Daniela, now the guard. What was it about his kissing Rosa that required people to ask if he was all right?

On the other hand, both times had left him off balance. It felt like something was shifting inside him— something deeper than sexual attraction. There was a yearning inside him that hadn't been there before, and, incredible as it sounded, Rosa was the trigger. If he didn't know better, he would think he was developing feelings for her.

Impossible. He'd already had the love of his life. His heart was buried with her. He hadn't felt anything for three years. Tonight was simply a product of traumatic confessions and Christmas lights. Nothing more. Turning on his heel, he headed back inside.

There had better be mistletoe hanging in that archway.

CHAPTER SEVEN

THE NEXT MORNING, instead of Christmas shopping like she planned, Rosa left her local coffee shop and headed for the palace. She needed a bit of grounding. After Armando had walked her to the car, she'd spent the entire ride home, not to mention most of the early hours, trying not to relive their kiss. No matter how hard she focused on other things, the memory of Armando's lips pressed to hers kept forcing its way to the front. For crying out loud, she even tasted him in her dreams.

Wasn't it just her luck? Three years of longing for someone to awaken the woman inside her, and it was Armando, the one man in Corinthia miles beyond her reach. If she didn't have interest in dating before, how would she ever now, having experienced the gold standard of kisses?

Which was why she needed a second shot of reality, to hammer home the fact that last night was nothing but a fantasy.

Despite the early hour, the lights in the grand archway were already lit in preparation for the day's tours.

Or maybe Armando never turned them off. Either way, the arrival of day had washed away last night's magic. Whatever spirits had been dancing along the walls were back in hiding as well, giving Armando and the rest of the royal family a rest from their presence.

The sight of plain gray walls put Rosa on firmer mental ground. Gripping the balustrade, she peered upward to find a sprig of green and berries hanging from the chandelier.

Did she really think there wouldn't be?

"Rosa?"

So much for grounded. One word from the familiar voice and her stomach erupted in a swarm of butterflies. Looking over her shoulder, she saw Armando walking toward her. Seemed impossible, but he looked more handsome than he did last night. His faded jeans and black turtleneck sweater were a far cry from the tuxedo, but he wore them as with the same elegance. Casual was a look he did well. Pity his subjects didn't get to see him like this—women would be storming the gate.

The closer he got, the faster the butterflies flapped. "What are you doing here?" he asked. "I thought you took the weekend off to finish your Christmas shopping."

"I left my list in my office," she lied. "Can't very well shop without one. Well, I could, but I might forget someone. Or something. What about you?" she asked, quickly changing subjects before her babbling got out of control. "What has you wandering the halls this early in the morning?"

"Oh, you know," he said with a shrug. "Paperwork, royal proclamations. Not to mention Arianna and her wedding planners have taken over the royal residence."

"In other words, you are hiding out."

"Precisely. If I stay, I'm liable to be asked my opinion on embossed napkins. My future brother-in-law can deal with that stress on his own.

"It's not the same during the day, is it?" he said, helping himself to the coffee cup in her hand. "The tree loses something when the lights are on."

Right. The tree. For a moment, she'd been distracted by the way his lips curled around the foam. If he kissed her now, she would taste the coffee on them. "Definitely. But then, most things aren't." She wondered if the rule applied to kisses, too. If Armando were to lean in right now, would she feel the same swirl of desire? Considering the way her insides buckled over watching him drink coffee, she was pretty sure the answer was yes.

Armando's lips glistened with liquid. "I'll tell you what's not the same," he said with a frown. "Coffee without sugar. I thought you were going to stop this diet nonsense."

"There's nothing wrong with watching your weight."

"Drinking bad coffee is not weight watching, it's torture. I forbid you from doing it anymore."

"I've got a better idea. Drink your own coffee," she

said, snatching back her cup. The banter felt good. She'd been afraid last night might taint their friendship.

At least it felt good until she went to take a sip and realized her lips were touching the same spot as his. Instantly, the butterflies returned.

"By the way, I—I had a great time last night," she said.

"So you said last night."

She knew that, but talking seemed a far better alternative to her other impulse, which was running her tongue along the cup rim.

"I just wanted to make sure you know how much," she said.

"I had a good time, too." To her surprise, pink inched along his cheekbones. "I was afraid you might regret opening old wounds…"

"No, not at all. In a weird way, telling you was liberating. I never realized how much the secret was weighing on me." Or rather, the shame of it. "Thank you, by the way, for not thinking me a complete failure."

"You're not a failure, period. Your taste in men could be a little better… I mean, I could have told you Fredo was a poor choice. For starters, the man eats far too much garlic."

"Yes, he does," Rosa laughed. "And too much dairy. What was I thinking?" Her smile faded. "Sometimes I could kick myself for being so stupid," she said.

"Not stupid. Naive, maybe, but never stupid." When he said it, she believed him. Maybe last night's magic hadn't completely dissipated after all.

The sounds of footsteps floated up from below. Beneath them, security guards were readying the archway for the public. Armando leaned his forearms on the stone railing. Rosa joined him, cradling her coffee and watching the activity on the first floor.

"Clearly there is only one solution," he said after a moment.

"Solution?"

"Regarding your terrible taste. From now on, you'll have to run all your potential dates by me, and I will decide if they are worthy of you."

"Is that so?" He was joking, but Rosa's spirits sagged slightly nonetheless. A tiny part of her had been hoping last night's kiss…

"Absolutely," he continued. "You're going to need my discerning eye. We don't want you falling for any old line. Just the ones I like." The sparkle in his eyes belied his seriousness. "I have to warn you, though. I have exceedingly high standards. In fact…" He pressed his shoulder against hers, and the wave of warmth that passed through her almost made her drop her coffee. "There is a very good chance I won't find anyone suitable at all."

"Is that so?"

"No. Very few men will measure up, as far as I'm concerned."

"None at all?" she asked.

His gaze aligned with hers. Between the shadows and his pupils, Rosa could barely make out the blue. "Maybe one or two," he replied.

She suddenly had trouble swallowing, the air from her lungs having stopped midway in her throat. "One would be enough," she managed to say. Had his pupils gotten even larger? The blue had been completely obliterated.

"One, then," he replied. "One very qualified candidate."

"Very qualified?"

"The best." Rosa didn't know a few inches could be so far away until Armando leaned in toward her. They were in their own private space. "We're standing underneath the mistletoe again," he whispered. "You know what that means…"

Most definitely. What's more, this time, there was no crowd or midnight confession to spur the moment forward. Just them. She parted her lips.

Armando's phone rang.

"You should answer," Rosa replied when he groaned. "It could be your father."

"If it is, he has horrible timing."

Still, no one in Corinthia ignored a phone call from the king, not even his son, so he reached into his breast pocket. One look at his expression told Rosa the caller wasn't King Carlos.

"It's Mona," Armando replied. There wasn't enough room in his eyes to hold their apology. "I'm sorry."

Rosa wasn't. As far as she was concerned, Mona's timing couldn't be more perfect. It saved her from making a very foolish mistake. So foolish, she almost laughed out loud.

With the walls of the archway closing in, she turned and hurried down the stairs. Once outside, she kept hurrying, through the front gate and down the block, stopping only when she reached the same coffee shop where she began.

Collapsing against the brick facade, she closed her eyes and told herself her heart was racing from exertion and not from the feelings swirling around inside her.

We're standing underneath the mistletoe again...

Heaven help her, she wanted to go back. Didn't matter if it was foolish or if Armando was making a joke, she wanted to go back, stand beneath that mistletoe and wait for Armando to take her in his arms.

She wanted him.

How? When did everything change? When did he stop being Armando, the man who married her sister, and become simply Armando the man? Last night amid the Christmas lights? Or earlier? Thinking back, Armando had always been one of two measures by which she rated others—Fredo at the low end and Armando at the top—and she'd told herself that when she decided she was ready to date, she would shoot for someone in the middle. After all, while she might not be the lump of clay Fredo thought her to be, she knew better than to put herself at Armando's level, either. So what did she do? Fall for Armando anyway. Could she be a bigger idiot?

Banging her head against the brick, she let out a loud sigh. Armando had just said she had terrible taste in men.

If only he knew.

* * *

Armando tried his best to focus on the voice talking on the other end of the line and not on the red-coated figure heading down the stairs.

"I wanted to apologize for missing the concert," Mona was saying. "I thought I would be well enough to travel, but I still have a fever. The doctor is afraid I might be contagious."

"Then it was definitely a good idea to stay home," Armando replied.

"Perhaps, but I am still sorry. I know how important this event is to you."

"There is no need to apologize. You can't control what your body is going to do." Sometimes your body wanted you to kiss a woman senseless. Confessions and Christmas lights, huh? What was his excuse this morning? Because he wanted to kiss her as badly as ever.

More than kiss her. He wanted to wrap her in his arms and not let go.

Below him, he saw Rosa crossing the tile, and his body clutched in frustration. He wanted to call for her to stop, but Mona was still talking.

"I swear I am normally very healthy. The doctor says this is one of the worst strains of flu he's ever seen," Mona was saying. "But I am definitely on the upswing, and will be one hundred percent as soon as possible. You have my word."

You have my word. Mona's statement was the perfect antidote to the spell that had gripped him as well as a reminder that Armando had made a promise of his own. "I'm looking forward to it," he replied, gripping the phone a little tighter. Rosa, meanwhile, had disappeared through the exit, leaving the archway cold and quiet. Just as well. "I also should be the one apologizing." For many things. "I didn't realize you were as sick as you are."

"I downplayed the situation when we spoke. I had the idea that if I told myself I was healthy, I would get healthy. Unfortunately…" She paused to cough. When she spoke again, her voice was raspy. "Unfortunately, I was wrong."

She certainly sounded terrible, Armando thought guiltily. "Why don't I fly in and visit? I promise to stay out of germ range. It would give us a chance to spend time together." Not to mention putting some distance between him and Rosa. Hypocritical, considering he'd admonished Rosa about avoiding him not five minutes ago.

His suggestion was met with a pause. "That is very nice of you, but I am afraid I would not be very good company. I wouldn't be able to show you around. Plus I look a sight."

"People with the flu often do," Armando noted.

"I know, but I would spend the entire visit feeling self-conscious. I hate whenever anyone sees me not looking my best."

Dear God, they were going to be man and wife. Did she think a fever and messy hair might send him running?

Armando thought of all the states he and Rosa had seen each other in, including one very embarrassing incident right after she started work when she vomited in his office waste receptacle. She'd been mortified. Spent the entire time apologizing and choking back feverish tears. Now that he remembered, she'd said she didn't want him seeing her in such a state, too. He'd ignored her. Instead, he sat by her side, rubbed circles on her back, passed her tissues and told her he was right where he belonged. "We're a team," he'd told her. "What's a little flu bug between partners?" Then he'd bundled her down the hall to one of the guest rooms, and they'd watched a movie until she fell asleep. Oddly enough, it was one of his fondest memories of their friendship.

He tried to picture rubbing Mona's back only to imagine being told to stay away.

"I would hate to think my company was causing you stress," he said, partly to the image in his head.

On the other end of the line, he heard a relieved sigh. "Thank you for understanding. We will enjoy our visit much better when I'm back to myself. Perhaps next week?"

"At the wedding?"

"That would be nice. I will let you know in a few days if I think I'll be feeling well enough so we can make arrangements."

"Sounds good." It struck him how formal and businesslike their conversation sounded. This was what he wanted, though, wasn't it? A business arrangement? A week ago he couldn't imagine thinking about anything more. His heart wasn't looking for more.

His eyes looked up at the mistletoe.

He squeezed them shut. Even if his heart was looking for more, he couldn't. He'd made a promise, and Corinthia's reputation rested on his honoring it.

He talked to Mona for a few more minutes, about the concert and what few details he knew about Arianna's wedding, then agreed to talk later in the week. He had just disconnected when he spied his father strolling the corridor. "There you are," Carlos said. "Your sister ordered me to find you."

"Funny," he replied. "I thought you were the one in charge."

"Of Corinthia, maybe. Of the bride…" He paused. "Is any father of the bride ever in charge?"

"In other words, my sister has you wrapped around her little finger." No surprise there.

"What can I say? She is my baby girl. I want her to be happy."

It might be early, but King Carlos was dressed as dapperly as always. He'd once told Armando a king needed to be on any time he stepped outside his private quarters. "The people expect their king to act like a king," he'd said. As his father drew closer, Armando noticed the older man's jacket hung looser than it used to. Seemed as if every week, he grew a little older. The weight of pending responsibility that rested perpetually on Armando's shoulders grew a little heavier.

"Surely you didn't think you could escape unscathed," his father remarked.

"I'd hoped."

"You might as well get used to it. This is only a small ceremony. Yours and Mona's will be far more elaborate."

"Must it? We are talking about my second marriage."

"Regardless, you are the crown prince," his father replied. "The people will want to celebrate."

Right, the people. Those thousands of candles relying on him to stay lit. The universe was certainly intent on reminding him of his duties today, wasn't it?

His father clapped him on the shoulder, breaking his thoughts. "I know what you are thinking, son."

"You do?" How, when he wasn't sure himself? A week ago yes, but now? Not so much.

"But of course," the king replied. "I know better than anyone how difficult it is to move forward when what you really want is to bring back the past. I know how much you loved Christina." Armando felt a stab of guilt. He hadn't been thinking of Christina last night— or this morning. Only of Rosa.

"When your mother died, it was all I could do to hold myself together, I missed her that much."

"I know," Armando replied. All too well he remembered the sight of his father with his face buried in his hands.

"I still miss her. Every day." He gave a soft laugh. "We Santoros love hard."

"So I've been told." At least his father did. Armando didn't know what he was doing anymore.

"What I'm trying to say is that I know what you are doing is difficult. You're putting your sister's happiness—not to mention the welfare of this country—ahead of your own needs." His hand still lay on Armando's shoulder, and so he gave a squeeze. "I hope you know how grateful I am. Grateful and proud. When I step down, Corinthia will be in wonderful hands."

For an aging man, he had an amazing grip. The pressure brought moisture to Armando's eyes. "Thank you."

"No, son, thank you. Now..." Lifting his hand, his father slapped him between the shoulder blades. "Let us go see what duties your sister has assigned to us, shall we?"

"I'll be right there. I just have to make a quick phone call."

"Don't dally too long. I don't want to go looking for you again."

Armando chuckled. "Five minutes."

"I will hold you to that," his father replied, waggling a finger. "I love my daughter, but I refuse to deal with her bridal preparations by myself."

"Coward."

"Absolutely. One day you will have a daughter, and you will understand."

He was probably right. "Don't worry, you have my word." And Armando always kept his promises.

His eyes flickered to the mistletoe. Unfortunately.

* * *

Instead of going shopping like she said, Rosa ended up spending the weekend at Christina's Home, helping the residents with their Christmas baking. Working with the other women helped ground her, reminded her there were worse things in life than unrequited feelings. Seriously, what did it matter if Armando didn't return her attraction? It wasn't as if it was a surprise. She was a chubby, average personal assistant. And that wasn't her insecurity talking. Those were simply the facts. She also had a job and a place to call home, which made her better off than a lot of people. To quote Fredo, which she hated doing even when he was right, she had it pretty damn good.

She'd get over her crush or whatever it was.

By the time she returned to work on Monday, she was in a much better place. In fact, she thought as she stepped into the elevator, she'd even go so far as to say her feelings were shifting back to normal. Why not? They crept up on her overnight—who's to say they couldn't disappear just as quickly? Right?

Right?

Armando was sitting at her desk when she walked in. Wearing one of his dark suits, his tie and pocket square a perfect Corinthian red, he was busy reading her computer screen and didn't see her. Rosa's insides turned end over end anyway. "Isn't that desk a little small for you?" she asked. She was not trying to sound flirtatious; his long, lean figure dwarfed the writing table.

Nor did the way his eyes brightened when Armando looked mean anything. "I was looking for the notes on last week's meeting with the American ambassador. He's coming by this afternoon, and I deleted the copy you sent me."

"You do that a lot."

"What can I say? I don't like a crowded inbox."

"Thank goodness you have me, then." She turned to hang up her coat on the coatrack in the corner.

"I know."

Rosa paused. It was the same banter they'd exchanged dozens of times, only this time, the words sounded different. There was a note of melancholy attached to the gratitude that unnerved her. Slowly she draped her coat onto its brass hook. "It's snowing outside," she said. "I heard one of the guards say we might even see accumulation on the ground. Might be the first time in years Corinthia could have a white Christmas."

Armando was looking at her now, not the computer. She could tell because her spine felt his attention and had begun to prickle. Still afraid to turn around, she made a show out of brushing the droplets of water from the blue wool. "Is something wrong?" she asked.

"I wanted…"

Hearing his exasperated sigh, Rosa stopped fussing with her coat and turned around. It wasn't like Armando to sound this uncertain. It made her uneasy.

The contrite look on his face didn't help. "I wanted to apologize…"

Oh, Lord, he was going to tell her he was sorry for kissing her. "It's all right," she cut in. "There is no need to apologize. It's a silly holiday tradition."

"Maybe, but my behavior the other morning crossed the line. I was inappropriate, and I apologize."

In other words, he was sorry he'd made the suggestion. "That's what happens during the holidays," she said, forcing a smile. "All the celebrating makes people say things they don't mean. Don't worry, I didn't take offense."

"It's not that I didn't mean it, I just…"

Just what? Rosa knew she should ask, but she was too stuck on the first part of his sentence to say the words. Was he saying he wanted to kiss her again?

Pushing himself to his feet, he moved around to the front of the desk. "You're a beautiful woman, Rosa. What man wouldn't want to kiss you?"

"You would be surprised," she murmured.

"That is Fredo talking. Believe me, any man with half a brain would kiss you in a heartbeat."

She would have smiled at his calling Fredo stupid if he weren't filling her personal space. Rejection would be so much easier with a desk between them. Or breathing room. Anything besides the scent of his skin teasing her nostrils. "There's no need to oversell your point," she told him.

"I mean every word."

She risked looking him in the eye. "But?" There had to be a *but*. After all, for all his sweet words, he was apologizing, not taking her in his arms.

Shaking his head, Armando stepped away. "I'm not dead," he said. "I see a beautiful woman, I am going to feel desire. It's only natural."

He started pacing, a sign that he was thinking out loud. Trying hard to move past his finding her desirable, Rosa leaned back and waited for him to work out the rest of the explanation. The part that would pour cold water over the rest of his words.

"It wouldn't be fair," he said. "To kiss you. Not when I don't... That is..."

"I understand." There was no need for her to hear the words after all. She'd heard them often enough. His heart was buried with Christina. He was emotionally dead.

He might as well marry a stranger and help Corinthia, because he would never love again.

That's what he meant by it not being fair. He might want her, but his feelings didn't—couldn't—go deeper.

Then there was Mona. Even if he could care, there was Mona.

At least he cared enough to worry about leading her on. She should take solace in that. Then, his sense of honor was one of the qualities that made him so special.

The least she could do was let him off the hook. Inserting a lightheartedness she didn't feel into her voice, she asked, "Aren't you being a bit egotistical?"

Armando stopped his pacing. "I beg your pardon?"

"We were flirting under the mistletoe. You might

be a good kisser, but that is still a big leap to go from a kiss to breaking my heart."

"So, you didn't feel—"

"I'm not dead," she said, throwing his answer back at him. "You're a wonderful kisser. But even I'm smart enough to know that one kiss does not a relationship make."

"That's good to know," he said, nodding. The note in his voice was embarrassed relief, Rosa told herself. It just sounded like disappointment.

"Now," she said, walking around and taking her seat, "if we are finished making needless apologies, would you like me to print out the notes for your meeting with Ambassador Wilson?"

His smile was also tinged with embarrassed relief. "Please. I'll be in my office. And, Rosa?" She looked up from her computer screen to find his eyes filled with silent communication. "Thank you."

"You're welcome." She dropped her gaze back to her screen before he could see her moist-eyed response. It had been for the best, this conversation. Better to be reminded of reality than to make a fool of herself pining for something that couldn't be.

Like she told herself when she got on the elevator, there were worse things than unrequited feelings. She couldn't think of any right now, but there were.

Didn't he feel like the proper fool? Blast his decision to keep the office door open, since right now Armando wanted to slap the back of his desk chair with all his might. Dragging a hand through his curls, he glared at the snow falling outside his window. Egotistical was right. Here he'd been worrying about whether he had been leading Rosa on and all this time she hadn't been the least concerned. From the sounds of it, she hadn't given their moments under the mistletoe a second thought.

Why the hell hadn't she? Surely she had felt the same frightening intimacy he'd felt on the stairs? Why then weren't her thoughts swirling with the same confusion and desire?

Don't look a gift horse in the mouth, 'Mando. Regardless of what Rosa did or did not feel, the arguments for his apology still applied. Rosa's lack of interest merely made closure that much easier. He should be relieved.

Check that. He was relieved, and now that matter was settled, his and Rosa's relationship could go back to the way it had always been.

"Here are your notes."

Or maybe not. Just like it had when she entered the outer office, his insides clutched the second he looked at her. So sweet and soft, he literally ached to pull her close. Desire, it appeared, needed a little more than an apology to disappear.

He gripped the back of his chair instead. "Thank you," he said as she dropped the papers on his desk.

Her eyes barely lifted in acknowledgment. "You're welcome."

With his fingers gouging divots into the chair leather, he watched her walk to the door. "Making things easier," he repeated with each sway of her shapeless jacket.

Still, why the hell wasn't she as affected as he was?

CHAPTER EIGHT

AMAZING HOW QUICKLY time went when you weren't looking forward to something. If Rosa had been excited for Arianna's rehearsal dinner, the days before the ceremony would have dragged on, but since she was dreading the event—as well as the wedding itself—time sped by in a flurry of activity.

Before she realized, it was the night before Christmas Eve and she was standing by herself in the east dining room. While the wedding was small, it was by no means unelaborate. They would be dining tomorrow off three-hundred-year-old royal china bearing the Santoro crest. Tonight they were using the more modern state china with its fourteen-karat edging and matching tableware. The gold gleamed bright amid the red and white table linen. Arianna counted the forks. Six courses. Her cream-colored gown tightened at the thought.

She made a point of arriving early, while the rest of the party was in the chapel. If anyone asked, her purpose was to help Arianna's assistant. The real reason was because she couldn't face any kind of wedding reference with Armando in the room. Actually, she was trying to avoid thinking of Armando in terms of weddings, period. New Year's Day was only a week away. Each passing day left a tighter knot in the pit of her stomach. Nine days and Armando would be lost to her forever.

Not that she'd ever had him, as he had stumblingly reminded her on Monday. No one other than Christina would ever have him. But the day he announced his engagement? That spelled the absolute end. The minute sliver of hope to which her heart continued to cling would cease to exist. One would think its demise would be a relief—that it would be better to have no hope than an improbable sliver—but in typical Rosa fashion, it wasn't.

And so, rather than sit in the chapel and face reminders of Armando's pending engagement, she decided to spend a few moments alone in the dining room preparing herself.

She was standing by the fireplace warming her toes when she heard the sound of approaching footsteps. A moment later, Armando entered at the far end of the room. Upon seeing her, he stopped short. "I wondered where you might be," he said. "I noticed you weren't in the chapel during the rehearsal."

Did that mean he had been looking for her? Rosa's pulse skipped in spite of herself. She needed to stop trying to read things into his comments. "I thought Louise might need help. She's had her hands full this week, what with the gifts and the preparations."

"You would think the wedding was ten times the size considering the number of people who have sent their regards. My sister will never want for silver ice tongs again."

"Nor soup tureens," Rosa replied. "At last count, she'd received three."

"I know, I saw the display in the other room." As per tradition, the gifts were lined up for guests to see. "I shudder to think what it would have looked like if the wedding was a major affair."

He'd know soon enough. His upcoming engagement hung between them, unmentioned. The conversation was reminiscent of others they'd had this week. Friendly, but with unspoken tension beneath the surface. Even their silences, normally comfortable, had an awkwardness about them.

Watching him watch the fire, she noted the black tie hanging loose around his neck. "Do you need assistance?" she asked. "With the tie?"

He glanced down. "Please," he said. "Damn thing keeps coming out crooked when I try." Rosa had to smile. "Arianna said she would help after rehearsal, but I have a feeling she will be distracted, and since you are here..."

"It's not as though I haven't done it a couple dozen times before," Rosa replied. Stepping close, she took hold of the ends and tugged them into place. The cloth was cold from being outside. His skin, however, emanated warmth. The heat buffeted her fingers, making them feel clumsy. "One of these days you're going to have to learn to do this yourself," she murmured.

"Why, when I have you to do it for me?"

"Who says I'm always going to be around?" In the middle of looping one end over another, she heard the portent in her words and fumbled. "I would think your bride would prefer she do this for you."

She felt his muscles tense. "Perhaps," he answered, rather distractedly. "But will she be as good as you?"

"Oh, I think most people are. It isn't as hard as you think."

"Or as easy," he replied.

"I'm not sure what you mean."

"Nothing." His Adam's apple bobbed up and down as he swallowed. "I imagine you'll be glad to be free of the duty. Taking care of me must get tiring after a while."

That was an odd choice of words. Rosa pulled the bow tight. "I've never minded doing things for you," she told him. In fact, it was one of the best parts of her job. She'd found a certain kind of symbiosis in taking care of him while he grieved. The more she did, the more she remembered how strong and capable she could be. Taking care of Armando had brought back part of the woman Fredo nearly erased.

She pulled the ends of the tie, then smoothed the front of his jacket. The planes of his chest were firm and broad beneath her fingers. "There," she said. "Perfect as always."

"So are you," he replied with a smile. "You look beautiful."

"My dress is too tight."

"Stop channeling Fredo. You look perfect. You always look perfect."

The sliver of hope throbbed inside her heart. He needed to stop making her feel special.

"Armando…"

"Rosa…"

They spoke at the same time, Armando reaching for her hand as she attempted to back away.

"I—" Whatever he was going to say was halted by a pair of deep voices. She managed to slip from his grip just as Max and another man strolled in.

"And you're telling me this is only one of the dining rooms?" the stranger was asking.

"One of three," Max replied.

"Damn. This place makes the Fox Club look like a fast food joint. Hello, who's this?" He smiled at Rosa. "You weren't at the rehearsal, were you? I would have remembered."

"Dial it back, cowboy. I don't need a scandal." Max clasped the man on the shoulder. "Rosa Lamberti, may I present to you my best friend, Darius Abbott. He just arrived from New York."

"Pleasure to meet you," Rosa replied, recognizing the name. "You're Max's best man, right?"

The African-American was slightly shorter than Max, but had a muscular build, the kind you might expect from a rugby player. The shoulders of his rented tux pulled tight as he lifted her hand to his lips. "They don't make them better," he replied, winking over her fingers. Rosa giggled at his outrageousness. Max's friend was a first-class flirt.

"Rosa is Prince Armando's assistant," Max told him. "She's been a huge help this week, too. Without her and Louisa, I'm pretty sure Arianna would have lost it."

"I didn't do that much," Rosa replied. "A little organizing is all."

"As usual, Rosa is underselling herself," Armando chimed in.

"Didn't I warn you, dude?" said Darius. Eyes sparkling, he leaned in toward her as though to divulge a dark secret. "I told him something about weddings make women crazy. Even good ones like Arianna."

"My sister didn't go crazy," Armando replied.

"Much," Rosa said. "Her nerves got to her at the end. But overall, she was pretty good," she added, looking over to Armando.

"Probably because she got such good help," Darius said. "I know I'm feeling calmer."

"What can I say, I have a gift."

"You certainly do."

Good Lord, but he was over-the-top. Rosa couldn't remember the last time a man—other than Armando— complimented her so audaciously. She would be lying if she didn't say she found his behavior immensely flattering.

Out of the corner of her eye, she could see Armando watching them with narrowed, disapproving eyes. Immediately she dialed back her behavior so he wouldn't be upset.

What was she doing? Max's friend was a charming, handsome man. If she wanted to flirt with him, that was her business. A little ego stroking was exactly what she could use right now.

It was definitely better than pining for Armando, who didn't—couldn't—want her.

Feeling audacious, she offered up her best charming smile. "Have you found where you're sitting yet, Darius?" she asked. "If you'd like, I can help you find your place setting. We don't assign places the same way as they do for American head tables."

"That'd be great." Darius's perfect teeth gleamed white as he grinned back. "Maybe I'll get lucky and you'll be sitting near me."

"You know what? I think that could be arranged." Hooking her hand through his crook in his elbow, she proceeded to lead him away from the group, patting herself on the back every step of the way. She didn't once turn back and look in Armando's direction. Even if he was boring holes in the back of her head.

Armando hated the American. Why did Max have to insist on his being the best man? So what if they were childhood friends? He could have been a peripheral guest; he didn't need to be front and center, grinning his perfect white teeth at everything Rosa said. And kissing her hand hello. Americans didn't kiss hands. He kept waiting for Rosa to shoot him a look over the man's outlandish behavior. Instead, she giggled and offered to find the man's seat. He was pretty certain they'd swapped placards as well, because there she was, four seats down next to him rather than by Armando's elbow, where she belonged.

"Do you plan to eat your soup or simply stir it all night?" his father asked.

Armando set his spoon down. "My apologies, Father. I'm afraid I don't have much of an appetite this evening." How could he with such completely inappropriate behavior going on?

"I'm just saying, it's weird to segregate one little fork. Put it on the left with all the others," he heard Darius remark.

Why was Rosa laughing? It wasn't that funny. Head tipped back, notes like the trill of a thrush…he thought that was the laugh she reserved for him.

"It is a shame Mona was unable to attend this evening," Father was saying.

"Yes, it is. I don't think she expected the weather to be as bad as it is in Yelgiers." On the inside, he was far less disappointed. Despite the fact the days were ticking closer to New Year's, he found himself fighting to stir interest in his future bride. He figured it was because they hadn't spent time together. After much persuasion, he had convinced her to chat by video the other evening. A perfectly nice talk during which she supported many—no, all—of his views and left him feeling strangely flat.

"She will be here in time for the ceremony tomorrow," he said.

"I look forward to seeing her as well as her father," King Carlos said. Down at the far end of the table, the sultan was happily engrossed in conversation with Armando's second cousin, who also happened to be the deputy defense minister. "I imagine you're eager to begin your formal courtship as well."

"Definitely," Armando replied. Perhaps when they met in person, there would be more of a spark.

Although if there wasn't one, he could hardly blame Mona, could he? Not when the reason for an arranged marriage was his inability to become emotionally involved. Funny that he should be worried about a spark all of sudden.

Soup became salad. He opted for wine. On the other side of Father, Arianna and Max were ignoring their guests in favor of gazing into each other's eyes. They'd been like that since Max stormed into the palace and declared his feelings. Eyes only for each other. His heart twisted with envy. He remembered what it was like to be that deeply in love, so everything around you faded when you were with that other person. To never feel lonely because you knew there was someone in this world who understood you, who recognized your flaws and cared anyway, about whom you felt the same.

Dammit, Rosa was laughing again. What was it about the American she found so amusing? Armando kissed her, and she told him he was reacting egotistically. This… Darius made a silly comment about oyster forks and she laughed as though it were the wittiest thing she ever heard.

"Poor tomato."

Arianna's maid of honor, Lady Tessa Greenwich, pointed to the salad. "I don't know what the vegetable did to upset you, but I'm glad you're mad at it and not me."

He looked down at the cherry tomato skewered on his fork. "That's what it gets for being the easiest to spear," he said.

"Here I thought you were angry with it."

"Angry? No," he replied. Just extremely irritated with people's lack of decorum. "Would you excuse me a moment?" He left the napkin next to his plate and stood up. "I'll be back a moment."

"Everything all right?" Lady Greenwich asked.

"It will be." Soon as he had a word with his assistant. As he walked by Rosa and Darius, he leaned in to her ear. "May I see you in the corridor?" he whispered. "Now?"

Naturally, she was smiling when he spoke. She turned the smile in his direction, which only fed his agitation. "Is there a problem?" she asked.

Rather than answer, he continued walking, knowing she would follow. Once in the corridor, he led her past two additional entrances. They ended up in the gallery next to the grand arch.

"What do you think you're doing?" he asked once he was certain they couldn't be overheard.

Her eyes widened, then narrowed. "What are you talking about?"

Dear God, but she looked beautiful tonight. Her silk gown looked like cream poured over her body. Even as irritated as he was, he wanted to run his hands along every curve and sensual swell.

"I'm talking about you and Max's friend," he replied. "The way you're laughing at everything he says."

"Because he's funny. Since when is that a crime?"

Since she wasn't laughing with Armando, that's when.

"Except that you're my assistant. You were supposed to be by my side in case I need anything." Not laughing it up with handsome foreigners.

"Come on, you're not that needy, are you? Are you serious? I'm four seats away, not on the other side of the country. An extra twenty feet will hardly make a difference. Besides," she added, folding her arms across her chest, "technically I'm not working. I'm here as a guest. That means I get to sit where I want."

"That doesn't mean you get to flirt with every man in the room."

"Flirt with…?" It was the first time he had ever seen her flare her nostrils. Unfolding her arms, she held her hands stiffly by her side and leaned in. "It's called enjoying myself."

"It's called flirting," Armando charged back. "Tossing your hair over your shoulder, laughing. Like a peacock showing her plumage," he muttered to the paintings on the wall. With Darius strutting in kind. Was it any wonder he'd lost his appetite?

"So what if I am?" Rosa asked, stepping up to his shoulder. "It's been a long time since a man has found me attractive."

Armando whipped his head around. "What are you talking about? I tell you that you're attractive all the time."

"I mean someone who isn't... It's nice, is all," she said. Their shoulders knocked as she pushed past him toward the archway.

Armando stalked after her. She stood with her back to him, staring up at the Christmas tree. For a moment, his annoyance faded as he lost himself in the skin exposed by the drape of her dress.

Until the way his fingers itched to trace her spine reignited it again. "It's inappropriate," he snapped. "You're making a spectacle of yourself."

"Says who?" she asked, turning.

Said him. It killed Armando to watch her encouraging Darius's attention when she had so easily brushed off his. "You're my personal assistant," he replied. "I expect you to behave with more decorum."

Again, she folded her arms. "What would you have me do, Armando? This is your sister's wedding rehearsal. Should I just ignore the man? Stop talking to him?"

That had been exactly what he wanted. Hearing the words aloud, however, he realized how unrealistic they sounded. "Just stop throwing yourself at him," he said.

Rosa inhaled deeply through her nose. Though they sparkled, her eyes had none of the warmth they'd had the other night.

"No," she said.

One word, spoken sharply like a slap. In fact, Armando's reflexes stiffened as if it was one. "I beg your pardon?" This was where she usually turned passive-aggressive, agreeing while showing her displeasure with a sarcastic *yes, Your Highness.*

"I said no," she repeated. The first time in three years that she had defied him.

It was the most arousing sight Armando had ever seen.

Taking another breath, she started walking toward him with careful, measured steps. "I'm not going to let people tell me what to do anymore. Not Fredo. Not you…"

"I am not Fredo," Armando shot out. "Do not compare me to that bottom dweller."

"Then stop acting like him!" she snapped back. "So long as I don't hurt anyone, who I find attractive and who I don't is none of your business. Now if you'll excuse me."

Armando grabbed her wrist. He regretted it as soon as she stiffened, but the agitation in his stomach had reached epic proportions. All he could picture was Darius's handsome face and his big hands curling over those creamy shoulders. "Are you planning to kiss him?" he asked.

"That's none of your—"

But he wouldn't be deterred. Some perverse part of him needed to know. "You just said you found him attractive. Does that mean you're planning to kiss him?"

"Maybe I am," she replied, yanking her arm free. "And so what? Unlike you, I can care again. Just because you've declared yourself dead doesn't mean I have to."

"Then you are planning to kiss him."

"Whether I do or don't is none of your business."

Armando wasn't sure if it was the assertiveness or the imaginings assaulting his brain, but he couldn't let her go. Grabbing her wrist a second time, he pulled her close. Caught off guard, her body fell into his, enabling him to slip his free arm around her waist.

"Let me go," she said.

The gentleman inside him was about to when he looked into her eyes. Beautiful, fiery eyes demanding answers. And all of a sudden, he had them. The emotions that had been swirling inside him since the concert came together with astonishing clarity. Before he could stop himself, he leaned in to kiss her.

She jerked her head back. "What do you think you're doing?"

"I—" He was acting on instinct. "I'm sorry."

Breaking their embrace, he walked over to the stairway and sat down, the irony of the location not lost on him. With his eyes focused on the floor, he listened to the sounds of Rosa straightening her dress. "I want you," he said simply.

She let out a noise that sounded like a snort. "Seriously?" she said. "Five days ago you stood in your office and apologized for wanting me, said you weren't being fair to me. And now all of a sudden you're doing everything you apologized about?"

"I know. My actions don't make much sense."

"They don't make any sense, Armando."

Seeing her standing there so gloriously indignant, Armando's stomach lurched. How could he have been so blind? "I only realized myself," he said.

"Realized what?"

"How much I care."

The color drained from her cheeks. "Care?" Her voice cracked with emotion as she repeated the word. The sound forced Armando to his feet, but when he reached out, she held up her hand. "For three years, I've listened to how your heart was buried with Christina."

"I thought it was." In fact, if someone had asked him eight hours ago, he would have given that very answer. "Then tonight, when I saw you and Darius…"

"That's your possessiveness talking," she said. "I've seen it before. Darius paid attention to me, so suddenly you decide you don't want to share. Then, soon as his interest wanes…" She shrugged.

"No." Damn Fredo. No doubt her ex was responsible for that kind of thinking. "I mean, yes," he continued. "I won't lie. I wanted to break Darius's finger every time he touched you. But my jealousy was only the final piece of the puzzle. What I'm feeling inside…"

She was facing away from him. Seemed that was her favorite position tonight, giving him the cold shoulder.

Curling his hands around those shoulders, he buried his nose in her hair for a moment before struggling to find the right words.

"Have you ever looked through an unfocused telescope, only to turn the knob and make everything sharp and clear?" he asked.

Rosa nodded.

"That is what it was like for me, a few minutes ago. One moment I had all these sensations I couldn't explain swirling inside me, then the next everything made sense. The way your kisses haunted me, the fact I wanted to deport Darius for kissing your hand—they weren't isolated sensations at all. They were my soul coming back to life."

"Just like that?" She still sounded skeptical, but she had continued leaning against him. Armando took that as progress.

"Like a bolt of lightning," he said, kissing her neck again.

She pulled away, leaving him standing in the middle of the archway by himself. "You don't believe me."

"I…"

"Or…" A second thought came to him. About how easily she brushed off his apology as his ego. "Is it that you don't care?"

So excited had he been about his revelation that he didn't stop to think that she might not share his feelings. He was ashamed of himself, although not nearly as ashamed as he was disappointed. Having come back to life, he desperately wanted her to feel the same intensity of desire and need that he felt.

Still, if she didn't, he had no choice but to respect her wishes. "I'm sorry if I've made you feel uncomfortable," he told her. "I let my enthusiasm cloud my judgment."

"No, you didn't," she said, turning. "Make me feel uncomfortable, that is. I do care. I'm not quite sure when things changed, but I care a lot."

"But?" There was no mistaking the hesitancy in her voice. As much as her proclamation made his spirits want to soar, Armando held them in check and prayed what came next wasn't rejection.

Rosa shrugged, palms up. "I don't know what to think," she said.

"Then don't think," he replied. "Just go with your heart."

"I—I don't know," Rosa replied.

He made it sound easy. *Just go with your heart.* But what if your heart was frightened and confused? She had come to terms with her feelings being one-sided, only to hear him say they weren't. How could she be sure this sudden realization wasn't a reaction to another man coveting his possession? After all, Armando was used to having her undivided attention. Who was to say that once he claimed her attention again he wouldn't lose interest? Chubby, divorced, insecure. Wasn't as if she had a bucket load of qualities to offer.

Nor had he said he loved her. He cared for her, needed her, wanted her. All wonderful words, but none of them implied he was offering his heart. For all his talk of coming to life, he was essentially in the same place as before, unable or unwilling to give her a true emotional commitment. He was simply done trying to be fair. Flattering to think his desire for her was great enough to override his sense of honor.

On the other hand, her feelings wanted to override her common sense, so maybe they were even. As she watched him close the gap between them, she felt her heartbeat quicken to match her breath.

"You do know that we're under the mistletoe yet again, don't you?"

Damn sprig of berries had quite a knack for timing, didn't it? Anticipation ran down her spine breaking what little hold common sense still had. Armando was going kiss her, and she was going to let him. She wanted to lose herself in his arms. Believe for a moment that his heart felt more than simple desire.

This time when he wrapped his arm around her waist, she slid against him willingly, aligning her hips against his with a smile.

"Appears to be our fate," she whispered. "Mistletoe, that is."

"You'll get no complaints from me." She could hear her heart beating in her ears as his head dipped toward hers. "Merry Christmas, Rosa."

"Mer—" His kiss swallowed the rest of her wish. Rosa didn't care if she spoke another word again. She'd waited her whole life to be kissed like this. Fully and deeply, with a need she felt all the way down to her toes.

They were both breathless when the moment ended. With their foreheads resting against each other, she felt Armando smile against her lips. "Merry Christmas," he whispered again.

Rosa felt like a princess.

Behind them, a throat cleared. "I beg your pardon, Your Highness."

The voice belonged to Vittorio Mastella, head of security. He stood in the doorway as statue-like as ever, dare she say even overly so, the way his hands were glued tight against his thighs. "I've been asked to deliver a message to you."

Armando tightened his hold on her waist, clearly afraid she might flee. "If it's Father, tell him I'm not feeling well, and I will see him in the morning," he said, smiling at Rosa. "I'm in the middle of a very important discussion."

"I'm afraid it's not from your father." The way his eyes flickered between the two of him made Rosa uneasy. Whatever the message, it sounded like unwanted news.

She couldn't have been more right.

"Princess El Halwani has arrived," Vittorio announced. "She's on her way to the dining room as we speak."

CHAPTER NINE

ENTER THE BIGGEST stumbling block of all. How on earth could Rosa have forgotten about Mona, the ultimate reason for holding back her heart? At the sound of her name, she broke free of Armando's embrace. Easy enough since his grip had gone lax.

"Thank you, Vittorio," Armando replied.

From his shell-shocked expression, it appeared he had forgotten about Mona as well. Small consolation, but Rosa took it nonetheless.

Vittorio bowed in response. "Again, I'm sorry for the interruption, Your Highness."

"No need to apologize, Vittorio. Your timing was fine."

Fortuitous even, Rosa would say. This was the second time she and Armando had been stopped from kissing. Maybe the universe knew the troubles that lay ahead and had stepped in to protect them. Certainly it had saved her from heartache tonight.

Partly, anyway.

The two of them stood listening to Vittorio's receding footsteps. Armando looked as dazed as she felt. His eyes were flat and distant.

She broke the silence first. "We'd best be heading back to the dining room as well. You don't want the princess wondering where you went."

"Yes, we should," he replied in a voice as far away as the rest of him. Then he coughed. The action seemed to shake him back to life, because when he looked at her, his eyes were sharper. Apologetic. "We should talk later."

"There isn't that much to talk about," she replied. Whatever they'd been about to discover was a missed opportunity.

They were met at the dining room entrance by both King Carlos and King Omar. While Armando's father wore a concerned frown, the sultan looked ready to burst with excitement. "There you are, my friend! I wondered where you had gone to for so long."

"I was feeling under the weather," Armando replied, "and went out for some fresh air."

"With your assistant?" King Carlos asked.

"I asked Rosa if she would get me something for my stomach. Vittorio told me Mona has arrived."

"Yes!" replied Omar. "The weather finally cleared, and our pilot was able to get clearance. She is freshening up after her flight and will be back momentarily. You do look pale," the sultan noted, cocking his head. "I hope it is nothing serious. This arrangement has been plagued enough by illness. Ah, here is my daughter now."

It was like a scene in a movie. At the sound of King Omar's pronouncement, all heads turned to the far end of the room to see Princess Mona walk in.

Not walk, float. She moved like she was moving on air with the amethyst color of her gossamer gown trailing behind her. "My deepest apologies, King Carlos," she said after executing a perfect curtsy, "for arriving so late. I hope I am not disrupting your daughter's special evening."

"You can blame me," Omar said. "Mona was going to go to a hotel, but I insisted she make an appearance. She and your son were long overdue to spend time together."

"You are most right, Omar," King Carlos replied before kissing Mona's fingers. "Your presence is welcome no matter how late. I've already instructed the staff to add a setting next to Armando."

"You're too kind, Your Highness." She cast her eyes down in appropriate demureness, her eyelashes fluttering like butterfly wings.

For a woman who wasn't planning to attend, she looked breathtaking. Her dark hair was pulled back tight to give accent to her almond-shaped eyes and high cheekbones. And her skin…her complexion looked like someone had airbrushed her.

The woman turned her curtsy to Armando. "Prince Armando, I'm so pleased to see you again."

Armando nodded. "I'm glad to see you are fully recovered. You…" He cleared his throat. "You look as lovely as I remember."

"I'm a fright from rushing to get here, but thank you for the compliment. I'm looking forward to our getting to know each other better over this next week."

"The same here." He coughed again. "Sorry. I think might need a glass of water."

"As good a cue as any to take our seats before your sister notices we are gone," King Carlos said. "Although I would say the odds are in our favor."

"They do appear very much enamored with one another," Omar noted.

"Indeed," said the king. "If we were to all go to bed right now, I am not sure they would care. In fact, we may have to tell them when dinner has ended."

Speaking of not being noticed… Rosa lagged behind as the royal quartet walked away. There was a brief moment when Armando looked back, but she purposely didn't catch his eye. Looking at him would only cause her to replay their conversation in the archway, and she felt cold and alone enough as it was.

"Hey, beautiful, I'd wondered where you'd gone. They're just about to serve the main course. Or so the forks tell me." Leaping to his feet, Darius pushed in her chair. "Everything okay with the boss man?"

She looked across the table to where Armando was introducing the princess to the rest of the guests. They made a good-looking couple, the two of them. They would make good-looking heirs as well.

"Why wouldn't it be?" she asked.

"The two of you were gone for a while. I was afraid something might have happened. Some kind of royal attack or something. We're not under attack, are we?" he whispered teasingly.

Rosa forced a smile. It wasn't Darius's fault she'd left her affinity for flirting back in the archway. "No attack. Yet," she replied. "His Highness had a problem he was trying to work out."

"Did he?"

"Turns out he forgot an important piece of information. But," she said as Mona laughed, making it her time to feel sick to her stomach, "now that he has it, I'm sure he knows what he has to do."

It was the longest meal of Armando's life. Bad enough before, when he was listening to Darius attempting to charm Rosa. But once Mona came, he was forced to be charming himself while listening to Darius. All the while wishing he was standing under the mistletoe with Rosa.

Rosa, who refused to catch his eye.

Just as well. It had been wrong of him to declare his feelings when he was obligated to Mona. Selfish and wrong. His only defense was that he'd been doing exactly what he'd advised Rosa to do: not think.

Now, as punishment for his greediness, he could spend the rest of the evening tasting Rosa's kiss. The sensation of her mouth moving under his overrode his taste buds, turning everything that passed his lips bland and lifeless. By the time dessert arrived, he wanted to toss his napkin on the table and tell everyone he was through.

He didn't, of course. One abrupt departure was enough. Besides, between his behavior and Mona's late arrival, he'd stolen the spotlight enough.

Well, he had wanted to give people something to gossip about besides Arianna's pregnancy. Sitting to his left, Mona dabbed her lips with her napkin. "Father was right," she said. "Your sister and her fiancé are very devoted to one another. No wonder your father is willing to be so…accepting…of the circumstances."

"What do you mean?"

"Please don't get me wrong," she said. "I only meant that Corinthia has a reputation for being almost as traditional and conservative as my country. That your father doesn't seem fazed by your sister doing things out of order, if you will, says something."

"The order doesn't matter. Max's devotion to Arianna is indisputable."

"She is very lucky. As you and I both know, love matches in royal marriages are rare."

Yes, they were. Yet again, he tried to catch Rosa's attention, but her profile was firmly turned toward Darius.

Armando flexed his fingers to keep from forming a fist. A lock of hair had fallen over her eye, loosened no doubt, when they'd kissed. He wanted to comb it away from her face simply so he could run his fingers through her hair.

He wanted to do a lot of things. Apparently being

haunted by her kiss wasn't enough—all his other buried urges returned as well.

Coming back to life was killing him.

"Over time…"

Mona was talking to him again. He jerked his attention back. "I'm sorry. I missed what you said."

"I was talking about royal marriages," she said. "That the absence of love in the beginning doesn't mean the marriage won't be successful. After all, if two people are compatible, there is no reason why they won't develop feelings for one another over time. Love doesn't always happen at first sight."

"No, it doesn't," Armando murmured. Sometimes love crept up on you over a period of years, disguising itself as friendship until your heart was ready.

"Especially when there are children and mutual interests involved," Mona continued. "When two people are committed to the same goals."

"Working as a team," Armando said.

"Precisely."

That's what he and Rosa were. A perfectly matched team.

You didn't break up a perfect team.

He would tell Mona tonight that their arrangement was off. There would be a scandal, which would divert attention away from Arianna and her child's illegitimacy. That had been the point of accelerating his marriage plans in the first place. Meanwhile he would court Rosa properly.

Fingertips grazed the back of his hand, causing him

to stiffen. Mona smiled apologetically. "You looked a million miles away," she said.

"I'm sorry. I was thinking about the future." One that looked bright for the first time in years.

"I'm glad to hear it," she replied, "because I have, too."

Sadly, they weren't thinking of the same future, and for that, he felt terrible. It wasn't Mona's fault love had a bad sense of timing. "Perhaps we should talk after dinner," he said.

"I would like that," Mona replied. She looked down at their hands, which were still connected, she having left hers atop his. "I hope you don't think me too forward, but I believe you and I could do a lot of good together."

The muscles along the back of Armando's neck began to tense. "Good?" he repeated.

"Yes. The flu I caught the other week. Father told you I caught it volunteering at the hospital? He lied. What he didn't tell you was that the people of Yelgiers are suffering from a terrible health care crisis. A lot of our citizens, mostly women and children, are without decent medical attention. The fact that women are still treated as second-class citizens in many parts of the country, and are therefore seen as undeserving of care, only exacerbates the problem. So many women suffer in silence."

"Too many," Armando noted, thinking of the women at Christina's Home.

"I've been reading up on how much your government

has done these past years to improve conditions for women and children. I'm hoping that when our countries are united," she said, squeezing his hand, "our countries' combined assets will help all our people."

Our people. Armando stared at his untouched dessert, the weight of Mona's speech pressing down upon his shoulders. With a few eloquent sentences, Mona had reminded him how much was at stake. Their engagement wasn't just about them. It wasn't even about protecting his family from scandal. It was about doing what was best for his people. Corinthia was counting on him to lead them to a prosperous future. To keep them safe and healthy. And now, thanks to his agreement with Omar, so were the people of Yelgiers.

Every single candle in every single window...

If he broke off the engagement, it would mean far more than some headlines and bad blood. While they might not realize it, there were people who needed his marriage to Mona to make their lives better.

How could he walk away knowing he was failing people? His people. Mona's people. As much as he loved Rosa—and, oh, God, he did love her, more than he thought possible—he could never live with himself.

Better to settle for kisses under the mistletoe and be able to look at himself in the mirror.

He'd been right earlier. Love really did have terrible timing.

For the first time in her life, Rosa couldn't find comfort in a chocolate dessert.

"Don't tell me you're pregnant, too," Darius joked. "You've got that same green-around-the-gills look the princess used to get when she first showed up in New York."

No such luck, she thought, putting a hand to her stomach. If she were pregnant with Armando's child, she would be doing cartwheels of joy. The only thing making her green was a bad case of jealousy. Brought on by seeing Mona holding Armando's hand.

"Just indigestion," she replied.

"I hear ya," Darius replied. "That was a lot of food. Makes me wonder what we're going to get at the wedding tomorrow."

Oh, Lord, the wedding. Maybe she could claim illness and stay home. That way she wouldn't have to face another eight hours of seeing Armando and Mona together.

The American leaned back in his chair with a satisfied sigh. "Thank goodness I've got till tomorrow night to digest everything. Otherwise, I might need some emergency tailoring on my tuxedo. Max would kill me. You sure it's indigestion?" he asked at her half-hearted laugh.

"It is." Rosa was still staring at the joined hands across the way. Whatever Mona was talking about had to be serious. Armando was frowning at his untouched plate.

"I don't know," Darius replied. "That prince of yours looks pretty green, too."

"He's not my prince," Rosa answered reflexively. Never was, but for five minutes under the mistletoe.

Now that Darius mentioned it, though, Armando did look pale. Good. Petty as it was, she wanted him to feel as terrible as she did. She also wanted Mona to trip over her floaty train and fall on her face.

No, she didn't. It wasn't the Yelgierian's fault she was beautiful and graceful and probably brilliant.

She wasn't even angry with Armando. Not much, anyway. It had been her choice to kiss him. He'd said to stop thinking, and she did. A smarter woman would have heeded her own warnings. Then again, a smarter woman wouldn't have fallen for Armando in the first place.

To think, she'd started dinner feeling empowered. The joke was on her. She was a bigger fool than even Fredo thought she was.

The wedding of Princess Arianna Santoro and Maxwell Brown, the newly named Conte de Corinth, went flawlessly. Not only did security keep the press away, but the bride's former boyfriend departed that morning on a lengthy trip to the continent. With all potential drama eliminated, the result was an intimate and beautifully romantic ceremony that even the people of Corinthia seemed content to let stay private.

Armando and his father had to be pleased. A week from now, Armando would announce his engagement, the country would be plunged into wedding fervor yet again and no one would ever remember the princess's pregnancy started before she met Max in New York.. Plus by this time next year, Mona would probably be pregnant—because she was no doubt amazingly fertile along with all her other qualities. Success all around. Long live the royal family of Corinthia.

Because it was Christmas Eve, the reception did double duty as a holiday celebration, only instead of trees, there were towers of poinsettias, each near ten feet high. People could be seen exchanging gifts by them when they weren't dancing and enjoying the wedding festivities. Seated at a table by one of the ballroom windows, Rosa triple-checked whether the decorations included mistletoe. Given her and Armando's recent track record with the plant, one could never be too careful.

There wasn't any. Meaning there was no excuse for even the most casual of kisses.

She cursed the way her heart fell.

"You should be careful. I hear there's a law in this country against outshining the bride." Darius handed her a glass of wine before helping himself to the seat next to her.

"Little chance of that, I'm afraid. Did you see Arianna?" She nodded to where the princess and her husband were posing for a photograph. Given the circumstances, Arianna had forgone a traditional gown in favor of simple pink satin, but her happy glow made her easily the most beautiful woman in the room.

"She looks good, but you're definitely a close second."

Rosa rolled her eyes. "Sounds like someone's been helping himself to the champagne."

"Sounds like someone needs to help herself to a little more." To prove his point, his added the remaining contents of his glass to hers. "Here, drink up," he said, sliding the glass toward her. "It'll make watching them a little easier."

"I don't know what you're talking about." Surely she wasn't that transparent.

Apparently she was, because the man immediately gave her a look. "Sweetheart, I'm a New York bartender. I know how to read people. In your case, it's not that hard. You've been watching the guy since last night's main course."

No sense pretending she didn't know what he meant. Directly across the dance floor, Armando and Mona were talking to her father, Omar. Mona was the one dangerously close to upstaging the bride. Her strapless gown looked sewn onto her body.

She paled compared to Armando, though. Both he and his father were in full regalia for the wedding, navy blue uniforms complete with sash and sword. He looked like he belonged on a white charger.

"For crying out loud, you're staring at him right now," Darius said. "Damn good thing I don't have self-esteem issues."

"I'm sorry. I don't mean to be rude. I..."

"Got a thing for the guy?"

Rosa felt her cheeks burn. Quickly, she grabbed her wine and swallowed. "I'm afraid it's complicated."

"I know. I met her last night. What's her deal, anyway?"

Rosa told him.

"Fiancée, huh? Then why were you two sneaking off last night? I told you, I'm observant," he added when she gasped.

Because Armando got jealous and said he wanted her. He kissed her like she'd never been kissed before, and probably never would be again. He let her pretend for a moment that a woman like her could be a princess, and now she was sitting at a wedding angry at her own foolishness.

"I told you," she said. "It's complicated."

"I bet. Complicated is why I'm glad I'm single. Come on." He stood up and held out his hand. "Let's fox-trot."

Rosa shook her head. "I don't think…"

"You really want to sit here looking like a sad chipmunk all night, or do you want him to see you enjoying yourself next time he looks in your direction?"

Rosa looked over to see Mona place a proprietary hand on Armando's arm. The woman certainly didn't waste time marking her territory. "There's a good chance I'll step on your toes."

"Good, that makes two of us."

Darius, it turned out, was a worse dancer than she was. By the second song, they were both laughing over how much they were tripping up the other. Rosa had to admit, it felt good to make mistakes and laugh about them. Made her forget her heartache for a little while.

That was, until a familiar hand tapped Darius on the shoulder. "May I?" Armando asked. His eyes, as well as his request, were directed at her.

Rosa could feel Darius tightening his grip in an effort to protect her. "It's all right," she told him. Actually, it was probably a mistake, but the chance to be in Armando's arms was too great a temptation to pass up.

"You two seem to be enjoying yourselves," Armando said when she stepped into his arms. "I'm sorry I had to interrupt." Rosa bristled at his barely disguised jealousy. What made him think he had any right?

"Isn't that the point of a wedding? To enjoy yourself?"

"I didn't mean that the way it sounded," he replied. He twirled their bodies toward a far end of the dance floor. "That's a lie. I meant it exactly as it sounded. It killed me to see you in his arms."

"Really? Because watching you with Mona is a picnic."

Her jab hit its mark, because he immediately winced. "You're right. I have no business saying anything, and I'm sorry."

"So am I," she replied. If these were to be the only moments Armando held her, she didn't want to waste them fighting. It was because the position reminded her too much of last night, and the memories were too raw to handle politely. She ached for him to close the distance between their bodies. A few inches, that was all. Enough for her to rest her head on his shoulder and pretend the rest of the world didn't exist.

Instead, the song ended. She started to step away, but Armando tightened his grip on her waist. "One more dance," he said. "There's something I need to say."

"Armando…" He was going to talk about Mona and obligations and all the other topics she wanted to forget.

"Please, Rosa."

Whatever made her think she had a chance? Letting out a breath, she relaxed into his touch. "You know I can never say no to you."

"I know," he replied.

While he spoke, his gaze traced a line along her cheek, performing the caress he couldn't do by hand. Rosa's insides cried for the touch.

They danced in silence for what felt like forever. Finally, just when she was ready to say something, Armando spoke. "Do you know what I did last night?" he asked.

She shook her head.

"I couldn't sleep, so I counted the lights I could see from my bedroom window. Seven hundred fourteen. In that one patch of space. Do you know how many there are in the entire country? One point two million."

"Oh, 'Mando." She knew where this was going.

"Never have I resented so many lights," he said, gazing past her.

"That's not true. You don't resent them," she replied. "You love them."

Still looking past her shoulder, Armando sighed.

"You're right. I wish I did hate them, though. I wish I didn't care what happened to any of them."

He pulled his gaze back to her, and she saw that the perpetual melancholy that clouded his eyes was twice as thick. "I do, though. Dammit, I do."

"I'm glad." Yes, a selfish part of her wanted him not to care, but it was Armando's love for his people that made him who he was.

"She wants to improve medical care. Mona. That's what she wants to do when we're married. Improve medical care in both countries. There will be thousands more candles to look after."

She could feel the responsibility pushing down upon him. Suddenly Rosa understood. He was backed into a corner. Choose duty and save lives. Choose for himself and fail two countries. Whatever anger she might still have began to fade. "You're doing the right thing," she told him. Like he always did. The responsible young boy who looked out for his sister on a bigger scale. "Corinthia—and Yelgiers—are lucky to have a leader who cares so much."

"Perhaps." He didn't look convinced. He looked… sad. "I had no right to kiss you, Rosa. It was wrong."

"Don't say that."

"But it's true. I knew I had obligations, and yet, like a selfish bastard, I went after what I wanted anyway. Who knows what would have happened if Vittorio hadn't interrupted us?"

They both knew what would have happened.

"How does that make me any different than Fredo?" he asked.

His self-loathing had gone too far. Halting her steps, she touched her fingers to his lips to silence him. "You are nothing like Fredo."

He smiled and kissed her fingertips. "Aren't I, though? You deserve better."

Except there wasn't anyone better. If the feelings in her heart were to be believed, there never would be. "In case you didn't notice, there were two people kissing," she told him. "We both ignored our common sense."

Armando shook his head. "Dear, sweet Rosa. You still won't admit you are a victim."

"Because I'm not a victim." Not this time. "Last night, you made me feel more special in five minutes than I had ever felt in my entire life. I would trade all the common sense in the world for that."

"If I could, I would make you feel special every day. You deserve nothing less."

"Neither do you."

He smiled sadly. "But apparently I do."

The song ended, but they had stopped dancing long ago in favor of standing in each other's arms. Rosa's first assessment was right—it was much too similar to last night's embrace. When Armando's eyes dropped to her mouth, common sense was again poised to disappear.

"I love you, Rosa. I'm sorry I didn't come to my senses sooner."

He pulled away, leaving her to shudder from the

withdrawal. She was still in a daze. Did he say he loved her? *Loved?*

The sound of a spoon against crystal rang across the ballroom. King Carlos had stepped up to the front of the room.

"Ladies and gentlemen, might I have your attention?" Instantly, the ballroom went silent.

"Arianna asked me to refrain from formal toasts and speeches during last evening's dinner, and as you all know, while I rule Corinthia, she rules me." Low laughter rippled through the crowd. Rosa sneaked a look at Armando and saw he hadn't cracked a smile. "However, I cannot let this evening end without saying a few words, not as your king, but as a father."

The king's smile softened. "This family has seen its share of loss over the past few years. My wife. Princess Christina." At the sound of her sister's name, Rosa looked to the floor.

"But now, as I look at the faces around the room and I see the smile on my daughter's beautiful face, my heart is filled with so much hope. Hope for new beginnings. Hope for the next generation, and the generations of Santoros to come. I've never been prouder of my children. Just as I am proud of my newest son, Maxwell. I hope also to add a new daughter soon as well." Everyone but she and Armando looked in Mona's direction. Armando kept his attention on his father, while Rosa lifted her eyes to watch Armando.

"I am getting older," the king continued. "Older and

tired. There may come a day in the future when I decide to step down."

A gasp could be heard in the crowd. King Carlos held up a hand. "No need to be upset. I'm not worried. Because I see the people who will be taking my place, and I couldn't be more pleased."

The rest of his toast was a flurry of well wishes for Arianna and Max. At least that was what she assumed. Armando had turned to her, and she found herself transfixed by his blue stare. *I'm sorry*, his eyes were saying. *I have no choice.*

All Rosa could hear were the words she'd convinced herself he wasn't going to say. *I love you.* A lifetime and she wouldn't hear three more beautiful words.

She loved him, too.

What was she going to do come Monday? And the Monday after that? What about when Armando announced his engagement? Knowing he loved her might sound wonderful today, but how was she going to face him day in and day out when he belonged to someone else?

Simple answer was, she couldn't. Not without the self-esteem she'd worked so hard to rebuild crumbling into pieces again.

There was only one answer.

CHAPTER TEN

"ALL ARE ONE…" The last words of the Corinthian national anthem rose from the crowd gathered below the balcony. Arianna and Max had been officially presented as a royal couple.

Leaving Father and the happy couple to greet their well wishers, Armando stepped back inside. There was only so much joy a man could take, and he had met his limit.

He was happy for his sister, truly he was, but if he had to watch her and Max gaze into each other's eyes a second longer, he would scream.

A few moments alone in the empty gallery would clear his head. Then he would be ready to tackle the rest of Christmas Day. Mona and her father were joining the celebration. Another day being reminded of the hole he'd dug himself into. At least he'd apologized to Rosa, taking that guilt off his shoulders. Somewhat. He doubted he would ever be completely guilt-free.

Because part of him would never regret kissing her.

To his surprise, Rosa was in the gallery when he

entered, studying one of the china cabinets. One look and his energy returned, even if she was wearing one of those ridiculous long blazers he hated. He hadn't expected to see her for a few days. He'd wanted to—oh, Lord, had he wanted to—but common sense had made a rare appearance and suggested otherwise. If he went to her apartment, he would be tempted to pull her into his arms. Much like he was tempted right now.

When she saw him, she smiled. "Merry Christmas," she greeted.

Something wasn't right. He could tell by the sound of her voice. "The crowd sounds thrilled with their princess's new husband" she said.

"So it would seem. If I were a gambling man, I would bet Max embraces his royal role very quickly."

"That would be good for Corinthia."

"Yes." That was what mattered, wasn't it? The best for Corinthia? "What are you doing here?" he asked. The question came out more accusatory than he meant. "I thought you were helping out at the shelter this afternoon."

"I wanted to come by and give you your Christmas present." She pointed to a wrapped box on the seat of a nearby chair.

Armando walked over and fingered the cheerful silver bow. He didn't know what to say.

"Don't worry, it's not booby-trapped, I promise," she said. A halfhearted attempt to shake off the awkward atmosphere.

It wasn't booby trapping that had him off balance—
it was wondering whether he deserved the kindness.

"My gift for you is under the tree upstairs," he said.
A gold charm bracelet marking moments from their
friendship.

"You can give it to me later. I can't stay long, and
I want to see you open yours. Go ahead," she urged.

He peeled back the gift wrap. It was an antique wood
statue of Babbo Natale. The colors were fading, but the
carving itself was flawless.

"I found it in a shop outside the city. The owner
thought he was handmade around the turn of the century. Silly, I know, but what else do you get the guy
who has everything? You've already got plenty of ties,"
she added with a self-conscious laugh.

"Don't apologize," Armando told her. "It's beautiful.
Truly handcrafted pieces are hard to find."

"When I saw him, I thought he looked a little like
you do when you're wearing the costume. Around the
eyes."

He turned the statue over in his hands. "I'll take your
word for it." It didn't matter if the statue resembled him
or the queen of England. She could have given him a
paper doll and he would have treasured the piece. Because it came from her.

He longed to pull her into a hug. "Thank you. I love
it." *And you.*

"I…" All of a sudden, she stopped talking and piv-
oted abruptly so she stood with her back turned to him.
Something was definitely wrong, he thought, his shoul-

ders stiffening. "I thought it would make a good memory to share with your child," she continued. "About those times you played Santa Claus at the shelter."

"You talk as if I won't be there anymore." That was never going to happen. The shelter and its mission were too important to him. More so now that he knew her story.

"Not you," Rosa replied, her back still turned. "Me."

Her? Armando's stomach dropped. "What are you talking about?"

When she didn't reply right away, he reached for her shoulder. To hell with not touching her. "What do you mean, you?"

"I-I'm leaving."

No. She couldn't be. Armando's hand fell away short of its goal. "You're not going to be my assistant anymore?"

"I can't." Finally, she turned around. When he saw her face, Armando almost wished he hadn't. Her eyes were damp and shining. "I can't come to work every day and see you. It's too dangerous."

"I don't understand." His mind was too stuck on her resignation to make sense of anything else. "Dangerous for whom?"

"Me," she replied.

She started to pace. Rosa being the one to mark paths on the carpeting for a change would be amusing if the circumstances were different. "I thought about what you said last night, about my deserving better," she said.

"You do. You deserve—"

She cut him off. "I know. Surprisingly. Fredo convinced me I would never deserve better than dirt, and for a long time I believed it."

He watched as a tear dripped down her cheek. "Then you said you loved me. Loved. And I started thinking, if a man like you thinks he loves me…"

"I do love you," he said, rushing toward her.

"Don't." With her hands in front of her chest, she shook her head. "This is why I have to quit."

"You don't want to be near me."

"Don't you understand? I want to be near you too much. You're marrying someone else, 'Mando.

"And I get it," she said when he opened his mouth to tell her she was—she would always be—his first choice. "I understand the responsibility you feel toward your country, and why you need to keep your word. I love your sense of honor.

"But if I stay, I'll be tempted to be with you no matter what the circumstances, and I can't be the woman you love on the side. I worked too hard on being myself again."

She was shaking by the time she finished. With tears staining her cheeks. It killed him to stand there when every fiber of his being wanted to steal her away to a place where they could be together. It killed him, but he knew it was what Rosa wanted. Just as he knew he couldn't fight her leaving.

"What will I do without you?" he asked instead.

"You survived without me for years, 'Mando. I'm

sure you'll survive again." Armando hated to think the last smile he'd see on her face would be this sad facsimile that didn't reach her eyes.

"Where will you go? What will you do?"

"I don't know yet. Right now, I'm going to focus on celebrating Christmas. I'll figure out the rest tomorrow."

"You survived once, you'll survive again," he repeated softly.

"Exactly." Her fingers were shaking as she wiped her cheeks. "Merry Christmas, Your Highness. Happy New Year, too."

Not without her in it.

With Babbo Natale cradled in his arms, he stood alone in the gallery and listened to the sound of the elevator doors closing. "Don't go," he whispered.

But like her sister had three years before, Rosa left anyway.

"Was that Rosa I saw getting on the elevator?" Arianna asked. She strolled in with Max and Father trailing behind. Her face pink from the cold, she shrugged off her coat and draped it over the arm of a chair. "I wish I'd known she was coming by. I have a Christmas present for her. Is that what Rosa gave you?" she asked, noting the wood carving. "It's lovely."

"What's lovely?" Max asked.

"The carving Rosa gave Max," Arianna replied.

"I'm not surprised," Father said. "She's always had impeccable taste." He went on to tell Max a story about an ornament Armando's mother bought the year Arianna was born. Armando continued to watch the doorway in case Rosa decided to return.

"She was determined to find the perfect ornament to mark Arianna's first Christmas. We must have gone to every shop, craftsman and artist in Corinthia, and nothing was good enough. If I'd thought I could learn fast enough, I would have taken up glassblowing myself so she could design her own. It has to be perfect for our baby, she kept saying."

Armando had already heard the ending. How his mother finally found the ornament in a gift shop in Florence, and it turned out to have been made by a Corinthian expatriate who insisted on giving the ornament as a gift for the new princess. The reverence in his father's voice as he spoke was at near worship proportions. His words practically dripped with love.

Armando's head started to hurt.

"I know she would be thrilled to look down and see the ornament on your tree, for your child."

"I'm only sorry she isn't here," he heard Arianna say with a sniff.

"We can only hope she is watching right now, happy and proud of both of you."

Would she be proud, Armando wondered. Would she be happy to know her eldest son had let the woman he loved walk away?

He worked up the courage to turn around, only to find a portrait of marital bliss. Max stood behind Arianna, arms wrapped around her to rest his hands on her bump. His father stood a few feet away, beaming with paternal approval. He tried to imagine himself in the picture, his arms around a pregnant Mona. Imagine himself content.

All he could see was Rosa's back as she walked away.

It wasn't fair. Father had said last night, their family had seen its share of dark days. Armando had buried his wife, for God's sake. He turned off a machine and watched her take her last breath! Did that moment truly mean he would never have love again? If that was the case, then why wake his heart up? Why torment him by having him fall in love with Rosa after he'd agreed to marry King Omar's daughter? Wouldn't it be better to keep his heart buried? Or was loving and losing another woman his punishment for some kind of cosmic crime?

"Armando!" Arianna was staring at him with wide eyes. "What is wrong with you?"

"You're choking Santa Claus," Max added.

He looked down and saw he had a white-knuckle grip on the statue. A more delicate piece would have snapped in two.

"I…" He dropped the figurine on the closest table like it was on fire. Babbo landed off balance and fell over, his wooden sack of toys hitting the table first with a soft thud.

Arianna appeared by his side, reaching past him to set the statue upright. "Are you all right?" she asked him. "You've been acting odd since late last night. Did something happen between you and Rosa?"

"Why would you ask that?"

"Because you and she are usually joined at the hip, and the past few days…"

"I have a headache is all," he snapped. The air in the gallery was feeling close. He needed space. "I've got to get some air."

Of course he would end up sitting in the archway, under the mistletoe. Trying to put your head on straight always worked best in a room full of memories. Sinking down on the next to last step, he scrubbed his face with his hands, looking to erase the night of the concert from his brain. Instead, he saw Rosa, her face bathed in golden light.

What was he going to do? Leaning back, he stared up at the mistletoe sprig. "You have been nothing but trouble, do you know that?"

If the berries had a retort, they kept it to themselves. Bastards.

A flash of gold and green caught his eye. A few feet to his left, he noticed an angel perched near the top of the tree. Unlike the other ornaments, which were ornate almost to the point of ostentation, the angel was simple and made of felt with a mound of golden hair surrounding her face. He really must be losing his mind; the way the angel was hung, it looked like she was watching him. "What do you think I should do, angel? Do I do the honorable thing and keep my promise to Mona? Or do I go against everything I've ever been taught to run after Rosa?"

Nothing.

That's what he thought. As if a Christmas ornament would know any more than a branch of mistletoe.

Why then did he feel as though the answer was right there, waiting for him to see it? "Why did Christina have to die in the first place?" he asked the angel. "Life would be so much easier if she had just taken the curve a little slower. I wouldn't have needed to enter an agreement with King Omar because I wouldn't need a wife."

And Rosa would still be with Fredo. Unacceptable. As much as he had loved Christina, he would never bring her back if it meant leaving Rosa married and fearful. Christina wouldn't want to come back under those circumstances.

But she would tell you to follow your heart. That life is too short to waste time feeling angry and unhappy. Not when happiness is within your reach. All you have to do is to be brave enough to take a chance. To sneak out after dark and turn on the Christmas lights.

To leave the abusive husband. If Rosa could be brave enough to walk away from Fredo, if the other women could walk away from worse, then surely he could summon up enough bravery to be happy.

"Armando! Are you here?"

Looked like he would be tested sooner than he thought. "In the archway, Father."

"I should have known." King Carlos appeared at the top of the opposite stairs. "I swear you are as bad as your sister regarding these lights," he said as he navigated the steps.

"It's too cold to go outside," Armando told him. "This is the next best thing."

"You are aware you are sitting under the mistletoe?"

"Believe me, I know. Damn plant is following me."

His father chuckled. "You, my son, might be the first person I have ever heard complain about kissing traditions. Or is it a more specific problem?" he asked, settling himself on the step as well. "Your sister is right. You've been out of sorts for a few days now. Did something happen?"

"You could say that," Armando replied. He stared at his palms. Maybe one of the lines had the words he needed to explain. "Did you mean what you said last night? About being proud of Arianna and me?"

Whatever his father had been expecting, that wasn't it. He leaned back a little so he could see Armando's face. "Of course I did. You make me immensely proud."

Would he still feel that way once Armando finished—that was the question. "Even if I dishonored Corinthia?"

"Considering your sister married a man who is not the father of her child, it would be hypocritical of me, don't you think? Besides, I doubt there's anything you could do that would dishonor Corinthia too much."

"Don't be so sure."

His father paused as what Armando said sank in. "What have you done?"

"More like what I can't do," Armando replied and looked up from his hand. He didn't need a love or life line to tell him what needed to be said. "I can't marry Mona."

"I see." There was another pause. "And why can't you?"

"Because I'm in love with someone else." He laid out the entire story, from why he contacted King Omar in the first place to his goodbye to Rosa a short time earlier. When he finished, he went back to studying his palms. "I know we're responsible for every light in Corinthia. I know that backing out of this arrangement means dishonoring our reputation and making an enemy out an important economic ally, but I just can't.

"It's selfish, but I'm tired of being unhappy, Father," he said, staring at the shadows flickering along the wall. "It's been three years of not being among the living. I need to live again."

By this point, he'd been expecting his father's silence, so it was a surprise when his father responded immediately. "Every light in Corinthia? Sounds like someone spent time with his grandfather."

He reached over and patted Armando's knee, something he hadn't done in Armando's childhood. "My father was a good man, but some of his advice could be heavy-handed. If I had known he was putting such notions in your head when you were young... Apparently I've failed you as well."

"No, you didn't," Armando said, shifting his weight to face him. "You have been an exemplary king..."

"And a mediocre father," he replied. "I wallowed in my grief and, as a result, taught you by example. Of course you should be happy, Armando. You can't lead a country if you're angry and bitter. If Rosa is the woman who will make you happy, embrace her."

Armando planned to. He took a deep breath. Perhaps his father had a point. Having made his decision, he no longer felt the pressing weight on his shoulders. Like on the night of the rehearsal dinner, the bits and pieces kicking around his head had solidified, making his thoughts clear. He could breathe.

"Omar is going to be furious," he said. Mona, too. And deservedly so.

"Omar is also pragmatic. His main concern is helping his people. If we offer economic aid, I think he and Mona will be willing to swallow their hurt pride. Although I wouldn't expect an invitation to stay at the Yelgierian palace any time soon."

If that was the only fallout, Armando would live. "I would like to start an initiative as well to encourage Corinthian and other EU doctors to set up practice in Yelgiers. From what Mona says, a dearth of doctors is one of their most pressing concerns."

"We'll make it a priority," his father replied. "Now, what are you doing sitting under a mistletoe with me? Don't you have a future princess to collect?"

Yes, he did. With his cheek muscles aching from the grin on his face, Armando jumped to his feet.

"Armando!" his father called when he reached the door. "Merry Christmas."

Impossibly, Armando's grin grew even wider. "Merry Christmas, Father."

* * *

Rosa was trying. She was serving food and reminding herself that her life could be a lot worse. She had her brain. She was strong and capable. Moreover, while she might be alone, Armando loved her. Wanted, needed and loved. She should take solace in the fact she was special enough to win the heart of the crown prince.

"I'd rather have Armando."

"Are you talking to your imaginary friend, Miss Rosa?"

Daniela, she who started everything by spotting the first mistletoe, yanked on her blazer. "I have an imaginary friend, too," she said. "His name is Boco. He's a talking elephant. Is your friend an elephant, too?"

"No," said Rosa, embarrassed to be asked about her imaginary friend. "She's an angel named Christina."

"Like the name of this place?"

"That's right. She's been helping me make sense of a very confusing problem."

"Is it helping?" Daniela asked.

"Not yet," Rosa replied. "But we'll keep trying." Broken hearts were never solved in one day. And when the person you loved had also been the center of your life…she suspected she'd be trying to sort things out for a very long time.

"Maybe cake would help," Daniela said. "When my mama needs to think, she always eats cake. And ice cream."

"Your mother is a very smart woman." Though in

this case, cake would only make matters worse. She'd already eaten her weight in Christmas cookies.

Sending the little girl back to play with the other children, Rosa stole a couple more cookies and made her way to the rear picture window. In the distance, Mount Cornier's snow-covered peak had been swallowed by clouds. She bit a cookie and imagined her sister's spirit sitting on a fluffy white cushion, watching over her legacy.

Holidays and heartache made her overly poetic.

If Christina was watching, the least she could do was tell her what to do next, since Rosa didn't know. In some ways, she was worse off than when she left Fredo. Then, she'd had Armando. This time she would have to lean on herself. Maybe she would go to the continent and find a job there. Or America. She didn't care so long as she could start fresh.

And someday forget Armando.

Maybe.

If she didn't—couldn't—forget him, she knew she would still survive. She wasn't the same woman who had scurried away from Fredo thinking she was a fat, ugly lump of clay. Oh, she still had days…but there were also days when she felt good about herself. The fact she made the choice to walk away from Armando said she was stronger.

In time, she would be all right. Sad. Lonely. But all right.

"If only you could make my heart stop feeling like it was tearing in two," she whispered to the glass.

"Ho, ho, ho! *Buon Natale!*"

The entire shelter burst into high-pitched squeals. "Babbo!"

It couldn't be. They must have hired a professional impersonator for the day, as a surprise for the kids.

The director hadn't mentioned anything to her, though.

"Is everyone having a good Christmas?"

Uncanny. They even sounded alike. She looked in the glass hoping to catch a reflection, but it was too bright out. All she could see was a darkened silhouette in costume.

"Babbo needs your help, boys and girls."

This was silly. Armando was not at the shelter playing Babbo. As soon as she turned around she would see that the person...

Was Armando.

Why? He was dressed in costume and surrounded by children. "There's a very special person whose present Babbo forgot to deliver," he was telling them in his boisterous Babbo voice, "and I'm afraid she thinks I decided to give her present to another girl. It's really important I find her, boys and girls, so I can tell her that I would never pick someone else. That she's the most important person in the world to Babbo. In fact, Babbo cares about her so much that he wants her to come back to the North Pole with him."

Throughout his speech, Rosa moved closer. Spotting her, he dropped his voice back to normal. "Her name's Rosa," he said. "Do you know where I can find her?"

"Right there!" the children screamed, two dozen index fingers pointing in her direction.

Rosa was too stunned to breathe. "What are you doing?" she whispered.

"What do you think I am doing?" Armando said. "I've come to bring you back home where you belong." He reached through the throng to catch her fingertips. "I love you, Rosa."

Beautiful as those words were to hear, they were still only words. "I told you, Ar—Babbo. I can't stay at the North Pole." Out of the corner of her eye, she saw the children watching intently and lowered her voice to a whisper. "It hurts too much."

"But you don't understand," he whispered back. "Mona's gone. Come with me." Grabbing her hand, he led her to the shelter's lobby and closed the community room door. "I told Mona I couldn't marry her."

She had to have heard wrong. "What about your agreement with King Omar? You gave him your word."

"It's a long story. What matters is I love you and I don't want to be with anyone else."

Rosa couldn't believe what she was hearing. It was too unreal. "Are you saying that you damaged relations with one of your closest allies for me?"

"When you put it that way...yes." He pulled off his hat and beard, leaving only his disheveled self. His beautiful, disheveled self. "I would do it again, too. Are you crying?"

"Like a newborn baby." All those years married to Fredo, believing she wasn't anyone special. How wrong she had been. Armando made her feel beyond special. Not because he'd nearly created an international incident on her behalf, or tracked her down dressed like Santa Claus, although both were amazingly romantic.

No, the reason he made her feel special was in his eyes. They were shining as clear and bright as a summer's day without a trace of melancholy to be found. He was happy being with her, and that was all she needed. "I love you," she told him.

Her reward was an even brighter shine. "Does that mean you'll come back with me to the North Pole?"

"Absolutely, Babbo. Right after you kiss me under the mistletoe."

"Forget the mistletoe," he said, tossing the beard over his shoulder. Rosa gasped as he pulled her into his arms and dipped her low. "All I need is you."

New Year's Eve

"Five minutes left in the year. Will you be sad to see it end?"

Rosa took one of the glasses of champagne Armando was carrying. "Yes," she said. "And no. I'll be sorry to see December end. For all the ups and downs, it turned out to be a pretty wonderful month."

"The last week certainly was." Armando gave her a champagne-flavored kiss that quickly deepened. "Have I mentioned how glad I am that we decided to skip a formal courtship?" he asked, lips continuing to tease hers.

"Well, it did seem a little silly, considering…"

"Mmm, considering," he said, kissing her again. What they were discovering was the intimacy that came from being friends before becoming lovers. There was a level of trust that made everything they shared feel deeper. Of course, the fact Armando was an amazingly enthusiastic lover didn't hurt, either.

"You know what else I'll miss," Rosa said, turning in his arms. "Once Epiphany passes, this will become a plain old archway again."

They were in their archway now, preferring to ring in the new year alone rather than in a ballroom full of dignitaries.

Armando kissed her temple. "If you'd like, I can insist the trees stay up by royal decree."

"Is this the same royal decree where you're going to ban the use of fake Babbo beards?"

"The fibers give me a rash."

"My poor baby. Too sensitive for synthetic fibers." She snuggled closer. "As much as I'll miss the decorations, they need to go. How else will they stay special?" Christmas decorations weren't like the man with his arms around her—Armando woke up being special.

While she woke up feeling like the luckiest woman in the world.

"Besides," she told him, "we still have tonight."

"Which switches to tomorrow in less than two minutes," he replied.

A brand-new year. Given how wonderfully this year was ending, Rosa couldn't imagine what the next year had in store. As far as she was concerned, she had everything she could want sitting next to her with his arms wrapped around her waist. She loved Armando, and he loved her. What could be better?

"Do you realize," she said, pausing to take a drink, "that if we hadn't gotten our act together, you would be announcing your engagement to Mona at this very moment?"

"You're right—I did plan to be engaged by New Year's, didn't I?"

"That was before." Armando's breaking the engagement to date his assistant turned out to be scandal enough to push Arianna's pregnancy out of the papers completely. Fortunately, Mona and King Omar, while hurt, didn't hold too big a grudge. Hard to be angry at a country that was funding doctors' relocation efforts.

"There is still the matter of my producing an heir, though," Armando said, shifting his weight.

"That can be arranged," Rosa said with a smile.

"Very amusing. If you don't mind, I would like to establish my family in the proper order. Marriage, then heirs. What do you think?"

"I think that's a very logical…" Armando had moved to his knee. In his hand was the most beautiful diamond Rosa had ever seen. "Are you—" She couldn't finish the sentence; her heart was stuck in her throat.

"I am," he whispered with a nod. "Rosa Lamberti, would you do me the honor of becoming my wife?"

She never did say the word *yes*. Instead, Rosa threw her arms around his neck and kissed him until there was no doubt as to her answer. "I would be honored," she told him.

Down the hall, the crowd began chanting a count-down to midnight. Rosa and Armando didn't care. Their time was already here.

* * * * *

If you loved Rosa and Armando's story,
find out where it all started with
CHRISTMAS BABY FOR THE PRINCESS
the first book in Barbara Wallace's festive
ROYAL HOUSE OF CORINTHIA *duet,*
available now!

"Jeez, Fallon—you're not actually hoping to stir up trouble, are you?"

"Maybe I am," she said. "Maybe I'm tired of every man I know treating me like a buddy. Maybe I want someone to look at me and realize I'm a woman, to want me as a woman."

And suddenly he got it. "You mean me," he realized. "You want me to see you as a woman."

She sighed as she shook her head. "No, Jamie. I think I've finally accepted that that is never going to happen."

"But I do see you as a woman," he assured her. "A genuinely warm, funny and smart woman."

"Maybe it's un-PC," she admitted. "But I don't want to be admired for my personality or my intelligence. I want to be wanted."

Jamie swallowed. "You're looking for a hookup?"

"That wouldn't be my first choice," she said. "But I've decided to open my mind up to any and all possibilities."

"A hookup should not be one of them," he told her. "You deserve better than that."

"What does the song say—we can't always get what we want, but we get what we need?"

"Don't go, Fallon." The words were out of his mouth before he realized what he was saying.

She paused with her hand on the door.

"Don't go out to the Ace tonight."

She slowly turned around, her expression carefully neutral.

"Are you making me an alternate offer?" she asked.

He nodded. "Stay here. With me."

* * *

Montana Mavericks:
The Baby Bonanza—Meet Rust Creek Falls'
newest bundles of joy!

THE MORE
MAVERICKS,
THE MERRIER!

BY
BRENDA HARLEN

MILLS & BOON

First Published in Great Britain 2016
By Mills & Boon, an imprint of HarperCollins*Publishers*
1 London Bridge Street, London, SE1 9GF

© 2016 Harlequin Books S.A.

Special thanks and acknowledgement are given to Brenda Harlen for her contribution to the Montana Mavericks: The Baby Bonanza continuity.

ISBN: 978-0-263-92039-0

23-1216

Brenda Harlen is a former attorney who once had the privilege of appearing before the Supreme Court of Canada. The practice of law taught her a lot about the world and reinforced her determination to become a writer—because in fiction, she could promise a happy ending! Now she is an award-winning, national best-selling author of more than thirty titles for Mills & Boon. You can keep up-to-date with Brenda on Facebook and Twitter or through her website, www.brendaharlen.com.

For Connor—it doesn't seem so very long ago
that we were celebrating your first Christmas.
Now you're in your first year at university, and I'm
counting the days until you come home for the holidays.
A lot has changed over the years, but there are
two things that never will: how very proud I am
to call you my son, and how much I love you. xo

Chapter One

Jamie Stockton turned the page on the calendar and stared at the letters that spelled out the month. D-E-C-E-M-B-E-R. The final month of a year that had mostly been a blur in his mind.

Twelve months earlier, he'd been anticipating the upcoming holiday and already thinking about this Christmas, when he and his wife would celebrate the holiday with their babies. Now Henry, Jared and Katie's first Christmas was only weeks away, but Paula was gone and instead of being excited about the event, he was simply exhausted.

His fingers automatically wrapped around the heavy mug that was thrust into his hand. He lifted it to his lips and swallowed a mouthful of hot, strong coffee. The caffeine slid down his throat, spread slowly through his system.

He turned away from the calendar to face his sister. "Thanks."

"You looked like you needed it," Bella said, as she started breaking eggs into a bowl.

He swallowed another mouthful of coffee. "Henry was up three times last night."

"Teething?"

"I don't know. His cheeks weren't red, he wasn't drooling and he didn't have a fever."

"Hmm." Bella turned and looked at the triplets, lined up in three high chairs beside the butcher block table, each of them focused on the cut-up pieces of fruit she'd offered to tide them over until she could cook breakfast. "He looks okay now—certainly a lot better than you do."

"Thanks," he said dryly.

She added a splash of milk and began whisking the eggs. "Did Jared and Katie sleep through the night?"

He shook his head. "Jared was awake once. Katie made it all the way through until her wet diaper woke her up at four this morning."

"And since you had to be up at five, you probably didn't even try to go back to sleep after she was changed." She poured the egg mixture into the hot pan on the stove.

"Nope," he agreed.

The truth was, even when the kids were settled in their cribs at night, sleep didn't come easily to him. When he tumbled into his own bed, unable to keep his eyes open a minute longer, his body would immediately shut down. His mind, not so much.

Although he'd always wanted to be a father, he never planned to be a single father. But that's what he was, and while the joys of being a parent to ten-month old triplets were countless, the trials were also numerous.

"I really think you should consider putting them into day care," Bella said gently.

It wasn't the first time she'd made the suggestion, and he understood that—for a lot of reasons—it was a valid one. Of course, he'd nixed the idea the first dozen times she'd mentioned it, vehemently when the town was in the midst of an RSV outbreak. But now that the epidemic had passed, maybe he would reconsider.

He nodded, because he agreed that socialization in a structured setting would be good for his children. And while the cost of day care for three babies was somewhat prohibitive, he also knew that he couldn't continue to rely on community volunteers to provide in-home care for his young family.

Since the tragic death of his wife after the birth of their babies, he'd been the grateful recipient of an outpouring of support and assistance from the residents of Rust Creek Falls. Under the direction of his sister, Bella, several volunteers had come together to create what she called a baby chain and help him take care of the triplets in rotating shifts.

For the past ten months, his sister had been the anchor of that system. Despite the demands on her, she'd somehow found the time to meet and fall in love with Hudson Jones. And Jamie knew it was time for him to take control of his own life so that she could get on with hers and the planning of her wedding.

"So you *are* thinking about day care?" she prompted, evidently surprised.

He lifted his mug again, to hide his smile behind

the rim. "I've heard a lot of great things about Country Kids."

Bella, who worked at Just Us Kids—the day care center managed by her fiancé—narrowed her gaze as she stirred the eggs in the pan.

He chuckled. "I'm kidding."

"I hope so."

"On the other hand, Fallon does work at Country Kids," he pointed out. "And they offer a discount for more than one child."

"Just Us Kids does, too," she told him, as she took the platter of bacon and toast out of the oven and set it on the table. "Plus, I'm pretty sure I can wrangle a family discount for you."

"I'm not looking for anything full-time," he told her, snagging a piece of bacon as soon as she turned her back.

"Of course not," Bella agreed, tearing a slice of toast into pieces for Henry, Jared and Katie to chew on. "Half days would be a better introduction for them. Any change in daily routine is an adjustment for a child, although the triplets do have something of an advantage in that they're accustomed to being cared for by different people."

Because they'd never had the benefit of a mother and a father to tend to their day-to-day needs, Jamie lamented silently. "That's an advantage?"

She winced. "I'm sorry. You know I didn't mean it like that."

"I know," he confirmed.

"So…half days," she said, attempting to refocus their conversation as she set a plate of eggs in front of him. "Mornings?"

He nodded as he picked up his fork to dig into his breakfast. "But not every day."

Bella sighed as she scooped smaller portions of egg into three bowls on the counter to cool off for a few minutes before she gave them to the babies. "Part-time only a few days a week isn't going to be very helpful to you when you're juggling so much," she pointed out. "You leave the house at the crack of dawn every morning, then you come back to have lunch with your kids, then you head back out to work and drop whatever you're doing to come back to check on them again in the afternoon."

"And yet I still feel guilty about relying on other people to care for them during so much of the time that they're awake," he admitted, adding a couple slices of thick, buttered toast to his plate.

She sat down with her own breakfast. "You'll feel less guilty when they're in day care—and less inclined to interrupt your day to check on them."

"Three days a week," he decided.

"Four," she countered, reaching out to snag a couple of pieces of bacon before he emptied the platter.

He scowled. "They're only ten months old."

"And I'll be at the day care every minute that they are," Bella assured him.

"I don't know," he hedged.

She didn't press any further as she finished her own breakfast, then gave the babies their eggs.

Jamie had just pushed his own plate aside when a brisk knock sounded on the back door, then Fallon O'Reilly walked into the room without waiting for an invitation.

He didn't mind. Fallon had been a friend of both

him and his sister since childhood and one of the first women to volunteer for the baby chain. She was also one of the most regular, and expediency had required that they dispense with the usual protocols months earlier.

"Good morning," Fallon greeted Jamie and Bella, her tone and her smile confirming that she believed it to be true. Then she turned to the babies, lavishly kissing each of their cheeks, making them giggle.

The sound filled his heart with joy and he looked at Fallon with sincere gratitude. She was so great with the babies—so natural and easy. She seemed to love them as he'd hoped their mother would have done, but Paula had never had the chance to be the mother he'd believed she could be—dying only hours after their babies were born by emergency C-section.

"I brought blueberry muffins." Fallon set a plastic container in the middle of the table, then moved across the kitchen to retrieve a mug from the cupboard. She brought it and the carafe to the table, offering refills to Jamie and Bella.

But Bella shook her head. "I should be getting into work."

Jamie picked up his mug and stood. "And I need to get out to the barn and check on Daisy. Brooks said she could foal any day now."

Fallon frowned at both of them. "Why are you racing off? It's barely seven-thirty."

"Hudson wants to expand Just Us Kids to offer a newborn group and I promised to help him review the applications and set up the interviews," Bella told her.

"And I've already had breakfast," Jamie said.

Fallon looked from sister to brother and back again,

her eyes narrowing. "This is about the coffee cake I made for the Fourth of July potluck, isn't it?"

Jamie and Bella exchanged a look.

Fallon huffed out an exasperated breath as she lifted the lid off the container. "I misread the recipe," she explained, selecting a muffin and peeling the paper off of the bottom half. "*Once.* And no one in this town will let me forget it."

"Because you served the cake at the potluck."

"*Three years ago.* And it wasn't really that bad," Fallon defended.

"You used two tablespoons of baking powder instead of two teaspoons," Bella reminded her, settling back in her chair. "The cake was tough and chewy."

"And tasted like metal," Jamie chimed in.

Color filled Fallon's cheeks as she tore a piece off the muffin. "Okay, it was bad," she acknowledged, as she popped the morsel into her mouth. "But these are delicious."

Jamie sat down again and reached into the container—because even after eating a full breakfast, there was room for a muffin. Bella continued to look dubious.

"I brought something else, too," Fallon said, as she broke up the bottom of the muffin into pieces and set them onto each of the babies' trays.

Henry, Jared and Kate showed no hesitation, gleefully stuffing the pieces into their mouths.

"What?" Jamie asked, nibbling tentatively on the muffin.

Fallon hesitated, not wanting to overstep. But she'd spent a lot of time with this man and his children over the past ten months, and although she understood that he was still grieving the loss of his wife, he needed to start to look forward instead of back—for the sake of his babies if no one else.

So she pulled the paper out of her pocket and unfolded it, then slid it across the table for Jamie to read.

He gave it a cursory—almost curious—glance, then looked away to focus his attention on the muffin that he suddenly couldn't shove into his mouth fast enough.

Bella leaned forward to peer at the words on the page.

"It's Henry, Jared and Katie's first Christmas," Fallon reminded Jamie gently, sliding the paper closer to him. "And I want to help you make it the best Christmas ever for them."

"They're not even a year old," he pointed out. "It's not as if they'll remember the occasion."

"Maybe not," she acknowledged. But she loved the holiday season almost as much as she loved the triplets, so she'd decided that she was going to do everything in her power to ensure that their first Christmas was a truly memorable one. That was why she'd come up with a list of suggested activities to introduce HJK—as Jamie affectionately referred to his children—to some yuletide traditions and get everyone in the holiday spirit.

Unfortunately, she knew that she would face an obstacle in their father. It was Jamie's first Christmas without his wife, and she understood it wouldn't be an easy one for him. She also believed that it wouldn't help him or his children to dwell on what they'd lost.

"But *you* will remember," Fallon told him. "And when they look back on the pictures you take over the holiday season, they'll see that you made it a wonderful one for them."

"I don't know—"

"Fallon's right," Bella interjected, reaching across the table to touch her brother's hand. "You need to do something special—for all of you. It's your first Christmas as a father—"

"And a widower," he pointed out.

"As a father," she said again, determined to emphasize the positive. "And that's a cause for celebration."

He glanced at the list again, his thick brows drawing together. "First Christmas photo with Santa? Am I supposed to ask the fat guy to pose with HJK after he squeezes down the chimney on Christmas Eve?"

"No," Fallon said, with what she thought was incredible patience. "You're supposed to take them to the mall in Kalispell."

He was shaking his head before she even finished speaking. "I don't do malls and I don't have the time—or the inclination—to bundle up three babies, strap their screaming, squirming bodies into car seats, and trek into the city to stand in line with dozens of other harried parents for a photo op with a phony Kris Kringle."

"Well, the real one is kind of busy at the North Pole this time of year," she shot back, deadpan. "And you need to make the time and fake the inclination if necessary, because this is important."

"To whom?" he countered.

"To me," Bella interjected, obviously attempting to play peacemaker. "I'd love a picture of my niece and nephews with Santa."

"Then *you* can take them," Jamie told her.

Fallon drew in a slow, deep breath and mentally counted to ten. It wouldn't help the situation if she lost her temper, but she was so frustrated with him—and for him. She knew he was grieving, but she also knew

he loved his babies and, when he finally stopped grieving, he would regret the opportunities he'd missed. She
wasn't going to let him have regrets.

"We'll put that one aside for now," she finally relented. "The outfits I've ordered haven't come in yet,
anyway."

His frown was back again. "You ordered outfits?"

"Wait until you see them. They're the—"

"I don't want to see them," he told her. "I want you
to send them back. I can afford to buy clothes for my
kids. I don't need your charity."

Fallon sighed. "It's not charity. It's a gift."

"And very thoughtful," Bella interjected again, with
a pointed look at her brother.

Jamie sighed. "Bella's right. I'm sorry."

"Prove it," she said.

His brows lifted. "How am I supposed to prove it?"

"By agreeing to fulfill the requirements of my list."

"I'm not *that* sorry." He pushed the paper away from
him.

She shoved it at him again.

With a sigh, he reached out to take it, his fingertips brushing against hers in the transfer. Little sparks
skipped through her veins in response to the brief contact.

She glanced up, to see if he'd experienced any kind
of reaction. His gaze remained focused on the page, his
expression neutral.

"I have no objection to a tree," he finally conceded.

Fallon ignored her own disappointment. "Great,"
she said. "We'll bundle the kids up this afternoon, take
them in the sleigh out to the woods and find an appropriate specimen."

"That's a wonderful idea," Bella agreed.

Jamie frowned. "This afternoon? What's the hurry? It's only the first day of December."

"A tree is the most obvious symbol of Christmas," Fallon pointed out reasonably. "Having one in the house will help you get into the spirit of the season."

Nothing in his expression hinted at the tiniest bit of holiday spirit, but he shrugged. "Fine. Whatever. If you want to take the kids out and chop down a tree, I'll see if one of the kids from next door is available to help you drag it back."

"Uh-uh," Fallon said, shaking her head. "I'm not taking the kids out to chop down a tree—*we* are."

"I don't have time—"

"Make time," she said, interrupting his familiar refrain.

He frowned. "When did you get to be so bossy?"

"She's always been bossy," Bella chimed in. "I don't know how it's possible that you've known her for more than twenty years and not known that."

But Fallon wasn't surprised that he hadn't noticed her ability to take charge and assert herself when the situation warranted. There were a lot of things that Jamie had never noticed about her. Most notably the Montana-sized crush she'd had on him since she was a girl experiencing the first stirring of adolescent hormones.

And while a part of her was grateful that he'd never discovered her feelings for him, another part continued to be frustrated that he'd always viewed her as his kid sister's friend. Sure, over the years they'd developed a friendship of their own outside of their mutual connection to Bella, but Jamie had only ever seen her as a pal to hang out with and an occasional confidante.

She was the only person he'd shared his anger and frustration with when he'd discovered that his wife had secretly been taking birth control while he'd thought they were trying to get pregnant. Of course, when Paula finally had conceived, Jamie had shared the good news with everyone in Rust Creek Falls. He'd been so thrilled, he'd practically shouted it from the rooftops. But he'd subsequently admitted to Fallon that Paula wasn't nearly as excited about having a baby as he was—and even less so when they learned that she would have three of them.

"I thought you were the bossy one," Jamie responded to his sister's comment while his speculative gaze lingered on Fallon.

"I'm not bossy," she denied.

His lips twitched. "Of course not. And now, I really do need to get out to the barn to check on Daisy," he said, suddenly remembering his expectant mare.

Fallon nodded. "Will we see you at lunch?"

"Not if I'm going to finish up early to go out hunting for a Christmas tree."

"I didn't ask you to do that," she pointed out.

"It gets dark early this time of year." He snagged a couple of muffins out of the container on the table, then winked at her on his way to the door. "These will tide me over."

She started to offer to wrap them up and fill a thermos with coffee, then clenched her teeth to hold back the words. She was pleased that he liked the muffins, but while offering baked goods was an acceptable and neighborly gesture, sending him off with a bagged lunch and a hot beverage was something a wife would do.

And Fallon wasn't his wife—she was his friend and his children's babysitter, nothing more. She needed to remember that—for the sake of her own heart.

Chapter Two

While Jamie was making his way to the door, his sister started clearing the breakfast dishes off the table.

"If you have to get to work, I can take care of that," Fallon offered.

"I'm not really in a hurry," Bella admitted.

"You don't have to meet Hudson to look at applications?"

"Not until this afternoon."

Fallon shook her head. "Really? You were so afraid to sample my baking that you made up that story?"

"I didn't make it up," her friend denied. "I just fudged the timeline a little."

"I've prepared lunch and occasionally dinner here numerous times over the past ten months and you never balked at eating anything I've cooked," she pointed out.

"You know how to put a meal together," Bella confirmed. "Dessert? Not so much."

"Ouch."

"You have a lot of talents," her friend soothed. "Baking just isn't one of them."

"But the muffins were good, weren't they?"

"They were very good, but one batch of muffins isn't going to make anyone forget the potluck experience."

Fallon scowled as she washed the babies' hands and faces, then she and Bella carried the triplets into the living room.

Because Henry, Jared and Katie were preemies—born almost two months ahead of schedule—they were a little bit delayed in their development and had only recently started to crawl and climb. Their sudden mobility had Jamie in a panic about childproofing the house, so there were now caps in all of the outlets, child locks and latches on all of the doors and drawers and baby gates to block off the rooms that were completely off-limits to the little ones.

He also had a play yard—which Fallon thought was intended to go *in* the yard, but he'd assured her was also suitable for indoor use and gave the babies a little more room to roam around than a traditional playpen. But for now, with Bella there to provide an extra set of eyes, they were letting the babies crawl around the floor.

While her brothers were playing with wooden toy cars, Katie was preoccupied with the sparkly ring on Bella's finger. "Pretty, isn't it?" Fallon said.

Katie, of course, didn't respond but continued to be mesmerized by the massive diamond.

"You're a smart girl," her Auntie Bella said. "You already know that diamonds are a girl's best friend."

"And her brothers are already obsessed with cars," Fallon noted.

"Whatever keeps them busy…and happy," Bella said, smiling as she watched them play. "For a long time, I didn't think they'd ever learn how to occupy themselves."

"It's amazing how much they've grown and changed over the past ten months," Fallon agreed. "And speaking of changes…have you and Hudson set a date for the wedding?"

"We have," her friend happily confirmed. "Saturday, June 10. We're having the ceremony at the church followed by a reception at Maverick Manor."

"Have you found a dress?"

"I've been looking at bridal magazines and browsing online, but that's it so far. I'm hoping to get to Mimi's Bridal in Kalispell on Saturday, but I have to make sure my maid of honor can go with me."

"Who are you having stand up with you?" Fallon asked.

"Hopefully my best friend," Bella said.

"Me?"

The bride-to-be smiled. "Of course you, if you're willing."

"I would be honored," Fallon told her sincerely.

"And are you up for wedding dress shopping on Saturday?"

"Absolutely. Have you decided who will be your bridesmaids?"

Bella shook her head. "I'm not having any other attendants."

"Why not?" Fallon wondered.

"Because I always imagined that I'd have Dana and Liza in my wedding party," the bride-to-be admitted softly, referring to the two sisters she hadn't seen in years. "And if they can't be there... I don't want anyone else."

Fallon reached over to squeeze her friend's hand in a silent gesture of comfort and support.

"So the wedding party is going to be very small," Bella continued. "Bride and groom, maid of honor and best man, flower girl and two ring bearers."

"Katie, Henry and Jared?" she guessed.

Her friend nodded. "Jamie thinks I'm crazy, but I want my niece and nephews in my wedding party."

"That's not crazy," Fallon assured her. "Crazy would be letting Homer Gilmore anywhere near the wedding punch."

Bella chuckled at her mention of the old man who had confessed to spiking the wedding punch with his homemade moonshine when Jennifer MacCallum and Braden Traub got married last Fourth of July. As a result, the celebration had resulted in several new romances and started the local baby boom. "Apparently he learned his lesson. Although I have to admit, I've found myself wondering if 'what happened at the wedding' wasn't much ado about nothing."

"I'm sure Will Clifton and Jordyn Cates, Lani Dalton and Russ Campbell, Trey Strickland and Kayla Dalton would argue otherwise."

"Hmm."

"I know that tone," Fallon said, sounding a little worried. "What are you thinking?"

"I was just thinking, if Homer Gilmore's moonshine really does have special powers, I should try to get my hands on some."

"Why do you want Homer's moonshine when all of your dreams are about to come true?"

"It wouldn't be for me, but for Jamie."

"I think your brother's hands are full enough with Henry, Jared and Katie," she said.

"I don't mean for him to have more babies," Bella said. "Although there was a definite rise in pregnancies for wedding guests who drank the spiked punch, there was also a noticeable increase in the number of couples falling in love," she pointed out. "That's what I want for Jamie—for him to fall in love, and for real this time."

Fallon didn't say anything. She wasn't going to ask, but her curiosity must have shown on her face because Bella's lips curved into a slow smile.

"Apparently Jamie doesn't tell you *every*thing," his sister mused.

"Maybe that's because he wants to keep his private life private," she suggested. Because she knew that Jamie and Paula's marriage hadn't been without its share of problems, but she also knew that Jamie had loved his wife.

Bella waved a hand dismissively. "If I've learned nothing else this past year, I've learned that keeping secrets doesn't help anyone. My brother needs a wife, his babies need a mother and most of the women in town are keeping a respectable distance because they think he's still mourning Paula.

"I'm not saying he didn't care for her," his sister hastened to explain. "He wouldn't have married her if he didn't believe he was in love with her. But even I could see that they were ill-suited. Paula might have wanted Jamie, but she never really wanted to live in Rust Creek Falls and…" she paused now, as if reluctant to say aloud what she was thinking "… I don't believe she ever wanted those beautiful babies.

"Of course, by the time my brother realized the truth about who she was and what she wanted, they were already married. And Jamie being Jamie, he was determined to make it work."

"She would have loved Henry, Jared and Katie," Fallon said. "If she'd been given a chance to be a mother to them, she would have loved them." Unfortunately, complications resulting from her pregnancy had taken that chance along with her life.

"You always did have a huge and forgiving heart," Bella told her. "And that's what I want for my brother— for him to find someone like you who will help him open his heart again."

She felt her own heart beat faster as she wondered if her friend had somehow guessed the truth of her feelings for Jamie.

But Bella continued, oblivious to Fallon's inner thoughts and deepest emotions. "Someone down to earth, preferably a Rust Creek Falls resident who understands life on a ranch and might be willing to become an instant mother to these precious babies." She grabbed a tissue from the box on the table to wipe the drool off Henry's chin. "Can you think of anyone who might fit the criteria?"

Me! Me! Fallon wanted to respond, while jumping up and down with her hand in the air like an eager second grader.

"I'm sure there are more than a few suitable candidates," she said instead, and hoped her friend didn't guess that her lack of enthusiasm was based on a reluctance to watch Jamie hook up with anyone else.

It had been difficult enough for her to see him with Paula, but she'd tried to be happy for him because she knew he was in love with his wife. She'd been sincerely pleased when he told her about his wife's pregnancy, because she knew how much he wanted to be a father, to have a family of his own. Her heart had ached, but she'd put a smile on her face because she loved him so much she valued his happiness above even her own.

But now, she wasn't sure she could go through that again. She didn't want to sit back and be a spectator while the man she loved fell in love with another woman.

"Has he indicated any interest in meeting someone new?" she asked cautiously.

"No," Bella admitted. "But why wouldn't he be content with the status quo when he's got someone here taking care of his babies every day and often putting a meal on the table? The only thing he's not getting is sex."

Fallon felt her cheeks flush. "How do you know he's not having sex?"

"Because he's too exhausted to ever leave the ranch and find a willing woman," his sister said matter-of-factly.

Which didn't preclude him finding a willing woman *on* the ranch, and that wasn't completely outside the realm of possibility considering that several of the baby chain volunteers were single women. On the other hand, it wasn't very likely with Jamie's sister living under the same roof.

"So what do you think?" Bella prompted. "Can you help me come up with some prospects for him?"

"Sure," Fallon agreed, because apparently she *was* enough of a masochist to play matchmaker for the man she'd been crushing on for more than a decade. Or maybe she was finally ready to face the truth and acknowledge that, if Jamie was ever going to show any interest in her, he would have done so years earlier. But aside from one single, solitary kiss the summer between his first and second years of college, their relationship had never been anything but platonic.

Henry crawled into Fallon's lap, stuffed his thumb in his mouth and dropped his head against her breast. "I think someone's trying to tell me that he's tired."

"Already?" Bella glanced at her watch. "I guess we've been gabbing longer than I realized."

Fallon nodded toward Jared, who had fallen asleep with his cheek on the carpet and a car in his hand. Only Katie was still upright, although Fallon could tell by the little girl's flagging movements that she wouldn't object to being put down for a nap.

Bella helped her get the babies changed and settled into their individual cribs before she headed off to work with a reminder to Fallon about their upcoming trip to the bridal salon.

She was genuinely happy for her best friend, and maybe feeling just a little sorry for herself, because she had no imminent plans for a wedding or a family of her own. But she would put a smile on her face, stand up beside the bride, continue to lavish Henry, Jared and Katie with attention and affection and, most important, pretend that she wasn't seriously infatuated with their father.

Jamie had more than enough work to keep him busy throughout the morning and most of the afternoon. After he checked on the mare and fed the heifers, he worked on fixing the fence on the north border that was in desperate need of repair. Though he couldn't say for certain, the look of the damage—combined with some talk he'd heard in town about Craig Garrison needing parts to fix his ATV—suggested to Jamie that his neighbor's idiot son had run into the fence while he was out joyriding, probably in the middle of the snowstorm a couple of weeks earlier.

He immediately felt guilty for the thought. Craig wasn't really an idiot; he was just a teenager. The spoiled youngest son of a successful rancher who didn't care that Jamie was struggling to keep on top of countless daily tasks without additional fence repairs added to the mix.

He'd bought the Circle K ranch from the bank when Dierk and Gretchen Krueger opted to walk away after the floods decimated their land three years earlier. They'd worked the ranch for almost forty years with the intention of passing it on to their own children someday. But none of their children was interested in the property—especially not after the floods—so they'd opted to sell and move to a more temperate climate for their golden years.

Jamie had been fresh out of school and eager to put down his own roots in Rust Creek Falls independent of the grandparents who had let him and Bella live with them in town but never showed them an ounce of affection. He was also familiar with the Circle K because he'd worked as a ranch hand for Dierk in the summers during high school. The old man had taught him a lot about ranch management, and though Jamie had felt uncomfortable taking advantage of his misfortune, Dierk assured him that he'd be happy knowing the ranch was in the hands of someone who cared about the land and wouldn't turn it into some kind of tourist attraction for the Hollywood types who had been flocking to Montana in recent years to pretend to be cowboys.

So Jamie had scraped together enough money for the down payment, financed the rest of the purchase and taken what was left of the Kruegers' herd on a consignment basis. He renamed the property The Short Hills Ranch in recognition of its topography, then he'd refurbished the house and moved in with his new bride.

He'd been happy then—and so full of hope for the future. Now he was just trying to get by, one day at a time.

That was the problem with physical work—it left his mind free to wander without direction. Usually he appreciated the mundane tasks that he could perform without thinking, but today, Fallon's desire to cut down a tree suddenly had him thinking of Christmases past.

He had fond memories of holidays with his family during the first fifteen years of his life, before his parents had been killed in a car wreck. Hiking out into the woods to find the perfect tree, arguing over who got to cut it down—and then who had to lug it back to the house.

While his father set up the tree, his mother would make hot chocolate, rich and creamy, and float little marshmallows on top. When the chocolate had been drunk, they'd work together to decorate the towering evergreen. Lights. Garland. Ornaments. And then, finally, the serious countdown toward Christmas would begin.

With seven kids in the family, there was always a pile of presents under the tree. Never anything too expensive or impractical, of course, but there was always something that was needed—like an extra pair of long johns or a new razor—and something that was wanted—a coveted toy or favorite treat. And his mother always knitted a new sweater for each of her seven children.

The first Christmas after his parents were gone had been starkly different for Jamie and all of his siblings. Agnes and Matthew Baldwin—their maternal grandparents—were their only living relatives, and they had not been pleased by the prospect of taking in seven grandchildren.

Luke, Daniel and Bailey made it easy on them—opting to leave Rust Creek Falls to make their own way in the world. Because the three eldest siblings were all of legal age, their grandparents couldn't stop them. But Jamie knew that they didn't even try, that they were relieved by this immediate lessening of their responsibilities.

And still, four kids were a lot for the older couple to take in, especially when they lived in a modestly sized house in the center of town. Without any consultation—or even any warning, Agnes and Matthew had signed the two youngest siblings over to the local child welfare authorities to be adopted. Jamie remembered saying goodbye to Dana and Liza before he left for school early one morning, and when he returned home that afternoon, they were gone.

Only Jamie and Bella—too young to be independent like their brothers and too old to be considered adoptable like their sisters—were left. Was it any wonder that he and Bella had adopted a "you and me against the world" mentality? Or that they'd never felt close to the grandparents who had reluctantly taken them in?

Their first holiday with the grandparents had been an eye-opener. Agnes and Matthew hadn't bothered with a real tree for years and didn't see any reason to change their tradition of putting out a ceramic tree on the coffee table. There were a few other decorations scattered around the house and a holly wreath on the exterior door.

He'd thought that was quite possibly the worst Christmas ever. He'd been wrong.

He scrubbed a gloved hand over his face as the cold wind swirled around him, making his eyes water, and forced his attention back to the fence.

A sound came from somewhere in the distance—something that sounded like a dog barking.

He didn't have a dog. He'd always planned to get one, but when he'd suggested to Paula that they make a trip to the nearest shelter to pick one out, she'd balked. If they were going to bring an animal into the house, she didn't want it to be what she called a flea-infested mongrel. And maybe that should have been one of his first clues that their differences were greater than their similarities, but he'd ignored the concerns, so certain that they could make their marriage work.

He heard the bark again—far in the distance. Near the end of the summer, he'd noticed a dog skirting the edges of the property. A once-beautiful golden retriever now with matted fur and distrustful eyes. He didn't know if she'd been abused or abandoned, but she hadn't let him coax her to come near. After a few weeks, he noticed that she hadn't ventured too far away, either.

So he'd put a couple of stainless-steel bowls outside of the barn, ensuring one was always filled with fresh water and the other with kibble he'd picked up when he was at the feed store. And he'd hammered together some spare boards into a makeshift shelter that he'd set out on the north side of the property, where she seemed to linger.

Though he'd never seen her inside, he felt better knowing that it was there, that she had an escape from the elements if she chose to use it. And though he'd never seen her at the barn, the water and food needed to be replenished on a regular basis.

He'd immediately thought of her as a she, though he didn't know for sure. But any uncertainty as to her gender had been put to rest early in October when he'd seen her hovering at the edge of the woods. She was pregnant.

So before the first snowfall, he'd tossed a couple of old blankets into the shelter he'd built, hoping she would take refuge there when her birthing time was near. He wished he could do more. He wished he had the time to track her down and bring her in out of the cold to ensure that she and her puppies were safe, but he had all he could handle taking care of his own kids—and then some.

And now Fallon had launched a Christmas campaign to get him in the spirit of the holidays. He appreciated that her heart was in the right place—he just wished he could make her understand that his was still battered and bruised. He did want HJK's first Christmas to be a memorable one, and he was confident that Fallon would make it so. He was less certain that anything could change his own "bah, humbug" attitude this year, though he was almost tempted to let her try.

Fallon had just finished programming the slow cooker when she heard one of the babies stirring. Wiping her hands on a towel, she quickly climbed the steps to the upper level, eager to get to whoever was awake before he or she woke the others.

She'd been part of the baby chain since the beginning and she'd fallen in love with Henry, Jared and Katie almost instantly. She loved taking care of them and, on the rare days that she didn't see them—and their dad—she missed them all unbearably. On days like today, while she was tending to the children, tidying the house and preparing meals while Jamie worked on the ranch, it was all too easy to pretend that this was her life—that Jamie was her husband and his children were her children, too. But that was only a fantasy. The reality was that when he came in from his chores at the end of the day, she would say goodbye and go back to her regularly-scheduled, lonely life. But today, the fantasy would be extended just a little bit longer, because when Jamie came back, they were going to cut down a Christmas tree together.

After caring for HJK for so long, she'd learned to distinguish the identity of the crier and the nature of their cries. This time it was Henry, she guessed. Either he was hungry, had a wet diaper or a tummy ache. She'd been pleased when he'd crawled into her lap earlier— and a little surprised, because he wasn't usually a cuddler, except when he was tired or sick. She'd assumed he was just tired, but now she wondered.

"How are you doing, big guy?"

He held his arms out to her, a silent plea to be picked up. And though his big blue eyes were swimming with tears, he smiled at her. A quick glance into the other two cribs confirmed that his brother and sister were both sleeping peacefully.

"You didn't nap for very long," she said, speaking

softly as she lifted him into her arms. She patted his bottom, checking his diaper. Though it didn't feel wet, she changed him anyway, then lifted him into her arms again. "You shouldn't be hungry," she said. "Auntie Bella said you had some fruit and eggs this morning, plus a piece of blueberry muffin and a bottle."

"Ba," he said, which was his word for 'bottle.'

"Are you thirsty?" She continued to chat quietly with him as she carried him out of the room and down the stairs. "Or hungry?"

She set him in his high chair and found some grapes in the refrigerator, already washed and cut up so they wouldn't be a choking hazard. She put a few pieces on his tray. He squished them between his fingers then smeared the broken fruit over his tray.

"Okay, not hungry," she decided, as she prepared a bottle for him.

Bella had created charts so that, at the end of the day, Jamie could clearly see each baby's input—the amount of food and drink—and output—the number of wet and dirty diapers. There was also a column for other notes. In the past few weeks, there had been a lot of other notes—explanations for red marks and warnings of possible bruises that attested to their increased mobility.

As Henry continued to muck around with the grapes, Fallon added a tally to the diaper column. Then she wiped off his hands and lifted him out of his high chair again and carried him to the living room.

Although all of the babies could hold their own bottles now, she'd read somewhere that human contact was important for a baby's development—and especially for preemies—and she liked to cuddle with each of them as much as possible. Since Jared and Katie were still sleeping, she took advantage of this one-on-one time with Henry, settling into the rocking chair and offering him the bottle.

He grabbed it with both hands and guided the nipple unerringly into his mouth and immediately began sucking.

"I guess you were thirsty," she noted.

As he continued to drink, she touched her lips to his forehead. Hmm...maybe he was a little warm. And in the late morning sunlight streaming through the window, his cheeks did appear a little blotchy and red.

"Maybe you're cutting some more teeth," she suggested. His bottom central incisors had broken through the gums only a few days earlier—two days later than Katie had cut hers, while his brother, Jared, was still waiting for his.

Henry continued to suck on the empty bottle until she gently eased it from his grasp and set it aside.

"Do you feel better now?" she asked him.

He responded by projectile-vomiting all over her.

Chapter Three

Fallon was having second thoughts about the tree-cutting plan before Jamie came back to the house that afternoon. She'd barely finished cleaning up Henry and herself—having to borrow a shirt from her friend's closet in order to put her own in the wash—when Jared and Katie woke up and began demanding their lunch. Of course, Henry's belly was empty, too, and though she was wary of what might happen with anything he ate, she couldn't let him go hungry.

Thankfully, whatever had upset Henry's tummy earlier seemed to be out of his system, and he dug into his pasta with enthusiasm. After they'd finished eating and she'd finished cleaning up the kitchen, she bundled them into their snowsuits and took them outside to play in the snow. It was fun to watch them crawl around in it, and as an added bonus, it tired them out quickly.

While they were outside, she scanned the property, looking for any sign of their father, but she didn't see Jamie anywhere. She knew he'd planned to fix the fence on the north border of the property, but unless the damage was worse than he'd suggested, he should have been finished by now.

When the babies finally collapsed in the snow, exhausted, she carted them back inside, wrestled them out of their snowsuits, changed their diapers, gave them their bottles and settled them back in their cribs. She touched the back of her hand to Henry's forehead, but whatever had ailed the little guy earlier seemed to have truly passed.

When they were finally all settled, she said a silent prayer of thanks that she was able to get them all to sleep at the same time. By that point, she was just as exhausted as they were.

But she threw another load of laundry into the washing machine, added a couple of items to Jamie's grocery list, and tidied up the toys in the living room because she knew if she sat down, she might not get up again.

She was accustomed to taking care of children all day long. When she wasn't helping with Jamie's babies, she worked part-time at Country Kids Day Care. But she worked with the preschool group, children who generally listened to instruction, sat happily at a table to complete an assigned task and enjoyed story time.

As much as she loved Henry, Jared and Katie—and she did—it wasn't easy trying to keep up with their demands. Although she couldn't deny that they were much easier to deal with now that their schedules were somewhat synchronized. For the first few months, it seemed as if one baby would go down for a nap, then the second would want to be fed, the third would need to be changed and by the time the second one was almost asleep, the first was waking up again.

In those early months, only a few hours with the babies had exhausted her. Thankfully, during that time, there had been a lot of volunteers in the baby chain so that no one had to do more than a four-hour shift and often there were two volunteers during a given period.

Over the past couple of weeks, however, as holiday preparations put more demands on everyone's time, the number of volunteers had started to dwindle. While Fallon understood that people had other responsibilities and obligations, she couldn't abandon Henry, Jared and Katie. Their father was already doing everything he could to keep the ranch running and there was no way he'd be able to do that if he was also responsible for the full-time care of his babies.

The dryer buzzed, signaling the end of the cycle and prompting her return to the laundry room. She knew Jamie appreciated the extra chores she did around the house, but as she folded diapers shirts and sleepers, she found herself wishing that he would—just once—see her as more than a link in the baby chain.

It wasn't quite three o'clock when Jamie returned to the house. After kicking off his boots at the back door, he was immediately struck by the unfamiliar sound of silence. Obviously HJK were down for their afternoon nap—but where was their babysitter?

"Fallon?" he called out.

There was no response. But he did hear water running and realized the sound was coming from the laundry room. As he headed in that direction, he was once again struck by the uncomfortable realization that he would never be able to repay her for everything she'd done for his family over the past ten months—and continued to do. Not only did she take care of his babies, but she also helped prepare meals, kept the house tidy and ensured that HJK—and he—always had clean clothes to wear.

But he could at least thank her, and with that thought in mind, he pushed open the partially closed door to reveal Fallon standing in front of the dryer, shaking out a garment that she'd just removed from it.

He didn't know what it was; he didn't note the shape or color or anything because he couldn't tear his gaze away from Fallon's naked body.

Okay, she wasn't actually naked.

Not even half-naked really.

She was only topless. And wearing a bra. But it had been a long time since he'd seen so much bare female skin. Temptingly smooth and pale. He wondered if it could possibly be as soft as it looked and, from out of nowhere, he was almost overcome by the urge to step forward and press his lips to her bare shoulder.

She turned slightly as she slid an arm into a sleeve, and he realized the garment was a shirt. And now he had an even better view of the bra she was wearing. A barely there scrap of lace with low-cut cups that hugged the curve of her breasts.

He swallowed. Hard.

He started to back away, so that she wouldn't know he'd caught her half-undressed. But he suddenly seemed to be having trouble with blood flow to his brain. Or maybe it was to his legs, because instead of backing out the doorway, he backed into the door, causing it to crash against the wall.

Fallon gasped and whirled around.

Now he had a perfect and unobstructed view of her front, and it was even more spectacular than her back. Because, of course, there were breasts front and center. Delicate swells of creamy flesh that were beautifully showcased by the white lace.

"Jamie!"

He lifted his gaze to her face, saw that her cheeks had turned the same color as her hair. "What?"

"Get out!"

"Oh. Right."

He backed into the door again, then turned around and fled.

Fallon's fingers were unsteady as she worked to fasten the buttons of her shirt. She could still feel the heat in her cheeks, though she didn't think the rush of blood to her face had been the result of embarrassment as much as arousal.

And it had been arousal she'd seen in Jamie's eyes, too. She was certain of it. Okay—*almost* certain.

But how would she know? When had a man ever looked at her with desire in his eyes? Maybe she was just seeing what she wanted to see, because she so desperately wanted to believe he might feel even a tiny bit of what she felt for him.

Aside from some flirting and a few kisses, she didn't have a lot of experience with the opposite sex. Yeah, she'd been hit on occasionally. Probably because there were a lot more men than women in Rust Creek Falls and any woman who walked through the doors of the

Ace in the Hole on a Friday or Saturday night could expect to be hit on. But now that she was thinking about it, she couldn't remember the last time that had happened. True, she hadn't been to the local bar in several months, but since the flood a couple of years earlier, there had been an influx of people from Thunder Canyon and other neighboring towns to help the residents of Rust Creek Falls. And while the majority of those people had gone back to their own homes, many had chosen to stay—most of them women. As a result, the local demographic had shifted. Now that there were a lot more young and single women in town, the local cowboys were happy to spread their attention and affection around.

Fallon had absolutely no objections. She'd never wanted anyone but Jamie. Unfortunately, except for that one kiss seven years earlier, he'd never given her any indication that he felt the same way.

She huffed out a breath and pressed her hands to her still-hot cheeks. Obviously she needed another minute or two before she could face him again. Thankfully, there was the rest of the load of laundry to be folded, which she did while trying not to think about what he'd been thinking when he'd looked at her.

Because it was possible that his wide-eyed, slack-jawed expression had been shock rather than arousal. Certainly he would have been shocked to discover her in his laundry room in a state of semiundress. Maybe even appalled—and wasn't that possibility like a bucket of icy water in her flushed face?

Before she'd finished folding the clothes, she heard, through the baby monitor that she carried with her everywhere she went, sounds of rustling and cooing that were the general precursors to any or all of the triplets waking up. And then she heard Jamie—the low, soothing murmur of his voice as he entered the room and began talking to his children.

She knew it wasn't easy for him—being both a father and a mother to three babies in addition to performing the majority of day-to-day chores that came with owning and managing a ranch. And yet, when he finally got back to the house at the end of his long days, his first thought was always of his children.

Of course, she knew how much family meant to Jamie, and she understood why it was so important to him to ensure that his children always knew how much they were loved. Because he'd been orphaned at fifteen and separated from his siblings soon after. And as far as she knew, neither Jamie nor Bella had heard a single word from any of the others since.

Losing most of his family in such a short period of time had made him determined to keep his own family together, no matter what. Which was why Jamie had been not just furious but deeply hurt when he ran into his grandfather at Crawford's a few months after the babies were born and Matthew Baldwin had suggested that the children might be better off if Jamie put them up for adoption, so they could go to homes with two parents to care for them.

Although Fallon believed the old man had offered this advice out of a sincere desire to help guide his grandson through a difficult situation, she didn't believe it was the right advice. And it renewed her determination to help in any way that she could to ensure that Jamie never needed to worry about losing his children.

When the laundry was folded, she headed upstairs

and found him in the babies' room, changing Katie's diaper. Henry was standing up, holding on to the bars of his crib and chewing on the top rail. Jared was still sleeping, his arms flung out at his sides. He was the only one of the babies who had hated being swaddled as an infant.

"Need a hand?" she asked.

He lifted Katie off of the changing table. "Sure— you can take her downstairs. I'll bring Henry and Jared when they're ready."

"Okay." She took the little girl from his arms, and he immediately turned toward Henry's crib without looking at her.

"Apparently this is going to be awkward," she said, standing beside the changing table with Katie propped on her hip.

"I'm sorry." He carried Henry to the table and began unfastening his overalls.

"Sorry this is awkward?"

He finally lifted his gaze to meet hers. "Sorry I walked in on you in the laundry room," he clarified.

"Forget it," she said. "It was just unfortunate timing."

One side of his mouth curved. "Or fortunate—depending on your perspective."

She felt heat rise into her face again.

"But I wouldn't have walked into the laundry room if I'd known you were in there. Naked," he said.

Her gaze shifted to the trio of cribs lined up along the far wall, settling on the closest one, in which Jared was still sleeping. Of course, none of the babies was paying any attention to their conversation. And even if they had been listening, they wouldn't have understood what the adults were saying. But that knowledge didn't prevent Fallon's cheeks from burning. "I wasn't naked."

"Close enough," he said.

"I was topless," she clarified. "And wearing a bra."

"White lace," he said, confirming that he'd noticed.

"A lot of women wear bathing suits that cover less," she pointed out.

He finished with Henry's diaper and turned back to face her. "Not in Montana in December."

"I'm just saying—it's not a big deal."

"It is to a man who hasn't seen an even partially naked female body in almost fifteen months."

Fifteen months?

He nodded, obviously having read the confusion on her face. "Yeah, the minute Paula found out she was carrying triplets, she shut me out of the bedroom."

Fallon didn't know how to respond to that, so she said nothing.

"So if I was staring—" He shook his head as he set Henry back in his crib so that he could perform the diaper routine with Jared, who was just waking up. "There's no 'if' about it—I was staring. And I'm sorry."

"It's okay," she said, and managed a small smile. "Truthfully, I'm flattered. My breasts are too small to garner much notice."

"Your breasts aren't too small, they're—" He broke off again, swallowed. "Wow, this is a really inappropriate conversation."

"Forget it," she said again. "Please."

"I don't know if I can," he admitted. "But I'll try."

The scent of something rich and savory teased Jamie's nostrils and made his mouth water as he made his way back down the stairs. After setting Henry and Jared in the enclosed play yard with their sister, he headed toward the kitchen, where he could hear Fallon moving around.

"Something smells good," he noted. And looks even better, he thought, surreptitiously glancing at her. Though she was fully dressed now, it was as if he could see right through her clothes to the creamy skin beneath, the tantalizing feminine curves, the peaked nipples pressing against white lace.

"I figured you would probably be ready for dinner by the time we got back from getting the tree," Fallon said, "so I put a roast and vegetables in the slow cooker."

He snapped a leash on his wayward libido and turned his attention to the pot. "We're not eating until we get back?"

"The plan was to go out before it gets dark," she reminded him. "And the roast won't be ready for another hour, anyway. But to be honest, I'm not sure we should get the tree today."

"Why not?" He had no objection to the reprieve, but he was curious as to why Fallon—who had been so eager to get the house decked out for the holidays—had suddenly changed her mind.

Was it his fault? Had his gawking at her nearly naked breasts made her uncomfortable? He mentally shook his head at the ridiculousness of the question. Of course, his gawking had made her uncomfortable. Unfortunately there was no way for him to unsee what he'd seen, even if he wanted to…and he wasn't certain that he did.

"Well, the reason I was doing laundry today—" she glanced away, her cheeks flushing prettily "—is that Henry threw up on me earlier."

"I'm sorry."

"It wasn't your fault," she assured him.

"But I knew he was feeling off," Jamie said, relieved that she didn't blame him for the incident, and especially that she didn't seem to feel uncomfortable after the laundry room encounter. "He was awake a couple of times in the night, not for any particular reason that I could tell, but he was definitely unsettled."

"Well, he seems fine now," she said. "But I'm not sure that being out in the cold for an extended period of time is a good idea."

"My mom always sent us out to play in the winter so the cold could kill off our germs."

The words were out of his mouth before he even knew what he was saying. If she realized the significance of his statement, the implication that she was as close to a mother-figure as his babies had, she didn't show it. In fact, she didn't react at all, except to ask, "What if it wasn't some kind of bug?"

"What else could it be?" he asked.

"Maybe…the muffins I made," she suggested tentatively.

Jamie shook his head. "Your baking did not make him sick."

"How do you know?" she challenged.

"Because all of the babies had the same thing and only Henry threw up."

"So far," she muttered.

"Besides, I ate four of those muffins," he pointed out. "And they were delicious."

She still looked dubious.

"He's fine, Fallon. If I've learned nothing else over the past ten months, I've learned that kids get sick—

and preemies more often than most. There's no way to prevent it," he assured her.

"I've also learned that three babies living in close proximity usually share germs and viruses much more willingly than toys—so it's quite possible that whatever caused Henry's stomach upset might already have been passed on to Jared and Katie."

She nodded in acknowledgment of that fact. "Which is another reason it might be a good idea to delay the tree-cutting."

"That will also give me a chance to haul down the boxes of decorations from the attic," he said. "Because I assume that, after we cut down the tree, you're going to want to decorate it."

"No, *you're* going to decorate it," she said, but softened the directive with a smile.

A smile that drew his attention to her mouth and made him wonder if her lips could possibly be as soft and sweet as they looked. He pushed the tempting question aside. "There you go, being all bossy again," he said, his tone deliberately light.

"But I *might* be persuaded to help," Fallon relented.

He lifted the lid on the pot and peered at the roast beef and vegetables in an effort to avoid focusing on her and the new and unexpected hunger that was churning inside him. "Are you sure it's going to be another hour before it's ready?"

She took the lid from his hand and set it firmly back on top of the stoneware. "Longer if you keep letting all the heat out," she warned.

Except he suspected that her proximity was generating even more heat than the cooking pot. He took a deliberate step away. "Sorry—but I worked through lunch, and dinner smells so good."

She plucked a muffin out of the container on the table and tossed it to him.

He immediately took a bite out of the top, because he was hungry and wanted to reassure her that he had no concerns about the treats she'd baked, but also because focusing on the muffin would help him resist the urge to reach for her. "These are really delicious."

"See? I'm not as inept in the kitchen as people like to believe."

"Hmm."

She narrowed her gaze. "What's that supposed to mean?"

"Well…that was a pretty awful cake that you took to the potluck." He couldn't resist teasing her a little.

She huffed out a breath and shook her head. "One mistake. *One.* And no one will let me live it down."

"On the other hand, the roast in that Crock-Pot smells really good."

"Crock-Pot cooking is easy," she admitted. "You just toss in the meat and veggies, add some liquid and seasoning, and it pretty much cooks itself."

"Still, I appreciate the effort," he said.

"If that's a 'thank you,' then you're welcome," she said, lifting her coat off the hook by the door.

"Where are you going?" he asked.

"Home."

He should let her go. He needed some time to catch his breath and think about the sudden and unexpected awareness between them—and he couldn't do that while her presence was wreaking havoc on his hormones. But instead of nodding and advising her to 'drive safely,' when he opened his mouth, the only word that came out was, "Stay."

Chapter Four

Fallon raised a brow. "Now who's being bossy?"

But she didn't protest when Jamie took the coat from her hand and returned it to the hook. "You went to the effort of making dinner, you should stay and eat it with us."

"I thought you might appreciate some peace and quiet after a busy day," she said.

"Yeah, me and the triplets—a definite recipe for peace and quiet," he remarked dryly.

Still she hesitated.

"If you don't have other plans, I would enjoy some adult company."

"Bella won't be home for dinner?"

"Not likely," he told her. "She and Hudson are pretty much inseparable these days."

"I guess that makes sense, considering that they're head over heels in love and planning to get married."

His only response was to snag another muffin.

"I thought a dozen of those would last more than a day," she noted, heading back to the living room where the kids were playing.

"I worked up an appetite today," he told her.

She lowered herself to the floor, near the play yard, using the sofa as a backrest. "Did you get the north fence repaired?"

He nodded as he sat down beside her, stretching his legs out in front of him.

She picked up a block that Henry tossed over the enclosure and dropped it back inside for him. "How's Daisy?"

"She seems to be doing okay, if maybe a little restless." He polished off the second muffin as his firstborn continued to play "catch" with Fallon. "How was your day—aside from being vomited on?"

As he'd expected, her cheeks immediately filled with color. "Aside from that, it was good," she said. "Bella asked me to be her maid of honor."

"I thought she would," Jamie said. "You're not just her best friend, you're like a sister to her. To both of us." It was an effort to keep his tone casual, to not reveal any of the inner turmoil he was feeling.

Because while Fallon was like a sister to Bella, she could never take the place of the actual sisters that she'd lost touch with eleven years earlier. And while he wanted to believe she was like a sister to him, their relationship wasn't quite that simple. Especially since he'd seen her half-naked in the laundry room. While he was still trying to get a handle on the feelings churning inside him, he was certain of one thing: those feelings weren't the least bit brotherly.

But maybe he hadn't been as successful at hiding his thoughts as he'd hoped, or maybe Fallon just knew him too well, because she touched his arm. It was simply a gesture of support, but the sight of her hand on his arm made him crave her touch on other parts of his body. He wanted those fingers gliding over his skin, her nails biting into his flesh as he—

Whoa! Not going there. Not with Fallon. No way.

"It's not easy for her, either," she said gently, drawing his attention back to the issue of his sister's wedding. "As excited as Bella is about starting a life with the man she loves, she's going to be thinking of all the people who won't be there on her wedding day."

He nodded. "I'm going to walk her down the aisle, but I'm not giving her away. Aside from it being an archaic tradition, it just doesn't feel right, so we're going to ask the minister to skip that part."

"She'd probably be happy to skip all of the parts that come before 'I now pronounce you husband and wife,'" Fallon said, in what he recognized as a deliberate attempt to lighten the mood.

"Because she knows I wouldn't approve of her moving in with Hudson until he's put the second ring on her finger."

"And you know she wouldn't just abandon you and the babies," she pointed out.

He nodded. "She's already put her life on hold long enough to help us out. And while I sometimes think I should have insisted that she stay at school to get her diploma, there's no way I would have managed this past year without her."

"She'll go back and finish," Fallon assured him.

"Even if she doesn't, she's got Hudson to take care of her now."

Fallon shook her head despairingly. "It's not his responsibility to take care of her," she chided. "When a man and a woman decide to join their lives together, they take care of each other."

She was right, of course. If he let himself think about his parents—which he rarely did—he knew that they'd enjoyed a mutually loving and supportive relationship. But his own experience with marriage had been very different.

At first, it hadn't been so bad. Paula had kept up the house and prepared the meals while he'd handled all of the ranch chores. And he was okay with that, because she was a city girl adjusting to life in Rust Creek Falls. But even that tentative arrangement had fallen apart after the two lines had appeared in the little window of the pregnancy test.

And when his wife had learned that she was carrying three babies, it had been the end of any cooperation or even communication between them. There had been no give-and-take with Paula after that—just a whole lot of unhappiness and anger.

Something beeped in the kitchen, and Fallon pushed herself up off the floor. "Are you still hungry?" she asked.

"Does today end with a *y*?" Jamie asked her.

She smiled at that. "Give me ten minutes to finish up the gravy."

He watched her walk out of the room, his gaze focused on the sexy curve of her butt and the gentle sway of her hips. Of course, when he realized what he was doing—ogling his best friend—he was appalled. But that brief glimpse of her mostly bare torso in the laundry room had reminded him of a simple fact that he'd denied for too long: Fallon O'Reilly wasn't a girl anymore.

Yes, she was his loyal friend and a dedicated caregiver to his babies, but she was also an attractive and appealing woman. Very attractive and incredibly appealing. And the acknowledgment of those simple facts made him a little uneasy, because he had no business thinking of her in those terms.

"Fa!" Henry demanded. "Fa-fa!"

Jamie saw that his son had made his way to the other side of the play yard and was looking toward the doorway through which Fallon had disappeared. All of his kids loved Fallon, but he'd recently begun to suspect that Henry had a little bit of a crush on his second-favorite caregiver—"Auntie Bella" being the favorite of all of them, of course, by simple virtue of the fact that she spent the most time with them.

"Fallon's making dinner for us," he told his son. "Are you hungry?"

"Fa-fa!" Henry said again.

"Fa-fa!" Jared echoed.

Jamie sighed. "What about you?" he asked Katie. "Are you going to join in?"

His baby girl looked up at him with big blue eyes. "Da-da!"

And the sweet sound made his lips curve and his heart swell. "That's my girl," he said, lifting her out of the play yard and into his arms.

Jared's little brow furrowed as he looked up at his sister, outside of the enclosure. He rocked the top rail, shaking the wall. "Da-da!"

"You think that's a get-out-of-jail card now, don't you?"

"Da-da!" Jared said again.

"Fa-fa!" Henry continued.

Chuckling, Jamie unlatched the gate so the boys could escape. Though all of the babies were now able to stand while holding on to something and had even begun to cruise around the furniture, none had yet attempted to take any unsupported steps. As he opened the gate, Henry and Jared dropped to their hands and knees and crawled out of the play yard and headed toward the kitchen.

Fallon was spooning the vegetables into a serving bowl when he walked through the doorway with Katie still in his arms. Henry's and Jared's palms slapped against the tile floor as they hurried to keep up with his pace.

"Perfect timing," she said, as she set the bowl on the table beside a platter of meat. The promised gravy had already been poured into a pitcher and there was a basket of warm dinner rolls, too.

Jamie buckled the kids into their high chairs and washed their hands while Fallon finished cutting up their meat and vegetables into bite-sized pieces. As he sat down across from her at the table, he realized that he was glad she was there. He'd invited her to stay because it seemed like the polite thing to do, but he was sincerely pleased that she'd agreed. Not just because he appreciated an extra set of hands to help with HJK, but because it was nice to have someone to talk to at the end of the day. *A friend*, he reminded himself firmly.

For a long time, it had been just him and his sister—and the three babies, of course, but they didn't yet add much to a dinner conversation. He was happy for Bella, that she'd met Hudson and fallen in love. And even if—according to Fallon—it wasn't Hudson's job to take care of Bella, Jamie knew that he would. Just as he knew that Bella would take care of Hudson, too.

If he had any concerns, they weren't about the upcoming nuptials but the practicalities of managing the triplets every day without his sister living under the same roof. He knew that she would continue to help in any way that she could, but he didn't want her to. She needed to focus on her own life, her own future, and her own happiness. The successful management and operation of the baby chain had allowed him to become complacent, but it was time for him to stop dragging his heels and make other arrangements for the care of his children.

But for now, he had different concerns. "So when do you want to get the tree?" he asked, as he sliced into a piece of roast beef. "Saturday?"

Fallon shook her head. "I promised to go wedding dress shopping with Bella on Saturday."

"They just got engaged. I didn't think she'd be rushing into that already," he commented.

"They're planning a June wedding," she reminded him. "And that's only six months away."

"Still, dress shopping won't take all day, will it?"

"A woman's wedding day is one of the most important days of her life," she pointed out to him. "And considering that all of the attention is on the bride and what she's wearing, I'm not going to rush your sister into making a decision."

"Okay, so Saturday's out," he conceded. "How about Sunday?"

"Attendance at my parents' house for Sunday dinner is mandatory, but I could maybe come by in the afternoon," she suggested.

"That sounds good," he agreed. "Plus it gives me a few days to haul the decorations down from the attic."

"You haven't said anything about the other items on my list," she noted.

He speared a chunk of potato with his fork. "Isn't it enough that I'm agreeing to put up a tree?"

Fallon shook her head despairingly as she chewed on a carrot. "Have you started your Christmas shopping yet?"

"Bella's picked up a few things for me to give to the kids."

"What about S-A-N-T-A?"

He lifted his glass to his mouth to hide his smile. "Santa?"

She scowled at him as she jerked her head toward the trio of high chairs, where Henry, Jared and Katie were intently focused on shoving food into their mouths and not paying the least bit of attention to the adults' conversation.

"Maybe you should clarify what you're asking," he suggested.

"I'm asking you who's going to help Saint Nicholas with his shopping," she told him.

"I'll figure it out." He slid another piece of the tender meat between his lips.

Of course, Fallon wasn't satisfied with that vague response. "When?" she pressed.

He shook his head. "You're relentless, aren't you?"

"I know a lot of guys take pride in doing all of their

shopping on Christmas Eve, but you can't do that when you have kids," she told him.

"Maybe not in a few years," he acknowledged. "But right now, they don't even know what Christmas is. Whatever Santa brings, they'll probably be more interested in the boxes than the toys."

Before she could dispute his point, the back door was flung open and Bella stomped in, kicking snow off of her boots. "It's really coming down out there," she said, as she pulled a knit hat off of her head and unfastened her coat.

Fallon turned to look out the window, her eyes widening as she noticed the thick, fluffy flakes illuminated by the porch lights. "When did the snow start?"

"About half an hour ago," Bella said, hanging her coat on an empty hook. Having taken off her boots, she now stuffed her feet inside a pair of fuzzy slippers. "A couple of inches have fallen already and we're supposed to get another eight to ten before morning."

"That's my cue to be heading home," Fallon decided, pushing away from the table.

"Do you want me to give you a lift?" Jamie offered.

She rolled her eyes as she dropped quick kisses on top of each of the babies' heads. "I've been driving in Montana for as long as I've been driving," she reminded him. "I'm not afraid of a little snow."

"Eight to ten inches is more than a little snow," he pointed out.

"Which is why I'm heading out now." She reached for her coat and turned to Bella, "Let me know what time you want to leave Saturday morning."

His sister nodded. "I will."

"And I'll see you guys Sunday," she said to Jamie,

encompassing the triplets with her remark and adding a wave for their benefit.

Henry lifted a hand, covered with the remnants of smushed potato and gravy, and waved back.

"Bu-bu-bu," Katie said, which was one of her favorite sounds and used to mean "bye-bye," "bottle," "ball" and "Bella."

"What's Sunday?" Bella asked, when Fallon had gone.

"We're going to get the Christmas tree on Sunday," Jamie told her.

His sister held a washcloth under the faucet, then wrung it out and wiped the triplets' hands and faces. "I thought you were planning to do that today."

"Plans changed."

Bella cleared away the babies' plates, then filled the kettle with water and set it on the stove to boil. "So what did I miss?"

Jamie mopped up the leftover gravy on his plate with a piece of roll. "Roast beef."

She shook her head. "I wasn't talking about that."

"What were you talking about?"

"I got the impression that I walked into the middle of something."

"Just dinner," he told her.

"Hmm," she said, clearly unconvinced.

"Did you eat?" he asked.

She nodded. "Hudson and I grabbed a bite at the Ace."

He frowned at that. "You know I don't like you hanging out there."

"I wasn't hanging out," she chided. "I was having a

meal in the company of my fiancé on a Thursday night. And you're changing the subject."

"What subject?" he asked.

"Fallon."

He carried his empty plate and cutlery to the dishwasher. "I didn't realize she was a subject."

"Neither did I, but there was a definite vibe between the two of you when I walked in," she told him.

"What kind of vibe?"

"That's what I'm trying to figure out," she admitted.

"Well, while you're doing that, I'm going to get HJK washed up and ready for bed," he said, and made his escape before his sister asked more questions he wasn't prepared to answer.

As he led the babies toward the stairs—because it was a lot easier to let them crawl than attempt to carry all of them—he wondered if she'd actually picked up on some kind of "vibe" between him and Fallon or was just toying with him.

Since Bella had accepted Hudson's proposal, she'd suddenly decided that he needed to find someone to share his life, too. More important, she believed that his children needed a mother. Jamie knew that she didn't mean to be insensitive—that she genuinely wanted what was best for his family. He also suspected that she knew more about the issues behind the scenes in his marriage than he'd ever admitted to her.

But he wasn't looking for anyone to share his life. In fact, as much as he appreciated the baby chain, he sometimes resented the presence of other people in his home and taking care of his children. Which was completely unreasonable, of course, but true nonetheless.

And yet, when he had the opportunity to share a meal

alone with his children, he'd invited Fallon to stay. But Fallon wasn't just a link in the baby chain. She was one of his best friends.

And now he'd seen her half-naked.

He hadn't been joking when he'd told her that he didn't know if he could forget seeing her topless in the laundry room. The tantalizing image seemed to be indelibly imprinted on his memory.

After the triplets were settled into their respective cribs and sleeping soundly, he spent some time in the main floor office paying bills and ordering supplies. He loved being a rancher—he didn't love the financial instability that came with the title. And he didn't love being dependent on other people to take care of his babies while he was busy with the numerous tasks required to keep the ranch running.

He wouldn't have made it through this past year without the baby chain, and especially without his sister. And while putting the triplets into day care would ease his reliance on community help, it wouldn't affect his daily routine very much—if at all. He would still be the one who fed them their dinner—even if the meals would likely be prepared by volunteers—bathe them and put them to bed.

But he knew the whole dynamic in the house would change when Bella married Hudson. And Jamie suspected it might not be too long after that before they'd want to start their own family. His sister deserved to be a mother to her own children, but he knew that her absence would leave an enormous hole in his life and the lives of his children.

Maybe he should think about finding a new mother for his children, but aside from the fact that he had no energy to get dressed up and go out when he finally finished his chores at the end of the day, he had less than zero interest in dating. Even if he had the time, he didn't know that he was willing to put himself out there again.

He'd made a major error in judgment with Paula. On his own for the first time, away from Rust Creek Falls and the rules and responsibilities that had been such an integral part of his life, he'd relished the freedom. And when he'd met Paula, he'd been blinded by her beauty and seduced by her charm.

They'd been together for almost three years and heading toward graduation when he asked her to marry him. They were both young, maybe too young to be thinking about lifetime commitments, but the alternative—going their separate ways—had been unthinkable to him.

His sister hadn't been thrilled when he'd told her about his imminent wedding plans. He'd thought Bella was just feeling out of sorts, or was still mad at him for going away to school and abandoning her in the care of their cold grandparents. Whatever her motivation, she'd warned him that Paula wouldn't enjoy ranch life. In fact, she'd questioned whether the Seattle native would be able to stick it out through a single Montana winter.

He should have listened to his sister. Because although Paula had endured three long and frigid winters, she hadn't been happy in Rust Creek Falls. She didn't like the weather or the isolation or even, by the end, the man she'd married.

If Jamie ever did decide to marry again—or even start dating again—he would choose a local girl. Someone who knew what it meant to live on a ranch, someone who loved the land—and especially someone who loved his children.

Someone like Fallon.

He shook his head, as if that might dislodge the thought from his mind. Fallon O'Reilly might be the perfect woman for him in a lot of ways, but she was also completely wrong for just one reason: she was his best friend. And that was a line he wasn't going to cross. Ever. No matter how much he was tempted by the image of her in white lace.

By the time he finally finished his paperwork, shut down the computer, checked on the kids and crawled beneath the covers of his bed, he was exhausted. Accustomed to the early mornings and long hours of running a ranch, he'd learned to fall asleep quickly even if he didn't sleep as deeply as he used to. He was so attuned to the sounds that his children made, he could often hear them stirring and tell when they were about to waken before they actually did so.

But tonight, his own sleep was elusive. Because every time he closed his eyes, he saw Fallon as she'd looked in the laundry room. Her back—long and narrow, the ridges of her spine visible beneath her creamy skin. The expanse of bare flesh broken only by the narrow band of white lace that stretched across her middle and tiny straps that went over her shoulders. The sweet little indent at the small of her back, just above the waistband of her jeans. The sexy slope of her strong shoulders. He could have stared contentedly at her back for hours—then she'd turned around.

He pressed the heels of his hands to his eyes. He shouldn't be remembering Fallon like this. They'd been friends for a lot of years. She'd been his confidante through some of the darkest periods in his life. She was the only person who knew about some of the worst days of his marriage. The one person he'd always trusted to listen and not judge. The one person who had always been there for him when he needed someone. And it would screw up everything if he let himself want her.

In the past ten months, he hadn't experienced even the most basic stirrings of physical attraction. He'd been too exhausted to feel much of anything. And that was okay. Every free minute he had, he spent with his kids. And every day, he sent up a prayer of thanksgiving that he'd been given the gift of three beautiful, healthy babies. He didn't think about romance except to think that he might be ready to start dating again around the time that HJK were ready to start school—as in college. He hadn't expected to feel any kind of sexual awakening before then—and especially not for his childhood friend.

Okay, so there had been that one kiss, more than seven years earlier. A kiss that never should have happened. A kiss that had, nevertheless, lingered in his mind for a long time afterward. The sweetness of her lips, the softness of her body, the absolute perfection of that one stolen moment.

Maybe he'd briefly considered the possibility of allowing that kiss to lead to something more. But even then, he'd valued her friendship too much to jeopardize that relationship for the sake of a sudden and unexpected attraction. Thankfully, he'd left the next day for his second year at college, grateful for the time and distance to get his head back on straight.

A few weeks later, he'd met Paula, and he'd pushed all non-platonic thoughts about Fallon to the back of his mind.

Neither he nor Fallon had ever mentioned the kiss

again. And when he'd told her that he was getting married, she wasn't anything but supportive. Even after the wedding, she'd continued to be there for him, listening to his hopes and dreams, worries and frustrations.

He'd told her things he'd never told anyone else, because she was firmly and unequivocally in the "friend" camp. Discovering her half-naked in the laundry room had apparently shifted her into the "want to get naked with" camp.

At the very least, he wanted to know if she was wearing white lace panties that matched her bra. And did she prefer bikinis or boy shorts or hi-cut briefs? The formation of the question in his mind proved that he'd spent too much time thumbing through the pages of the Victoria's Secret catalog his sister had left on the kitchen table.

Maybe he wasn't ready to think about getting married again. Maybe he wasn't even ready to start dating again. But his body was definitely in favor of ditching the celibacy phase that had never been his idea. Thankfully, his rational mind knew that thinking about Fallon in conjunction with that plan was a very bad idea.

Unfortunately, his subconscious didn't agree. And when he finally fell asleep, he dreamed about her in his arms...and in his bed.

Chapter Five

Jamie pulled HJK's sleigh over the snow, toward the woods on the west side of his property, while Fallon walked beside him, dragging an empty toboggan onto which he would secure the tree that they cut down. The air was cold and crisp, typical of Montana in December, the snow crunching beneath their feet.

Fallon was wearing slim-fitting jeans tucked into knee-high winter boots, a navy ski jacket with a pink pom-pom hat and matching mittens. The color should have clashed horribly with the red curls that peeked out beneath her cap, but it didn't. Instead, she looked like she'd walked off the front cover of an L.L. Bean catalog—a woman as comfortable in her clothes as she was in her surroundings.

He wondered how it was that he'd known her forever, but every once in a while, he would look at her as if he was seeing her for the first time and be struck by how truly beautiful she was. Today was one of those days. While he viewed this outing as a chore, she was obviously excited about their purpose and it showed in the color in her cheeks and the sparkle in her eyes.

He halted at the edge of the tree line and turned to her. "Okay, pick a tree."

"Me?" she said, obviously surprised.

"Isn't that why we're here?"

"No, we're here because you need a Christmas tree," she reminded him. "I only agreed to tag along because I knew there was no way you could chop down a tree and get it—along with three babies—back to the house on your own."

"No, you're here because you didn't trust that I'd comply with your list," he guessed.

"That, too," she confirmed, not even attempting to hide her smile. "But this is really about sharing—or starting—family traditions with your children."

"If you expected three ten-month-old babies would have any input in selecting a tree, you're going to be disappointed."

"Why would you say that?"

He gestured to the sleigh, where Henry, Jared and Katie had all fallen asleep.

Fallon sighed. "I should have remembered that the motion of the sled knocks them out."

"Looks like it's up to you and me," Jamie said.

She didn't let herself read too much into his words. Didn't want to admit—even to herself—how much she wished there was a "you and me" that included her and Jamie.

"It's your tree," she reminded him. "So you should pick."

"Okay. How about that one?"

Of course, he was pointing to the closest one for, she suspected, no reason except that it was the closest one. She looked the tree up and down, then walked around it, emerging again from the other side shaking her head. "It's too big."

He pointed to another undoubtedly random tree. "That one?"

She immediately nixed that suggestion, too. "That one's too small."

"Make up your mind, Goldilocks."

"Goldilocks?"

He reached out and tugged on the end of one of her curls. "Your hair might be the wrong color," he acknowledged. "But you've mastered the picky part."

"There's a difference between being picky and discerning," she told him. "And this shouldn't be an impulsive decision. You have to think about where you're going to put the tree, you should check to ensure there aren't any big gaps between the branches, that the trunk is relatively straight and the needles are healthy."

He swept his arm out, gesturing to the wooded area. "Pick a tree—please."

She performed a quick visual scan of the area, then did another walk around a different tree. "This one," she decided.

He glanced from the one she'd selected to his original choice and back again. "That's the same size as the first one I picked."

"The same height," she allowed. "But it's not as full, so it won't take up as much space in the living room."

Though he still looked skeptical, he shrugged. "Okay."

He picked up the saw and moved closer to the tree. Before he started cutting, though, he reached between the branches to grab hold of the trunk and give the tree a good shake to dislodge any critters that were making it their home.

The branches were pretty low to the ground, so Jamie cut off the lowest ones before he crouched down to attack the trunk.

Fallon stood out of the way, keeping an eye on the still-sleeping babies, while Jamie got started. Though she would never admit it to him, she enjoyed watching him work—especially in the hot summer months when he'd strip down to his jeans and T-shirt. Well-worn jeans that molded to the strong muscles of his butt and thighs, and simple T-shirts that stretched over his broad shoulders.

Today, in deference to the frigid winter weather, he was wearing a sheepskin-lined leather jacket over a flannel shirt over one of those T-shirts. Despite the layers, she couldn't help appreciating the width of those shoulders, the obvious strength in his arms. He was incredibly and beautifully built, with the kind of rock-hard muscles that were honed through years of ranch life and could never be replicated in a gym.

It always made her heart sigh to see this strong man being so gentle with his babies. To watch those big hands fasten the tiny snaps on a diaper shirt or affix a miniature barrette in Katie's wispy hair. And whenever she caught him snuggling one of those tiny babies against his broad chest…well, if she'd been the type to swoon, that scene would have made her do so.

Thankfully, he seemed oblivious to the effect he had on her. Not just because of their long-time friendship but because she knew he was grieving the loss of his wife, and it would take time for his heart to heal. But she also knew that he had an incredible capacity for love, because she saw evidence of it every time he was with his babies. And there was a tiny blossom of hope inside of her heart that maybe, someday, he might love her, too. In the meantime, she was content to be part of his life and shower all of her love on his children.

When the tree was strapped down on the sled, with the saw secured beneath it, they headed back toward the house. Henry, Jared and Katie never woke up. Not until Fallon helped Jamie lift them out of the sled and extricate them from their snowsuits.

After they were settled in their play yard with an assortment of favorite toys, Jamie wrestled the tree into the living room. The pungent scent of fresh pine filled the air and filled Fallon's heart with nostalgia. Christmas truly was her favorite time of the year. She had so many wonderful memories of the holidays with her family, so many traditions they still shared—shopping and wrapping, baking and caroling—and those were what she wanted to help Jamie create with his family.

She understood his reticence. The holidays hadn't been a lot of fun for him in the years following his parents' deaths. And, of course, this was his first Christmas without his wife. But it was also his first Christmas with his babies, and she knew that if he could be convinced to make an effort for them, he would find joy in the celebration, too.

And putting up a Christmas tree was, she believed, a first step in the right direction. Which was why she was on her stomach on the floor in the middle of the room, holding the base while he maneuvered the stump in place.

Thankfully, he'd had the foresight to cut off some more of the lower branches before bringing the tree into the house, so she wasn't completely suffocating beneath it. When it was finally in place, she tightened the screws, then wriggled out from beneath the branches and stood up beside him. "What do you think?"

He tilted his head and considered. "I think it's a little crooked."

"It looks great," she assured him.

"Maybe if I—"

"No."

He frowned. "You don't even know what I was going to say."

"It doesn't matter," she said. "You don't need to do anything. The tree is perfect just the way it is."

"Perfect?" he echoed skeptically.

"Perfect doesn't have to mean without flaws," she told him. "Sometimes it only refers to what fulfills your need in the moment."

He held her gaze for a long moment, and something in the depths of his blue eyes made her suspect that he was thinking of needs unrelated to the upcoming holiday. The intensity of his stare made her heart pound and her blood pulse.

Then his attention shifted to the tree again. "In that case, I'd say this perfect tree doesn't need any lights or decorations."

"And you'd be wrong," she said, pleased that her even tone gave no hint of her inner turmoil.

"I figured you would say that," he admitted.

Fallon opened one of the boxes he'd brought down from the attic, looking for lights. The boxes were clearly labeled, but for some reason the contents didn't match the tags. She finally found the lights in the third box she opened—the one marked "Tree Decorations." She had yet to find the actual tree decorations. As for the lights—

She sighed.

"What's wrong?"

Jamie winced when she held up a tangle of wires and miniature bulbs.

"Oh."

"Who put these away like this?" she asked.

"I guess I did," he admitted.

She tossed him the knotted mess. "Then you can untangle them."

He didn't grumble too much about the assigned task. Of course, she ended up helping, because nothing else could go on the tree until the lights were on.

"How was shopping with my sister yesterday?" he asked, as he picked up a second strand of lights.

Thinking back to the hours she'd spent in Kalispell with Bella made her smile. "It was a lot of fun."

"Did she find a dress?" he wondered.

"She didn't tell you?"

"I've hardly seen her," he admitted. "I heard her come in late last night, then as I came in from the barn this morning, she was on her way out again."

"Yes, she found a dress," she told him, replacing a burned-out bulb while he continued working at the knots. "After trying on about thirty different styles—and looking fabulous in every single one—she finally went back to the first one that had caught her eye. Then she had to choose her veil and shoes and…well, you probably don't want to know what your little sister's going to be wearing under her gown, but I can confidently assure you that she's going to be the most beautiful bride Rust Creek Falls has ever seen."

Too late, Fallon remembered that Jamie and Paula had been married in town, at the same church where Bella and Hudson planned to exchange their vows. And, of course, his wife had been stunning—a veritable fairy-tale princess in an elaborate white gown with a full skirt heavy with crystals and beads. Unfortunately, their marriage had not led to happily-ever-after.

"Or at least the most beautiful bride next June," she amended.

"You don't have to watch what you say around me," Jamie told her. "We've been friends too long for you to worry about censoring your words now."

"I know," she agreed. "But I also know this whole year has been incredibly difficult for you, and it must be hard to feel happy for Bella when your own marriage didn't turn out the way you hoped it would."

"I can't deny that my marriage wasn't what I'd hoped, but it isn't hard to be happy for my sister," he said. "Maybe I am a little concerned that everything seems to be happening so fast, but there's no denying how much Hudson adores her or how happy they are together, and that's all I want for her—to be happy."

"She says the same thing about you," Fallon told him.

"I know," he admitted. "But right now, I'm focusing on being grateful. I've been blessed with three wonderful kids and I feel like it would be selfish to want anything more."

"Wanting to win the lottery might be selfish. Wanting to be happy is human."

"Are you happy?" he asked, looking up from the tangle of wires and meeting her eyes.

She stood up with a strand of lights in her hand. "How did this get to be about me?"

"I know you've always wanted to get married and have kids of your own," he continued, turning his attention back to his task. "But you've put that dream on hold for the better part of ten months to take care of my family."

"Maybe." She climbed onto the step stool he'd set up by the tree. "But I don't regret a single minute of it."

"What are you doing?" he demanded, dropping the lights and crossing the floor in three quick strides until he was standing by the stool.

"What does it look like I'm doing?" she countered.

"It looks like you're trying to kill yourself," he said, lifting his hands to her hips to hold her steady.

Except that she'd been steady—until he touched her. Now she could feel the imprint of his hands through the denim, and her knees felt weak and shaky.

"You're not supposed to stand on the top step," he admonished.

"I can't reach the tree top if I don't," she pointed out.

"Then get down from there and let me do it," he suggested.

"If you want me to get off the stool, you need to move away."

"If I move away, you're going to fall," he countered.

She rolled her eyes as she shifted her feet to turn around. And realized her new position left Jamie looking directly at her crotch. And while he'd loosened his grip enough to let her turn, the lighter touch of his hands on her hips felt almost like a caress. Now her legs started a full-on wobble.

"I, uh, need to get down," she said.

"I've got you," he promised.

If his words were intended to reassure her, they had the opposite effect. She took one step down, then another, but he didn't shift away, which meant that by the time her feet were firmly on the floor, their bodies were so close they were nearly touching.

She tipped her head back to look at him, and found his eyes—those deep blue eyes—were fixed on hers. This his gaze dipped to her mouth, and her breath caught in her lungs.

"Fa-fa!" Henry called, the familiar and impatient demand finally breaking the spell that seemed to have woven around Fallon and Jamie.

She attempted to step back, and stumbled against the stool she'd actually, stupidly, forgotten was there. But Jamie still had his hands on her hips, so she didn't fall. His lips twitched at the corners, as if he was trying not to smile. Not to laugh at her. She felt her cheeks flush—the curse of being a redhead. Embarrassed and annoyed, she shoved the strand of lights at him.

"Fine, you put these on the tree while I finish untangling the rest."

He had to let go of her to catch the lights, and then he finally stepped away from her.

"Fa-fa," Henry chanted again.

She shifted her attention to the baby, who was standing up and holding on to the top of the gate. "What's up, big guy?"

He pointed to the rubber ball he'd thrown to her.

"You want to play catch?"

He grinned, showing her his six tiny white teeth. She scooped up the ball and tossed it back into the enclosure. He let go of the gate to clap his hands together.

Fallon gasped softly. "Jamie!"

"I see him," he said, his voice close behind her.

"He's standing up without holding on to anything."

The words were barely out of her mouth before he wobbled, then fell back onto his butt. His eyes opened wide, as if he wasn't sure what had happened, and then his lower lip began to tremble.

"You're okay," Fallon told him, deliberately employing the sing-song tone of voice that was usually effective in diverting a meltdown. "You were up, and then you went down, that's all."

His lip stopped trembling.

"Up then down," she said again, then clapped her hands together. "Yay!"

He clapped his hands together, too.

Jamie reached over the wall of the enclosure to ruffle his son's hair. "Way to go, big guy."

Henry grinned, obviously proud of himself even if he wasn't sure why.

"Make sure you note the date in his baby book," Fallon said.

"I will," he promised. "I missed the first time he rolled over—actually, the first time each one of them rolled over—so there's no way I'll forget this milestone."

He stepped up onto the bottom step of the stool—because he was at least six inches taller than she was and had longer arms, too—and began winding the lights around the tree.

"Don't just hang them off the ends of the branches," Fallon admonished. "Wrap them around each branch, up one side and back down the other."

"What's wrong with the way I'm doing it?" he wanted to know.

"Aside from the fact that it's sloppy and lazy, you won't have any light emanating from inside the tree."

"You're being picky again," he told her.

"Discerning," she countered.

"And these needles are prickly."

"Just like your attitude."

His lips curved at that. "Fine. I'll do it your way," he relented. "But as soon as I get the highest branches done, I'm letting you take over."

She handed him another strand of lights. "Are you sure you can trust me to stand two feet off the ground?"

"No, but it's unlikely you'd break a leg falling from that height."

She continued to untangle lights while he worked at wrapping the tree, muttering under his breath whenever the needles poked his skin.

"Did you grumble this much when you put the lights on your tree last year—or did Paula do it?"

He snorted. "Paula wasn't exactly in the holiday spirit last year, so I picked up a tree from the lot down by Crawford's."

"I guess, being five months pregnant with triplets, she wasn't up to hiking half a mile through the snow to chop down a blue spruce," she said, wishing she hadn't mentioned his wife's name.

"Or even decorate it," he admitted.

"She didn't tell you what ornaments she wanted where?"

He shook his head. "By December, we were barely on speaking terms."

"I know you went through a rough patch," she said softly. "But I didn't know it was that bad."

"It wasn't something I wanted to talk about, with anyone," he admitted. "And, of course, everyone thinks I've spent the past ten months mourning the loss of my wife, but the truth is, our happy marriage was an illusion. Even if she hadn't died, we wouldn't be celebrating this holiday together."

"What do you mean?"

"She was planning to leave after the babies were born."

Fallon shook her head. "I don't believe it."

"It's true," he told her. "You remember how I told you that she wasn't happy to discover that she was carrying triplets?"

"Sure," she agreed. "But any woman would be daunted by the prospect of birthing and caring for three babies. I imagine you were a little apprehensive yourself."

"More than a little," he admitted. "The difference is that I always wanted a big family—even if I assumed they would come one at a time."

She lifted a hand to his arm, drawing his gaze to her. "She was scared and overwhelmed, but she would have come around," she said softly.

"I'm not so sure," he confided. "Before Christmas last year, she made it clear that the babies would be my responsibility because she was going back to Seattle and filing for divorce."

"I don't believe it," Fallon said again. "I mean, I believe that she said it," she clarified. "But I don't believe she would have done it. She loved you, Jamie."

He appreciated the sentiment, but he no longer believed it was true. Maybe Paula had loved him when she married him, but any affection she'd felt for him in the beginning was long gone before her premature labor. Pushing the unhappy memories aside, he turned his attention back to the lights.

Although he'd threatened to make Fallon do the lower half of the tree, by the time he was halfway, it seemed easier just to finish the task. When the lights were on, she handed him the garland, and he draped that along the branches while she found the boxes of decorative bows and balls and other ornaments.

She chatted to HJK while she was opening boxes and unwrapping ornaments, carrying on a one-sided conversation that kept them engaged while they played. Watching her with his children, Jamie never ceased to be amazed by her natural ease with them. She had an innate ability to anticipate their wants and needs, offering comfort and support while also encouraging them to push their own boundaries and try new things. He had no doubt she'd make a great mother one day.

He hung a red cardinal-shaped ornament on a branch in the middle of the tree and stepped back. "That's the last one."

"Not quite," Fallon said, handing him a medium-sized square box with a red bow on the top.

"What's this?"

"Open it and see."

He lifted the lid to uncover three frosted ornaments nestled in separate compartments. Two of them were adorned with sets of blue footprints on the front and the third with pink footprints. He lifted one from the box and turned it over to see that there was a date and an inscription on the other side: Henry's First Christmas.

The other ornaments were similarly marked with Jared's and Katie's names and the date.

"These are great, Fallon."

"I saw the woman who makes them at a craft show in Kalispell last month and immediately put in my order," she told him. "They look like glass but they aren't. I didn't see any point in a keepsake ornament that would break the first time it fell off a branch."

"I never thought about getting something like this... something to commemorate the occasion," he admitted, moved by her thoughtfulness.

"You would have," she said confidently. "But I saw them first and couldn't resist."

"You give me too much credit."

She shook her head. "You don't give yourself enough. I can only imagine how hard it must be to keep the ranch running and take care of three babies all by yourself."

"I don't do it by myself," he reminded her. "There's no way I could manage without Bella and all the baby chain volunteers...and you."

"You don't have to," she assured him.

He managed a smile at that. "I can't expect the baby chain to operate forever."

"Of course, it won't be forever. In another four years, the triplets will be ready for school."

"Only another four years?"

She bumped her shoulder against his playfully, and the soft curls on top of her head brushed against his jaw. "You're going to make it."

"I appreciate your vote of confidence," he said,

breathing in the scent of her shampoo—strawberries and cream, sweet and tempting.

She glanced at the clock on the mantel and winced. "And if I'm going to make it home in time for family dinner, I need to run."

After a quick check on the babies, he followed her to the door, where she was already zipping up her coat. She tugged her pom-pom hat onto her head again, and he lifted a hand to her hair.

She went completely still. "What are you doing?"

"You've got a pine needle caught in your curls," he told her.

"Oh."

He attempted to work it free—without much success. He was trying to extricate it without pulling her hair, but the curls seemed reluctant to let go of the needle, and he found himself reluctant to remove his fingers from her soft tresses.

"Don't worry about it," she said, after about half a minute had passed with no apparent success. "My hair is—"

"I've got it," he assured her. "Just give me a second."

It probably wasn't much more than that before he lowered his hand from her curls with the long green needle pinched between two fingers.

"Thanks," she said, a little breathlessly.

"Thank *you*," he countered. "I wasn't really looking forward to the tree decorating but you made it fun."

"Only the first of many fun activities on my list," she promised.

Which somehow started him thinking of fun activities that he knew weren't on her list. Activities of a much more personal nature.

He blamed those thoughts for what he did next: he dipped his head toward her, tempted almost beyond reason by the sexy curve of her lips. Tempted to sample her sweetness, to taste and take like a starving man at a banquet until he was finally sated by her flavor.

But at the last moment, he shifted and touched his lips to her cheek instead.

Because kissing her would change everything between them, and he wasn't sure that he was ready for things to change—or if he ever would be.

Chapter Six

"Sorry, I'm late," Fallon said, kissing her mother's cheek as she hurried past her to wash up at the sink.

Maureen O'Reilly glanced up from the potatoes she was mashing. "Where have you been?"

"At The Short Hills Ranch." She turned on the faucet, squirted some soap on her hands and rubbed them together to create a foamy lather.

Her mother punched the masher into the potatoes again. "With Jamie Stockton," she said, her statement of the obvious spoken in a tone of disapproval.

"Yes, with Jamie and the triplets," Fallon clarified, focusing all of her attention on rinsing the soap off of her hands and willing the heat to fade from her cheeks—one of which had recently been brushed by Jamie's lips. "We chopped down and decorated their Christmas tree."

"It's nice that you were there to help," Maureen acknowledged. "But maybe you should let Jamie celebrate those kinds of family traditions with his family."

"His sister spends most of her time with her fiancé, the rest of his siblings are scattered, he barely speaks to his grandfather and his children are more of a hindrance than a help at their age." She grabbed a towel to dry her hands and tried not to think about the kiss—if the brief contact could even be considered a kiss. "Not everyone is fortunate enough to have a family like ours."

The explanation seemed to appease Maureen, at least a little.

"Well, now that you're here, you can finish setting the table. Brenna got it started, but then she got a text from one of her friends who just broke up with her boyfriend and she's been on the phone ever since."

She was happy to be given a task that would allow her to escape the scrutiny of her mother's eagle eye, but had to ask, "Where's Fiona?"

"She ran into town to pick up ice cream for the apple crisp."

"Mmm, I thought I smelled apples baking."

Fallon peeked into the dining room to see how much Brenna had accomplished and discovered that she'd put plates around the table—that was all.

As she retrieved cutlery from the drawer, she didn't ask what her brothers were up to. While Maureen wouldn't hesitate to conscript her husband and sons if she needed their help, she generally considered the kitchen a woman's domain—not a woman's responsibility so much as her sanctuary.

When Fiona got back with the ice cream and Brenna managed to extricate herself from her phone, the

O'Reilly family gathered around the table. Conversation flowed freely and steadily as everyone piled their plates with the roast chicken, mashed potatoes and buttered corn, with topics ranging from ranch issues to town gossip.

Fallon hadn't been kidding when she told Jamie that attendance at Sunday night dinner was mandatory. Although the kids were adults now, they continued to live on the ranch. The girls still slept under their parents' roof, but the boys had converted an old barn into their own living quarters. Throughout the week, it was rare for all of them to be able to sit down at the same time, which was why Maureen and Paddy insisted on them all being together on Sunday.

After everyone had eaten their fill of dinner and dessert, Fiona went out to the barn with Paddy to check on her mare, who had stumbled while they were out riding earlier and had some minor swelling in her right foreleg. Keegan and Ronan headed to the barn, too, to complete the evening chores, and Brenna slipped away to visit her inconsolable friend. Which meant that the responsibility for clearing away the dishes and cleaning up the kitchen fell to Maureen and her youngest daughter.

Fallon didn't mind the chores or hanging out with her mother. Unlike some of her friends, she had a good relationship with both of her parents and she felt fortunate that there wasn't anything she couldn't talk to them about.

Unfortunately, it also meant that her parents didn't consider any topics off-limits. After she'd filled the sink with soapy water and started to wash the pots and pans, Maureen said, "I don't think you should continue to take care of the Stockton triplets."

"What?" Fallon picked up a towel and turned to look at her mother. "Why would you say something like that?"

"Because I'm worried about you," Maureen admitted.

"You don't need to worry," she told her. "I'm fine."

"You're exhausted."

"I'm a little tired," she acknowledged. Okay, she was a lot tired, but that wasn't the sole responsibility of Jamie or his babies. And while her days were busy, she would rather give up her job at Country Kids Day Care than give up a single minute of the time that she spent at The Short Hills Ranch. Especially if that brief, almost-kiss Jamie had given her was a prelude to better things.

"And when was the last time you were on a date?" Maureen asked.

Fallon frowned at the question. "What does that have to do with anything?"

"You don't even know, do you?" her mother challenged.

"It's been awhile," she admitted, because the truth was, she couldn't remember the last time she'd been out on a date. But not dating didn't mean she was missing out on anything, either, especially since the last few dates that she'd had were obviously not very memorable.

In fact, feeling the touch of Jamie's lips on her cheek had affected her more deeply than any other man's kiss had ever done. Or maybe it was the anticipation that had tied her insides up in knots. Because for a brief moment, she'd actually thought that he was really going to kiss her. The way his gaze had dropped to her mouth and lingered there, she'd been almost certain he intended to touch his lips to her own.

But, of course, he hadn't. Because Jamie didn't see her as a woman but as a friend.

"Because every free minute you have is spent taking care of Jamie Stockton's babies," her mother continued, oblivious to the direction of Fallon's wandering thoughts.

"I'm not the only one who helps out," she felt compelled to point out. "There are at least half a dozen people who are still part of the baby chain."

"I know," her mother acknowledged. "But you spend more hours over there than anyone else, except maybe Jamie's sister, who lives there."

"Because I have more time than anyone else. Cecelia Pritchett and Margot Crawford both have husbands waiting for them at home at the end of the day. Paige Dalton has a husband and a baby."

"Which is exactly my point," Maureen said gently. "The other women have husbands and/or children of their own. And soon Bella is going to be married, too. But as long as you make Jamie Stockton and his babies your priority, you're never going to find a man to marry and raise a family with."

"Considering that I'm only twenty-four, it might be a little premature to slap the 'old spinster' label on me," she said lightly.

"You were twenty-three when you started helping with the triplets," her mother noted. "And you'll be twenty-seven before they're ready for preschool. And maybe that is still young, but not as young as many of the women who have recently moved to Rust Creek Falls looking to marry handsome cowboys."

"I appreciate your concern, but there's no reason to

worry about me," she insisted. "Besides, Jamie's planning to start the babies in day care in the New Year."

"Well, I think that's a good idea," Maureen said. "For a lot of reasons."

Fallon nodded, because she knew her mother was right. But she also knew she was going to miss HJK—and their father—terribly when she wasn't seeing them four times a week.

"Speaking of good ideas, Presents for Patriots is coming up," her mother reminded her.

Fallon wasn't sure that was a natural segue, but she was happy enough about the shift in topic that she didn't question it. "I'll be there."

"Good. It's a popular community event."

"I'm aware of that," she acknowledged.

"And it might be a good opportunity for you to meet some single men," her mother pointed out.

"Really, Mom? You want me to hook up with some guy at a local gift-wrapping event?"

Maureen flushed guiltily. "I'm not suggesting a hookup."

"I didn't realize you were so eager to marry me off," Fallon said. She didn't dare tell her mother that she'd already invited Jamie to attend the event with her. She knew that he didn't like to go into town except if absolutely necessary, because he was weary of the pitying glances he always received. But she wanted to coax him out of his comfort zone, get him involved in something for the community.

"I'm not trying to marry you off," her mother denied. "I just want you to be happy. You're working at Country Kids because you love children—and I know that's one of the reasons you were so quick to sign up for the baby chain when Bella was looking for volunteers."

Fallon opened a cupboard to put away the pots and lids she'd finished drying.

"You're not asking me what I think the other reasons are," her mother noted.

"Jamie and Bella have been friends of mine since we were all kids."

"That's true," Maureen acknowledged. "It's also true that you've had a crush on Jamie for a lot of years."

She kept her face averted so her mother wouldn't see the color that flooded her cheeks. "That was a long time ago—before he went away to college."

"And you were devastated when you found out that he was marrying Paula," her mother said gently.

"And all this time, I thought I'd done a pretty good job hiding my true feelings."

"You did. From everyone else. But a mother knows when her child is hurting," Maureen said. "And it hurts a mother, too, when there's nothing she can do to help."

"Well, I got over it," Fallon told her.

"Did you?"

She sighed. "Okay—I'm trying to get over it."

"Do you really think that's going to happen when you see him three or four times a week?" Her mother pulled the plug in the sink to drain the water, then turned to face her daughter. "Or are you hoping that seeing *you* three or four times a week is going to somehow change Jamie's feelings for you?"

"Maybe I am," she finally acknowledged.

Maureen brushed a strand of hair away from her face, tucking it behind her ear as she'd done so many times over the years. "I'm not going to say it couldn't ever happen—because if the man had half a brain in his head, he'd be head over heels in love with you," she said. "Unfortunately, I think he's got so much going on in his life right now, he just can't see the beautiful, incredible woman who is in front of him, and I don't see his situation changing anytime soon."

Fallon nodded, accepting the truth of her mother's words.

"And I don't want you to miss out on falling in love with some other terrific guy who is capable of loving you the way you deserve to be loved because you're hung up on Jamie," Maureen continued.

She felt the sting of tears behind her eyes. She wished she could tell her mother to mind her own business, but she knew that her concern was sincere. And truthfully, Fallon wanted what her parents had—a loving, supportive relationship that had endured through five kids and thirty years of marriage.

Her mother was right—things were going to change in the New Year. Which meant that she had less than four weeks to get Jamie to see her as a woman instead of a friend. And if she had any hope of succeeding, drastic measures were required.

When Jamie made his way downstairs Monday morning, his gaze automatically went to the corner of the living room where the Christmas tree was standing. Though he wouldn't have thought it was possible, seeing it there did lift his mood a little. Or maybe seeing the tree made him think about cutting it down and decorating it with Fallon, and that was what lifted his mood.

He was still thinking about her as he rode the fence-line Monday afternoon, checking for any new problems, when he heard something unexpected. He strained to listen, but the sound—a whimper?—was too quiet and distant to ascertain the direction.

Or maybe it was just the wind that he'd heard.

But as he continued to ride, he heard it again. A low and plaintive sound.

Definitely not the wind.

"Do you hear that?" he asked his mount.

The mare tossed her head, as if in agreement.

"Should we check it out?"

He loosened the reins to let Willow take the lead, trusting that she would lead them in the right direction.

She turned toward the shelter he'd built for the expectant stray who had been hanging around the property.

That's where he found the puppies.

He scanned the horizon, looking for the mother, but she was nowhere to be found and the puppies sounded scared and hungry. Though they were huddled together for warmth, they weren't newborns. At least six weeks old, he guessed, which meant that if he scared them, they could—and likely would—scatter. And there was no way he could chase down six puppies.

His attention was snagged by a movement at the corner of the shelter.

Ah, hell—there were seven.

"Looks like you've got your hands full there," Brooks Smith said when he entered the exam room and saw the crate of puppies on the table.

"Not my hands," Jamie denied.

After he'd discovered them, he'd called his neighbor and asked if he could borrow a dog crate. While he didn't like to think that the mother had abandoned them, it was obvious the puppies were scared and alone and hungry, and there was no way he could leave them outside with the temperature steadily dropping. Dallas Traub had provided not just the crate but helped round up the animals so that Jamie could take them to the Buckskin Veterinary Clinic to be checked out.

He'd called ahead to let Brooks know that he was bringing in a whole litter of puppies, and the vet had apparently assumed they were his—an assumption he was eager to dispel. "I've seen a stray golden wandering around the north side of the property for the past several months—I'm guessing they belong to her. Or they did before she abandoned them."

"They weren't abandoned," Brooks told him.

"How do you know?"

"The mother was brought in yesterday afternoon by Gene Strickland. He and Melba were out for a drive yesterday and the dog darted out into the road in front of them. He slammed on his brakes but the vehicle didn't stop in time. Both Gene and Melba were devastated that the dog didn't make it. And though we could tell she was a nursing mother, we had no idea where to begin looking for her pups."

"So now they're orphans," Jamie realized.

Brooks nodded.

"How old?"

"Between six and seven weeks," the vet said, confirming Jamie's initial guess. "The mom was definitely a golden retriever but, looking at the puppies, I'd guess the dad was a shepherd."

"In other words—they're going to get a lot bigger than they are right now?"

"Probably between sixty to eighty pounds." Brooks made some notes in a file, then glanced up at Jamie again. "You thinking of keeping them?"

"No way," he said immediately. Firmly. "I can't. I've already got three babies." And the only way he was managing to take care of them was with a lot of help.

"I'll have Jazzy come in to take some pictures," he said. "We'll post an ad in the waiting room, another at Crawford's and maybe one at the community center."

Jamie nodded, because he agreed the vet's plan was the best idea.

But still he lingered, thinking that he'd always wanted a dog at the ranch. That a ranch needed a dog.

He looked down at the little bundle of fur that was attempting to climb up his leg, desperately trying to snag his attention. While its siblings were wrestling with one another, this one—the first one to tentatively come forward out of the makeshift shelter to sniff his boots—seemed eager for human contact.

Even though he knew he shouldn't, he reached down and scooped up the little guy, rubbing the soft fur beneath his chin with a knuckle. The puppy panted happily. "You're going to do just fine wherever you end up," he said.

"They'll find homes quickly," Brooks said. "Puppies always do."

Jamie nodded, but he made no move to put the little furball down.

"So if you're thinking that maybe you'd like to keep one, you'd better decide fast," his friend warned.

"I'd have to be crazy to take on the responsibility of a puppy," he said.

Brooks just grinned.

Jamie watched the other puppies playing together on the floor, attempting to climb over one another, chewing on ears and chasing tails. He knew it was ridiculous to hope that they would stay together. He couldn't imagine anyone wanting to take in seven puppies that would grow up to be seven fairly large dogs.

But maybe he could keep just one.

No. He immediately discarded the thought of tearing one of these adorable puppies away from its siblings. Maybe it wasn't a reasonable comparison, but he remembered how he'd felt when he'd been separated from his siblings after their parents had died. How lonely and alone he'd felt when they were gone. But at least he'd had Bella.

So how could he possibly keep one puppy and force it to say goodbye forever to its six siblings?

The answer was simple: he couldn't.

He also couldn't keep them all…but maybe he could find room for the little guy in his arms…and one more.

It was snowing again.

Fallon glanced at the clock and then out the window and tried not to worry too much about the fact that Jamie wasn't home. He'd sent her a quick text message more than an hour earlier, just saying that he'd needed to run an errand in town but shouldn't be long.

She didn't mind staying late, but the way the snow was blowing around outside, she was beginning to worry whether he would make it home at all. The eight to ten inches that had fallen last week had laid a pretty blanket of white on the ground, but the storm that was blowing through town now was hitting Rust Creek Falls with both fists and visibility was practically nonexistent.

Since he was going to be late, she'd fed the kids and put them in their play yard while she tidied the kitchen. A plate of leftover steak pie had been set in the oven to stay warm for Jamie when he got home. *If* he got home.

She glanced out the window again, exhaling a shaky sigh of relief when she saw, in the distance, a set of headlights turn into the drive. She checked on the babies again, then slid her hand into an oven mitt and removed Jamie's dinner from the oven.

She set the plate on the table, beside the bowl of salad, as she heard the creak of the back door opening. She heard him kicking the snow off his boots, then soft murmuring.

Puzzled by the quiet tone and words indecipherable over the howl of the wind, she glanced toward the door and saw him holding two tiny, furry bodies close to his chest.

Puppies.

The first one had butterscotch-colored fur with brown ears, white paws and a white tipped tail. The other had slightly darker fur, with a lighter patch around its muzzle and down its throat.

"Oh. My. God." The words were a whispered squeal of excitement. "They're beyond adorable."

He grinned. "They are, aren't they?"

She eagerly took the soft, wriggling bodies from his arms so that he could shed his coat and boots. The puppies, happy to make her acquaintance, tried to climb up her chest to swipe at her mouth with their tiny pink tongues. "You found them?" she guessed.

He nodded.

"And you're keeping them?"

"That's the plan," he admitted.

Fallon shook her head as she nuzzled the puppies. "You're crazy. You know that, don't you?"

"Quite possibly," he agreed.

"What do you think your sister's going to say when she comes home and finds you've added two puppies to your family?" Though the question was obviously intended as an admonishment, the effect was negated by her cuddling with and cooing over the puppies.

"She'll probably say that I'm certifiably insane," he guessed. "And then she'll take one look at them and fall head over heels in love—like you did."

Fallon didn't doubt it was true. Her friend had always loved playing with Duke when she hung out at the O'Reilly house, which she'd done as often as she could. Bella had confided in Fallon about her wish for a dog—although, in retrospect, Fallon suspected that what her friend had really wanted was the love and affection that a dog gave so readily and easily. Whatever her reasons, her wishes had been denied. Agnes and Matthew Baldwin had refused to allow any animals in their house.

"Yeah, she'll love the puppies," Fallon agreed. "But that doesn't preclude the possibility of her killing you."

"I can handle my sister," he assured her.

"I hope so."

The lights flickered as the windows rattled their protest against the howling wind.

"It sounds nasty out there," she noted.

He nodded. "That's another reason I'm so late—I could barely see two feet in front of the truck while I was driving home."

"Then I should head out before the storm gets worse."

"No," he said. "You should stay here tonight."

She'd been waiting a long time to hear those words, though whenever she'd imagined him saying them to her, it hadn't been because of unsafe road conditions.

But regardless of his reasons for issuing the invitation, there was only one answer she wanted to give. "Okay—I'll stay."

Chapter Seven

When Fallon called to let her parents know she would be staying at The Short Hills Ranch rather than drive home in the storm, she knew they would approve of her decision if not the situation. So she was relieved when Brenna answered the phone and told her that both Paddy and Maureen were out at the barn, alleviating any guilt about leaving the message with her.

She played with the puppies while Jamie spent some time with the triplets before he gave them their bath and got them ready for bed. Conscious of the fact that little puppies had little bladders, Fallon decided to take the pair of them outside. In the knee-deep drifts, she got no further than the corner of the porch, where she set the puppies down.

She was surprised—and grateful—that both puppies actually squatted and peed. When she scooped them up again, their little bodies were shivering, so she tucked them close to keep them warm.

She could smell the familiar comforting scent of wood-smoke when she stepped back inside the house and knew that Jamie had lit a fire in the hearth. The way the wind was howling, it wasn't just possible but likely that the house would lose power and though he had a generator—as most ranchers did—the fire would help keep the house warm so that he didn't have to use it for that purpose. He'd also set candles in holders around the room, although they remained unlit.

"Did you get in touch with your folks?" Jamie asked, when she set the puppies on the floor in the living room.

"I talked to my sister," she said.

"Good. I wouldn't want your family to think you were on your way home in this storm."

"What about Bella?" she asked. "Do you know where she is?"

He nodded. "Hudson took her to Maverick Manor for dinner, before the storm hit, so they've decided to spend the night there."

"Why do you sound so disapproving?"

"Because she's my little sister—and yes, I know that she and Hudson are engaged, but they're not married."

"And, of course, you never had sex with your fiancée before you were married?" she teased.

He winced. "Please. I do not want to even think that word in conjunction with my sister."

Fallon laughed. "Okay, big brother, I'll leave you with your delusions."

"Thank you," he said sincerely.

"I can't help but wonder, though…if you're this protective of your little sister, what are you going to be like when Katie is old enough to date?"

"I don't know," he admitted. "But at least I've got thirty years before I need to worry about that."

"Thirty years, huh?"

"At least," he confirmed.

"So maybe it's not unreasonable for my parents to worry about the fact that I'm spending the night here," she mused aloud.

"Why would they worry about you spending the night here?"

She felt her cheeks flush as she spelled it out for him. "Because you're a man…and I'm a woman."

"But they know me," he said. "And they know I would never take advantage of our friendship in that way."

"Thanks," she said dryly. "You sure do know how to boost a girl's ego."

"I didn't mean—" He scrubbed his hands over his face. "I'm going to go out and shovel off the porch and walkway, so that when Bella makes her way home in the morning, she'll hopefully be able to find her way to the door."

Fallon just nodded.

She knew that she had no right to be upset with him for saying aloud what she'd always suspected—that he didn't see her as a woman. But she was upset and frustrated, and now she was trapped under the same roof with him for the night.

After checking on the babies to make sure they were content and secure in their play yard, she headed upstairs to borrow a pair of pajamas from Bella's drawer. Poking through the cupboard of her friend's bathroom, she also found a new toothbrush that she appropriated for her own use. She hurriedly changed and cleaned her teeth, then headed back downstairs.

Since the power wasn't out yet, she decided to turn on the Christmas tree lights. And because she suspected that Jamie would want something to warm him up when he came inside—and because she couldn't seem to stop taking care of him even though she knew it was a habit she needed to break—she put on a pot of decaf coffee.

When Jamie returned, she was on the sofa with the babies beside her, reading a story to them. Though they rarely sat still for long, Fallon believed it was important to teach children an appreciation of books at an early age. Recently, she'd been reading them stories about Christmas—particularly books with pictures of Santa Claus so that he wouldn't seem like a complete stranger when they went to the mall in Kalispell to have their photo taken with him.

After a quick shower, Jamie came back downstairs wearing a pair of flannel lounge pants and a long-sleeve thermal tee that hugged his torso in a way that made her mouth go dry. Because no matter how many times she tried to tell herself that he was a friend, she couldn't stop seeing him as a man.

The only man she'd ever wanted.

Despite the storm still raging outside, it was undeniably cozy inside the house. Carrying a mug of the coffee that Fallon had brewed for him, Jamie paused in the arched entranceway of the living room, a fist squeezing his heart when his gaze settled on the Christmas card-worthy scene in front of him.

A brightly lit Christmas tree topped with a sparkling

star beside the stone fireplace with flames flickering in the hearth, a beautiful woman sitting cross-legged on the sofa with one baby in her lap and another on either side of her, reading aloud to them a story about Santa and a snowman. Looking at Fallon with Henry, Jared and Katie, he was overwhelmed by gratitude to her, for everything she'd done for his babies.

He felt a glimmer of something else, too—an awareness of Fallon as more than a childhood pal and favorite caregiver to his children, an appreciation of her as a beautiful and captivating woman. But he wasn't ready to acknowledge those feelings. He didn't want to see her as anything more than the steady and true friend she had always been.

Instead, he focused on the crucial role she'd played in the baby chain. He knew there was no way he would have made it through the past ten months without the community volunteers—and Fallon in particular. She'd gone above and beyond for him and his babies, taking care not just of their basic needs but lavishing them with attention and affection, loving them as easily and naturally as he would expect a mother to do. It didn't surprise him that Henry, Jared and Katie absolutely lit up whenever she was around, greeting her with big smiles and outstretched arms, vying for her attention. It did surprise him that her presence had the same effect on him, though he was careful not to show it.

Fallon finished the last page of the book and closed the cover.

"Now that's what I call a successful bedtime story," he told her.

She glanced at the babies cuddled against her and

discovered they were asleep. "One of these days, they'll stay awake until the end."

He set his coffee down on the table and picked up Jared and Henry, one in each arm. Fallon stood up with Katie in her arms and followed him up the stairs. Taking care of the babies was—if not easy, at least natural for her, and he knew that she would be a great mother someday. The kind of mother he'd always hoped his children would have.

When the babies were settled in their cribs, he stayed in their room for another minute, just watching them sleep. "I used to do this all the time when I first brought them home from the hospital," he confessed to Fallon. "Stand here watching them sleep and listening to them breathe, alternately thanking God for giving me three perfect babies and cursing Him for taking away their mother."

Fallon stood beside him, not saying anything, just listening to him talk.

"But it wasn't anyone's fault except Paula's," he admitted. "If she'd gone to her doctor's appointments, the preeclampsia would have been diagnosed, arrangements made for the safe delivery of the babies, and she would have lived." He shook his head. "I'll never understand why she skipped those appointments and jeopardized not just her life but our babies' lives, too."

"She didn't do it on purpose," Fallon said to him now. "Whatever her reasons for not having regular checkups, I don't think she truly understood the risk she was taking. If she had, if she'd even suspected how dangerous the consequences could be, she never would have done so."

"I wish I could believe that was true, but in those last few months, she was so angry with me."

"With you? Why?"

He only shook his head, because he couldn't repeat her words aloud. Not even to Fallon.

Thankfully, she didn't press him for a response. Instead, she laid her hand on top of his, curled over the side rail of Katie's crib, and squeezed it reassuringly. "Maybe you need to stop looking back and focus on the future and your babies."

"They're the reason I get up at way-too-early o'clock every morning," he admitted. "I need to make this ranch a success so I can provide for them. And yet, I spend so much time working, I feel as if I'm missing out on their childhood."

"You've mostly just missed out on a lot of dirty diapers," she teased.

He felt a smile tug at his lips, for just a moment. "I wouldn't have been able to keep them if I hadn't had the baby chain volunteers helping out every day." He lifted his eyes to hers. "I wouldn't have been able to do it without you."

"No one in this town would have let you lose your family."

Again, Jamie thought, but he didn't say the word aloud.

He didn't need to.

He sat up for a while with Fallon, talking about the upcoming holidays. She again hassled him about all the "great Christmas ideas" she'd enumerated on her list, such as visiting Santa, baking cookies, singing carols and taking part in the Candlelight Walk. Although he liked to tease her about her obsession with the holidays, he couldn't deny that she had a way of making everything fun. She found pleasure in the simplest things, and her pleasure was infectious. Over the past ten months, he hadn't found many reasons—aside from his babies—to smile. Being with Fallon made him smile.

When he finally headed upstairs to his bed, leaving her on the sofa with a pile of blankets, he found sleep elusive. Maybe it was because he'd been talking to Fallon about Paula earlier that thoughts of his ex-wife continued to linger in his mind. But Fallon was the only person he could talk to about so many things. As a result, she knew almost all of his secrets. She certainly knew more about the problems in his marriage than anyone else, but even she didn't know everything...

Moving to rural Montana had been a major adjustment for his Seattle-born wife, but during her first summer in Rust Creek Falls, she'd made an effort to meet people and fit into the community. During that time, he was working almost from sunup to sundown, trying to take care of the ranch without relying too much on outside help he couldn't really afford.

But after they'd been married almost a year, he'd broached the idea of starting a family. They hadn't talked about children before they were married, because he hadn't thought such a discussion was necessary. In his mind, a wedding was a natural prelude to a family.

But when he suggested that they could stop using birth control, Paula balked. As far as she was concerned, their life was perfect and adding a child to the mix could mess up everything. Besides, she wasn't really the maternal type, anyway.

Jamie had been stunned. How could she possibly

think that a baby would mess up anything? And why would she question her motherly instincts? Rather than actually answer any of his questions, Paula agreed to stop taking her birth control pills to "see what happens."

And Jamie, excited by the prospect of having a child with his wife, didn't push for answers because he believed that, when they finally had a baby together, she would see that all of her worries and concerns had been for naught.

Except that another six months went by and *nothing* happened. He'd always envisioned himself having a house full of children—like the loving home his parents had provided before their deaths—and he wasn't prepared to give up on that dream. Instead, he suggested that they make an appointment with a fertility specialist. Paula agreed, albeit with obvious reluctance.

By that time, he'd realized there was more going on than his wife was telling him, but he still believed they could work through whatever was bothering her. Until a few days before the wedding of Braden Traub and Jennifer MacCallum, when he was searching for a pair of tweezers to remove a splinter from his thumb and found a package of birth control pills hidden in a zippered compartment in his wife's makeup case.

"I shouldn't have lied to you," she admitted, swiping at her tears with the back of her hand. "But I was afraid that, if I got pregnant and fat, you wouldn't want me anymore."

He was sincerely baffled by her response. "Why would you ever think any such thing?"

"Because that's what happened in my parents' marriage, when my mom got pregnant with me."

"Whatever problems your parents had, had nothing to do with you," he assured her.

But she shook her head. "Everything was fine, until I came along. They were happy and in love, and then her body started to grow and change, and my dad lost interest. That's when he started looking at other women—and sleeping with other women. And I didn't want to risk the same thing happening to us."

Jamie's heart ached for her: the little girl who had felt responsible for the problems in her parents' marriage, and the woman who believed that he would ever be unfaithful to her. And though he felt he understood her better now, he wasn't sure he could forgive her actions. She'd lied to him—for more than a year, every time they'd made love, every time he'd asked about her cycle, she'd deliberately and continuously lied to him.

"When I promised to love, honor and cherish you, I meant every word of it," he said, then dropped the package of pills on the desk and turned away.

She pushed away from the desk and rushed toward him. "Please, Jamie. Give us another chance to be a family."

Of course, those words wrapped around his heart like a lasso over the head of an errant calf, and yanked him right back into line.

And then Paula took his hand and led him to the bathroom, where she dumped the pills into the toilet and flushed them all away.

Jamie knew that the issues between them couldn't be solved that easily, but he let himself believe that it was the first step toward getting their life back on track.

And when they attended Braden and Jennifer's wedding a few days later, he couldn't help but remember their wedding day, when they were head over heels in love and confident in their future together. Listening to the exchange of vows reminded him of the promises that he and Paula had made to one another, and he knew that he owed them a second chance.

When they went home after the wedding, they were both drunk on love and intoxicated by joy, and they made love all through the night. It wasn't until several weeks later that he heard about the spiked wedding punch and realized they might have been drunk on more than love. Regardless of the reasons, that night signaled a turning point in their relationship—the new start they both claimed to want.

Four weeks after the wedding, after Paula had been feeling dizzy and sick for about a week, Jamie encouraged her to take a pregnancy test.

The test was positive, and he was ecstatic. His wife was a little less so, but she seemed willing to believe his promises that they would have a wonderful life together with their baby. Then she found out that there wasn't just one baby—there were three.

And the bigger Paula's belly grew, the more miserable she became. She refused to let him accompany her to her monthly check-ups, insisting that he'd done enough. Maybe he should have insisted, but the truth was, by that time, he was weary of the arguing and bickering, so he relented and let her go to the doctor's appointments on her own. Because it never occurred to him that she wasn't going.

And she never missed out on an opportunity to remind him that having three babies was *his* choice not hers.

He'd wanted to believe that as soon as their babies

were born and she held them in her arms, she would love them as much as he did.

Unfortunately, she'd never had that chance.

Chapter Eight

Fallon hadn't slept very well. Despite the fact that it was late when Jamie said good-night and finally turned out the lights, she'd had trouble falling asleep. Because as soon as she closed her eyes, she pictured Jamie upstairs in his bedroom. Alone in his big bed. And though she would never dare tiptoe up the stairs and crawl beneath the covers with him, there was no denying that she wanted to. The tantalizing thought teased her mind and stirred her body, and when she finally did sleep, she dreamed of him.

And then she'd awakened twice in the night to howling winds that rattled the windows and urged her to add more wood to the fire. So far, the power had not been lost, but better safe than sorry. She'd awakened three more times to put the puppies outside.

Jamie had lined a laundry basket with a towel for

them to sleep in, and Fallon had set the basket close by so that they wouldn't feel abandoned and alone. As a result, she'd heard every soft cry and whimper and, worried that every little sound might be an indication of a full bladder, she'd scooped them up, shoved her feet into her boots, and taken them out onto the porch.

The last time she'd ventured out into the frigid air, the first light of dawn was just starting to shimmer on the horizon.

She'd obviously fallen into a deeper sleep after that, because she didn't hear anything else until a warm, masculine voice whispered close to her ear.

"Wake up, Sleeping Beauty."

And she did—jolting awake and abruptly upward, the top of her head smacking Jamie in the chin.

She winced, he swore.

"Ohmygod. I'm so sorry."

He dropped to his knees beside the sofa and rubbed his chin. "I don't think you broke anything, but damn, you have a hard head."

"And you have a hard jaw," she told him, rubbing the top of her head.

He carefully wiggled the disparaged part of his anatomy.

"Are you okay?" she asked.

"I'm not sure. I think you might need to kiss it better."

She blinked, certain that she hadn't heard him correctly. "What?"

"When Jared fell down and banged his knee yesterday, you kissed it better."

"Well, yes," she admitted. "Because he's a baby."

"I bet my jaw hurts more than his knee," he told her.

Fallon rolled her eyes but leaned closer to brush her lips gently to his jaw, telling herself that it would be just like kissing Jared's knee. Except it was nothing like kissing Jared's soft, chubby knee. Jamie's jaw was hard and strong and rough with stubble that made her lips tingle, and he smelled like fresh hay and clean soap with an underlying hint of something that she recognized as uniquely his scent. Apparently he'd been out to the barn already, as he was every morning before the kids were even awake.

"Better?"

She drew back, but he was still close. Close enough that his lips were mere inches from her own. His gaze dropped to her mouth, lingered. She held her breath, waited.

"I think so," he finally said, and wiggled his jaw again.

Then he lifted a hand to her head, his fingers gently sifting through her hair in search of a possible bump. "How's the noggin?"

"I don't think I'm concussed," she said, trying to make light of the situation when just his nearness was making her heart race and her knees weak. Or maybe those were effects from the knock on her head.

"You're a dangerous woman," he teased.

"That's what all the guys say," she quipped back.

Despite the casual tone of their banter, there was something else in the air, something exciting and new and—

"It's like a Winter Wonderland out there," Bella announced, striding into the room.

It was a testament to how mesmerized Fallon had been by Jamie's nearness that she didn't hear any of the telltale signs of her friend's arrival. Apparently he'd been equally oblivious, because he quickly dropped his hand away and rose to his feet.

"How was the driving?" he asked his sister.

"Good," she said. "The plows must have worked through the night, because the roads are all clear."

"Which is my cue to be heading out," Fallon decided.

"You might want to change out of my pajamas first," her friend teased.

"Oh. Right." As she headed upstairs to do that, she heard Bella say to her brother, "That better not be a puppy in that laundry basket."

"Well, actually," he began.

And that was all Fallon heard before she closed the bathroom door.

Fallon wasn't surprised to find her mother sitting at the kitchen table with a cup of coffee on the table in front of her and a worried expression on her face when she walked in the door.

"Good morning," she said, kissing Maureen's cheek and hoping that her greeting would make it so.

The furrow between her mother's brows warned her otherwise. "I don't approve of you spending the night at Jamie Stockton's house."

"Did you really want me to drive home in the storm after the sheriff had made a public announcement asking all residents to avoid unnecessary travel?"

"Of course not," Maureen admitted. "I just wish you'd been home before the storm hit."

"That wasn't an option, because Jamie wasn't home before the storm hit."

"You know there will be talk if anyone saw your vehicle parked in his driveway overnight."

"People who want to talk will always find a reason to do so."

"Well, I'd prefer that they not talk about *my* daughter."

"You don't need to worry," Fallon assured her. "No one could have seen my SUV in Jamie's driveway because it was buried in snow."

"You shouldn't be so flippant about your reputation."

She sighed. "You can't have it both ways, Mom. Either Jamie is oblivious to the fact that I'm a woman, which all outward signs confirm, in which case there's no reason for you to fret about the fact that I spent the night under his roof."

"I don't fret," Maureen said, sounding a little miffed by the label her daughter had put on her concern.

"Or he's secretly but wildly attracted to me," she continued to make her point, "in which case you should worry that we spent all last night tearing up the sheets. But then your concerns that I'm wasting my time with a man who will never notice me are unfounded."

"When you have children of your own, you'll understand," her mother said.

Fallon sighed. "I know you're only looking out for me, Mom, which is why I'm going to tell you that absolutely nothing inappropriate happened and I spent the night looking after the puppies."

"What puppies?"

Having anticipated the question, Fallon already had her cell phone in hand to pull up the pics she'd taken of the puppies.

"Oh, my goodness." Maureen's voice was a whisper now. "Aren't they just the cutest things?"

"And there are five others who are just as adorable." She told her mother the story about how they came to be found on Jamie's ranch.

"Puppies are a lot of work—the housebreaking and obedience training," Maureen said, her tone a little wistful.

"Well, Brooks and Jazzy are keeping the others at the clinic until they can find good homes for them."

"I don't imagine they'll have to wait long."

"So you'd better make up your mind quickly," Fallon teased, knowing exactly what her mother was thinking.

"I'll talk to your father about it," Maureen decided. "I think he's been a little bit lonely since old Duke died." She looked up at her daughter then, a glint in her eye. "But don't think that story managed to distract me from our previous topic of conversation."

"I didn't imagine it would," she said, because her mother was like a dog with a bone when she got her teeth into a subject.

"And while you're busy taking care of another man's babies, the marriageable men of Rust Creek Falls are going out with other girls your age, falling in love and planning to marry them."

"Then clearly none of them were ever meant to be my husband."

"How can you possibly know that when you haven't gone out with any of them?" her mother challenged.

"This has been a really fun conversation," Fallon noted sardonically. "And as much as I'd love to continue it, I really need to shower and get ready for work."

Maureen immediately pushed her chair back from

the table. "Do you want me to make you some break-fast?"

As she grabbed a mug from the cupboard and filled it with coffee from the carafe to take upstairs with her, Fallon was reminded once again why she couldn't stay mad at her mother. Because whatever Maureen said or did, it was always with the best interests of her children in mind.

"Thanks," she said. "But I'm okay."

"Will you be home for dinner tonight?"

"If I ever get out of here, I will be home for dinner," she promised, and kissed her mother's cheek as she moved past.

Jamie had anticipated his sister's reaction to the puppies. He knew she'd be furious—for about two minutes. She'd chastise him for taking on more responsibility than he could handle, then he'd tell her the story of how he found them, and she'd cautiously lift one of them from the basket and fall head over heels in love.

What he didn't anticipate, after she'd gotten over being mad and the babies were dressed and fed and she was sitting with both of the puppies in her lap, was her completely out-of-the-blue comment: "There seemed to be a little bit of tension between you and Fallon earlier."

"What do you mean?"

She rolled her eyes. "You aren't really that oblivious."

"Oblivious to what?"

"Whatever's going on between the two of you."

"There's nothing going on between us," he said, de-liberately blocking the tantalizing memories of soft lips and lace-covered breasts from his mind. "I've known Fallon forever—we're friends."

"That doesn't mean you can't be more."

"Neither of us is looking for anything more," he told her.

"Are you sure about that?" Bella challenged.

"Of course, I am."

She shook her head. "Then you're completely oblivious."

"Oblivious to what?"

"The way she looks at you," she said.

"She looks at me like everyone else in this town looks at me—with sympathy and pity."

"If that's what you see, then you're not very observant," his sister remarked.

"I know that she loves Henry, Jared and Katie," he said. "And I'm more grateful than I could ever express for everything she's done for my babies."

"Is that really all you feel—gratitude?" she asked, sounding a little disappointed.

"Of course not," he denied. "Aside from you, she's my best friend."

"Have you ever considered that you might be something more?"

"No," he said, but his gaze slid away as the memory of a long-ago kiss teased the edges of his mind.

"Well, maybe you should," Bella told him.

"I have my hands full enough with Henry, Jared and Katie—and now two puppies," he acknowledged. "The last thing I need is a woman in the mix."

"The fact that your hands are full with the babies is exactly why you should think about finding them a mother."

He flinched as if she'd struck him.

She immediately put a hand on his arm. "I'm sorry, Jamie. I didn't mean to sound insensitive."

He shrugged.

"I know that losing Paula devastated you, but you can't mourn her forever."

"It hasn't even been a year," he pointed out to her.

"I know," she said again, more softly this time.

But she didn't know all of it.

For example, she didn't know about the conversation that had taken place in the exam room when Paula had her first ultrasound.

"Is there a history of multiple pregnancies in your family?" the doctor asked, as he moved the wand over the barely-there curve of Paula's belly.

"No," the mom-to-be responded immediately, vehemently.

The doctor glanced at Jamie. "Your family?"

He shook his head, his gaze fixed on the monitor where he could clearly see the outline of not just one—and not even two—but three separate blobs.

"There's only one, right?" Paula asked, staring at the screen. "Something's wrong with your machine thing and the picture's broken, right?"

The doctor shook his head. "The machine isn't broken," he assured both of them, his tone calm and soothing. "You're pregnant with triplets."

Paula opened her mouth as if to reply, but closed it again without saying a word. And when she looked at him, her eyes were filled with fear and anger and tears.

"I can't have three babies," she told him. "I wasn't even sure that I wanted to have one."

"Well, it's not as if we really have a choice," he pointed out, determined to remain reasonable and calm

despite the fact that he was feeling a little bit of panic over the thought of three babies, too. But in addition to the panic, there was joy. A lot of joy.

"We do have a choice," she insisted. "We can reduce the number."

He stared at her, not wanting to comprehend what she was saying.

When he didn't respond, she turned to the doctor. "Doctors do it all the time, don't they?" she said to him—pleaded with him.

"Not all the time," he replied cautiously. "And not without a valid medical reason."

"My body can't possibly support three babies," Paula insisted. "Isn't that a valid medical reason?"

"There is no evidence to suggest that's true," the doctor denied.

In the end, she'd been right, but only because she hadn't made any effort to help her body support their babies.

That was the part of the story that no one knew, and Jamie wanted to keep it that way.

Fallon changed her mind at least half a dozen times on the trip from Rust Creek Falls to Kalispell. While the whole makeover thing had worked pretty well for Cinderella, she was less optimistic about her own prospects.

Yes, desperate times called for desperate measures and all that—but she didn't want anyone to know she was desperate. On the other hand, the conversation with her mother had made her face some hard facts, and the reality was that she had a very small window of opportunity to catch Jamie's eye. Maybe she was already too late, but with her self-imposed New Year's Eve deadline in mind, she took a deep breath, walked up to the counter of the fancy salon and said, "I need a makeover."

The girl seated at the computer—whose name tag identified her as Leila—barely glanced up from her phone as she continued texting. "What were you thinking? Hair? Nails? Makeup?"

"All of the above."

Leila reluctantly set aside her phone and shifted her attention to the computer screen. "We're currently booking for the middle of January. Is there a particular—"

"The middle of January?" Fallon interjected, her hopes immediately deflating. "Don't you have anything available today?"

The receptionist finally lifted her gaze to give the obviously despondent customer her full attention. "Honey, we're one of the top-rated salons in Kalispell and it's barely two weeks before Christmas."

Fallon released a weary sigh. "I'm guessing that's a no."

But Leila held up a hand—a silent request for Fallon to wait a moment—as she scrolled through the schedule displayed on her computer screen.

If Fallon couldn't get an appointment today, she didn't want one. And the middle of January was way too late to fit in with her plans.

"I almost forgot that we had a cancellation," the receptionist told her. "One of our top clients who regularly books a full array of services was scheduled to come in at twelve-thirty today, but her husband surprised her with an impromptu pre-holiday Mediterranean cruise."

Fallon held her breath. "I can have her appointment?"

Leila scanned the computer screen again. "Twelve-thirty with Cindy for hair," she confirmed. "Then Gina's available to do a mani-pedi at two, and Tansley can do your makeup after that."

"That all sounds perfect." She didn't even ask what it would cost—because she didn't care. If changing her outward appearance succeeded in finally getting Jamie Stockton to look at her like a woman instead of a pal, every penny would be money well-spent.

Fallon usually had her hair done at Bee's Beauty Parlor in Rust Creek Falls, where she got a family discount if Brenna washed and cut her hair. At La Vie Salon, the stylists had assistants who escorted clients from the waiting area—where orchestral music played quietly in the background and cold and hot beverages were offered to those lounging in the butter-soft leather chairs—to the prep area. There Fallon was turned over to a designated shampoo girl, who didn't just wash her hair but gave her scalp such an incredible massage she didn't ever want it to end. But of course it did, and when her hair was rinsed and conditioned and rinsed again, the assistant returned to escort her from the prep area to Cindy's work station.

After a brief introduction and a few minutes of general conversation that immediately put Fallon at ease, Cindy surprised her by asking, "What's his name?"

"Who?"

"The man." The stylist gently combed out her wet hair. "Whenever a woman comes in here for a makeover, it's usually because of a man."

Fallon wished she could lie. She didn't want to be the cliché, but Cindy's question confirmed that she was. And since she would probably never see this woman again, she confided the truth. "He's a friend who refuses to see me as anything but a friend."

"And you think—if you look different—he'll finally see you," the hair stylist guessed.

"I'm hoping," she admitted.

Cindy continued to snip the ends of her hair. "Do you realize how beautiful you are?"

She managed a wry smile. "I've been called cute, and occasionally pretty, but never beautiful."

"You are," the stylist insisted. "You've got those gorgeous blue eyes, which will be framed nicely with the wispy bangs I'm going to give you, and gloriously thick auburn hair."

"It's red."

"It's more than red. There are so many shades of copper and gold, and the curls—"

"The curls have to go," Fallon interjected.

Cindy looked horrified by the thought. "I think that would be a mistake."

"I need to look different," she said again. "If I don't get rid of the curls, he'll just think that I got my hair cut—if he even notices that much."

"This guy must be pretty special," the stylist said.

"He is."

"Then I'm going to do everything I can to help you knock his socks off," Cindy promised.

By the time Fallon walked out of the salon, she felt like a different woman—if not a less nervous one. When she stopped at the makeup counter to pick up some of the mascara and lip gloss Tansley had recommended, she did a double take when she saw her reflection in the mirror.

Although she'd given Cindy specific instructions on what she wanted—"to look different"—it still gave her a jolt to see how well the stylist had done her job. Yes, she'd had her eyebrows tweezed and her makeup done, but the biggest and most significant change was her hair. Without the mass of curls around her face, she almost looked like a completely different person.

And yes, that had been her purpose in requesting the makeover, but she found that she was nearly as apprehensive as she was excited about the changes. On the other hand, once she looked past the sleek curtain of hair and perfectly made-up face, she was still the same old Fallon in the same old plaid flannel shirt tucked into well-worn jeans with her favorite cowboy boots on her feet. If she wanted Jamie to see her as an attractive woman, she was going to have to overhaul her wardrobe, too.

Chapter Nine

He never should have agreed to this.

When Fallon had asked him to attend Presents for Patriots with her, Jamie should have declined the invitation. Instead, he'd said yes, partly because he'd long been a supporter of the event and partly because he had a hard time saying no to Fallon.

The original plan had been for him to pick her up so they could drive over together, but as he'd been getting ready to leave the house, Fallon had sent him a text message suggesting they meet at the community center because she was already out running errands.

Now he was here, but he didn't see her anywhere. He felt obviously and awkwardly alone and uncomfortable. Since the birth of the triplets and the death of his wife, he'd avoided trips into town as much as possible. Bella accused him of being an antisocial recluse, but he didn't agree with that assessment. If he chose to stay close to home, it was because of the responsibilities that he had there. It was also a convenient excuse to avoid the hushed whispers and pitying glances that seemed to follow his every step whenever he walked down Main Street.

Bella had been pleased when he'd told her that he would be attending the gift-wrapping event, and she'd immediately offered to stay home with HJK. While he appreciated her willingness to babysit and knew that his children adored Auntie Bella, he couldn't help thinking that he should be at home with them. Of necessity, much of his day was spent away from his kids so that he looked forward to spending any free time he had with them. And considering that the community center was rapidly filling up with volunteers, he didn't think he'd be missed if he decided to slip out the door.

Except that he'd promised Fallon he'd be here. And he was—but where was she?

He looked around again, but he still didn't see her. Of course, there was already quite a crowd gathered. It seemed that every year, there were more and more people who came out in support of the event. He recognized Tessa Strickland, looking pretty and pregnant, with her fiancé Carson Drake, and Dr. Jon Clifton with Dawn Laramie, obviously and happily in love.

Then a glimpse of copper hair snagged his attention, and he automatically turned. The color was exactly the same as Fallon's, and he'd never known anyone else whose hair was as pretty and shiny as a new penny. The woman was about the same height as Fallon, too, with the same slender build, but the similarities ended there. Instead of Fallon's tumble of curls, this woman's hair was straight and sleek; instead of Fallon's customary—and eminently practical—jeans and flannel shirts, this woman was wearing a short denim skirt with high-heeled boots and a soft green sweater that molded to her distinctly feminine curves.

Definitely an out-of-towner, he decided. Because no Montana native would venture out on a frigid December night without long underwear. But even while he shook his head at the woman's complete lack of common sense, he couldn't deny that her long, shapely legs sure were a pleasure to look at.

As if sensing his perusal, the woman slowly turned around. And Jamie's jaw nearly hit the floor when he realized the woman he'd been ogling *was* Fallon.

But he'd never seen Fallon looking like *this* before. She was hot enough to melt the snow on top of Falls Mountain, and he could tell by the way several other men in attendance were checking her out that he wasn't the only one who thought so.

Justin Crawford whistled under his breath. "Is that Fallon O'Reilly?"

"Yeah," Jamie reluctantly confirmed.

"She looks…different." The cowboy continued to stare at her. "Hot."

"Yeah," he said again, not at all happy to realize it was true. She was his friend—he didn't like the idea of other guys ogling her. And he especially didn't like to admit that *he'd* been ogling her, too.

He crossed the room to where she was chatting with Nina Traub. She glanced over as he approached, her lips curving in a familiar and welcoming smile.

Except that even her mouth looked different today—slicked with something peach-colored and shiny. Something that tempted him to want to taste her lips. The hint of a distant memory teased the back of his mind. Of a sweet and innocent kiss that had stirred some not-so-sweet-and-innocent yearnings. Yearnings he'd ignored then and needed to again now.

With a brief wave of acknowledgment in his direction, Nina headed the opposite way.

His dark mood must have been reflected in his expression, because Fallon's smile slipped as he drew closer. "Is everything okay?" she asked.

"Everything's just—" his gaze dropped to her mouth again "—peachy."

"Then why are you scowling?"

His only response was to shrug out of his jacket and drape it over her shoulders.

His action made her scowl, too. "What are you doing?"

"It's cold in here," he told her, inwardly cursing the fact that his jacket barely covered the curve of her butt. It certainly didn't come close to the hem of her short skirt—or the mile of shapely leg on display beneath that hem.

"I'm not cold," she said, pulling his jacket off her shoulders and holding it out to him.

He took her arm instead of the jacket.

"Come on," he said, and guided her over to a vacant table. He held out a chair for her to sit down, so that her legs would be hidden from view beneath the table.

"What's going on with you?" she asked him.

"I've been waiting half an hour for you to show up," he said, which was a slight exaggeration and not even close to being the reason for his irritation.

"Sorry," she said. "I was in Kalispell today and ran into some traffic getting back."

"What were you doing in Kalispell?"

Fallon looked at him for a long minute, then shook her head. "Apparently I wasted a lot of time and money."

"Shopping?" he guessed.

"That, too," she agreed, managing to keep her tone light despite the fact that his obliviousness had caused her ever-hopeful and pathetic heart to sink into the pit of her stomach.

"For Christmas?" he guessed, because apparently this inane conversation wasn't yet close to being done.

"Actually, most of my Christmas shopping is done and my gifts wrapped," she told him. "I was looking for an anniversary present for my parents. They're celebrating thirty years of marriage on Christmas Eve."

"That's impressive," he said.

She nodded. And proof that her mother was obviously a lot more knowledgeable than Fallon when it came to matters of the heart. *If the man had half a brain in his head, he'd be head over heels in love with you. Unfortunately, I think he's got so much going on in his life right now, he just can't see the beautiful, incredible woman who is in front of him, and I don't see his situation changing anytime soon.*

Fallon had thought—hoped—she could change it. She'd honestly believed that changing her hairstyle, putting on some makeup and buying new clothes would make him look at her differently. A five-minute conversation had disabused her of that notion.

They worked together wrapping the gifts that were piled beside their table. Jamie didn't say much as they worked. Fallon found herself humming along to the

Christmas music that played softly in the background. There were a lot of people in attendance to help out with the event and much happy chatter as people talked with their friends and neighbors while they worked.

Jamie hardly said a word, and when he did speak, it was only to ask her to pass the scissors or tape.

"How were the kids today?" she asked, attempting to break the unexpectedly awkward silence.

"Good." He folded the corner of the paper, secured it with a piece of tape, and didn't look up at her.

"How is Jared doing with his new teeth?" she asked, having noticed that the little guy's first two teeth had finally broken through his bottom gums a few days earlier.

"Fine." Fold. Tape. Repeat.

"Are the puppies still sleeping in the laundry basket?"

"Fine," he said again.

She affixed a bow to the present she'd finished and set it aside. "You're not listening to anything I'm saying, are you?"

Now, finally, he glanced up. "What?"

She huffed out a breath. "If you don't want to be here, why did you agree to come?"

"I do want to be here," he said.

"Well, you're not acting like it," she told him.

"I'm just…thirsty."

She blinked. "You're thirsty?"

He nodded. "I'm going to grab a cup of hot apple cider. Do you want one?"

Though she was as baffled by his sudden interest in a beverage as she was by his lack of communication, she decided that cider would be good. "Sure," she agreed.

Jamie pushed his chair back and stood up to head toward the refreshment table.

Shaking her head at his inexplicable mood, she returned her attention to her task. Or pretended to, while she surreptitiously watched Jamie move across the room. There was just something about the way the man filled out a pair of jeans that made her blood hum in her veins. But she was tired of being a solo act. She wanted to be with a man who wanted to be with her, and since that obviously wasn't Jamie Stockton, she should follow her mother's advice and start looking in another direction.

Jamie hadn't quite reached the refreshment table when Bobby Ray Ellis slid into the chair he'd recently vacated.

She'd gone to high school with Bobby Ray and they'd occasionally hung out together in a group of friends, but they'd never dated. Probably because, like most of the other guys in Rust Creek Falls, he'd seen her as a good pal rather than a potential mate. And that had never bothered her before, because she'd been too infatuated with Jamie to want to go out with anyone else.

But now she was starting to accept that her mother was probably right. That it was time to give up hoping that Jamie would ever see her as anything more than a friend for himself and a babysitter for his children.

"You look awfully pretty tonight, Fallon," Bobby Ray said, drawing her attention back to the table.

She smiled, grateful that *someone* had noticed the effort she'd gone to with her appearance. "Thank you, Bobby Ray."

"And I was wonderin'," he continued, "if you've been dating anyone recently. Exclusively, I mean."

She shook her head as she cut a piece of paper from the roll. "No," she said, not wanting to admit that she hadn't been dating at all—exclusively or not.

"Because I wouldn't ever want to encroach on someone else's territory," he assured her, "but I sure would like to take you out sometime, if you were interested in goin' out with me."

And while a part of her bristled at the idea of being considered any man's "territory," she knew Bobby Ray too well to be offended by his choice of words. "Are you asking me out on a date, Bobby Ray?"

"Yes, ma'am, I am. Or at least, I'm tryin' to."

"I don't know what to say," she admitted.

"I can help you with that," he said. "Say yes."

She smiled at his polite earnestness. He really was a good guy and more than pleasant to look at. Maybe he didn't make her heart feel all fluttery inside, but since no one other than Jamie had ever had that effect on her—and since Jamie had shown less than zero interest in asking her out—she decided to follow her mother's advice and go out with other people. "Okay, yes," she finally agreed.

Bobby Ray's smile stretched across his face. "How about tomorrow night? They're showin' *National Lampoon's Christmas Vacation* at the high school."

Despite the impressive growth of the town in recent years, Rust Creek Falls still didn't have an actual movie theater. Instead, movies were shown on Friday and Saturday nights at the local high school. "That sounds like fun," she decided.

"Great. Give me your number and I'll get in touch with you in the mornin' to firm up plans," he said.

So she added her number to the contacts list in his phone as he did the same to hers.

Her former classmate had just slipped away when Jamie came back carrying two paper cups of hot apple cider. "What did Bobby Ray want?"

She accepted the cup Jamie offered and wrapped her hands around it, because maybe it was a little chilly in the room and tights weren't nearly as warm as long johns. "He asked me to go out with him."

Jamie scowled. "Like on a date?"

"You don't have to sound so surprised," she told him. "I do occasionally go out." Which okay, was a bit of a stretch considering that she hadn't had a date in more than a year. Still, his question and tone were both a little insulting.

"But... Bobby Ray?" he said skeptically.

"Why shouldn't I go out with Bobby Ray?" she challenged.

"He just doesn't seem like your type."

"Really? Then who do you think *is* my type?"

She held her breath, waiting for his response. Waiting for some hint that he'd finally recognized that they should be together.

But he only lifted a shoulder, a casual gesture of indifference. "I don't know."

She was oh-so-tempted to pick up the roll of wrapping paper from the table and whack him upside the head. Was he being deliberately obtuse? Or was he trying to let her down easy? Well, to hell with that.

"Just because you don't find me attractive doesn't mean that other men don't," she told him.

His scowl deepened. "What are you talking about?"

She shook her head. "Nothing. Forget it." She fought

against the tears that burned the backs of her eyes. "I think I'm going to go home now."

"What?" He seemed genuinely startled by her sudden announcement. "Why?"

"Because it's been a long day and I'm tired." And she knew that if she didn't make her escape quickly, she would likely do something she would regret—though it was a toss-up as to whether that "something" might be hitting him with the wrapping paper roll or kissing him senseless.

"But... I thought we were going to wrap presents together."

She pushed her chair away from the table. "There are enough other people here that I won't be missed."

Jamie watched her pull on her coat—a heavy, full-length garment that covered from her chin to the top of her boots—and wondered why he felt as if she'd directed that last comment at him. As he watched her go, he couldn't shake the feeling that he'd done something wrong, even if he had no idea what that something might be.

And though he'd only been fifteen years old when he lost his parents, they'd made a point of teaching him manners and responsibility, and it was all too easy to imagine what they'd say about him allowing Fallon to walk out into the darkness of the night alone.

He pushed his chair back and hurried after her.

The night was cold—the type of cold that seared the lungs and crunched beneath the feet. It did both as he jogged across the parking lot in an effort to catch up with her hurried stride.

"Fallon, wait."

"It's too cold to stand around outside," she told him, not even adjusting her pace.

"Let me apologize."

She paused beside her SUV and stuffed her hands into the pockets of her long coat. "Why do you think you need to apologize?"

"I don't know," he admitted. "But obviously I said or did something to upset you, and I'm sorry."

She shook her head. "No," she said, maybe a little sadly. "You didn't do anything."

"Fallon," he tried again.

She waited, expectantly, but he didn't know what else to say.

After a moment, she opened the door of her vehicle and stepped up onto the running board. "Good night, Jamie."

He moved closer and caught the top of the door before she could close it. "Bobby Ray's a good guy," he finally said.

She nodded. "I know."

"And if you really want to go out with him…well, I hope you have a good time."

She responded by shoving her key in the ignition and starting the engine—a clear indication that their conversation was over.

Have a good time.

Fallon drove home with Jamie's parting words echoing in her head and tears stinging her eyes. But she refused to let them fall. She refused to let herself cry any more tears over a man who was too blinded by his responsibilities and grief and guilt to see that she was in love with him.

There had been moments over the past couple of weeks—when he'd held her steady as she tried to loop the lights around the Christmas tree and when she'd kissed his chin after bashing it with her head—that she'd been certain he felt *something*. If not desire at least awareness. But apparently she'd been wrong about that, too.

And maybe she should be grateful that he'd never figured out the true depth of her feelings. Because as much as it hurt to acknowledge his disinterest, she knew it would be infinitely more painful to accept his pity.

She was almost home before she remembered that Bella had asked her to keep an eye open at the community center for any single women who might be interested in marrying Jamie and becoming an instant mother to his three babies. It wouldn't be too difficult to come up with a list of names for her friend. There were a lot of suitable candidates and many of them had been at Presents for Patriots tonight to check out the unmarried men in attendance—including Jamie Stockton.

Hadley Strickland was the first name that came to mind. Hadley was a beautiful young veterinarian from Bozeman who was visiting with her grandparents— Melba and Old Gene—over the holidays. She'd also spotted a couple of women she didn't know by name but who she guessed were cousins of the Daltons and definitely pretty enough to snag any man's attention. It certainly wouldn't take much effort for her to generate a list for Bella, but that didn't mean she was going to do it. She'd stood back and felt her heart shatter as Jamie married another woman once already. She wasn't masochistic enough to want to experience the same thing again.

* * *

"You weren't gone very long," Bella said, when Jamie walked into the house before nine o'clock. She was sitting on the sofa with Jared in her arms; both Henry and Katie were on a blanket spread out on the rug, sleeping. The puppies, confined to the play yard, immediately started jumping up at the walls of the enclosure, yipping for attention when he entered the room.

"There were a lot of people there. They didn't need me," he told her, scooping up the puppies before they woke the sleeping babies.

"But I thought you were meeting Fallon there."

"I was. I did."

"So where is she?" Bella asked.

"She went home."

His sister continued to rub circles on Jared's back. "Did something happen between the two of you?"

"Nope." He lowered himself into an armchair and lifted his feet onto the coffee table.

Bella narrowed her eyes. "What aren't you telling me?"

"Nothing."

She waited.

"I can't figure her out," he admitted. "She shows up looking like a completely different person, and half the guys there are drooling over her as if they'd never seen her before. And she's smiling at them and flirting with them. Bobby Ray even asked her out on a date—and she said yes."

"Does that bother you?"

"No," he lied. "Why would it bother me? She can date whoever she wants."

"Then why are you yelling at me?"

"I'm not yelling," he denied.

But when Katie lifted her head, he knew that his annoyance had been reflected in his volume.

"And what do you mean—she looked like a different person?" his sister pressed.

He set the puppies down again and picked up his daughter, rubbing her back until her eyes drifted shut again.

"Her hair," he finally responded to Bella's question in a quieter tone. "And her face. And her clothes."

"Could you be a little more specific?" she suggested, not even attempting to hide her amusement.

"She was wearing a skirt," he muttered, unable to banish the image of those endlessly long, shapely legs from his mind.

"A skirt?" Bella feigned shock. "I didn't know those were legal in Montana."

"A short skirt," he clarified.

She gasped. "Maybe we should call the sheriff."

"I'm glad you think this is funny," he said, though he wasn't glad at all.

"I don't think the situation is funny. I think your extreme response to the situation is funny."

He scowled at that.

"Fallon's decision to alter her appearance a little isn't cause for concern," she said gently. "And you need to realize that not all change is bad."

"She's going out with Bobby Ray," he said again, for some reason unable to get past that fact. "They've been friends since high school, and suddenly she's going on a date with him tomorrow night."

"No relationship is stagnant," Bella pointed out to him.

"But dating a friend—" He shook his head. "It seems to me an easy way to ruin a friendship."

"I guess that's why Fallon's going out with Bobby Ray and not with you," she said, pinning him with a look. "Because you wouldn't ever cross that line, would you?"

Chapter Ten

"I thought he was exaggerating," Bella said, her gaze skimming over her friend, from the top of her head to her toes and back again. "When Jamie came home last night, babbling about your hair and face and clothes, I actually thought he was making a big deal out of nothing."

"And now?" Fallon asked, wanting her friend's honest opinion of her makeover.

"Now I think I owe him an apology," Bella said.

"But what do you think of my new look?" she prompted.

"I think you look fabulous. Not that you don't usually look fabulous—because you do," her friend hastened to clarify. "But this is a very different look."

"Good. I wanted something different."

"But…why?" Bella asked.

"Because I'm tired of looking the same—and of everyone else looking at me the same way."

"*Everyone* else?" her friend queried. "Or *someone* in particular?"

Fallon had always wondered if her friend suspected that she had deeper feelings for Jamie than friendship, but if she did, she'd never voiced those suspicions aloud. So maybe this was a hint to Fallon that she could finally confide the truth to her friend. But before she could figure out how to say the words, Bella spoke again.

"Because I heard that Bobby Ray Ellis asked you out on a date."

She was surprised by her friend's remark. Not just the fact that Bella was somehow aware of her plans but the obvious enthusiasm in her tone. Almost as if she was steering Fallon toward Bobby Ray—and away from Jamie.

Was her friend trying to subtly warn her that the single dad was a bad bet? Or was Fallon reading too much into a simple comment?

"So…is it true?" Bella asked.

"It's true," Fallon confirmed. "We're going to see *National Lampoon's Christmas Vacation* tonight."

Her friend made a face. "At the high school?"

She nodded.

"That's not a real date," Bella lamented. "He could at least take you to an actual movie theater in Kalispell for a current feature."

"I like the *Vacation* movies," Fallon told her. "Besides, it's a long drive back from Kalispell if the date turns out to be a dud."

Her friend frowned. "But you don't think it will be a dud, do you? I mean, you do like Bobby Ray, right?"

"Sure," she agreed. "I mean, I've always liked Bobby Ray, even if I've never *liked* Bobby Ray."

"I'm confused," Bella said. "If you don't *like* him, why did you agree to go out with him?"

"Because he asked and I'm tired of sitting at home every night," she admitted.

"Then this whole makeover thing wasn't part of a plan to attract his attention?"

"No," Fallon said.

"But it was part of a plan to attract someone's attention," her friend guessed. "So whose?"

She shook her head. "It doesn't matter."

"Some guys are too blind to see what's right in front of their eyes," Bella said sympathetically. "And if your mystery man doesn't know how lucky he would be to have you, then it's his loss."

Fallon took her time getting ready for her date with Bobby Ray. Though he wasn't the man she wanted to be going out with, his apparent interest was a balm to her wounded ego and she wanted to repay him by showing that he was worth the effort to look nice.

She wore a knitted sweater with a low V-neck over a lacy camisole and another skirt, but this one was much longer, falling to mid-calf. Bobby Ray wasn't quite as tall as Jamie, but he was still several inches taller than her so she didn't worry about her cowboy boots adding an inch to her five-foot-eight-inch height.

She straightened her hair with the iron she'd bought for that purpose and carefully applied her makeup. A light dusting of powder to even out her complexion and mute the sprinkling of freckles across the bridge of her nose, some mascara to lengthen and darken her lashes and peach gloss to highlight her lips. After only a brief moment's hesitation, she spritzed on some of her favorite perfume.

The way that Bobby Ray's eyes lit up when she descended the stairs told her that he appreciated the effort. Her mother, too, smiled her seal of approval. In fact, she'd been overjoyed ever since Fallon had told her of the upcoming date. "I knew you'd meet someone if you made an effort to put yourself out there. And Bobby Ray is such a nice boy," she'd said.

She ushered them out now and waved goodbye to them from the door.

"Sorry about my mom," Fallon apologized as Bobby Ray pulled out of the driveway. "I haven't dated much in the past year and tonight has given her renewed hope that I won't die a spinster."

Bobby Ray chuckled. "I think you've got a few years before you need to worry about becomin' a spinster."

"She worries anyway—for some reason, more about me than my sisters, who are both older," she admitted.

"Well, I'm really glad you agreed to go out with me tonight," Bobby Ray said. "Even if it was only to appease your mother."

"It wasn't to appease my mother at all," she denied. "I was happy to accept your invitation."

"When I saw you at Presents for Patriots, I wasn't sure if I'd be steppin' on any toes by askin' you out."

She shook her head. "You definitely didn't step on any toes."

"Well, you were there with Jamie Stockton," he noted. "And I know you spend a lot of time helpin' out with his kids, so I thought maybe you and he were like...a couple."

"No." She shook her head. "We're just friends."

"That's good," he said. "Because he's a good guy, and I know he's had some hard knocks, so I didn't want to poach but I really wanted to ask you out."

He was right. Jamie was a good guy, and he had been dealt some hard knocks—and she was tempted to deal him another one to his thick skull, but she'd accepted that she couldn't make him acknowledge feelings that didn't exist.

"Now, I have a question I want to ask you," she said to Bobby Ray.

"Shoot."

"Was it the new hairstyle or the skirt that made you ask me out?"

"That's a pretty direct question," he said, the tips of his ears turning red. "Probably both. I mean—I always thought you were pretty, but we've known each other for so long, I didn't ever see you like a girl I'd want to go out with, until you looked different. If that makes any sense."

"It does," she agreed. And it was, after all, the reason she'd decided to change her appearance. Unfortunately, the man she'd hoped would look at her differently still didn't seem to see her at all.

Bobby Ray parked his truck outside the high school and immediately came around to open her door for her. She was touched by the gesture, pleased to be treated like a lady.

He paid their admission at the table set up in the foyer, then they took their tickets and walked down the hall toward the gymnasium.

"Do you want popcorn?" he asked.

"I can't imagine watching a movie without it," she told him.

He grinned at that. "Me, neither."

They lined up at the concession table, then carried their snacks and drinks into the makeshift theater.

She took off her coat and hung it over the back of her chair. "I'm just going to slip out to the ladies' room before the movie starts."

"I'll be right here," Bobby Ray promised.

She used the facilities, then washed her hands, exchanging pleasantries with a few other people she knew who came in while she was there—including Margot Crawford, Vanessa Dalton and Jordyn Clifton. On her way back to the gymnasium, she nearly bumped into the absolute last person she expected—or wanted—to see tonight: Jamie Stockton.

"What are you doing here?" she asked him.

He lifted one shoulder in a gesture of bafflement that matched the expression on his face. "Bella kicked me out."

Fallon frowned at that. "Your sister kicked you out of your own home?"

He nodded. "She said I needed to do something besides ranch chores and diaper changes, and since she knows that this is one of my favorite Christmas movies, she firmly nudged me in this direction."

"Are you here with anyone?" she asked, then held her breath while she waited for his answer.

He shook his head. "No. Just me."

Deeply ingrained manners warred with the instinct for self-preservation. On the one hand, she felt bad that he was alone. On the other, she was on a date. If she'd been with friends, inviting him to join them would be the polite thing to do. To invite him to sit with her and Bobby Ray would just be a whole lot of awkward—especially when Bobby Ray had already asked about her relationship with Jamie.

"Are you here with someone?" he asked.

She nodded. "Bobby Ray."

"Oh. This is your…uh…date?"

"Yes, Jamie. As inconceivable as it may seem to you, I am on a date."

He frowned. "I don't think it's inconceivable. I'm just… It doesn't matter," he decided. "And I should let you get back to your date. The movie's going to be starting soon."

She nodded. "And you need to find a seat. This movie seems to be a popular one."

Jamie smiled at that, and she inwardly cursed the skip of her pulse. Bobby Ray had a nice smile, too, and he was every bit as handsome as Jamie, but his smiles didn't affect her the same way. His nearness didn't make her feel hot, and his touch didn't make her skin tingle. On the plus side, he'd never broken her heart, either.

"It's a Saturday night and the only movie in town," Jamie pointed out.

"True enough," she agreed. "Well…enjoy."

"You, too," he said.

As she made her way back to her seat, Fallon promised herself that she would enjoy the movie and Bobby Ray's company. And she hoped Jamie would find a seat far away on the other side of the gymnasium so she could forget he was even there.

But because he was only looking for one empty chair, he managed to snag a spot only a few rows back from where she and Bobby Ray were sitting. And she was aware of him, of his eyes on her, throughout the whole movie.

Of course, she was probably only imagining his scrutiny. After all, he'd made it clear that he had no interest in anything more than a platonic relationship with her.

When the movie finished, Fallon and Bobby Ray decided to go to Daisy's Donuts for a hot beverage. The café was a popular destination for the post–movie night crowd, and there were already several other people ahead of them in line when they got there. Fallon was relieved that Jamie wasn't one of them. She was also pleased to see Tessa Strickland, hand-in-hand with her fiancé, Carson Drake. The sheriff, Gage Christensen, and his wife, Lissa, as well as Jordyn and Will Clifton were also there, confirming her mother's claim that everyone in town was pairing up, falling in love and making plans for their futures.

And while she liked Bobby Ray well enough, Fallon couldn't imagine falling in love with him and marrying him. Or maybe she wasn't being fair. Maybe she couldn't see him as her future husband because she'd never let herself imagine anyone but Jamie Stockton in that role. And since Jamie had made it clear that he wasn't ever going to see her as a potential wife, she needed to erase that image from her mind and open herself up to other possibilities.

"Do you know what you want?" Bobby Ray asked, as they stepped up to the counter.

I want the man I love to love me back.

But of course the girl behind the counter couldn't serve that to her in a tall mug, so she ordered a café mocha instead. Bobby Ray ordered a regular coffee, and they carried their drinks to a narrow booth. While they sipped their hot beverages, they chatted casually about his ranch, her job at the day care, the movie they'd just seen and upcoming holiday plans.

"You seem preoccupied," Bobby Ray said to her, when she lifted her empty cup to her lips.

"I'm sorry," she said. "It's been a long week and I think I'm more tired than I realized."

"As long as it's not the company that's puttin' you to sleep."

"It's not the company at all," she promised.

"Then let's get you home," he suggested.

He was being so attentive and sweet and she really wanted to *like* him, but if tonight had served no other purpose, it had confirmed that her thoughts—and her heart—were elsewhere.

She looked over at him in the dim light of the truck. He really was a handsome guy. Tall, dark blond, deep green eyes and the broad shoulders that came from honest physical labor. He'd been popular in high school and had dated a lot of girls before he hooked up with Jillian Landers at the beginning of their junior year.

For the last two years of high school, they'd been pretty much inseparable and everyone expected an engagement announcement would follow soon after their graduation. Instead, Jillian had run off to Billings with someone else.

Curious, and a little bit wary of picking at a scab over old wounds, she asked, "Do you ever hear from Jillian Landers?"

Bobby Ray seemed surprised by the question, but after only a brief hesitation, he said, "We keep in touch on Facebook."

"Is she still in Billings?"

He nodded. "Married with three kids already and a fourth on the way."

"Why aren't you married, Bobby Ray?"

"Is that a hypothetical question or a proposal?" he teased, not taking his eyes off the road in front of him.

"A purely hypothetical question," she assured him.

He shrugged. "I guess I never met anyone else who made me want to take that next step."

She nodded her understanding.

"Now it's your turn," he said. "Why aren't you married?"

"Probably the same reason," she said. Then she surprised herself as much as him by confiding, "Or maybe because the only man I've ever loved doesn't feel the same way about me."

"Unrequited love sucks," he said bluntly.

"It sure does," she agreed.

He parked behind her SUV and walked her to the front door. As he'd been driving her home, it had started to snow again—thick, fluffy flakes that seemed to dance and twirl in the sky, adding a decidedly romantic touch to the end of the evening.

She stopped at the front door and held her breath, waiting for him to say good-night, wondering if he would try to kiss her—and if she would let him.

"I had a really nice time tonight," he told her.

"Me, too," she said.

Then he leaned down and touched his lips to her cheek. And it was a perfectly nice kiss, but there was absolutely no zing or zip.

She looked into his eyes, and saw her own disappointment reflected there.

"We're never going to fall in love, are we?" she asked regretfully.

He shook his head. "I don't think so. But that doesn't mean we can't hang out sometimes to help keep the gossip mill churnin'—because I'd much rather people speculate on what we're doin' together than feel sorry for us because we're two singles in a town where everyone else seems to be pairin' up."

"I would, too," she agreed.

He followed her home.

As Jamie sat in his truck, pulled over to the side of the road with his headlights turned off, and squinted through the window toward the distant and dimly lit front porch of the O'Reilly residence, he realized he'd officially crossed the line from friend to stalker.

He wasn't proud of himself, but he couldn't make himself pull away, either. Not until he knew that her date had gone.

He'd thought he was okay with Fallon going out with Bobby Ray Ellis. Truthfully, he had no right or reason to object to her going out with anyone. But what he'd realized when he saw her at the high school with Bobby Ray, the other man's arm draped across the back of her chair while the movie played on the screen in front of them, was that while the idea of Fallon being on a date didn't bother him, the reality had a very different effect.

And when he realized he'd pulled out of the parking lot behind Bobby Ray's truck after the movie was over, he decided that he would follow her home, just to be sure that she made it there safely. Except that Bobby Ray's truck had unexpectedly pulled into an empty spot by Daisy's Donuts.

Of course, Jamie had no intention of sitting in his truck and waiting for them to come out again. But somehow, that's exactly what happened. For almost forty minutes, while Fallon and Bobby Ray were cozied up together drinking coffee or hot chocolate or whatever, he'd sat in his truck and waited, periodically idling his engine so he didn't freeze his butt to the leather seat.

And then, when they finally left Daisy's Donuts, he'd followed Bobby Ray's truck to the O'Reilly property to ensure the man was taking Fallon home. Of course, from his position on the road, he couldn't see what they were doing or hear what they were talking about. He could only tell that they stood close together on the porch for three minutes, which wasn't a very long time but not a quick good-night, either.

Only when he saw Bobby Ray's truck pull away in the swirling snow did he call it a night.

He made a point of being gone before Fallon showed up Monday morning, and he stayed away until his grumbling stomach insisted that it was time for lunch. He got back to the house just as she was grilling cheese sandwiches for the kids. She buttered four more slices of bread and dropped his sandwiches into the hot pan while she cut the others into bite-size pieces.

"So…did you and Bobby Ray have a good time at the movie the other night?" Jamie finally asked her.

"Yes, we did," she said. "Did you?"

"It was good to get away from the ranch for a while," he said, because that was true. But he didn't remember anything about the movie despite the fact that he'd seen it at least a dozen times before. He couldn't keep his focus on the screen because his gaze kept slipping to the back of Fallon's chair and the other man's arm draped across it.

He had nothing against Bobby Ray. He'd known the guy casually for a lot of years and generally liked him well enough. But he didn't like the idea of him touching Fallon. Or kissing Fallon. And he couldn't bear to consider the possibility of anything more than that.

He knew his feelings were both irrational and unreasonable. But she wasn't just his friend, she was his best friend, and if she and Bobby Ray became a couple, she would spend more time with the other man and less time with him. Okay, so he was irrational, unreasonable *and* selfish.

He knew that Fallon wanted to get married and have a family of her own, and if anyone was meant to be a wife and a mother, it was Fallon. She was so warm and kind and giving—the type of woman he should have married.

He helped himself to a mug of coffee, surreptitiously watching her while she flipped his sandwiches. He'd noticed that she was dressing differently these days. Instead of her usual plaid flannel shirts, she was wearing more fitted styles in more feminine colors.

The top she was wearing today was cream-colored, with tucks at the side that helped it mold to her shape and dozens of tiny hooks down the front to hold the two sides together but made him think how easy it might be to spread them apart. Her jeans looked new, also, and hugged her shapely curves a little more closely than he was accustomed to. She was decorating herself with jewelry, too—sparkly stones in her ears and jangly bracelets on her wrists.

"When is your hair going to go back to normal?"

She blinked at the abrupt question as she plated his sandwiches. "What?"

"You curls are gone," he said.

"They're not actually gone," she admitted. "I've just been straightening my hair."

"Why?"

"Because I wanted a change."

"Why?" he asked again, sincerely baffled by her decision.

"Do I need a reason?"

"Well, generally if something isn't broke, you don't fix it," he said.

She frowned at the irritation in his tone. "How does that apply to my hair?"

"It was just fine the way it was."

"Just fine," she echoed.

"The other way suited you."

"And this doesn't suit me?"

He looked at her again. "I guess it looks okay," he relented. "It just doesn't look like you."

"Bobby Ray seems to like it," she told him.

"So are you like dating him now?"

"We've had one date," she pointed out. "I don't think either one of us is in a hurry to put a label on our relationship."

He scowled. "What does that even mean?"

"It means that my relationship with him is none of your business," she told him.

"Is it wrong for a friend to express concern?"

"No," she acknowledged. "But there's no reason for you to be concerned."

"He hasn't dated anyone exclusively since he broke up with Jillian."

"So?"

"So I just don't want you to get hung up on a guy who's still hung up on someone else," he said.

"Yeah, falling for a guy who isn't capable of reciprocating my feelings would be a stupid move on my part, wouldn't it?" she noted dryly.

"I'm not saying he's not a good guy. I'm just saying that you should be careful."

"Maybe I'm tired of being careful."

He scowled. "What kind of a statement is that?"

"An honest one," she told him. "All my life, I've been a good girl. A good daughter. A good student. A good friend. I've followed the rules without question or complaint, accepting what was offered to me instead of going after what I wanted."

"And Bobby Ray is what you want?"

Her response wasn't at all what he'd expected. Instead of a yes or a no, she took a step closer to him, then lifted herself up onto her toes and kissed him.

Shock held him immobile for about two seconds, then the soft seduction of her lips penetrated the haze that enveloped his brain. Heat pulsed through his system, and he forgot all of the reasons that this was a bad idea and kissed her back.

Just one taste, he promised himself. But her lips were warm and sweet, and one taste wasn't enough. His hands were clenched at his sides, because he knew that if he touched her now, he wouldn't be able to stop. But he really wanted to touch her.

While his head warred with his hormones, she eased her mouth from his and stepped back.

"What was that?" he asked, when enough brain function had been restored that he was able to put words together and form the question.

She ran the tip of her tongue slowly over her bottom lip, as if savoring his flavor. "A test," she said lightly.

His brows rose. "Did I pass?"

Her mouth turned up, just a little at the corners. "I haven't decided yet if I'm grading on a curve."

"Grading on a curve?" he echoed, torn between insult and amusement. "In that case, I want a redo."

But she turned away from him to grab her coat off of the hook by the door. "I have to go."

"You can't just kiss a guy like that and walk away," he protested.

"Watch me," she said.

He stood there, stunned and aroused, and did just that.

Chapter Eleven

"I thought you were going to make my brother do this," Bella said to Fallon, as they stood in line with the babies at the center court of the mall Wednesday afternoon, waiting for their turn to see Santa.

"That was the plan, but Jamie's been so busy with the ranch…and now with Andy and Molly, too," she said, referring to the puppies by the names he'd given them—names apparently inspired by the characters in one of Bella's favorite childhood movies.

"He didn't have to bring those puppies home," his sister pointed out.

Fallon slid her friend a look. "Really? Knowing your brother as well as you do, you can actually say that with a straight face?"

"You're right," Bella acknowledged. "I guess I should be proud of the fact that he only kept two of the seven."

Fallon inched forward with the stroller as two more kids scrambled toward the sleigh, eager to share their Christmas wishes with jolly old St. Nick. She was impressed with his appearance and demeanor. If his beard was fake, it certainly didn't look it. And he seemed incredibly patient with all of the kids—even the screaming babies and toddlers. And there had been a lot of screamers.

Thankfully, HJK didn't seem to be bothered by the other kids' crying. Maybe because, in the first few months, one or more of them had always been in tears, so they'd learned not to be swayed by the others' emotions.

They inched forward in the line again. Fallon reached down and unfurled Katie's fingers from the hem of her dress and pulled the skirt away from her mouth, swapping it for a pacifier. Since she'd started teething, she would chew on anything and everything she could get her hands on.

Behind Katie, Jared was trying to take his shoes off his feet, playing with the laces and knots. Henry was happy just to watch the people go by. He was, of the three babies, the most content and easy to please. Jared was a little more high energy and Katie was downright demanding at times, but Fallon loved the individual personality of each of them.

When it was finally their turn to see Santa, Katie balked for a moment when she heard the booming "Ho Ho Ho," but Bella and Fallon coaxed her into overcoming her apprehension and letting herself be perched on Santa's knee.

It took half a dozen attempts to get a picture with all three kids looking at least in the general vicinity of the camera, and Fallon would have been happy with that—as would the dozens of parents waiting in line behind them. But Santa seemed content to chat with the kids while the photographer kept snapping away. It was probably more by luck than design that he did end up with a picture in which Henry, Jared and Katie were all looking into the camera and smiling—and which Fallon decided would be a perfect Christmas present for their daddy.

"Aside from putting up a tree, has my brother complied with any of the other requests on your holiday cheer list?" Bella asked, as they made their way through the mall.

"Well, he hasn't objected to listening to the Christmas music I usually have on."

"I don't think the absence of an objection earns a check mark," Bella said dryly.

"He's been eating the Christmas cookies I've baked."

"Okay, he gets points for bravery."

Fallon narrowed her gaze on her friend.

"I'm kidding. I'm sure they were...edible."

"They were delicious," she insisted.

"But he didn't help you make them and he didn't eat them because they were shaped like bells or wreaths," Bella pointed out. "He ate them because they were cookies."

"Still...baby steps," Fallon said.

"Any luck convincing him to attend the Candlelight Walk?"

"Not yet," she admitted.

"I can't figure out if you're incredibly patient or extremely stubborn," Bella said. "But I'm grateful that you're not giving up on him."

Fallon wasn't sure of her motivation, either. The only thing she knew for certain was that giving up on Jamie had never been an option.

When Jamie walked into the house at the end of a very long day on Wednesday, he discovered that Fallon was wearing one of those skirts again. The short kind that showed off a mile of leg between the bottom of the hem and the top of her boots. Her sweater had a modest neckline and long sleeves, but it hugged her torso like a lover's hands.

He tore his gaze away from her tempting feminine curves and focused his attention on his babies, giving them lots of love and cuddles because coming home to them was always his favorite part of the day. Of course, the puppies wanted their share of attention, too, so he scratched their ears and rubbed their bellies.

"There's a lasagna in the oven for your dinner," Fallon said. "It should be ready in half an hour."

He nodded. "Thanks." And though he didn't intend to say anything else, the next words spilled out of his mouth of their own volition. "Why are you dressed like that?"

"I'm going for dinner with Bobby Ray," she told him.

"Where are you going?"

"Just over to the Ace."

He scowled. "You can't go to the Ace dressed like that."

"I'm twenty-four years old," she reminded him. "I don't even let my mother tell me what to wear anymore."

"Do you want to start a brawl?"

"I'm hardly the type of woman who inspires that kind of behavior," she retorted.

"You're a woman," he said. "Sometimes that's the only inspiration a drunk cowboy needs."

"Thank you for that incredibly flattering assessment," she said dryly.

The furrow in his brow deepened. "You don't need me to tell you that you're an attractive woman."

"Maybe I do."

"Well, you are," he said. "You should be able to see that for yourself every time you look in the mirror."

Her lips curved. "Do you really think so?"

"Geez, Fallon, you're not actually hoping to stir up trouble, are you?"

"Maybe I am," she said. "Maybe I'm tired of every man I know treating me like a buddy. Maybe I want someone to look at me and realize I'm a woman, to want me as a woman."

And suddenly he got it. "You mean me," he realized. "You want *me* to see you as a woman."

She sighed as she shook her head. "No. I think I've finally accepted that that is never going to happen."

"But I do see you as a woman," he assured her. "A genuinely warm, funny and smart woman."

"Maybe it's un-PC," she admitted. "But I don't want to be admired for my personality or my intelligence. I want to be wanted."

He swallowed. "You're looking for a hookup?"

"That wouldn't be my first choice," she said. "But I've decided to open my mind up to any and all possibilities."

"A hookup should not be one of them," he told her. "You deserve better than that."

She walked to the door, then turned back. "What

does the song say—we can't always get what we want, but we get what we need?"

"Don't go, Fallon." The words were out of his mouth before he realized what he was saying.

She paused with her hand on the doorknob.

"Don't go out with Bobby Ray tonight."

She slowly turned around, her expression carefully neutral. "Are you making me an alternate offer?" she asked.

He nodded. "Stay here. With me."

She held his gaze for a moment, considering his invitation. "What would we do?"

His mind immediately filled with possible answers to her question, none of which she'd go home and tell her mother about. And while he wasn't just ready but eager to explore each and every one of those possibilities, he realized that he needed to be smart—to think about what would happen after and the potential consequences to their relationship. Getting personally involved with Fallon was a risk he couldn't take.

"Forget I said anything," he decided. "Go out with Bobby Ray tonight."

Fallon shook her head. "You flip-flop more than a fish out of water."

"I'm sorry," he said, and meant it. "I'm trying to be smart here and your friendship is too important to me to risk jeopardizing it."

"Forget about being smart and tell me, honestly, what you want."

"I want you to stay," he admitted. "I want…you."

She pulled her cell phone out of her pocket, tapped her fingers over the keypad, then tucked the phone away again. "I'll stay."

* * *

Jamie opened a bottle of wine to go with the lasagna they had for dinner. After they'd finished eating, they cleaned up the kitchen and spent some time playing with the babies. It was all part of a routine that she'd performed with him countless times before. But tonight, after Henry, Jared and Katie had been bathed and changed and were asleep in their cribs, Fallon wasn't getting ready to leave.

Jamie poured some more wine into her glass, and her hand shook as she lifted it to her lips.

"You're nervous," he noted.

"A little," she admitted.

"Have you changed your mind?"

She shook her head. "No, but I can't help thinking about how this is going to change our relationship," she confided.

"Change isn't always a bad thing," he said, taking the wine glass from her hand and setting it down on the counter beside his. Then he put his arms around her and drew her toward him.

Now, she thought. Finally now he would kiss her and she could stop thinking about what was going to happen and enjoy the experience of letting it happen.

But he bypassed her mouth in favor of her temple, gently skimming his lips over her skin. Then he brushed a kiss on her cheekbone, another near her ear, and her jaw. He wasn't kissing her so much as caressing her face with his lips, and every fleeting touch was incredibly and shockingly arousing.

His hands slid beneath her sweater, his fingertips danced over her skin. He was a rancher with big hands and tough skin, but his touch was infinitely and almost unbearably gentle. No, he wasn't touching so much as teasing, hinting at the promise of so much more.

His hands moved around to her front, stroking gently over her belly, tracing the edge of her bra. He hadn't touched her breasts, but her nipples were already peaked, aching.

"Are you trying to drive me crazy?"

"Is it working?"

"Yes."

He smiled. "I like the feel of your skin." Then he nuzzled her throat. "The scent of your skin." Then he pressed his lips to the ultra sensitive spot where her neck met her shoulder. "And the taste of your skin."

"You could touch, smell and taste a lot more if you took me upstairs to your bedroom," she told him.

Jamie didn't need to be told twice.

Upstairs, he pulled back the covers on his bed, then laid her down on the mattress.

It had been a long time since he'd been with a woman. He didn't remember exactly how long, except that the last time Paula had let him touch her had been in the early stages of her pregnancy, before she discovered she was carrying triplets.

He pushed those unhappy memories aside to focus on the joy that filled his heart here and now.

Fallon was passionate and eager, responding to his kisses, his touches, with wild abandon, meeting his demands with her own. He knew she was self-conscious about what she considered to be her too-small breasts, but to him they were perfect. Round and firm with dark pink nipples at the center.

He took one of those nipples in his mouth, then the other. She squirmed beneath him as he suckled her flesh, her breath coming in short, shallow gasps that assured him she was enjoying the attention. He proceeded to pay the same careful attention to the rest of her body. He moved slowly down her torso, his mouth trailing kisses over her silky skin.

He slid his hands along the inside of her thighs, urging them apart. Then he parted the soft folds at her center, to reveal her sweet glistening core. She sucked in a breath, her fingers curling into the sheet. He interpreted her silence as acquiescence and lowered his head to taste her.

Her heels dug into the mattress, her hips instinctively tilting to provide easier access. He took advantage of what she was offering, using his lips and his tongue to give them both pleasure.

"Jamie. Please." She was writhing beneath him, gasping for breath. He knew what she was asking for, because he wanted the same thing. He was rock-hard and aching, desperate for her.

He shifted away from her only long enough to dig a little square packet out of the drawer in his night table, then huffed out a frustrated breath.

"What's wrong?" Fallon asked.

"It's been a long time since I've had any need for birth control, and I'm pretty sure this condom is past its best before date," he admitted.

"Oh," she said, the single syllable heavy with disappointment.

"I don't suppose you have any in your purse?" he asked hopefully.

"No, I—wait. Actually, I do," she admitted, and even in the dim light, he could see her cheeks flush. "But they're, uh, glow-in-the-dark condoms."

"Aren't you full of surprises?" he teased.

"I'm not. I mean, they're not mine." She lifted her hands to cover her face. "Brenna tucked them in my purse, as a joke, before I went out with Bobby Ray Saturday night."

He absolutely was not going to ask if she'd used any of the condoms, because he definitely did not want to know. "If you could not talk about other men while you're naked in my bed, that would be great," he suggested.

Her next words ignored his advice and rekindled his ardor.

"I didn't sleep with Bobby Ray," she told him. "I wouldn't be here with you if I had."

He brushed a quick kiss on her lips. "Where's your purse?"

"In the kitchen."

"I'll be right back," he promised. Then he slid from the bed, quickly wrapped himself in his robe and took the stairs two at a time.

He was gone less than a minute. When he handed her the purse, she unzipped the side pouch of her purse and pulled out a handful of condoms.

He took one and set the others on top of the night table, then tore open the package and quickly sheathed himself.

"Wow," Fallon commented. "It really does glow."

"Give me a minute," he said. "And you'll be saying 'wow' for a different reason."

Her lips curved as she reached for him, her hands eagerly exploring his body, sliding over his chest, his shoulders and down his back.

The muscles in his arms quivered with the effort of

holding himself over her as he fought against the primitive instinct to drive into her, hard and deep. Instead he slowly eased into her. Despite her obvious arousal, his entry wasn't easy. She was tighter than he'd expected, and he could feel the tension in her body as she braced herself to take him.

He was a little tense, too, trying not to think about the fact they were passing the point of no return. Then he kissed her again, slowly and deeply until he felt some of the tension leave her body, and he eased in a little deeper.

He was trying to hold onto his patience, to show some restraint, but Fallon apparently decided that she was having none of that. She lifted her legs to hook them at his back and tilted her hips to pull him deeper, gasping with shock as he finally pushed through a barrier he hadn't expected to encounter.

He froze, as shocked disbelief penetrated the euphoria of his arousal.

"You were a virgin," he realized.

"Can we save the talking for later?" she suggested.

His fingers curled into the comforter, and he gripped the fabric tightly in his fists. "I think we need to talk about this."

But she shook her head. "Not now. Please, Jamie. I've waited too long for this—for *you*—to stop now."

Then, just in case the words weren't sufficient to make him lose the tenuous grip on his self-control, she started to move her hips again. Whatever she lacked in experience, she more than made up for with enthusiasm, and he finally gave himself over to the passion that consumed them both.

* * *

Fallon had dreamed of making love with Jamie, but even her most vivid and erotic dreams did not compare to the reality. Even without knowing he was her first, he'd been a careful and attentive lover, ensuring her pleasure before taking his own. She exhaled a contented sigh, though she knew the blissful peace of the moment wouldn't last.

Jamie would have questions, and he'd demand answers, and though the last thing she wanted to do was dissect the most amazing experience of her life, she understood that she at least owed him an explanation.

"You should have told me," he said.

"I figured you already had enough reasons for not wanting to get naked with me without adding any more to the list."

"I don't know that I would have been able to stop myself from making love with you," he admitted. "But I do know I would have been more careful."

She stroked a hand down his back, because now that she'd finally had the opportunity to touch him, she didn't want to stop. "You didn't hurt me, Jamie."

"Are you sure?"

"I realize that I'm the inexperienced one here, but I would have figured the fact that I climaxed a few times and bit down on your shoulder so that I didn't shout would be clues that I had a pretty good time."

His lips curved. "A pretty good time, huh?"

"But maybe I should be asking how it was for you," she realized.

"It was amazing. *You* were amazing."

"Of course, it has been fifteen months since you've had sex," she reminded him.

He brushed his lips against hers, softly, sweetly.

"You were amazing," he said again.

But she could tell by the slight furrow in his brow that he was still worried about something, and she had a pretty good idea about the cause of his concern.

"I wasn't saving myself for anyone—or for any particular reason," she told him, unwilling to admit—even to herself—that she had done exactly that. "So please don't make this into something bigger than it is."

"It is pretty big," he told her.

"Now you're just bragging," she admonished.

It took him a second, then he chuckled softly. "You really are full of surprises, aren't you, Fallon O'Reilly?"

"In a good way, I hope."

He brushed his lips over hers. "The very best way."

When Jamie slid out of bed a short while later to check on the kids and let the puppies outside, Fallon decided to sneak into his shower. She wasn't embarrassed by or ashamed of what had happened between them, but she didn't want to advertise it, either. She turned on the faucet and adjusted the temperature, then stepped beneath the spray.

She had just lathered up a washcloth with soap when the curtain was yanked back, making her yelp.

"What are you doing?" she demanded, when Jamie stepped into the shower with her.

"I'm a conservationist and I'm saving water."

She instinctively crossed her arms over her body.

Jamie chuckled. "Have you forgotten that I've already seen every inch of your body?"

"Not under bright lights," she argued.

"A definite oversight," he said, wrapping his fingers around her wrists and pulling her hands away.

"You are so beautiful, Fallon. So perfect."

"I'm not even close to being perfect," she denied.

"A wise woman once told me that perfect doesn't have to mean without flaws but only what fulfills your need in the moment."

"Didn't I already fulfill your need?"

He smiled as he slid his hands up her back. "Yeah, but I need you again."

"Do you now?"

"I have a feeling that you could become an addiction," he told her.

She wanted to believe he was telling her the truth, that his desire for her could be even half as deep and real as her need for him. At the same time, she was trying to tread carefully. Because while the physical aspect of their relationship was new territory, she'd accepted her feelings for him a long time ago.

She was still trying to decide on an appropriate response when he lathered up his hands and began to spread the soap over her body, effectively scrubbing all rational thoughts from her brain.

"What are you doing?" she asked instead.

"Showing you there are more benefits to sharing a shower than just saving water."

He nudged her under the spray, to wash away the suds, then dipped his head to touch his lips to the cluster of freckles on her shoulder, then trailed his mouth across her collarbone. "Your skin is so soft."

"Your body is so hard," she noted, letting her hands explore the rugged contours of his shoulders, his pecs, his abs. And lower. She boldly wrapped her fingers around the rigid length of him. "All over."

He slapped a hand against the shower wall behind her and closed his eyes. "You're a fast learner, aren't you?"

"Actually, I think I'm a pretty slow learner. In fact, we're probably going to have to practice over and over again before I really figure this out."

"Over and over again?"

"Over—" she stroked him again, slowly, from base to tip, and back again "—and over."

A long time later, after they'd made love again—this time in the bed—and his heart rate had finally slowed to something approximating normal, Jamie wrapped a strand of damp hair around his finger and tugged gently. "There they are."

She blinked slowly, as if trying to bring the world back into focus. "What?"

He smiled, gratified to know that he'd rocked her world as completely as she'd rocked his. "Your curls," he said. "I thought they were gone forever."

"I wish."

"I don't. I like your curls."

She seemed surprised by that admission. "You do?"

He nodded. "And as much as I like the way you look in a short skirt, you're every bit as appealing in a pair of jeans."

She made a sound of disbelief. "You never looked at me twice until I started wearing skirts," she pointed out to him.

"I always looked," he told her. "I just never let you see me looking."

"Why?"

"Because I was afraid that if I tried to turn our friendship into something more and it didn't work out, I'd lose my best friend."

"And now?"

He tucked a strand of hair behind her ear. "I'm still worried," he admitted. "I don't ever want to lose you, Fallon."

"You won't lose me," she told him. "But I do have to leave your bed right now."

"Why?"

"Because it's late and we both have to get up early."

"It's not that late," he said, though she could tell he was having trouble keeping his eyes open.

"And your sister's going to be home soon."

"Maybe," he acknowledged.

"Do you really want to explain this—" she gestured between the two of them "—to Bella?"

"Not tonight," he admitted.

She brushed her lips to his. "And that's why I need to go."

He slid a hand up her thigh to settle at the curve of her butt. "Are you here tomorrow?"

"Ten months," she said, shaking her head. "And you still don't know the schedule."

"The schedule keeps changing," he said in his defense.

"I've always done Monday and Thursday mornings, full days on Wednesdays and the occasional Saturday."

"So I'll see you in the morning?"

"Yes, you'll see me in the morning," she assured him.

"Good." He framed her face in his hands and brought his mouth down to hers, kissing her softly, deeply.

"And if you want to see me the following night, you

could give me a call and ask me to go to the Candlelight Walk with you, Henry, Jared and Katie," she suggested.

"You're determined to drag us out to that, aren't you?"

She shrugged. "It's just an idea, but I know that's where I'm going to be Friday night."

"I'll give you a call," he promised.

Chapter Twelve

She was twenty-four years old and sneaking into her house as if she were a teenager out past curfew.

Fallon had no experience with that kind of subversive behavior. As a teenager, she'd never broken curfew. She'd always been a good girl, a rule follower. Tonight, she'd broken a lot of rules, and she couldn't deny that it felt pretty darn good.

How many times had she sat in the high school cafeteria listening to her friends and classmates recount and evaluate their sexual experiences, without having anything to add to the conversation? Truthfully, she'd always suspected that sex was overhyped. She knew better now.

Tonight, she'd made love with the man she loved, and the experience had surpassed every one of her expectations.

The only tiny niggling concern was that she didn't know how Jamie felt about her. Suggesting that he might become addicted to her was the closest he'd come to any kind of emotional declaration, and that was okay. She understood that men didn't engage their emotions as readily as women did. She also understood that he might still be grieving the loss of his wife. Maybe he was even still in love with his wife.

That possibility took a little bit of the spring from her step. She'd never believed that Paula deserved him, but she'd supported his choices because he was her friend, because she loved him and wanted him to be happy. She'd sincerely hoped that Paula would make him happy, and she had—for a while. But Fallon knew there had been issues and tensions in their marriage—as there were in any marriage—and Paula had died before they could be resolved, one way or another.

As a result, it wouldn't surprise her to learn that Jamie had some lingering feelings for his wife—the mother of his children. She only hoped those feelings wouldn't prevent him from letting himself fall in love and be loved again.

She was tiptoeing toward the stairs when she heard the scrabbling sound of paws and a trio of excited yips from Duchess—the puppy her parents had chosen from Andy and Molly's littermates.

"Shh," she admonished, crouching to scratch behind the pup's ears.

Duchess dropped to the ground then rolled onto her back, a not-so-subtle demand for Fallon to rub her belly—which she did, because she knew it would keep her quiet.

After she'd fussed over the animal for a few minutes, she pointed toward the kitchen. "Now go back to bed."

Surprisingly, the dog obeyed her command and Fallon headed up the stairs. At the top, she turned automatically toward her bedroom—and nearly bumped into Brenna, who had just stepped out of the bathroom.

Her sister blinked, as if trying to focus in the darkness. "Fallon?"

"Hey, Brenna," she whispered softly.

"What time is it?"

"Late," she hedged.

"Obviously." Brenna grabbed her arm and steered her into her bedroom, where she glanced at the clock on her bedside table. "It's almost three a.m."

"Early rather than late then," she said lightly.

Brenna pushed her toward the bed. "Sit."

And though she wasn't a child and her sister had no right to boss her around or interrogate her, she sat.

Brenna perched on the edge of her desk chair, facing Fallon. "Now spill."

"Can't this wait until morning?"

"As you pointed out, it is morning."

Fallon sighed. "Come on, Bren—I just want to catch a few hours' sleep before I have to get up."

"This conversation can be long or short, depending on how willing you are to answer my questions," her sister said.

"You're not my mother, so don't try to act like you are."

"Would you like me to wake Mom up so you can have this conversation with her instead?" Brenna challenged.

She sighed. "No."

"Where were you?" her sister prompted.

"I was at The Short Hills Ranch," she admitted.

"With Bella?"

She lifted her chin to meet her sister's gaze. "With Jamie."

To her surprise, Brenna smiled. "So maybe he's not as much of a clueless idiot as I was beginning to think."

Fallon just stared at her.

"Did you think I would judge you for being with the man you've loved for most of your life?" her sister asked softly.

"Is there anyone who doesn't know how I feel about him?"

"Probably Jamie," Fiona said, as she slipped into the room and sat on the edge of the bed beside her youngest sister. "Men can be so oblivious about certain things."

"She's right about that," Brenna confirmed.

"Did we wake you up?" Fallon asked, worriedly.

"No, I was awake," Fiona assured her.

"Maybe our big sister has a man on her mind, too," Brenna teased.

Fiona's only response was a shake of her head— whether a denial or an indication that she didn't want to talk about it, Fallon never had a chance to ask before Fiona spoke again. "Are you okay?" she asked gently. "Were you careful?"

"Yes and yes," she said, more touched than embarrassed by her older sisters' questions and concern.

"Good." Fiona kissed her cheek. "Now go to sleep so the rest of us can, too."

The Candlelight Walk was exactly that—a leisurely stroll from one end of Main Street to the other, under-

taken by residents carrying lighted candles and singing along with the Christmas music that accompanied
their journey. At the end of the processional, there was
a big bonfire and refreshments were served.

The first Christmas after their wedding, Jamie and
Paula had attended the event, and Paula had griped that
it was cold. Even with two sets of mittens, she'd com-
plained that her hands were icy. The second year, they'd
skipped the event entirely. And last year, they'd barely
been on speaking terms.

Which was probably why he'd resisted Fallon's efforts to embrace the holidays—because all of his memories from the previous year had been unhappy ones. But
she'd refused to let his "bah, humbug" attitude dampen
her own holiday spirit. She'd surrounded him with all
the sights and sounds and scents of Christmas—not just
the tree in his living room but decorations around the
house, holiday music pumping out of her iPod, the scent
of gingerbread baking (and though he had initially been
wary, the cookies had been really tasty). And now, with
Christmas less than two weeks away, he found that he
was sincerely looking forward to celebrating the holiday—his first with Henry, Jared and Katie. And hopefully his first with Fallon, too.

But venturing into town and celebrating with all the
residents of Rust Creek Falls? He wasn't sure he was
quite ready for that.

"Are you sure it's not too cold out for HJK?" he
asked worriedly.

"They're wearing three layers beneath their snowsuits," she pointed out to him. "Plus hats on their heads
and mittens on their hands. They'll be fine."

"Katie's nose was running this morning."

"Because she's teething."

"I'm not sure about this," he said. "It wasn't so long ago that there was an RSV outbreak in town, and the immune systems of preemies are more fragile than other babies'."

"Why don't you tell me what's really going on here?"

"What do you mean?" he hedged.

"Why don't you like taking your kids into town?" she asked.

"My reluctance isn't really about the kids," he admitted.

She considered his response for a moment before hesitantly asking, "Is it that you don't want to be seen with me?"

"What? No," he responded immediately, eager to dispel her concern. "It's not about you, either."

"Then what is it about?" she pressed.

"The way people look at me," he finally acknowledged. "The sympathy and the pity."

"The respect and admiration," she interjected.

He raised a brow.

"Do you really not see that?" she asked him. "Everyone in town knows how hard you're working to provide for your family, and they respect you for it."

"Not everyone thinks I made the right choices," Jamie told her. "The first time I saw Gramps in town after the babies were born, he told me that they'd be better off in a home with two parents."

She touched a hand to his arm. "I'm sorry—but you have to realize his opinion isn't a popular one."

He nodded. "And when I got over being angry and hurt, I wondered if he was trying to explain to me why they sent Dana and Liza away—because they believed it would be better for them."

"Maybe," she said dubiously. "But then why didn't they find a better option for you and Bella?"

He shrugged. "Maybe because we were too old to appeal to adoptive parents and too young to be left to our own devices."

Whatever the reason, he and his sister had been caught in the middle, living with grandparents who didn't want them and didn't seem to know how to love them. It was no wonder they'd had trouble opening up their hearts. Of course, when he'd finally done so, he'd ended up with his heart broken.

Still, he was sincerely happy to know that Bella had finally fallen in love. His sister deserved to be happy, and it made him happy to watch her planning her future with Hudson. Even if it didn't make him eager to open up his own again. No, thanks—been there, done that, bought the ill-fitting T-shirt and not going back again.

"I could go for a hot chocolate," Fallon said to Jamie, when they'd come to the end of the processional and the crowd had begun to disperse.

"If you want to stay here with HJK, I'll brave the line at the refreshment table to see if there's anything left."

"Thanks."

"Whipped cream or marshmallows?"

"Are you asking what I want in my hot chocolate or is this a question for later?" she teased.

"I was asking about the hot chocolate, but now you've got me wondering," he admitted.

"Marshmallows…for now," she told him.

"And later?"

She smiled. "Whatever you want."

* * *

She went back to Jamie's house for a few hours after the Candlelight Walk, where he made love to her slowly, thoroughly and quietly.

Afterward, he fell asleep with her in his arms, feeling—for the first time in a long time—both happy and optimistic about the future.

He didn't often dream. Or maybe it was more accurate to say that he didn't often remember what he dreamed. But when he woke up in the night, his heart hammering against his ribs, his breath shallow and ragged, the dream was still vivid in his mind.

Not a dream—a nightmare.

He sat up and scrubbed his hands over his face, trying to reassure himself that it was only a dream. That none of it was real.

But it had felt real.

He'd heard Paula's voice as clearly as if she'd been right beside him, telling him that she hadn't really died in the hospital but only pretended to so that she could escape from him and a marriage she'd never really wanted. And now that she'd had some time to think about it and had seen their sweet, beautiful babies, she'd decided that she wanted them after all.

When he told her that she couldn't have them, she just laughed. But she did turn to walk away, and he exhaled a sigh of relief as he watched her go. Until he noticed that Henry, Jared and Katie were following her.

He tried to go after them, but his feet were stuck to the ground. He tried to reach for them, to pull them back, but no matter how far he stretched his arms, it wasn't far enough. He couldn't get to them and they continued to move away, following Paula until they all disappeared into the mist.

Then he heard a sound from another direction and turned to find himself face-to-face with Fallon. She smiled at him sweetly and kissed him softly, then told him she was going to check on their babies. And he had to tell her that they were gone.

She hadn't understood at first. His voice was hoarse and broken and the words didn't make any sense to her. They didn't make any sense to him, either. He didn't want to believe that they were true. But somehow he could see through the window as she hurried into the house and raced up the stairs and into the babies' room. She'd stared at the empty cribs, tears sliding down her cheeks.

"How could you let them go?" she demanded.

He tried to explain. "I didn't let them go, but I couldn't stop them."

"You had only one task—to keep your family together and safe. And you failed. You failed, Jamie."

"I'm sorry."

She shook her head. "Being sorry doesn't change anything."

And then she turned and walked away, following the same path as his ex-wife and his babies, disappearing into the same mist.

Jamie shuddered. It had felt so real, so terrifyingly real. But it was only a dream. A nightmare.

He sucked in a deep breath, then exhaled slowly, attempting to reassure himself that none of it was true.

Except that Fallon was gone.

He'd fallen asleep with her in his arms, and when he'd awakened, she wasn't there.

Logically, he understood that she couldn't stay with him through the night. But he wasn't feeling logical right now. He was feeling alone and abandoned, because she'd left him—just like everyone else he'd ever loved.

Loved?

Now his heart was pounding for a different reason.

No, it couldn't be true. It was too soon. Wasn't it?

He'd only been in love once before. He'd fallen fast and hard for Paula, and he'd felt so lucky that she'd fallen for him, too. And look how that had turned out.

He didn't regret the years they'd spent together. How could he when she'd given him Henry, Jared and Katie? But loving and losing Paula had changed him. And though he knew that Fallon wasn't anything like his former wife, he wasn't the same man anymore, either.

He wasn't eager to toss the dice and gamble that this time love would endure. This time, he had too much to lose.

Chapter Thirteen

Fallon had hated leaving the comfort of Jamie's arms and the warmth of his bed, but she knew that any concerns Maureen O'Reilly had about her youngest daughter's relationship with the single father would not be alleviated by her staying out all night. So she'd slipped out of his bed in the early hours of the morning, drove home in the darkness, and slid under the covers of her cold, empty bed, already counting the hours until she would see him again.

Only six more hours, she promised herself, and drifted off to sleep with a smile on her face.

It was a relatively short period of time, but when Fallon walked in the back door of Jamie's house six hours later, she instinctively sensed that something had changed.

Or maybe it was just that the house was unusually

quiet, the three high chairs in the kitchen empty and no sign of Henry, Jared or Katie anywhere around. Only Jamie was there, sitting at the table with a mug of coffee in his hands and a grim expression on his face.

"Where are the kids?" she asked.

"Bella and Hudson offered to take them for a few hours this morning."

"Oh." It was a perfectly reasonable explanation, but there were too many things that didn't add up. They'd made love just last night…they were alone in the house…and he hadn't even kissed her.

"What aren't you telling me?" she finally asked him.

He refilled his mug with coffee, then set it down again without drinking. "I don't know how to say it," he began.

Her heart did a freefall into the bottom of her stomach. "You're breaking up with me," she realized.

"No," he denied, though not very convincingly. "I'm just suggesting that we…take a step back."

"A step back," she echoed hollowly. "What, exactly, is that supposed to mean?"

"Everything happened so fast. I just think we should take some time to think about what we really want from one another."

Fast? She almost laughed. Only if seven years after their first kiss was fast.

But maybe, from his perspective, it was fast. His wife—the mother of his babies—had died only ten months earlier. Maybe it wasn't unreasonable for him to need some more time to adjust to the changes in their relationship.

"How much time?" she asked, her tone carefully neutral. "A few days? A couple of weeks?"

He didn't meet her gaze. "I don't know."

She suddenly felt hollow and empty inside, drained of all happiness and hope. "Do you really want time—or are you trying to get out of a situation you wish you'd never gotten into?"

"I don't regret being with you, Fallon."

"But you don't want to be with me anymore," she guessed.

"I don't want to lose my best friend," he told her.

She nodded. "That's always a good one—hard to argue against."

"It's true," he insisted. "You are one of few people in my life that I know I can count on."

"And, somehow, sharing your bed makes me unreliable?"

"You're determined to make this difficult, aren't you?"

"Forgive me," she said. "I've never been dumped by a lover, so I'm not entirely sure how I'm supposed to react."

"I'm not dumping you," he denied.

"No? Because that's what it feels like from this end."

"You deserve someone who can give you what you want," he told her. "And that's not going to be me."

"How do you know what I want?" she challenged.

"Because I know *you*. Because I know that you've always dreamed of having a husband and a family, and maybe you look at me and the babies and think we're the quickest route to everything you've ever wanted."

"Apparently you don't know me at all," she shot back, her tone practically vibrating with suppressed fury. "Because I don't think of you and the babies as a 'route' to anything, but as the man and the children I love."

He shook his head regretfully. "I'm not a good bet, Fallon."

"Oh, this one I know," she said, still fuming. "The 'it's not you, it's me' speech."

"It's not a speech—it's the truth," he insisted. "I've been married, and it didn't turn out well."

"We slept together a few times," she pointed out to him. "I may be naïve and inexperienced, but I'm not holding my breath for a proposal."

"Maybe not yet," he acknowledged. "But you can't tell me that you weren't hoping our relationship was headed in that direction."

She felt the sting of hot tears behind her eyes, but she refused to let them fall. "You're right. I did think, considering our history of friendship, common interests and goals, that we might have a future together."

"And I can't go down that road again," he said. "I've loved and lost too many people in my life to risk losing you, too."

Too many people.

Those words successfully defused her anger, because she realized now that this wasn't just about their relationship or even the loss of his wife—this went back much further and much deeper. Unfortunately, the words did nothing to staunch the bleeding of her heart.

She understood that he'd been scarred by the loss of his parents, the abandonment by his brothers and the disappearance of his youngest sisters, which was why she'd wanted to help him reunite with his siblings. But any time she'd broached the subject with him, he'd shot it down.

Just as he was shooting down her feelings and her hopes for a future for them together now. "So what do you want—for us to go back to being just friends again?"

"I think that would be for the best," he said.

But it wasn't. Not for her, anyway. She didn't want to be "just friends" with the man she loved—the man she'd always loved. She'd given him all of her heart, and he was handing it back to her like an unwelcome gift.

Tears welled in her eyes again, and she turned away so that he wouldn't see them. "I don't know if that's possible now."

"It is," he insisted. "You just have to be willing."

Was she willing?

She wanted so much more than he was offering, but if all he could give her was friendship, she would take that rather than lose him forever.

"Please, Fallon," he implored.

And because she'd never been able to deny him anything he wanted, she nodded.

But before they could go back to being "just friends," she needed a little bit of time to pick up the pieces of her broken heart. "Okay," she finally responded. "I'm going out of town for a few days, but we can talk when I get back."

He frowned at that. "You're leaving town?"

"Just for a few days," she told him.

"Because of this?"

"No," she denied. "This has been in the works for a while. In fact, I've already talked to Bella to ensure that the baby chain has you covered."

"You're really going to abandon Henry, Jared and Katie," he said, more of a statement than a question.

"I'm not abandoning them," she said gently. "And I'm not abandoning you, either."

Maybe she didn't see it that way, but from where Jamie was standing, it certainly felt as if he was being abandoned.

"When will you be back?" he demanded.

"I'm not sure."

He wanted to ask her not to go, but he knew he had no right. Instead, he asked, "Where are you going?"

She lifted herself onto her toes and touched her lips to his cheek. "I'll see you soon."

Then she turned, and he was left standing there, watching her walk away and wondering if he'd just made the biggest mistake of his life.

When Jamie headed back to the house after completing his morning chores, he found his sister had returned and was sitting at the kitchen table looking at sample wedding invitations while the babies played.

He poured himself a mug of coffee and sat down across from Bella. "Fallon told me that she talked to you about her plans to go out of town."

She nodded. "Since school is on break for the holidays, Paige Traub is going to cover Fallon's usual shifts, which will give the kids a chance to hang out with her son, Carter. And Cecelia Pritchett had to cancel her Thursday afternoon because she's got an appointment in Kalispell, but Margot Crawford can fill in for her. The revised schedule is on the fridge."

He didn't really care about the revised schedule. He wanted to know where Fallon had gone—and when she'd be back. But if he started asking his sister all kinds of questions, she'd figure out that he'd screwed things up with Fallon, and he wasn't prepared to talk about it. Not until he'd figured out how he was going to fix it.

So far, he didn't have any ideas in that direction, and sitting around thinking about the mistakes he'd made would drive him crazy. Instead, he reached for the box of invitations Bella had set aside, deciding that he could distract himself by helping her.

She snatched the box away from him. "Don't you have stables to muck out or something?"

"Already done," he told her.

"Fence to fix?"

"Finished that last week."

"Then you obviously don't need me to hang around here," she said pushing her chair away from the table. "Which is good, because Hudson and I are going in to Kalispell to see about a cake for the wedding."

"Your wedding isn't until June—won't the cake be stale by then?"

"Ha-ha." She kissed his cheek. "Have a good day, big brother."

"Actually, I might head into the city today, too," he decided impulsively.

"For what?" she asked suspiciously.

"To take HJK to the mall."

Bella's brows drew together as she touched the back of her hand to his forehead, as if checking for a fever. "Are you ill?"

He scowled at her. "No, I'm not ill."

"But it's eight days before Christmas—and a Saturday—and you want to take three babies to a shopping mall in the city?"

No, he didn't really *want* to, but he remembered Fallon's repeated urgings for him to have the kids' first Christmas commemorated by a photo with Santa—and his repeated brush-offs.

He lifted a shoulder. "Fallon seemed to think it was important for Henry, Jared and Katie to see Santa, and I thought she might like a picture of them with the big guy."

Bella opened her mouth as if she was going to say something, then apparently changed her mind and closed it again.

"You don't think I can handle an outing with my own children?" he challenged.

"I'm sure you can handle it," she finally said. "But I think you might benefit from an extra set of hands. Why don't I go with you, then Hudson can pick me up at the mall and we'll do our rounds of the bakeries afterward?"

Which was her way of saying that she didn't think he could handle a trip into the city with his own kids. And while his pride urged him to decline her offer, his rational mind reminded him that three babies were a handful on the best of days. "I don't want you to change your plans on my account," he said.

"I'm not changing my plans, just adjusting the timeframe," she told him.

"In that case, I'd appreciate those extra hands."

"I guess we'd better get the babies washed up and changed for their big photo shoot." She lifted Katie out of her high chair first. "And Jamie—"

He glanced up as he unfastened the sticky buckle around Henry's middle—evidence of the pancakes their aunt had made for them for breakfast earlier. "Yeah?"

"This is a really great idea. Fallon will love it."

He sincerely hoped his sister was right.

It was not a great idea.
In fact, it was a terrible idea.

Jamie cruised around the parking lot looking for a vacant space. Anywhere. But it was as if every single resident of Kalispell had decided to come to the mall today—and many more from neighboring towns, too.

"There," Bella said, pointing toward a woman and her daughter, both loaded down with shopping bags, who were making their way across the parking lot.

He paused in the middle of the lane, then crawled along behind them, putting his indicator on as a sign to other drivers that their parking spot—wherever it might be—was his.

It took the woman forever to load up her parcels, get into the car, and buckle her seatbelt. Then God only knows what she was doing, because she sure as hell didn't hurry to leave. Maybe she was fiddling with the radio, maybe she was programming a GPS or making a phone call. It took her two full minutes to finally decide to put her vehicle into Reverse and ease out of her narrow space.

As Jamie unfolded the triple stroller, Bella started to unbuckle the babies from their car seats so they could be loaded into their wheeled carriage and buckled up again. He was definitely grateful for her extra set of hands.

Thankfully Santa had a lot more patience than Jamie did.

Bella occupied the kids, who were now hungry and cranky, while he stood beside one of the elves to select from the digital images on the computer screen. Jamie was hungry and cranky by now, too, and tempted to walk away without a picture because none of them was the perfect shot he'd wanted for Fallon.

On the other hand, the one with Jared smiling at the camera was pretty good—even if Katie was looking in the opposite direction. But none of them was screaming and there were no tears and they were all wearing the cute little outfits she'd bought for them.

Okay, he'd forgotten Katie's shoes, so she was wearing her snow boots on her feet, and there was a wet spot on Jared's vest, where he'd spit up while they were waiting in line, and Henry's cowlick refused to be flattened. So it wasn't a perfect picture, but it perfectly captured his kids and he was confident that Fallon would love it.

When the picture had been finally printed and Bella had helped him pick a suitable frame, they went to the food court to get some French fries for the kids to nibble on while they waited for Hudson, who'd got caught in a meeting in Rust Creek Falls.

"So what kind of cake do you want?" Jamie asked his sister, when they'd found a vacant table and had finally sat down.

She smiled at him. "It's enough that you're going to walk me down the aisle—you don't have to pretend to be interested in any of the other details."

"My interest in cake is not a pretense," he told her.

"I'm thinking three or four layers, each one a different flavor—and yes, one will be chocolate."

"I want my piece cut from that layer."

"I'll make sure of it," she promised.

"So you're really going to marry this guy?"

She nodded. "I want to spend every day of the rest of my life with Hudson."

Jamie nibbled on a fry before he asked, "How did you do it?"

"What did I do?"

"Let yourself fall in love again."

His sister smiled. "I didn't 'let' myself fall in love,"

she told him. "I did, finally, let go of all the heartache from my past, and then the falling in love just happened."

"I don't think I can let go," he said. "And I feel like an idiot admitting that to you, because you've experienced as much heartache as I have."

"I'm not saying it was easy, but it was necessary," Bella said gently.

"Everyone I've ever loved has gone away." He heard the depth of emotion in his voice, and was shocked by its intensity.

"I'm still here," his sister said, as she put her hand over his. "And Fallon will be back in a few days."

"Where is she?" he asked again.

"It doesn't matter where she is now. What matters is that she'll be back."

He wasn't convinced, but he let that topic drop. Instead, he brought up another subject that had been bothering him of late. "Do you ever think about Gramps?"

"Not if I can help it," she admitted.

"You don't think we abandoned him?"

Bella frowned. "Really? You can actually ask that question after everything *he* did? He made his choices long before either of us was even born when he turned his only daughter—our mother—out of her home because she was pregnant."

"I know. But then Mom and Dad got married, and they had a great life together," he pointed out.

"Until they died," his sister said bluntly, bitterly.

He nodded, a silent acknowledgment that the car accident that had taken the lives of Rob and Lauren Stockton had significantly altered the lives of their seven children, as well.

Bella's cell buzzed and she glanced at the screen. "Hudson's here—and he's illegally parked so I've gotta run."

Jamie nodded.

She gave him a brief hug, then dropped quick kisses on the top of each of the babies' heads as she made her way past them.

"Chocolate," Jamie reminded her.

She responded with a nod and a grin before she disappeared into the crowd.

By the time he pulled into the driveway of The Short Hills Ranch and parked in front of the house, he was exhausted. Physically, from wrestling the kids in and out of their stroller, and emotionally, as a result of the conversation he'd had with his sister afterward. Of course, as soon as he turned off the ignition, all three children—who had slept in their car seats all the way from Kalispell to Rust Creek Falls—woke up, and now they were eager to play.

Since they were already bundled into their snowsuits, he decided to let them roll around in the snow for a while, opening the house to let Andy and Molly come outside to play with them.

Babies need fresh air and exercise.

His mother's voice, from so long ago, echoed in the back of his mind.

Apparently Fallon subscribed to the same idea, because he'd often seen her outside with HJK. Even when they were infants, she'd put them in their carrier or stroller or sleigh—depending on the weather—to ensure they had some outdoor time.

And there she was again—not just on his mind but

in his heart. Of course, she'd been a steady presence in his life for a lot of years, so maybe it was inevitable that he would think about her, about how it had felt to hold her, kiss her, love her.

And he did love her, but he'd been too much of a coward to admit his feelings to her. It was hard enough acknowledging the truth to himself, and his brief marriage had taught him that love wasn't a magical cure-all. Because he had loved Paula, but he'd made a lot of mistakes in their relationship.

He wasn't just afraid of making another mistake with Fallon. He was afraid of losing her forever. Ironically, it was that fear that had caused him to push her away.

But he trusted that she would be back. Not just because Bella had said so, and not even because Fallon had promised that she wouldn't abandon him, but because his heart told him that it was true.

And this time, he was going to listen to his heart.

Fallon had told him that she'd be gone a few days.

A few days wasn't so long—or so Jamie tried to convince himself.

But a few days without any word from Fallon felt like an eternity. On the fourth day, he stopped by her parents' ranch.

"Jamie—hi." Fallon's mother's greeting was pleasant enough, though she was obviously surprised to see him.

"Hi, Mrs. O'Reilly. Is Fallon here?"

"No, she isn't," Maureen said. "Didn't she tell you that she was going away?"

"She did," he confirmed. "But I thought she would be home by now."

"When I talked to her this morning, she was still in Oregon."

Oregon? "What's she doing there?" he wondered aloud.

"A personal errand," Fallon's mother said, a response that sounded deliberately vague to him.

But Jamie took solace in the fact that she didn't seem concerned about her daughter's whereabouts. "Did she say when she'd be back?"

Maureen rubbed her hands briskly up and down her arms to warm them. "It seems silly to have a conversation standing on the porch in this cold weather," she said. "Did you want to come in for a cup of coffee?"

"Coffee sounds good," he told her.

She moved away from the door so that he could enter. As soon as he stepped inside, a wriggling bundle of gold fur pounced on his boot and attacked the laces.

"Leave it, Duchess," Maureen admonished.

But Jamie only chuckled as he crouched to give the pup a scratch. "There's no doubt she's related to mine," he said. "They like to chew on anything they can sink their teeth into."

"She needs a close eye at this stage, but she's been a wonderful addition to the family."

"I was happy to hear that Brooks found good homes for all of the pups—and so quickly."

"I can't bear to think what might have happened if you hadn't found them," Maureen said, making her way to the kitchen with Duchess trotting along happily at her heels.

She took two mugs from a cupboard and filled them both with steaming brew from the carafe. "Is your sister watching your little ones this morning?"

"Yes. She was taking them to the day care, so that they could see what it's all about before they show up for their first day."

"Fallon mentioned that they were going to be starting at Just Us Kids soon," Maureen said. "Cream or sugar?"

He shook his head. "Black works for me."

She handed him one of the mugs and doctored the other for herself. He waited to sit until she had done so.

"This must be a bittersweet time for you," Maureen noted, not unkindly. "The triplets' first Christmas—and your first without your wife."

"I thought it would be," he agreed. "But I'm trying to focus on the good stuff, on making this holiday a memorable one for the kids. Of course, Fallon has been a big part of that."

"She loves the holidays—and children—so she'd want to do everything possible to help make this Christmas special for them."

"It's not just the holidays, though," he admitted. "I don't think I would have made it through the past ten months without Fallon."

"I know she's spent a lot of time with your children, but one of the greatest benefits of living in a close community like Rust Creek Falls is that neighbors always do step up to help neighbors. If Fallon hadn't been there, someone else would have been."

"I'm getting the impression you wish someone else had been," he noted.

"My youngest daughter sometimes gives too much of herself with little regard for what it may cost her," she confided.

Jamie suspected she wasn't just referring to Fallon's help with Henry, Jared and Katie.

"She's an incredible woman," he said sincerely. "And I think, for a long time, our friendship prevented me from appreciating how truly incredible."

"Are you telling me that you do now?" Maureen asked him.

He nodded. "I don't just appreciate her—I'm in love with her."

"Oh." For a moment, Fallon's mother seemed at a loss for words. Then her lips curved, just a little, into the same half smile he'd seen countless times on her daughter's face. "I have to admit, this is surprising, but not unwelcome, news."

"I hope Fallon feels the same way when I tell her," he said worriedly.

"You haven't told her?"

"By the time I realized how I felt, she was probably halfway to Oregon," he admitted.

"Well, she'll be back before Saturday," Maureen assured him. "Because it's Paddy's and my thirtieth anniversary on Christmas Eve and there's no way she'd miss that."

"No, she wouldn't," he agreed.

"We're hosting an open house to celebrate—and I know Fallon would be happy to have you and your family join us."

"Thank you," he said, grateful for the invitation and already planning how to make the most of the opportunity she'd given him.

Chapter Fourteen

When she got behind the wheel of her SUV and drove away from Rust Creek Falls, Fallon only expected to be gone a few days. But what had been intended as a three-day journey had turned into four, then five. Now on the sixth day, she was finally on her way home again.

In the past six days, she hadn't spoken to Jamie at all. He'd called, left voice mail messages and sent numerous texts, but she hadn't responded to any of them. Not because she was mad or trying to punish him for dumping her—though she still wasn't very happy about that—but because she was concerned that any communication on her part might somehow reveal the surprise she'd planned for him.

As she drove past the familiar Welcome to Rust Creek Falls sign, the excited anticipation that had fueled her through most of the long journey turned into knots of apprehension in her belly.

It wouldn't be very much longer now before she found out whether following her heart had been a brilliant move or a big mistake.

It was December 23 and Fallon still hadn't returned to Rust Creek Falls.

She hadn't even returned any of Jamie's phone calls or text messages. He wasn't worried about her—he knew that she was in contact with her family—but he was worried about *them*.

The last time he'd talked to her, he'd stupidly told her that he just wanted to be friends. She'd said she needed some time to think. What if she'd decided that he was right and that it was better for them to be friends than lovers?

The possibility tortured his mind during the day and kept him awake at night.

"You look like hell," Bella said, when he came in from the barn for lunch.

"I didn't sleep very well last night," he admitted. Or the night before, and the night before that. In fact, he'd barely slept since Fallon had abruptly left Rust Creek Falls without a word to him about where she was going or when she would be back.

"Were the babies up?" Bella asked.

He shook his head. "No, they've slept through for the past several nights."

"So why didn't you?"

"I'm worried about Fallon," he admitted.

"She'll be back today," his sister assured him.

"How do you know?"

"I spoke to her briefly this morning," she said.

"You talked to her?"

"I've talked to her—or at least texted her—almost every day since she's been gone."

He was relieved to know that Bella had been in communication with Fallon—and frustrated that his sister had deliberately withheld that information from him.

"She hasn't answered any of my calls or replied to any of my text messages," he confided.

"And why is that?" Bella wondered aloud.

He scowled. "I'm sure you know why."

"If I had to guess, I'd say it probably has something to do with the fact that you slept with her—then told her you just wanted to be friends."

He winced at the accusation in her tone. "She told you that?"

"She's my best friend—and I thought she was one of yours, too."

"I was an idiot," he admitted.

"I'm not going to argue with that," she said.

"There's no excuse for my actions, but there is an explanation. But how can I explain to Fallon if she won't even talk to me?"

"She'll listen to you," Bella told him.

"How do you know?"

"Because she's not the type to hold a grudge, and because she cares about you too much to not want to mend the rift between you."

"I hope you're right."

"I am right," she insisted. "And that's her vehicle coming up the driveway now."

He was out of the house almost before she finished speaking, without even pausing to grab his hat or jacket.

Fallon had barely shifted into park when Jamie yanked open the driver's side door and hauled her out of the SUV and into his arms. Though he squeezed all of the air from her lungs, she didn't complain. For the past six days and nights, she'd dreamed of being in his arms just like this.

You deserve someone who can give you what you want...and that's not going to be me.

With those words echoing in the back of her mind, she forced herself to pull back and deliberately kept her tone light and friendly when she said, "Do you greet all your friends this way when they return after a few days out of town?"

His arms still around her, he tipped his head down to rest his forehead against hers. "You're so much more to me than a friend," he admitted gruffly. "You're the woman who owns my heart."

Her own heart skipped a beat. "I am?" she asked cautiously.

He nodded. "I was a fool and a coward, unwilling to recognize and admit the truth of my feelings, but I'm telling you now. I love you, Fallon."

She'd almost given up hope that he would ever say those words to her and, hearing them now, she was swamped by such a wave of emotion she couldn't speak—she couldn't even breathe.

"Say something, please," he urged when she remained silent. "Tell me I'm not too late—that denying my feelings for so long didn't ruin my chance with you."

"You didn't ruin anything," she finally said. "I love you, too. I think I always have. I know I always will."

He kissed her then, with an intensity and purpose that told her even more than his words that the feelings he'd professed were real.

"Don't ever leave me like that again," he said, when he finally eased his lips from hers.

"I didn't—I wouldn't—leave you," she promised.

"It felt like you'd left me," he said. "And I don't ever want to feel so empty and alone again."

As he was talking to her, she registered the sound of another car door opening, and then closing. She pulled back, just a little, her cheeks flushing. "You almost made me forget the whole purpose of my trip," she chided gently.

But he still didn't look away from her. It was almost as if he didn't want to take his eyes off her for a single second in case she disappeared again. "You didn't just go away to punish me for being an idiot?"

"I didn't go away to punish you at all," she said, extricating herself from his embrace. "And I brought you back a present."

"You're the only present I need," Jamie assured her.

But he turned then, to follow the direction of her gaze, and was surprised to see another woman—young and blonde—standing on the other side of the car. Though she was bundled up in a long coat with a knit cap on her head, there was something vaguely familiar about her, something that stirred long ago memories buried in the back of his mind.

He sucked in a lungful of icy air as that vague familiarity shifted to hopeful recognition. But still, he was afraid to let himself believe—

"Hi, Jamie."

Her voice, when she spoke, was cautious but familiar, confirming his own tentative hope.

"Dana?" he said, speaking the name of his youngest sister who had been turned over to the child welfare authorities to be adopted more than eleven years earlier, when she was barely eight years old.

The name sounded rusty on his lips after so long, but it was all she needed to propel herself forward. And then she was in his arms. When she'd left Rust Creek Falls, she'd been a child and now she was a young woman, but holding her somehow felt the same. And so did the love that filled his heart to overflowing. Apparently he wasn't the only one feeling a little overwhelmed, because Dana clung to him as she wept. He looked over his sister's head toward Fallon, and though his mind was swirling with questions that needed answering, for now he was content to mouth a silent "thank you."

She just nodded, her own eyes bright with unshed tears.

After another moment, Dana pulled back. "I'm sorry. I promised myself that I wouldn't bawl like the baby you probably remember me to be, but I just couldn't help myself. I've missed you—all of you—every single day since I was taken away."

"I've missed you, too," he told her.

"Is Bella here?" Dana asked. "Fallon said that I'd get to see her, too."

"She's inside," Jamie said. "Which means the babies must be keeping her busy, because if she'd even peeked out the window and caught a glimpse of you, I know she'd be out here, too."

"Fallon showed me pictures of your triplets, and I can't wait to meet them."

"Then let's go inside so you can." He started toward the house, but turned back when he realized Fallon wasn't beside him. "Bella and the babies will want to see you, too."

But she shook her head. "We'll catch up later. I don't want to intrude on your family reunion."

"Which wouldn't be happening at all, if not for you," he pointed out.

. "My sisters have been texting me nonstop for three days, sending me lists of all the things we need to do before our parents' anniversary party tomorrow."

He didn't want to let her go, but he understood that she had things she needed to do—and that she'd fallen behind schedule because she'd gone out of town for him, to give him back a piece of his family.

"Okay," he finally relented. "But I'll see you tomorrow."

"I'm counting on it," she said.

He hugged her again. "I want to know how and why, but for now, I'll just say thank you."

"The how is kind of complicated," she admitted. "But the why is simple—I wanted you to know that even when the people we love go away, the love endures."

Jamie didn't know if he could process all of the thoughts and feelings that were clamoring for prominence inside him.

Of course he'd thought about tracking down his siblings. Over the years, he'd thought about it a lot. Reconnecting with his brothers and sisters was something he'd dreamed about ever since the day they were separated.

But in the past year, the idea had been shoved to the back of the mind. With so many other and much more immediate concerns, he hadn't let himself think about or miss his other siblings. Or maybe that was just an excuse. Because the truth was, Luke, Daniel and Bailey had chosen to go off on their own. They knew where

Jamie and Bella had been living with their grandparents and they'd chosen to let eleven years pass without making contact in all of that time.

But Dana and Liza had been taken away and he didn't know where they'd ended up. Again, he would have expected they were old enough to remember the time they'd spent in Rust Creek Falls, but after they'd gone, they'd never made any attempt to communicate with him and Bella.

And now, after all of that time, Dana was here. Not through her own initiative and not because of any effort on his part, but because Fallon had tracked her down and brought her to Rust Creek Falls. He didn't know how long Dana would stay—or could stay—but she was here now. Fallon had brought one of his little sisters home, and he knew he wouldn't ever be able to repay her.

He thought about what she'd said—the words she'd whispered in his ear when she'd hugged him. *Even when the people we love go away, the love endures.*

She'd proven that to him twice today—by bringing his sister to Rust Creek Falls and by coming back herself. And now that she was finally home, he was going to do everything in his power to ensure that she never wanted to leave again.

Fallon was up early the next morning to help Fiona and Brenna with the hors d'oeuvres. Her hands went through the necessary motions, but her mind—and her heart—were at The Short Hills Ranch with Jamie.

Jamie. She felt her lips curve as she thought of the man who had held her in his arms as if he never wanted to let her go. The man who had kissed her as if he wanted to kiss her forever. The man who had told her—finally—that he loved her.

Fiona snapped her fingers in front of her face. "Earth to Fallon. We're expecting upwards of a hundred guests between four and seven, which means that we're going to need a lot of meatballs, sausage rolls, shrimp skewers, pinwheel sandwiches, vegetable crudités, platters of cheeses and crackers and fruit, and I need your attention on this planet."

Fallon resumed her chopping. The girls were in charge of the food and the boys were in charge of the setup, which meant rearranging the furniture to accommodate the folding tables and chairs borrowed from the community center, and all the while Duchess was running around, doing her best to trip up everyone as they performed their assigned tasks.

Surrounded by her family—whom she loved with every fiber of her being despite the fact that they often drove her crazy—it was natural that her thoughts would drift to Jamie and Bella, that she would wonder how the reunion with Dana was going. She'd been relieved to witness the success of the initial meeting, pleased that the siblings were happy to be together again after so many years. But Fallon knew that a lot had happened during the time they'd been apart and it was possible that, when all the tales had been told, old wounds would be reopened and tender feelings hurt.

"Fallon—" it was Ronan who interrupted her musing this time "—can you give me a hand with these chairs?"

"Where's Keegan?" she asked.

"I sent him to pick up the flowers and balloons."

"Mistake," Brenna told their oldest brother.

"Why?"

"He had a total of three things to pick up at Crawford's yesterday and he forgot one of them," Fiona piped in.

"Although I don't think he actually forgot," Brenna said. "I think he wanted an excuse to go back and flirt with Natalie Crawford."

"I don't care how much flirting he does as long as he's back with the balloons and flowers before Mom and Dad get home," Ronan said.

"Where are they?" Fallon asked.

"Mom went to Bee's Beauty Parlor to get her hair done and Dad's on his way back from Kalispell."

"Why did he have to go into the city today?" Brenna asked.

"Probably to find an anniversary present for Mom," Fallon guessed.

"To pick up her anniversary present," Ronan clarified. "A strand of Akoya pearls."

"Pearls are the traditional gift for a thirtieth anniversary," Fiona noted.

Fallon nodded. "And Mom's always wanted real pearls."

"Well, I guess Dad decided that thirty years was long enough to wait," Ronan said.

"She's going to cry," Fiona warned.

Fallon's own eyes were a little moist as she imagined Maureen's reaction to the gift, as she considered how it might feel to be part of a couple that had endured for three decades. No, not just endured but flourished.

"What did Mom get for Dad?" Brenna wondered.

"Super Bowl tickets," Fiona told her.

Fallon laughed. "Not traditional, but definitely something Dad's always wanted."

"Which just goes to show how perfectly suited they are for one another," Brenna said.

"Put the sentiment on hold until the party," Ronan advised. "The clock is ticking."

As a result of her oldest brother's constant prompting and nagging, everything was set up and ready for the party when the guests of honor got home. Since she hadn't really had a chance to talk to her mother since her trip to Oregon, Fallon offered to help Maureen get changed.

"You look beautiful," Fallon said, after she'd zipped up the back of her mother's dress.

"Bee has a knack with hair," her mother said.

She shook her head. "Your hair looks nice, but it's more than that. You're glowing." And she knew it was love that put the color in Maureen's cheeks and the sparkle in her eyes. Not just being in love but knowing that she was loved in return. Fallon suspected that she had a little bit of a glow herself and wondered if her mother could see it.

Maureen laughed softly. "I've been reminiscing a lot today," she admitted. "Paddy and I have made a lot of memories together over thirty years and five children."

"You've definitely shown us what a good marriage should look like," Fallon told her.

"I hope so," her mother said. "Your dad and I don't always agree about everything, but hopefully that showed our kids the importance of navigating stormy seas, the value of compromise and, at the end of the day, the necessity of working together.

"That's what I want for all of my children," Maureen continued. "An enduring lifelong partnership with someone who loves, respects and supports them."

"It doesn't sound like so much, does it?" Fallon noted wistfully. "But it's huge, and I know how lucky I am to have grown up in this family."

"You're thinking of Jamie again, aren't you?" her mom asked gently.

"Jamie, Bella, Dana and the rest of their family," she admitted.

"It was such a tragedy for all of them, losing their parents the way they did. And Agnes and Matthew—" Maureen shook her head "—I can't begin to know what they were thinking, letting the older boys go off on their own and sending the younger girls away, but I think you've helped Jamie and Bella see that even broken pieces can fit back together."

"You don't think I overstepped by bringing Dana to Rust Creek Falls?"

"I don't think it's ever wrong to follow your heart."

"I love him, Mom."

Her mother smiled. "I know you do."

"I tried not to," she admitted. "But he's it for me."

"That's how it was for me with your father," Maureen confided, lifting a hand to tuck a wayward curl behind her daughter's ear. "I'm glad you didn't straighten your hair today—I like the natural look."

"I thought I had to change to get Jamie's attention," she confessed. "But as it turns out, he likes the real me. He loves the real me."

"Because he's as smart as he is handsome," her mother remarked.

"Speaking of smart and handsome men—let's go find your husband before the guests start arriving."

It seemed as if all of the residents of Rust Creek Falls showed up to wish Paddy and Maureen O'Reilly a happy anniversary. Some folks just passed through to offer a brief "congratulations" while others settled in for a longer visit with friends and neighbors and to enjoy the food and drink provided. Even Homer Gilmore stopped by to offer his best wishes. While the old man was in the house, Fallon kept a close eye on him to ensure that he never got close enough to the punch bowl to spike the fruity drink Brenna had prepared.

It was close to five o'clock when Jamie showed up.

She hadn't been certain that he would come. She'd invited him and Bella and Dana, but she knew the three siblings had a lot of catching up to do and she wouldn't have blamed them for skipping the party.

Hudson and Bella came in first, with Bella carrying Henry. Dana followed with Jared in her arms, then Jamie walked through the door with Katie. It was readily apparent that the newly found Stockton sister had already fallen head over heels in love with her niece and nephews, and it warmed Fallon's heart to see them all together, to see that the bond they'd shared as children had not been broken by the time or distance that had separated them.

There were still four other siblings to be found, but she knew that Jamie would find them. She'd helped him take the first step; now it was time for her to step back and let the Stocktons figure out their family.

She tried to make her way to him through the crowd but was halted in her tracks when Paddy put his fingers between his lips and whistled to silence the crowd.

"Sorry to interrupt, folks, but I wanted to take a few

minutes to thank you all for coming today to celebrate our anniversary with Maureen and me."

The crowd cheered and applauded, but Paddy—an Irishman to the bone—wasn't even close to being done.

"I'd also like to make a couple of toasts," he said, "so make sure your glasses are full.

"First, and most important on this day, to my always beautiful and amazing wife. These first thirty years have been a heck of a ride, and I'm looking forward to the next three decades—and more."

The crowd applauded and cheered.

"I'd also like to toast our children who, through the many challenges they presented to us over the years, taught Maureen and me a lot about the trials and tribulations of parenting."

There was, predictably, some laughter to follow that.

"But seriously, when Maureen and I exchanged our vows, we were united in our desire not just to spend our lives together but to fill our home with children. We were fortunate to be blessed with Ronan, Keegan, Fiona, Brenna and Fallon, who have enriched our lives in more ways than we ever would have thought possible. And who will hopefully further enrich our lives by giving us the wonderful gift of grandchildren someday."

There was more laughter and the clinking of glasses again, then Fallon saw Jamie hand his daughter to Hudson and step forward. Her heart hammered against her ribs as her mind wondered, what was he doing?

"Since you brought up the topic," Jamie said, addressing her father, "I was wondering if you'd mind having your lives enriched by grandchildren sooner rather than later?"

Paddy's bushy brows lifted to meet his hairline. "I'd

guess that would depend on the circumstances," he said. "What, exactly, are you asking?"

Fallon held her breath, waiting for Jamie's response. Thankfully, he didn't make her wait long. Through the crowd, his eyes found and held hers as he said, "I'm asking for your daughter's hand in marriage."

And Fallon's heart swelled to fill her chest.

But it was Brenna who piped up to say, "And I accept."

Paddy chuckled as several other guests began to whisper about this unexpected turn of events and Jamie's face turned red.

"I guess you should have been more specific," the O'Reilly patriarch suggested.

Jamie nodded. "I would like to ask for *Fallon's* hand in marriage," he clarified.

Brenna let out an exaggerated sigh. "You're dumping me already?"

Fallon elbowed her sister sharply in the ribs as laughter sounded around the room. She couldn't imagine it had been easy for Jamie to make a public declaration of his feelings and she didn't want him to shy away now. Not when he was so close to finally asking the question she'd been waiting to hear for so long.

She looked toward her father and saw Paddy offer his hand to Jamie.

"You and your children would be a welcome addition to the family," he said, then he raised his glass again. "And now we have another reason to celebrate today— not just an anniversary but an engagement."

Everyone cheered again.

Everyone except Fallon who, when the murmur of the crowd died down, finally spoke up. Because while the moment was pretty close to being perfect, she still wanted an actual proposal. "I'm pleased to see that everyone is having a good time, but I think some of this revelry might be a little premature."

"So long as he's not…premature…in the bedroom," Winona Cobbs piped up.

Which, of course, made Fallon's face turn red, but her gaze didn't shift away from Jamie.

He took a ring out of his pocket, lowered himself to one knee in front of her and finally offered her what she most wanted in the world—and it wasn't a diamond in a band of gold, it was his heart. "Fallon, will you do me the honor of becoming my wife?"

Her eyes misted and her heart, already full, overflowed with love and happiness. "I feel as if I've been waiting my whole life for you to ask me that question," she confessed.

"Is that a yes?" Keegan interjected. "Because when a guy asks a yes-or-no question, he just wants a yes-or-no answer."

"And he'd probably appreciate the rest of her family butting out so that she can answer the question," Fiona said pointedly.

Fallon continued to hold Jamie's gaze as she shook her head in response to her family's antics. "I'll bet you're regretting the public proposal now, aren't you?"

"My only regret would be if you said no," he told her sincerely. "Because I don't want anything so much as I want to spend the rest of my life with you."

"Yes," she finally said. "My answer is yes, because I want exactly the same thing."

He took her hand but paused with the ring—a stunning princess-cut diamond solitaire—at the tip of her finger. "You do understand that marrying me will mean becoming an instant mother to three adorable, messy and demanding children?"

"I do," she agreed. "And I love those adorable, messy and demanding children every bit as much as I love you."

He smiled and slid the ring onto her finger.

"I love you, Fallon O'Reilly," he said, whispering the words against her lips.

"And I love you, Jamie Stockton."

And then, finally, he kissed her.

"Well, it's official," Jamie said, dropping onto the sofa beside his fiancée and surveying the disaster zone that had once been his living room.

In the middle of the floor littered with discarded paper, Henry was trying to pull off his socks, Katie was banging on a drum, Jared was collecting all the green bows—and only the green ones—in a toy shopping cart, Molly was chewing on a red bow and Andy, apparently worn out from all of the excitement, was sprawled on his back beneath the Christmas tree.

On the coffee table were two framed photos: similar but different pictures of the babies with Santa, one wrapped up for Jamie by Fallon and the other for Fallon by Jamie. They'd both had a good chuckle over that.

Fallon tipped her head back against his shoulder. "What's official?"

"This was undoubtedly The. Best. Christmas. Ever."

She smiled. "Only until next Christmas," she promised.

"Well, while we're still celebrating *this* Christmas, I have one more gift for you."

She took the small, flat package and peeled away the paper, then opened the lid of the box to reveal a silver snowflake ornament decorated with sparkling crystals.

"It's beautiful," she said.

"Turn it over."

She did as he suggested and found that it was inscribed on the back with a date and the words: Fallon & Jamie—First Christmas Together.

"I love it," she said, softly, sincerely.

"The first of many," he told her.

"I'm already looking forward to each and every one," she assured him.

"I'm hoping that next Christmas I'll get to wake up with you in my arms."

Because although they were engaged, engaged wasn't married, and Paddy and Maureen had made it clear that they expected their unmarried daughter to wake up under their roof and spend Christmas morning with her family. Which she had done, then she'd come over to The Short Hills Ranch to celebrate with Jamie and the babies.

"Me, too," she said.

"Does that mean you're ready to set a date for our wedding?"

"We haven't even been engaged twenty-four hours," she pointed out.

"Is there some kind of required waiting period that I don't know about?" he teased.

"I just thought you might want to wait until all of your brothers and sisters could be at our wedding."

But he shook his head. "I want to find them—I *am* going to find them—but I have no idea how long that's going to take and I'm not willing to put our wedding on hold until it happens." He kissed her softly. "Because I want to spend every day of the rest of my life with you, and I want the rest of our life together to start as soon as possible."

"That sounds like a perfect plan to me," she agreed.

Epilogue

Three months later

"That's a lot of cupcakes," Jamie commented, looking at the miniature frosted cakes that had been assembled on the table to spell out Happy 1st Birthday.

"There are a lot of babies celebrating today," Fallon reminded him.

Although Henry, Jared and Katie had celebrated their birthday two months earlier, they'd been invited to this party, along with everyone else in town, to celebrate the first anniversary of the Baby Bonanza—as many residents had taken to calling the population explosion that had occurred nine months after Braden and Jennifer's Fourth of July wedding.

"They look like they're all vanilla," he said, sounding disappointed.

"There's leftover chocolate cake in your fridge from the bakery that's going to make our wedding cake," she reminded him.

They'd decided on May twentieth as the date for their wedding, because it gave them a few months to make the arrangements and would allow them to take time for a honeymoon before Bella and Hudson exchanged their vows.

Maureen had initially been a little concerned that they were rushing their nuptials, but Fallon assured her mother that she didn't feel rushed at all. She'd been in love with Jamie since she was seventeen years old and she was excited about finally starting their life together.

"I can see now why so many women who want to have babies believe there's something in the water in Rust Creek Falls," Fallon commented, as more families and more babies entered the community center for the celebration.

"Except it wasn't the water but the wedding punch," Jamie reminded her. "I'm not sure if Homer Gilmore should be given the key to the city or put in jail and the key thrown away."

"No doubt that's a topic that has been widely debated around town, but I'd vote for the key to the city," Fallon said. "Because if it wasn't for Homer spiking the wedding punch, we wouldn't have Henry, Jared and Katie."

"True," he acknowledged. "But when we decide to expand our family again, I'd be content to let nature take its course."

It was the first time he'd mentioned having another child, and Fallon was both pleased and surprised. "You want to have another child?"

"I'm not in any hurry," he assured her. "Especially

considering that we aren't married yet and already have three babies in diapers. But I loved growing up with so many brothers and sisters, and I'd be thrilled to add to our family in a couple of years."

"I'd like that, too," she told him. "But I really hope we grow our family one baby at a time."

"How would you feel if you did end up pregnant with twins or triplets?" he asked curiously.

She looked at Henry, Jared and Katie, playing with the toys that had been scattered in the middle of the room, and thought back to the early days when they'd been so tiny and fragile and demanding. The first few months had been incredibly hard, and there had been days when she'd wanted to cry right along with them. But for every one of those days, there were countless more during which she'd felt nothing but pure and un-adulterated joy simply because Henry rolled over or Jared clapped his hands or Katie smiled at her— simply because they were a part of her life. And that was even before they'd stopped calling her 'Fa-fa' in favor of 'Ma-ma.'

"Blessed," she finally responded to his question. "I would feel doubly or triply blessed."

He smiled and slid an arm across her shoulders. "Let's gather up our kids and go get some cupcakes."

* * * * *

MILLS & BOON®

Cherish™

EXPERIENCE THE ULTIMATE RUSH OF FALLING IN LOVE

A sneak peek at next month's titles...

In stores from 15th December 2016:

- **Slow Dance with the Best Man** – Sophie Pembroke
  and **A Fortune in Waiting** – Michelle Major
- **Her New Year Baby Secret** – Jessica Gilmore
  and **Twice a Hero, Always Her Man** – Marie Ferrarella

In stores from 29th December 2016:

- **The Prince's Convenient Proposal** – Barbara Hannay
  and **His Ballerina Bride** – Teri Wilson
- **The Tycoon's Reluctant Cinderella** – Therese
  Beharrie *and* **The Cowboy's Runaway Bride** –
  Nancy Robards Thompson

Just can't wait?
Buy our books online a month before they hit the shops!
www.millsandboon.co.uk

Also available as eBooks.

MILLS & BOON®

EXCLUSIVE EXTRACT

When Eloise Miller finds herself thrown into the role of maid of honour at the wedding of the year, her plans to stay away from the gorgeous best man are scuppered!

Read on for a sneak preview of
SLOW DANCE WITH THE BEST MAN
by Sophie Pembroke

Maid of honour for Melissa Sommers. How on earth had this happened? And the worst part was—

'Sounds like we'll be spending even more time together.' Noah's voice was warm, deep and far too close to her ear.

Eloise sighed. That. That was the worst thing. Because the maid of honour was *expected* to pair up with the best man, and that would not make her resolution to stay away from Noah Cross any easier at all.

She turned and found him standing directly behind her, close enough that if she'd stepped back a centimetre or two she'd have been in his arms. Suddenly she was glad he'd alerted her to his presence with his words.

She shifted further away and tried to look like a professional, instead of a teenager with a crush. Looking up at him, she felt the strange heat flush over her skin again at his gorgeousness. Then she focused, and realised he was frowning.

'Apparently so,' she agreed. 'But I'm sure I'll be far too busy with all the wedding arrangements—'

'Oh, I doubt it,' Noah interrupted, but he still didn't sound entirely happy about the idea, which surprised her. Perhaps she'd misread his flirting earlier. Maybe he really was like that with everyone and, now the reality of having to spend time with her had set in, he was less keen on the idea. 'Melissa has quite the packed schedule for the wedding party, you know. She's right—you're going to have to find someone to take over most of your job here.'

Eloise sighed. She *did* know. She'd helped Laurel plan it, after all.

And, now she thought about it, every last bit of the schedule involved the maid of honour and the best man being together.

Noah smiled, a hint of the charm he'd exhibited earlier showing through despite the frown, and Eloise's heart beat twice in one moment as she accepted the inevitable.

She was doomed.

She had the most ridiculous crush on a man who clearly found her a minor inconvenience.

And—even worse—the whole world was going to be watching, laughing at her pretending that she could live in this world of celebrities, mocking her for thinking she could ever be pretty enough, funny enough...just *enough* for Noah Cross.

Don't miss
SLOW DANCE WITH THE BEST MAN
by Sophie Pembroke

Available January 2017
www.millsandboon.co.uk

MILLS & BOON®

Why shop at millsandboon.co.uk?

Each year, thousands of romance readers find their perfect read at millsandboon.co.uk. That's because we're passionate about bringing you the very best romantic fiction. Here are some of the advantages of shopping at www.millsandboon.co.uk:

* **Get new books first**—you'll be able to buy your favourite books one month before they hit the shops

* **Get exclusive discounts**—you'll also be able to buy our specially created monthly collections, with up to 50% off the RRP

* **Find your favourite authors**—latest news, interviews and new releases for all your favourite authors and series on our website, plus ideas for what to try next

* **Join in**—once you've bought your favourite books, don't forget to register with us to rate, review and join in the discussions

Visit **www.millsandboon.co.uk**
for all this and more today!